THE FLOWER SHOP

Caldron of Conspiracy

a novel

by H. Christopher Quinn

This is a work of fiction, although many of the persons mentioned and the places described in the book were real and existed at the time of the story. A few of the characters' names have been changed

Copyright © 2012 by H. Christopher Quinn
First Edition – November 2012

ISBN
978-1-77097-945-1 (Hardcover)
978-1-77097-946-8 (Paperback)
978-1-77097-947-5 (eBook)

All rights reserved.

No part of this publication may be reproduced in any form, or by any means, electronic or mechanical, including photocopying, recording, or any information browsing, storage, or retrieval system, without permission in writing from the publisher.

Produced by:

FriesenPress
Suite 300 – 852 Fort Street
Victoria, BC, Canada V8W 1H8

www.friesenpress.com

Distributed to the trade by The Ingram Book Company

*Dedicated to my Wife Donna,
for her help, her understanding,
and her patience*

CHAPTER 1

Harry was the first one on the bus. He stuffed his duffel bag into the overhead rack, sat down in the first seat by the window and spread his coat on the aisle seat, staking claim to these two seats for the duration of the trip. With no one in front of him, Harry would have a clear line of vision straight ahead, and he would be able to see anything worth seeing along the side of the road. A perfect, unobstructed view.

The man at the ticket window said the trip could take about twenty-four hours, depending on the traffic and the weather and the roadblocks. Harry had asked the ticket man what kind of road blocks, and the man said "all kinds ... falling rocks, construction, cows crossing the road, maybe a cow that didn't make it across, bandits, car crashes, perhaps a car that went over the side of the mountain, maybe a fire or two, military convoys, police barricades. A lot of things can happen on those winding roads. A lot of things can happen in those mountains."

I've got the best seat on the bus, Harry decided. If there's something in the road, I'll be the first one to see it—the driver and I will. If we hit something, I'll be the first one to feel it. And if we have to get off the bus in a hurry, I'll be the first one off. Right now, I'll just sit back and relax.

But Harry could not relax. There was too much on his mind. The rush to make it this far, the anticipation of his journey, and the uncertainty about what lay ahead kept him on the edge of his seat. So he stood up and turned to survey the interior of the bus. He knew it would be best to look around now rather than later, when the other seats were occupied and the passengers would think he was being nosey. Nothing unusual, just an empty bus.

Then Harry spotted a coat in the overhead rack across the aisle, behind the driver's throne. The coat, neatly folded, obviously had been placed there with great care. It was a light tan corduroy blazer with a dark brown leather elbow patch and one leather-clad button visible. Looked like it might be a college professor's jacket, with maybe a pipe and a pouch of tobacco in one of the pockets.

The driver climbed aboard with a red leather case in one hand, a large red-and-blue thermos in the other, and an olive green jacket draped over one shoulder. The jacket matched his pants. Must be the bus company uniform, so the coat in the rack probably is not his.

"Someone left a coat, up there in the luggage rack," Harry said to the driver, gesturing up at the unclaimed coat. "It must've been one of the passengers on an earlier trip."

The driver arched his eyebrows, shrugged his shoulders, and mumbled something Harry didn't understand. He fumbled in his case for some papers, checked the gauges on the dashboard, and got off the bus without ever looking up at the coat in the overhead rack. He didn't seem to understand a word Harry said.

Now the other passengers began to board, a few at a time, and Harry turned so he could watch as they jostled down the aisle, cramming luggage and boxes and baskets and coats into the overhead racks. Some were family groups, others were solitary travelers. Five or six of the newcomers paused in the aisle, glanced at Harry's jacket spread across the empty seat, and moved on back. Harry's jacket was doing its job.

Harry listened carefully to the laughter and the chatter, trying to pick up snippets of conversation. He recognized a few scattered words, but the people were speaking in hushed tones, talking so fast he couldn't make out a complete sentence. Harry realized he was on his own, alone in a foreign country.

The bus was filling up, and Harry knew he would not be alone for long. Someone would ask about that vacant seat. So far, his diversion had worked well. The fat man with three-alarm halitosis, the old man with a chihuahua puppy under his arm, and the young mother with the baby in desperate need of a fresh diaper—all those folks had noticed his coat on the seat, hesitated, and moved on back. Harry was in control, and he would decide who was going to sit next to him.

"*Perdóneme Señor, ¿está ocupado el asiento?*"

Harry looked up, and there she was, his seatmate for the rest of the journey. Young, about his age, maybe a little younger. Attractive, with a pleasant smiling face. High arching cheekbones accentuated her blue eyes. Blond hair fell neatly over her shoulders. Nice figure. Dressed in modest clothing—navy blue suit with a three-quarter length jacket, a white blouse open at the neck, small flowers on the lapel of the jacket. Ideal for traveling. Just a little bit of jewelry, nothing fancy. A simple silver cross on a silver chain around her neck, a silver charm bracelet on one wrist, a silver watch on the other.

The girl was not what Harry expected to see on this long cross-country bus ride. Most of the other passengers were peasants, the men dressed in simple work clothes, sandals and straw hats, the women in multi-colored flowing skirts.

She repeated her question, this time in English. "Pardon me, sir, is this seat occupied?"

Harry was already on his feet. He gave her his best smile, and he answered her in English. "No, no, it's not, but it's your seat now. I've been saving it just for you." He helped her place a satchel in the overhead rack, which by now was nearly filled to capacity, and then he crammed his coat into the last remaining space up there.

And he smiled again, thinking what a corny response he had just made. 'Saving it just for you' might be a good pick-up line in a bar, but it's probably a lousy way to make friends with a pretty girl on a bus.

"Here, you sit by the window," he invited, "so you can see the scenery, and I'll take the aisle seat."

It's the gentlemanly thing to do, he told himself, and it'll give me more freedom to move around, or get off the bus in a hurry if I need to. And it might even score a few points.

The bus driver hopped back on and looked down the aisle to do a quick head count. Satisfied he had his complement of paying passengers, he closed the door, put the bus in gear, and pulled away from the depot. He turned his head slightly and called out, *"¡Vámonos amigos! ¡Rumbo a México!"*

"What did he say?" Harry asked the girl. "My Spanish is a little rusty."

Actually, Harry's Spanish was pretty good, and he knew exactly what the driver said, but he figured this might be a better way to strike up a conversation, and he wanted to keep the conversation in English a little longer. The less she knew the better.

"The driver said, 'Let's get going to Mexico City.' Are you going all the way to Mexico City, Señor? You do speak Spanish, no? Are you on a business trip?"

"Yes, I'm going to Mexico City. How about you? Do you live there?"

"Yes, I am looking forward to arriving home," she said, "although I do not look forward to such a long ride on this bus. The journey on a bus can be so exhausting. It's so crowded, and so noisy and so dusty. Why are you going to our Capital, Señor? Are you a tourist?"

"Yeah, I guess it can be a long trip, but I hope nothing happens along the way to delay us. The man at the ticket window said you never can tell what might happen on these roads. But where are you coming from? Have you been on vacation? Were you in Texas?"

"Dios mío, Señor, what was that man suggesting? What could possibly go wrong on a major highway such as this? Did he say what things could possibly delay us? Or perhaps you did not understand him correctly?"

"Well, I might have misunderstood him. Like I said, my Spanish is a little rusty, and his English wasn't so good, either." Harry laughed. "He said maybe a dead cow in the middle of the road, or maybe a car that went off the side of the mountain. But you should know how long it takes. You've made this trip before, right?"

The girl's face flushed and her eyes closed briefly. She shifted in her seat, and took a moment to speak. "Oh, I hate to think of a car going over the side of the mountain. That would be horrible—so horrible for the driver of the car. The driver would not survive." She adjusted her feet atop her makeup kit on the floor in front of her. "Do you like to ride the bus, or do you prefer to travel by train, or perhaps by airplane? Do you do a lot of traveling in your business, Señor? Where do you come from? Have you been to Mexico before?"

She's dodging my questions, Harry thought, and she's throwing a lot of questions right back at me. But what the hell, I haven't been answering her questions, either. I'm not about to give her my life story. She's nervous, or she's afraid to get too chummy with a stranger on a bus. Or maybe she has something to hide.

"I prefer to fly," he said, "but it costs too much. The bus is cheaper, and the long ride gives you a chance to see the scenery, but the bus makes too many stops. But please," he said, realizing he was running off at the mouth, "you don't have to continue calling me 'Señor.' You can call me Harry. I respond better when I hear my name. And what can I call you?"

"My name is Rosa."

Harry had the best seat on the bus for looking at the road ahead, but he had to turn his head, or rely on peripheral glances, to see the girl's face. Right now, when she said, "My name is Rosa," he could see a faint smile, and he also thought he heard a quiet sigh of relief.

CHAPTER 2

Rosa settled in for the long ride. This seat is an excellent place to sit if you want a clear view of the road ahead, she thought, and it's also a good place to be if you have to leave the bus quickly. The lack of space for my feet is a disadvantage, but sometimes you have to make adjustments when you travel. I know nothing about this man sitting next to me, except that he must be a North American, or perhaps Canadian. I don't think he's English, he doesn't sound English. I'll have to be alert at all times, although he does appear to be a gentleman.

He's been avoiding my questions. Perhaps he doesn't want me to think he's being forward. Or perhaps he has something to hide. He seems to be thinking about something off in the distance. I'd like to know more about him, although I do feel a sense of relief now that I know his name, and he knows mine. But it's a long trip, so here goes. "Harry, you say your Spanish is rusty. Perhaps I can help you. I would be happy to help you during our long ride."

"Hey, that would be great, I could use the help. From now on, I'll speak nothing but Spanish, and you can correct my grammar when I make a mistake. Or you can fill in the correct word when I stumble for a Spanish word." Harry switched to Spanish. "But please, don't laugh at my mistakes."

Rosa smiled, and she replied in Spanish. "Okay, from now on we speak nothing but Spanish, and I'll try not to laugh at your mistakes."

"So where've you been?" he asked.

"I've been visiting my sister in Nuevo Laredo. Yes, I live in Mexico City, and I work in a flower shop, selling flowers and designing floral arrangements for customers. I love flowers, and I love making people happy with beautiful things. But you haven't answered my questions. Have you been to Mexico before? And why are you going to our Capital now?"

Nice teeth, Harry thought. Kissable lips, nice body. I'd like to see more of her when we get to Mexico City. You never know what might develop.

"You're right, I guess I haven't answered your questions. I'm just a tourist, going down to Mexico City on a little vacation, to see the sights, take in a bullfight or two, and play some golf. And I'll take a side trip down to Acapulco and do some deep sea fishing, or just lie on the beach and soak up the sun."

Rosa sat up straight and beamed. "Oh, you'll love Mexico City, there's so much to see and so much to do, and you certainly will love Acapulco. Everybody loves Acapulco. And of course, you must go to Taxco. Taxco is an ancient silver-mining town. I love to visit Taxco and shop for silver items, like this charm bracelet I'm wearing now." She held up her right hand so Harry could admire the silver charms dangling from her wrist.

Yes, he thought, this girl certainly does have charm. "That's very beautiful. What are all those little charms on your bracelet? What do they mean?"

"Oh, these are just little mementos of my country. See, this one is a sombrero—that's the big straw hat men wear to keep the sun out of their eyes. Here is a burro, the little animal that does so much work for us, and this one's a guitar, representing the musicians who play mariachi music. You've heard our mariachi bands?"

"I've heard their records a few times. Lively music, lots of spirit."

"Yes, it's our national music. I love mariachi music, although not all their music is lively. Some of the songs are very sad. And see this one. This is a dahlia, our national flower." Rosa laughed. "Of course, a real dahlia, with all its brilliant color, is much prettier than this tiny silver charm. It's such a beautiful flower. And what do you do when you're not on vacation?"

"Well, I guess you could say I'm a newspaper reporter, and you could say I'm between assignments right now."

"Between assignments?"

"Yes, that's just a polite way of saying I'm unemployed, I don't have a job. I figure I'll be in Mexico for two or three weeks, or as long as my money holds out."

"And what happens when your money runs out?"

"That depends. I may have to leave, but if I still haven't seen everything I want to see, or if I haven't done all the things I want to do, I may try to pick up some kind of part-time work so I can stay longer, but I'm really not interested in going back to work full time right now. I just want to have a good time. Like I said—a little golf, a little beach time, see the sights, and a lot of relaxation."

"Oh, I'm sure you'll find plenty to see and to do here in Mexico," she said. And then she added, with a sincere, friendly laugh, "Just don't drink the water."

"I've heard that. Is that what you tell all the tourists?"

"Oh, we don't drink the water, either. No one in Mexico drinks the water."

Harry laughed too. She's a nice girl, he thought, and maybe she can help me in Mexico City. She mingles with the public in her flower shop, so she might be able to show me around, show me the night life. "So what do you drink instead of water?"

"Oh, we do drink water, but it's always bottled water. It's much safer. Or maybe we drink a little wine. The men like to drink tequila or beer, or sometimes pulque."

"Pulque?"

"Yes, it's like tequila, only stronger. It's made from the leaves of the maguey tree."

"The maguey tree?"

"Yes, the maguey is native to Mexico. Fiber from the stalk is used to make rope, but the fiber from the leaves also is used to make pulque."

Harry curled his lip, and uttered a guttural growl. "A drink of rope doesn't sound very appealing, but I suppose I'll have to try pulque sometime. Meanwhile, maybe you and I could have a drink when we get to Mexico City, maybe a glass of wine, or even tequila or beer?"

She smiled. "Yes, that would be nice, thank you, but I think I would prefer wine."

The bus was making good time on the open highway. Most of the passengers were dozing or sleeping. A muffled murmur of conversation was interrupted now and then by a subdued bit of laughter, the cry of a fussy baby, or the cluck of a chicken. The only other sounds were the constant hum of the engine and the whir of the tires on the road.

"*¡Ay, caray!*" the bus driver cried out in full voice. "*¡Miren por allá! ¡el incendio!*" He pointed to a brilliant light in the sky, straight ahead, just over a rise in the road. Plumes of thick black smoke were silhouetted against bright balls of vibrant red and orange flames lighting up the night sky. As the bus got closer, the smell of smoke drifted in through the open windows.

"That's great, we're headed right for it," Harry said with a touch of sarcasm. "Just like the man at the ticket window said, bad things can happen along this road."

But as the bus crested the hill, the highway veered off slightly to the right, putting the fire now to the left of the bus. A side road, turning off to the left, seemed to lead directly to the source of the flames. A police car blocked access to the feeder road, and the bus driver waved to the police officer as he drove on past.

Someone near the front of the bus spoke up. "It's probably just a crop burn, clearing the fields."

"Maybe they're burning bagasse in the sugar fields," another passenger volunteered. "They do a lot of that around here."

"But why are they doing it at night?" a woman asked.

"Perhaps it's a controlled burn that got out of control," the first passenger suggested. "The wind is brisk tonight."

A man in the row behind Harry said, "No, I believe it's some kind of an oil fire. It might be a derrick in the oil fields, or perhaps something at a refinery or a storage tank. Fires like this are dangerous, especially when they get out of control. There was a pipeline fire a week or two ago, not far from here. Anyway, it smells like an oil fire."

The driver turned his head, looked at Harry, and grinned. "No, I think they must be burning gringos again." He burst into a raucous laugh, and everyone within earshot laughed with him.

When the laughter subsided, Harry asked Rosa to explain the joke. She smiled faintly, and said, "I think our driver has a very strange sense of humor."

Harry wasn't sure if it was a joke or not. He decided it must mean that the driver, and a lot of the other passengers, did not like Americans.

CHAPTER 3

The excitement of the fire soon passed, and most of the passengers went back to sleep, but Harry and Rosa continued to talk. Small talk, mostly. They talked about the villages they passed. The weather in Mexico City and Acapulco. Flowers. The water. She explained some of the scenes picked out by the bus's headlights. Advertising signboards. Roadside shrines to memorialize victims of the auto accidents the ticket man had warned about.

"What are those big white letters painted on walls and buildings?" Harry asked. "I see them everywhere, even on the sides of the mountains. Somebody goes to a lot of trouble to climb up there and paint them. What do they mean?"

"Those are the initials of our political parties," Rosa explained. "PRI is the Institutional Revolutionary Party, the most important party in Mexico. They're the people who run the country. Our president, Miguel Alemán, is a member of the PRI, and so is Adolfo Ruiz Cortines, the man Alemán picked to succeed him."

"You say he 'picked to succeed him.' Wasn't there an election?"

Rosa laughed. "Oh, of course. There was an election last month, but the outcome was automatic. It's all determined ahead of time. President Alemán picked Ruiz Cortines with the *dedazo*."

"The dedazo?"

"Yes, the 'pointing of the finger.' Toward the end of his six-year term, the president points his finger at his favorite and says 'I want him to succeed me.' Then we have the election, but it's just a formality.

The opposition parties have their candidates, but they don't provide much opposition, and they don't have a chance of winning. And look, there's a sign for PAN, the National Action Party. Those letters up ahead on the left, PCM, those initials stand for the Communist Party in Mexico."

"Are there are many Communists in Mexico?"

"Oh, yes, I guess there are a few, but they don't have much political power."

Harry and Rosa talked about many things. He asked her questions she didn't answer. She asked him questions he didn't answer. Small talk doesn't always come easy.

After a lull, Harry asked Rosa about the fire. "The man in the row behind us said there was a fire a few weeks ago. Is this unusual?"

"Well, I guess fires do happen from time to time. That fire was not very big. Harry, your Spanish is not so rusty. You speak Spanish like a native. Where did you learn to speak our language?"

"I learned it in school, and picked up more just traveling around. But what caused the fire a few weeks ago?"

"Oh, you hear a lot of different things. You know how it is, people just like to talk."

"Yes, but what are they saying?"

"Well, some people say it was just an accident, careless workers at Pemex."

"Pemex?"

"Petróleos Mexicanos. That's the government petroleum company."

"The government owns the oil company?"

"Yes. Back in 1938 Mexico nationalized the oil industry. Before that the oil companies were controlled by foreigners, but for the past fourteen years Pemex is just one big company run by the government. And now, many people say careless workers at Pemex were the cause of that fire a few weeks ago. Pemex is plagued by absenteeism, and sometimes there aren't enough workers available to handle a crisis.

"But many people say the real problem is the bureaucrats who run Pemex," she continued, "that they don't know how to manage the company, and they're going to ruin the company. Not everyone is happy with the government, and not everyone is happy with Pemex. People like to talk. No one seems to know anything for certain, but everyone seems to have an opinion. So much talk over one little fire."

"And what do you think?"

Rosa put her head back and smiled. "I don't think about it too much. There are more important things to worry about."

Harry looked over at Rosa. Her blue eyes sparkled in the soft glow of the dashboard lights. "But what could a pretty young girl like you have to worry about?"

"Oh, we all have our secrets," she replied, smiling.

Rosa closed her eyes. Soon she was asleep. As the bus rounded a curve, her head rolled onto Harry's shoulder. He shifted his weight to provide a more secure pillow for her head, and he gently took her hand.

CHAPTER 4

The bus was moving along, right on schedule. Between stops the passengers slept when they could, and they talked when they could. More small talk, mostly. Rosa talked about flowers and music, and she talked about Acapulco. She said when you take the bus to Acapulco you go right through Cuernavaca and Taxco. Harry said he would like to make that trip.

Harry asked her about the newspapers in Mexico City.

"Well, *The News* is an English-language daily paper," she said, eager to provide whatever helpful information she could to this affable stranger. "Many of the people working at *The News* are North Americans, and many are bi-lingual Mexicans.

"Also, several of the major newspapers in Mexico City print a page in English each day. They publish a few news and sports stories, but a lot of what they print is society news of the American and the British communities. Those pages are prepared by an English-speaking editor on the staff of the newspaper. Say, Harry, maybe you could find a job at *The News*."

"I'll keep that in mind, but right now I'm really not interested in getting wrapped up in a regular job. Life's too short. I've got plenty of years ahead of me for work. But tell me, where would be a good place for me to stay in Mexico City?"

"Oh, you would like the Hotel Comé, or perhaps the Geneve. Many tourists stay at those hotels, because they're clean and pleasant and well-located, and they're not too expensive. Wealthy tourists, and even wealthy Mexicans and businessmen with expense accounts, like to stay at the Reforma or the Del Prado, for a lot more money but also more luxury and convenience. Or if you like history, you could try the Cortes."

Harry laughed. "Well, I'm not wealthy, and I don't have an expense account, so I guess I'd better take your advice and try one of those first two places you mentioned."

Rosa laughed with him. "Or maybe you can win a million pesos in the *Lotería Nacional*, and buy a big house in the Lomas de Chapultepec, where the rich people live."

The bus, now getting closer to Mexico City, stopped at a bustling cantina on the edge of Pachuca. Inside the cantina, passengers chatted and bought snacks, coffee, soft drinks, and beer. Some sat at tables, others preferred to stand or walk around, stretching their legs. Many lined up to use the restrooms.

Harry came out of the men's room and went straight to the parking lot in front of the building to catch the fresh air. He looked back through the doorway and saw Rosa talking to a man in a rear corner of the cantina. A blond, fair-skinned man, maybe in his mid-forties. Tall, dressed in a dark double-breasted suit, white shirt and maroon-and-blue rep stripe tie.

That's odd, Harry thought, I don't remember seeing him on the bus. He must have been sitting all the way in the back. But how did I miss him? I'm sure I saw everyone who got on. Is this guy making a pass at her? No, it's more than that. They're arguing about something, and she's furious.

Suddenly the rep stripe tie guy grabbed Rosa by one arm and pulled her toward the rear door. She swung her free hand, slapping him on the cheek. He let go in a hurry. Then three burly cantina customers seized the man by both arms, dragged him to the rear door, and threw him out. The rest of the people in the cantina broke into applause and laughter and cheers of *¡Olé!* Rosa turned and headed for the front door.

When Harry saw the ruckus, he was ready to run back into the cantina to help Rosa, but the whole thing happened so fast he didn't get a chance. He waited for her by the steps of the bus and glanced back over his shoulder, just in time to see her slip a white envelope into her purse as she hurried toward the bus.

When the bus got rolling again, Harry and Rosa resumed that inevitable small talk about Pachuca and the cantina and the soggy *taquitos*. Then he asked the question. "Rosa, what was that all about back there? Who was that guy? What did he want? You can't be too careful in a roadside joint like that."

Rosa didn't answer, so he repeated the question. "Rosa, what was going on back there at the rest stop? And who was that man?"

"Oh, pardon me, Harry. I'm sorry, I didn't hear you. My mind must have been drifting. I guess I'm exhausted from such a long bus ride. I don't know who he was, just one of the other passengers on the bus."

"But you were arguing. He grabbed you by the arm. And he gave you something." Harry laughed, and tried to add a bit of levity to his probing. "And you really let him have it—*pow*, right in the kisser."

"Harry, I don't know what you're talking about. He didn't give me anything. I don't know what you mean. I don't know who he was."

Harry didn't press her for more information. He figured he could learn more later on, when they meet for dinner in Mexico City.

Rosa put her head back, closed her eyes, and drifted into a restless half-sleep. Harry was wide awake, thinking about what happened back there in Pachuca. That guy was not just one of the other passengers. Wearing a suit coat and tie on this hot, breathless bus? No way. From my catbird seat up here in the front of the bus, I watched people getting on and getting off, at the start of the trip and at all the stops along the way, and I know damned well that son of a bitch was never on the bus.

CHAPTER 5

As the bus worked its way to the terminal, Harry realized why oil must be such a burning concern in Mexico. Gasoline, diesel fuel, kerosene and motor oil were the lifeblood of this sprawling city of three million people, if not the entire nation. The highways, streets, alleys, avenues and boulevards were the arteries that kept the throbbing economy alive. The late-afternoon traffic in Mexico City was as boggling as anything he had experienced in New York or London or Buenos Aires or anywhere else in the world.

Taxis, trucks, buses, motor cycles, motor bikes, passenger cars, limousines, mini cars, delivery vans—all were fighting to be first through an intersection, first around a traffic circle, or the last one through a yellow traffic light. Adding to the congestion were the bicycles, streetcars, trams, pedestrians, and the occasional horse.

At the bus station, Harry collected his luggage—two suitcases, a Sunday bag of golf clubs, and the duffel bag. "I'll get a taxi," he said, "and I'll drop you off at your house, and then we'll meet later for dinner."

"No, no—I live so far, and it would be better if I drop you at the hotel."

"Are you sure?"

"I insist. After all, you're a stranger in our city. Then I'll join you in one hour at the Restaurante 33."

"Okay, if you're sure it's not out of your way, that'll work. By the way, is this Restaurante 33 a fancy place? I mean, will I have to wear a suit coat, or can I come in just a sport shirt?"

"You should wear a suit coat and tie, or at least a sport coat and tie. In Mexico City, all the businessmen wear a coat and tie most of the time." Rosa laughed. "Some men wear a black suit every day because it's the only suit they own, but they're always prepared to go to a funeral if a friend or a relative dies."

Rosa anticipated his question. "And, of course, many men like to wear just a *guayabera*." That's the tropical white shirt that men wear hanging outside the belt. With the guayabera you don't need a coat."

In his room at the Hotel Comé, Harry opened one of his suitcases and hung a gray flannel suit on the back of the bathroom door. He shaved, took a quick shower, and let the hot water continue to run in the tub to steam his suit. When he was half-dressed, he placed a telephone call to the reception desk at the Hotel Del Prado.

"This is Harry Banister speaking. I'm running a little behind schedule, but I'll be there soon. Is my room ready?"

"Ah, good evening, Señor Banister, and welcome to Mexico. Yes, your room is ready, you've been pre-registered, and there is an envelope waiting for you here at the desk."

"An envelope?"

"Yes, Sir, a messenger delivered it this afternoon."

"Okay, I'll pick it up when I check in. I'll be there in thirty minutes."

Harry finished dressing, took the unopened suitcase and the duffel bag, and left the room. He stopped at the reception desk and exchanged fifty U.S. dollars for Mexican pesos. As he left he told the desk clerk, "I have to deliver these bags, but I'll be back later." He got a taxi and headed for the Del Prado.

On the way, Harry asked the taxi driver if he knew the Bar Restaurante 33. "You're in luck, Señor. The Bar 33 is on Avenida Juárez, just a short walk down the street from the Del Prado. You won't need to take a taxi to go there."

So Harry checked in for the second time that evening, unpacked, and settled into a lounge chair by the window. This room definitely was larger and more luxurious than his room at the Comé, which didn't surprise him—like Rosa said, the rate was higher.

The envelope was marked "delivered by hand." Harry opened it and read the message:

Welcome to Mexico. Hope your room is okay
Stop by tomorrow and say hello

Harry considered his priorities for tomorrow: have a leisurely breakfast, buy a street map, get oriented, maybe take a sightseeing tour, be a tourist. Check with the Del Prado concierge about golf. Stop by later and say hello to Bob, and thank him for making the reservation. And maybe see Rosa again—depending, of course, on how things turn out tonight.

Like the taxi driver said, the Bar Restaurante 33 was right up the street from the Del Prado. Harry was afraid Rosa might see him coming from the hotel, so he walked fast. He assumed 33 would be the street address of the restaurant, but as he approached he noticed that the buildings had even-numbered addresses and he realized the number 33 must have some other significance. So he asked the doorman.

"Yes Sir," the doorman replied in English. "That 33 is a pretty important number, all right. Refers to Article 33 of the Constitution, which says the Mexican president can kick out anyone he thinks is undesirable."

Harry switched to English. "You mean deport them?"

"Yes, Sir. Deport them. Kick 'em right out."

"And what do they mean by 'undesirable?'"

"Well, Sir, they mean criminals, revolutionaries, spies, foreign agents—you know, really dangerous people like that." The doorman's English carried a noticeable Dixie accent.

Harry switched to Spanish. "How about gringos, like you and me?"

The doorman smiled. "Oh, I'm not a gringo. Gringos are white Americans, and I don't quite fit that description. I came down twenty years ago from Memphis, and I'm a Mexican now.

"But I don't think they mean you either, Sir, as long as you're not a threat to the peace of the country, as long as you don't break any laws or cause any problems. No, the government's looking to apply The 33 to really dangerous foreigners, like rapists and murderers, you know, or revolutionaries, or spies, or smugglers.

"But you know what else, sir? The owner of this establishment, he likes to apply The 33 to any customers he thinks are out of line. Throw them out. Deport them from the premises. You know what I mean, when they're drunk, or noisy, or fighting, or anything like that. Or when a guy really annoys one of the ladies, and causes trouble. The owner doesn't tolerate any kind of trouble or scandal in his restaurant."

"Does that happen very often?"

"Oh, from time to time he has to do it, throw out a drunk, maybe. Like I say, he doesn't tolerate any kind of trouble."

Harry went in and got a table near the door, with a good view of the bar and the rest of the dining room. Just like when you're riding the bus, he thought, it's a good idea to take in as much of the scenery as you can. It was still early, but quite a few tables were occupied, and several men were at the far end of the bar. Musicians were setting up and tuning their instruments next to the dance floor. Harry ordered a beer and, as he waited for Rosa, he studied the room, studied the customers, and recalled what the doorman said about Article 33 and the undesirables. And he wondered how Rosa happened to pick this place for dinner.

CHAPTER 6

"So tell me, Rosa, how did you happen to pick this place for dinner?"

"Well, it's a pleasant restaurant, and the food is good, and the prices are reasonable, but mostly I picked it because I thought it would give you a chance to see Avenida Juárez and the beautiful Alameda across the street. Avenida Juárez is a very important street in our city, and it leads past the Palacio de Bellas Artes—oh, Harry, you must visit our Palace of Fine Arts while you're here. It's such an architectural splendor, and so many important events take place there. And then the Avenida continues right down to the Zócalo and the National Palace and the Cathedral."

Now Harry smiled. "You must really know this town inside and out, just like a tour guide."

Rosa blushed. "Oh, I don't mean to sound like a tour guide, but I do love this city. This is my city. It's so vibrant. There's so much life, so much excitement here. And while there's life, there's also much fascinating history." She paused briefly and smiled, and then continued. "It's important for me in my work to know my way around, and to understand the city and its principle buildings and its parks and historic locations. And our Alameda is such a lovely park. There's always something exciting going on there."

"Yes, I noticed the park when I got to the restaurant," Harry said as the waiter delivered vodka and orange juice for her and another beer for him. He didn't think it necessary to tell her he could see the Alameda from his hotel room.

"And did you hear the mariachi music when you arrived?"

"I could hear the music, but I couldn't see the band. They must've been playing somewhere back inside the park."

"Oh, you must see the mariachis. We Mexicans love our mariachi music. It's so colorful, and so exciting. Mariachis are part of our heritage. You hear them everywhere. Oh, Harry, you should go to the Plaza Garibaldi—the mariachis play there every night, and people come to listen to them and to hire them for a party. Or a man might hire a band or a trio to serenade his sweetheart." Rosa blushed again.

"Serenade?"

"Yes. They'll go to her house and play a song outside her window."

"Just like the movies. Sounds romantic," Harry commented, thinking he might be able to do a little romancing later tonight. "I'd like to see them up close some time."

"Of course, you didn't see them tonight, but mariachis play regularly here in the Alameda, and often there are artists in the park in the daytime, sketching and painting and displaying their work, and people are sitting on benches, just talking and relaxing. And many of these people on the benches are young couples holding hands." She smiled at Harry, and blushed, and lowered her eyes. "Oh, pardon me, Harry, but there I go again, sounding like a travel brochure, or a tour guide."

"That's all right, you go right ahead." He reached across the table and took her hand. "I want to learn all I can about your city, and I love to hear you talk. You must know everything there is to know about Mexico City, all the history, and where all the bodies are buried."

Rosa pulled her hand away and sat up straight. "What do you mean? Are you saying the cemeteries? Of course, I know where all the important cemeteries are located, but more important, perhaps, are the monuments. Like the Monument to the Revolution, or the Caballito, or the Monument to the Boy Heroes—oh, there I go again, just like a tour guide."

Harry laughed. "What I said about buried bodies was just my poor translation of an American figure of speech. I just meant that you really know your way around, you know all the important places. Like this restaurant, for instance. Do you come here often?"

"I've been here a few times with customers of the flower shop, but it was not always pleasant, because all they wanted to talk about was their business, and the men wanted to seduce me, and they really didn't care about the flowers, as long as they were fresh and delivered on time." She smiled again as she looked at Harry. "And it's much more pleasant being here with you tonight."

Rosa's beauty had caught Harry's eye the moment she boarded the bus at the border. Now she was absolutely dazzling. She had changed from her rumpled travel clothes to something more fashionable, a tailored light blue suit and an open-collar white blouse. A boutonniere of three small white roses was pinned to the lapel on the left side of her jacket. Her hair was down, falling loosely over her shoulders. A silver cross, hanging from a silver chain, nestled comfortably in the cleavage of her ample breast. A silver watch hung from her left wrist, and her silver charm bracelet dangled once again from her right wrist. All that silver jewelry, Harry decided, complimented her blue eyes and blond hair.

"You know, I was thinking about your name. It's a perfect name for a girl who works in a flower shop. And those three roses on your jacket—do you always wear them?"

She laughed, and adjusted the flowers. "Yes, I wear three miniature white roses every day. They're like a name badge. Sometimes, when strangers come into the shop, they see me and they see my roses and they say, 'Oh, you must be Rosa—my friend so-and-so told me to ask for Rosa.'" She blushed, and added, "I must confess that I'm known to close friends and a few other people as *La Rosa Blanca*. My father gave me that sobriquet when I was just a little child."

"The White Rose. That's very fitting. Your father's a very perceptive man—the name suits you so well. You must be very close to your father."

Rosa bowed her head, touched her forehead with the fingertips of her right hand, as if to make the sign of the cross, and pulled her hand away. "My father, may God bless him, died when I was very young," she said softly.

"Oh, I'm sorry, I didn't know. I'm sure you miss him very much."

"Yes," she said, "I miss him. I was only seven years old when he died, and most of my memories of him are sketchy, like seeing him through a cloud of smoke, or perhaps seeing his reflection in an old dust-coated mirror. But I cherish those few memories that are vivid and happy. I didn't see much of him that I can recall, because he was away from home so much, often for weeks or even months at a time, but when he was home I had many happy times with him, playing little games and sitting on his lap and listening to his stories about animals. He loved animals so much."

Rosa paused and smiled, as if she suddenly remembered a particular moment in her childhood.

"I do recall that he and my mother were very close," she continued, "and they loved each other very much, although there were times when they had great disagreements. Sometimes at night, when I was supposed to be asleep, I could hear them arguing. I didn't understand what it was all about, I didn't know what they were arguing about, but as I grew older I came to understand. And when I was old enough, my mother explained it all to me."

Rosa paused again, taking a silent slow sip of her drink. Then she sat up straight and continued. "My mother was a wonderful, loving person, and I know she cared for him very much, but she didn't like him being away from home so much of the time. And, as I came to understand later, she certainly did not approve of what he was doing when he was gone."

My God, she realized, I'm revealing my life history to a man I just met. Barely twenty-four hours ago he was a stranger sitting next to me on a bus, just another passenger, and I didn't even know his name. Now I'm telling him some of the darkest secrets of my past. Dear God, what is happening?

CHAPTER 7

"After my father died, my mother raised me," Rosa continued, speaking very softly, "and she saw to it that I had a good education in the best schools. She was very strict with me, and she wanted to instill in me her morals and her religious values and traditions. She also is gone now, just a few months ago, God rest her soul. I live alone now, in the same house she and I lived in for many years."

She must live close by, Harry decided. She not only went home to change her clothes, but she also had time to stop by her flower shop to pick up those fresh roses. "But where is your flower shop, in case I want to drop in to see you some time? And I'll be sure to ask for La Rosa Blanca when I come."

Rosa beamed, and leaned forward to touch Harry's hand. "Oh, yes, please do come." A bright smile filled her face as the conversation now turned to a happier subject. "I would love to have you see where I work. It's not too far from here, close to the Hotel Geneve. It's called the Florería Roma. We're not a large shop, but we do a very good business, and we're busy all the time. Many of our customers are families, or perhaps men who buy flowers for their wives, or whoever it is that men buy flowers for." She blushed when she said that.

"And, of course, the funeral parlors. They're steady business for us because people are dying every day. We make beautiful floral arrangements for the funerals, all in good taste." She paused to catch her breath, and to take a sip of her vodka. She was excited, talking now about her beloved flowers.

"But we also provide beautiful flowers for weddings, and there are many weddings, so there always will be people to replace the ones who are dying. And, of course, we provide flowers for *quinceañeros*."

"Quinceañeros?"

"Yes, a quinceañero is a party for a young girl when she reaches her fifteenth birthday. It's her debut, you might say. It's a very important day for a young girl, a festive occasion."

Harry could tell she really enjoyed her job. When she talked about flowers, her eyes sparkled like bright blue dew-topped flowers in the morning sun (he could see the flower in his memory, but he couldn't recall the name).

"And I suppose you had a quinceañero?" Harry asked.

"Oh, yes. A modest one. My mother planned it for me, and of course, the Florería Roma supplied the flowers. It was a very happy occasion."

"And when was that?"

Rosa laughed. "Now that would be telling, wouldn't it? A woman never likes to reveal her age. But permit me to continue. We also provide flowers for offices and stores and small shops, and also for many of the government offices when they want to look nice for a reception or a press conference or some other special event." She paused again to take a quick breath. "Oh, I'm sorry Harry, I'm talking too much."

"No, not at all. I like to hear you talk. I like the sound of your voice. Please, go on."

"Well, flowers are so important here in Mexico, Harry, so much a part of our lives, and so much a part of the natural beauty of Mexico, ever since the days of the ancient Aztecs. When I'm surrounded by flowers—the blossoms, the colors, the aromas—I think this must be the best of all possible worlds."

Harry laughed a sympathetic laugh. "You're a very busy girl." He wondered how the hell she could waste a whole day on that hot, dusty, smelly Red Arrow bus. He wondered the same thing about himself.

"Well, I guess you'll have to go to work tomorrow," he continued, "but I'm going to relax, and see some sights, maybe take a tour, just like any other gringo tourist. But how about if we meet for lunch, and you can introduce me to another restaurant."

"Yes, I'll have to go to the shop in the morning, and find out what I'll be doing the next few days. I know we have a quinceañero coming up the end of next week. There are other people working in the shop, but Pedro, the owner, seems to rely on me for some of the important assignments." She frowned when she said that, and then she smiled as she thought about tomorrow. What a wonderful thing it would be to see Harry again, and how fortuitous it had been meeting him today. In fact, it would be wonderful seeing him every day. He's not at all the way I expected a Yankee to be. He's such a gentleman.

"Yes, let's do that. I'll give you the name and address of a place on Morelos where we can meet and have a delightful *comida corrida*. It's a little restaurant owned by a family from Spain."

Rosa fumbled around in the depths of her purse and, after a bit of searching, pulled out a piece of paper and a pencil. Typical woman's purse, Harry thought, big enough for everything she needs plus a lot of things she sure as hell does not need. Must be heavy to lug around.

"And what's a comida corrida?"

"Oh, the comida corrida is practically a full-course meal for only three pesos. Just about all the restaurants serve a comida corrida at mid-day." She beamed as she scribbled the address and handed him the slip of paper. "You'll love it there. It's so picturesque, typically Spanish, and the food is so good."

Then, in a sudden burst of enthusiasm, she blurted "Xochimilco! Oh, Harry, you must go to the floating gardens at Xochimilco while you're here. The flowers are so beautiful, and the mariachis are playing as they float by on little flat-bottom boats, and vendors are selling beer and tacos and tamales from their little boats. Xochimilco is such a lovely way to pass a Sunday morning or afternoon. And I have a wonderful idea! Perhaps you and I could go together next Sunday."

"Hey, that's a great idea," he replied, surprised by her sudden suggestion. "It so happens that I'm going to be free Sunday. I haven't made plans that far ahead, although I had thought about going to the bullfight."

"Well, maybe we can go to Xochimilco in the morning and have lunch on one of the little boats and then go to the bullfight in the afternoon," she said with a laugh.

My God, Harry thought, someone once told me I was a fast operator, but this girl's really on a fast track.

When dessert was served, Harry decided it was time to get serious with the big question. After all, that's what any good reporter should do. He leaned forward, reached across the table, and took Rosa's hand. "I hope you don't mind if I ask you again, but I have to know. You didn't level with me on the bus."

"What do you mean?"

"You weren't completely honest with me, and I was worried about you back there in Pachuca. That man in the cantina, he wasn't a passenger on our bus. You knew him, didn't you? You two were arguing about something, and he gave you an envelope. I saw you put it in your purse. What was that all about?"

Harry caught her by surprise. The conversation to that point had been light and pleasant, with talk about flowers and mariachis and food. She wasn't prepared for this sudden change of direction, and she freed her hand, picked up her dessert fork, and took a bite of her flan in an obvious gesture of delay.

Then, visibly flustered, she replied. "Yes, Harry, I knew him, and yes, we were arguing, but I didn't want to talk about him on the bus." She paused, and took another bite of flan. "That was my ex-husband, and yes, we were arguing, and that's the reason he no longer is my husband, because we were always fighting and arguing about something or other."

"But what was he doing up there in Pachuca? Was he following you? How did he know you were on that bus?"

Rosa hesitated, and took a sip of her coffee. "He must have known I was coming back today, and he must have called the bus terminal to get the schedule."

Harry could tell she didn't want to talk about it. Her voice was soft and choked, her breath was short, and she was at the point of tears.

But she continued. "We were arguing over the alimony. We always argue about the alimony because he never wants to pay. He gets angry that he has to pay, and he always tries to avoid it." She took a sip of coffee. "And that's what was in the envelope. The alimony. Now you understand, don't you?"

"Yes, I understand," he lied.

Rosa sat for a moment, silent but obviously agitated, her moist eyes downcast, her hands fidgeting with the coffee cup. Then she got up abruptly, slung her purse over her shoulder, and blurted, "Excuse me, Harry, I must go to the ladies' room for one little minute. You're asking me about something I didn't want to talk about. I must calm down, and collect my thoughts, and I must fix my makeup."

Harry finished his flan. He drained his wine glass and checked his watch, and he realized that it's been more than just 'one little minute.' It's closer to four or five minutes—so where the hell is she?

Then, just as the waiter returned with the check, Rosa hurried back to the table. Harry's first thought when he saw her was that she never made it to the ladies' room. Her hair was tousled, her jacket was open, and the flowers of her name badge were hanging limp from her lapel.

"I'm sorry to spoil such a wonderful evening this way, Harry, but I really must leave. I'm afraid I must be over-tired from the long bus ride, and I have to be up in the morning for my work. But I want to thank you for such a wonderful supper. I'll get a taxi out in front."

And she was gone.

CHAPTER 8

Harry didn't have a chance to ask Rosa any questions, and he couldn't follow her—the waiter was standing by the table, waiting with the check. Harry quickly paid the tab, went out the front door, and asked the doorman if he had seen the blonde lady leave.

"Yes, Sir, she just left in a taxi."

"Did you hear where she was going?"

"No, Sir, I couldn't hear what she said, but I did see the driver hold up two fingers, so it couldn't have been very far away."

"Two fingers?"

"Yes sir, two fingers for two pesos. It's two pesos for a short distance, or three pesos for a longer ride. You always want to settle on the fare before you get into the cab."

Harry went back into the restaurant and headed toward the restrooms. Something happened back there, and he wanted to find out what. Cute as she is, he thought, that girl sure has a way of attracting trouble.

Five or six employees and customers were crowded around a partially-closed door. Harry called on his training and experience as a reporter—plus a dose of congenital gall—and pushed through the blockade and opened the door. He found a dimly-lit hallway, the walls lined with bullfight posters. On one side was a door with a plaque bearing a man's name. The manager's office, Harry decided, or the owner that the doorman described as a guy who doesn't tolerate any kind of trouble in his restaurant. The door was ajar. Beyond it were two more doors, both closed, that looked like they might be offices or storage rooms.

On the other side of the hallway was the door to the ladies' room, and beyond that the door to the men's room. Tri-fold screens, each about eight feet tall and colorfully decorated with scenes of ancient Aztec rituals, stood by the restroom doors, providing additional privacy. To the rear, at the end of the hallway, was another door that Harry figured might lead out to the alley. A third Aztec screen was flat on the floor next to the door.

Two men were huddled in agitated dialog near the door to the men's room. "What happened?" Harry asked.

"There's a body in the men's room," a waiter whispered. "Dead. Very dead."

"What happened? Who is he?" Harry reacted with shock in his voice and on his face, but somehow he didn't really feel surprised. He was ready for anything right now, after everything that had happened so far today. "How did he die?"

A man who looked like he might be the manager or perhaps the owner replied in a hushed but authoritative voice. "We don't know for certain. I believe he was shot, but there's so much blood I think perhaps he could have been stabbed. We don't know for certain. The police will know. But be careful where you step, Señor. There is much blood on the floor, right there in front of you. You must be careful where you step."

Harry looked down at several pools of blood, the largest about the size of a dinner plate, some the size of a saucer, and others the size of a twenty-centavo piece. Some were perfect, undisturbed circles, others were shaped like teardrops. Two or three of the spots already had been stepped in. The spots reminded him of the bloody Aztec heart-removal sacrifices portrayed on the towering tri-fold screens.

On the wall next to the men's room door was a poster for a bullfight featuring the great Spanish matador, Manolete. On the poster, in the sand behind the charging bull, was a splatter of fresh, moist blood—definitely not the bull's blood and not Manolete's.

Harry determined that the victim was shot while he was standing in front of the poster, but hidden from view by the elaborate tri-fold screens. There could be a bullet buried in the poster. The circular drops indicated that the victim must have remained standing there for a moment or two, perhaps uttering a few last words to his assailant, perhaps pleading for his life, perhaps even struggling with the assassin.

The teardrop-shaped pools of blood laid a trail to the door of the men's room. Several of these spots were smeared, as if the victim had a hard time making it into the restroom before collapsing. Or perhaps someone had assisted him, or dragged him, toward the restroom.

Harry could see the victim's shoes and pant legs through the partly open door. There was blood on the bottoms of both shoes. "Who is he?" Harry asked again, as he edged closer.

"We don't know," the manager replied. "A customer perhaps, a stranger for certain."

"Is there anyone in there with the dead man now?" Harry gave the door a nudge with his elbow, opening the door just enough to give him a glimpse of the victim's upper body and face. The dead man was on his back and his suit coat was open, exposing a bloody white shirt.

"I need to use the facilities," Harry said as he pushed the door open wider. He stepped carefully over the body and into the room, crouching, nearly falling, and touching the floor with one hand to catch his balance.

"*Cuidado, Señor,*" the manager protested, alarmed by the audacity of this gringo. "Be careful! I cannot permit that. You should not be in there now! You could trip and fall. We don't need another body in there." He reached in to grab Harry by the arm as Harry tried to stand up straight. "You may use the ladies' room, if you must."

"That's all right, I guess I can wait," Harry said, backing slowly out of the room, once again crouching and stepping carefully backward over the body. He hesitated by the door, making mental notes as he studied the face and the body and the clothing.

The hallway group was growing, and the manager told his employees to return to their work. He also suggested that the customers return to their tables. "The police will be arriving any minute now, and they'll want to question everyone when they do arrive. Right now, you must clear this hallway to make their work easier. The police do not like crowds."

Harry went out and sat on a stool at the end of the bar. His perch gave him a view of the hallway and those Aztec screens. He also had a good fix on the front door. He saw the police when they arrived, and he watched as they began bustling around, questioning employees, talking to customers, and questioning the manager. Nobody saw anything, of course, because of the door at the opening to the hallway and because of the tall Aztec screens, and nobody heard anything, they claimed, because of the loud music.

"Take the body out the back door," the manager demanded. "I don't want any scandalous activity in my restaurant. Our patrons are enjoying their dinner."

"You already have had scandalous activity here this evening," the officer in charge said, "and most of your customers already have left. The customers who remain, I'm sure, are not enjoying their supper any longer. But we'll want to question the ones who are still here."

When Harry heard that, he recalled what the doorman had told him earlier, and he quickly and quietly left the Bar 33, melting into the commotion of the curious on the sidewalk in front of the restaurant. After a few minutes of lingering and listening, he left.

CHAPTER 9

Rosa instinctively pushed down the lock as she closed the taxi door, and she leaned back and tried to figure out what had just happened. Everything's a blur, she thought. Everything happened so fast. What in God's name went wrong? I can't go home right now, I'm shaking with fear. I wouldn't be able to get to sleep.

And it's been such a long day—a happy day, in part, because I met such a delightful man. Harry is so kind, so considerate. He seemed genuinely concerned about me when we left Pachuca. Yes, some of his questions were annoying, but I think he was sincere. He was asking those questions because he wanted to help me. He's a thoughtful man, a gentleman. But also he is *muy macho,* a real man. He's a man I would like to get to know better, a man I could spend the rest of my life with.

But what a dreadful episode in Pachuca. What a surprise, what a shock. How did he find me? He was so persistent, and I was so frightened. And what a horrible ending to supper. Dear God, why does my life have to be so complicated?

A block from the restaurant Rosa sat up, cleared her throat and spoke to the driver. "I've changed my mind. Please take me to the Florería Roma, on Calle Londres."

"Sí, Señorita," the driver replied, examining her rumpled appearance in the rear view mirror, "but I believe the flower shop must be closed at this late hour."

"Yes, I'm sure it is, but take me there anyway." She rolled down a window and slid closer to the open window to get the full effect of the fresh night air flowing through the back of the taxi. She tucked in her blouse, buttoned her jacket, and brushed her hair with her hand in the semi-darkness of the taxi. She took a compact from her purse and checked her makeup as the taxi passed under a street lamp. And in the dark, she deftly adjusted the roses that hung limply from her jacket lapel.

This would be an ideal opportunity to stop by the shop, Rosa thought, and take time to smell the flowers, as the saying goes. This has been a long and harrowing day.

Of course, the shop was closed when she arrived, and the metal shutters were down, protecting the windows that always displayed such beautiful flowers in the daytime. It's such a pity that we have to hide these lovely flowers from the public at night, she thought. Flowers are meant to be seen, and appreciated.

Rosa used her front door key to enter, and the sweet aroma in the shop immediately raised her spirits. Things cannot be all that bad, she decided, as long as flowers such as these continue to blossom and thrive. Flowers always put me at ease at the end of the day.

Rosa was startled to see lights in the back of the shop. She stepped cautiously till she heard familiar voices.

Pedro and María Elena were at the table in the workroom, cutting and arranging flowers. "Ah, good evening, Rosita," Pedro called out when he saw her. "Welcome home. I didn't expect to see you until tomorrow morning. How was your trip?"

Pedro, a balding, heavy-set man in his mid-forties with a soft, easy-going disposition, had known Rosa since she was a child, and he treated her like a daughter, or at least like a niece. Rosa thought of him as the uncle she never had, and from time to time she called him Tío Pedro. He let her work part time in the shop while she was going to school, and he taught her how to feed and prune and care for the flowers and how to arrange them artistically in vases and urns and baskets. Because of her intellect and her quick appreciation of the beauty of flowers, she learned rapidly. He gave Rosa a full time job after her mother died.

"Good evening, Pedro, and hello, María Elena. Oh, it's good to be home. The bus ride was long and tiresome, but you two are working late tonight."

Pedro reacted with a nod, then a smile and a laugh. "Ah, yes. We've been very busy. Late this afternoon I received a phone call from our friends at Pemex with an order for flowers for a press conference tomorrow. María Elena came in to help me prepare, and now these table-top bowls are nearly ready. In the morning we'll finish the baskets that will go on the dais, in front of the podium."

María Elena, a part-time sales clerk who normally worked just a few hours each day in the front of the store, was at Pedro's side helping him trim a bouquet of flowers, handing him bits of string and ribbon and wire.

Rosa admired Pedro's dedication. He always takes such great care preparing flowers for his customers, she thought, and his work with the shop and the flowers always seems to come first, regardless of whatever distractions he might encounter. "Oh, Pedro, the bowls look so beautiful," she said, "but isn't that short notice? They called you late today and the press conference is tomorrow?"

"It was a last-minute decision. Something important. That's the nature of our business. We must always be ready to serve our customers. But tell me, where have you been this evening, my Rosa Blanca? You must be tired from your trip. I didn't expect you to come in now, so late."

"Oh, yes, I am tired. When I got home from the bus station I thought I deserved a good meal. The food at those rest stops along the road was so bad." She laughed, and patted her stomach. "After I freshened up and changed, I went out for supper, but I stopped in here on the way to pick up fresh roses for my jacket. I feel almost naked without them."

Rosa didn't want to tell Pedro about Harry. Not just yet. She didn't want to tell him about the problem at the Pachuca rest stop. She certainly couldn't tell him about the horrible incident at the Restaurante 33. And of course, she couldn't mention any of these things with María Elena standing there at the work table.

"But I wanted to come here now, on my way home, for just one little minute. What time is the press conference tomorrow?"

"At two o'clock. Miguel will have to be there by one o'clock to set up the display, and I would like you to go with him to help. We want the flowers to look their best. Pemex says they have some very important news to disclose, and I'm curious to know what could be so important." He laughed. "It's ironic, isn't it?"

Rosa was puzzled by Pedro's question. She wasn't sure what he meant by "ironic," but she agreed anyway. She often agreed with Pedro when she didn't understand him, just because it seemed like the proper thing to do. "Yes, it is," she said.

"And later tomorrow," he continued, "is the reception at the Brazilian embassy. You have another busy day ahead of you, my Rosa Blanca. Go home now. You must be exhausted. And you too, María Elena. I don't want to have to broom you ladies out the door with these cuttings," he said, laughing as he swept the workroom floor. "I'll be leaving just as soon as I finish cleaning this room." Pedro smiled and hummed as he busied himself with the broom.

Of course, Rosa thought, he smiles all the time when he's with his flowers. It's his nature to smile. It seems like flowers are the soul of his life. He's such a pleasant man, and it's such a pleasure to be with him when he's working with his flowers. But sometimes, even though he might be smiling, his eyes reveal that he's somewhere else, a million miles away, in a distant land. At these times, it seems like he's living in two different worlds.

"Yes, I am exhausted, but I'll be here in the morning. And I'll go with Miguel to the press conference. Good night, I'll see you both in the morning."

A most unfortunate thing, Rosa realized, I won't be able to meet Harry for lunch. I was looking forward to seeing him again, after the disastrous way our evening ended. It's imperative that I see him again. I must explain things to him. But how can I tell him what happened? I'm not sure I can even explain it to myself. Could it be that I, too, am living in two different worlds?

CHAPTER 10

When he left the Bar Restaurante 33 Harry returned to the Del Prado and ordered a Carta Blanca in the lounge. I'll give the cops twenty minutes or so, he thought, to clean up the mess and get the body out. Meanwhile, I'll do what I usually do in a place like this, I'll listen and observe.

Harry bought a pack of Camels from the cigarette girl and studied the room and the customers as he sipped his beer. At the table to his right were two men in pin-stripe suits with white silk handkerchiefs cascading from the breast pockets of their coats. Mexican entrepreneurs. One scotch on the rocks, one scotch neat. Conversation about business.

At the table to his left were a man and two blonde women, all speaking English. Two gin and tonics and one scotch. Ice for all of them. Americans, Harry decided. The women called the man Ed. Conversation about a barbacoa at the American ambassador's house. He wondered how the hell Ed rates two good-looking blondes.

After thirty minutes and a second quick beer, Harry headed back toward the restaurant, but the sight of two police cars and a gaggle of gawkers in front of the place changed his mind. He hailed a taxi and went directly to the Hotel Comé, hoping Rosa would call him there, hoping she would tell him what happened.

Harry fell asleep in the chair by the window, waiting for the telephone to ring.

By nine o'clock the next morning Harry was back at the Hotel Del Prado. He stopped in the lobby to pick up a street map and a copy of *Excelsior*, and continued down to Sanborn's for breakfast. Just like the lounge last night, the restaurant was crowded with a mixture of well-dressed Mexicans and foreigners.

Harry took a seat at the counter and ordered an American-style breakfast of ham and eggs, toast on the side. With a few minutes of eavesdropping he picked up bits of conversation in Spanish, English, German and French. Nothing sounded very important, just quiet breakfast talk and laughter.

In his room, Harry sank into the chair by the window, the one with the view of the Alameda. He picked up the newspaper and, as usual, he glanced first at the sports pages. Mostly soccer, baseball, horses and bulls. Up in New York, the Yankees had the day off, and will face the Senators today.

Turning to the main news section, Harry stopped on a bold headline halfway down an inside page, and translated as he read:

Horrible assassination: unknown man killed in men's room at famous Bar 33

By Alberto Duarte

An unidentified man was shot and killed last night in the famous Bar Restaurante 33 on Avenida Juárez, across from the Alameda. The horrible crime occurred while customers were eating their supper and enjoying the music of the band.

Police Detective Captain Victor Gonzalez Moreno said the unfortunate victim's body was discovered by a restaurant porter, stretched out on the floor of the men's bathroom. The victim had been shot twice in the chest at close range, Detective Gonzalez Moreno told *Excelsior*.

Detective Gonzalez Moreno said robbery appeared to be the motive for the horrible crime. The victim's wallet was missing, and there were only seven pesos in one of his pockets.

Also, there was no wristwatch on the victim, but fresh red marks on his wrist indicated he had been wearing a watch that had been forcibly removed.

Detective Gonzalez Moreno said there was nothing in the pockets or on the body of the victim that would reveal his identity or where he lived, but Detective Gonzalez Moreno assured us that the Federal District police will continue to pursue a "vigorous investigation."

Detective Gonzalez Moreno declared that "we will discover who this unfortunate man was, and we will discover the identity of the killer, and we will apprehend him and prosecute him."

Sr. Enrique Fernandez, the manager of the Bar Restaurante 33, told *Excelsior* he did not recognize the victim, and that he was not a regular client of the restaurant.

But Detective Captain Gonzalez Moreno said there was a possibility that . . .

Harry reached over to answer the phone, tossing the newspaper on the bed. Hell, he thought, there's not much in that story I didn't already know, except the names of a cop, a restaurant manager, and a newspaper reporter.

"Good morning, Harry, and welcome to Mexico. You made it in all right last night?"

"Hey, hello Bob. Yeah, everything's fine. And thanks for making the reservation for me. Nice place, the Del Prado. Nice room with a great view of the park. They put me on a floor right up near the top."

"Good. I thought you'd like it. I wanted to be sure you made it without any problems."

"No problems. I'm glad you called. I was going to give you a call in just a little bit. Like I said, no problems, but I'll just have to get used to the thin air in Mexico City, up here in the clouds."

"Oh, you'll get used to it, and it won't take long. Just don't do too much running and jumping at this altitude."

"Don't worry about that, I'm not planning any strenuous physical activity. I'm here to relax and have a good time."

"I know, that's what you told me. What do you have planned?"

"Nothing definite yet. I want to play some golf, and I'd like to get down to Acapulco and relax on the beach, maybe do some deep-sea fishing, but first I want to take in the sights here in Mexico City."

"Well, there's plenty for you to see right here in the Valley of Mexico, but do you think you might want to do a little work for me while you're here? I'm short-handed now."

"Thanks, Bob, but I'm not really interested in going back to work just yet."

"I thought maybe I could give you a few assignments, but nothing permanent, you understand. Why don't you stop by the office later this morning? We can talk about it then."

Harry smiled when this sudden opportunity popped up. The subject of work never had been mentioned in any of his earlier telephone talks with Bob.

"Like I said, I'm really not interested in going to work, but I'll be there in a little while and we can talk about it. I've got a few things to do before I can stop in."

As he hung up, Harry considered what those "few things to do" should be. I could go back to the Bar 33 and nose around, or better yet, go down to he lobby and see if the concierge could set up a golf game for me, or set up a sight-seeing tour. I could go to the Florería Roma and see Rosa, I could phone her now, or wait till we meet for lunch and question her then.

Harry picked up the phone and called the Hotel Comé.

"Yes, Señor Banister, there was one call for you just after you left this morning, but the lady did not leave her name, and she did not leave a message."

"Okay, thank you. Thanks very much."

That answers one question, Harry thought. Rosa wants to tell me what happened last night.

Harry put on his suit coat and left the room, heading toward the elevators, but he stopped short, turned, and walked briskly back to the room. He picked up the newspaper and continued reading the story on the "horrible assassination" in the restaurant:

But Detective Gonzalez Moreno said there was a possibility there was more than one person involved in the shooting. "I cannot say any more about it at this point," the veteran detective told *Excelsior*, "but we have retrieved certain clues that point to the possibility of the presence of a third person in the hallway.

"And although we do not know the identity of the victim, because he was robbed of every bit of his personal belongings and identification, we do have one clue that might tell us something about where he lived, or where he came from."

Detective Gonzalez Moreno gave no indication of what that mysterious clue might be, but he assured us he would continue to pursue this investigation with great vigor.

When Harry left the hotel he looked up the street and saw a police car parked in front of the Bar Restaurante 33. He got a taxi and headed for the Florería Roma.

In the cab, Harry thought about the shooting and sorted through the myriad possibilities as if he were interviewing the cop for a newspaper story:

Detective Gonzalez, can you tell me why you think there might have been a third person involved? Are you perhaps referring to my dinner companion, Rosa? If not, who?

Did this third person shoot the guy, or did Rosa shoot him? Was he alive when she got there, or was he already dead?

Did the killer, or this third man, if it was a man, slip out the rear door to the alley? Or did he (or she) blend in with the customers at the bar or in the dining room?

And please tell me, Captain Gonzalez, what was the dead man doing there in the first place? Was he having dinner, or was he drinking at the bar? How could I have missed seeing him sitting at the bar?

What did you see, Detective Gonzalez, that I didn't see? What clue tells you where the dead man came from?

And who do you think the killer might have been"

My God, Gonzalez, are you thinking about me? Did the manager tell you about the gringo who was snooping around back there, asking a lot of questions and sticking his nose into the scene of the crime, almost tripping over the corpse while he was at it?

For Christ's sake, Gonzalez, am I your prime suspect?

CHAPTER 11

A little bell over the door tinkled, announcing Harry's arrival. He was greeted by a waft of sweet fragrance that told him he was in the right place. The pleasant aroma immediately cleared his mind of all thoughts of death and intrigue. It was like being in another world, a world of perpetual springtime and tranquility, far removed from his world of saloons and, since the bus trip down here, cantinas. No wonder Rosa enjoyed her job so much.

He next was greeted by a woman who smiled and said, *"Buenos días, Señor,* and welcome to the Florería Roma. How can I help you?"

Harry was further set at ease by the warm smile and hospitality of this woman. Yes, perhaps Rosita was right—perhaps this is the best of all possible worlds. Whatever happened last night never really happened, it was just a bad dream. "Good morning, Señora. I'm looking for La Rosa Blanca. Is she here this morning?"

"But of course, Señor. I'll call her for you. She'll be most happy to serve you."

A rustle at the curtain in the back of the store told Harry it wouldn't be necessary to call Rosa. Two faces peeked out, Rosa's and that of a rotund, slightly bald man. Rosa was smiling, although it seemed to be a nervous, restrained smile.

Rosa stepped out from behind the curtain and quickly moved toward the front of the store. The man stepped out slowly but remained in the background, snipping something or other with a pair of clippers. The woman who had greeted Harry retreated to the room beyond the curtain.

"Good morning," Rosa said with a subdued voice, still nervous as she approached Harry. "Welcome to the Florería Roma. So good of you to come." She was wearing a colorful smock with a bright floral print. She always wanted to look her best when customers came in from the street. Harry's arrival had caught her by surprise, and she extended her right hand to shake hands in a business-like manner. Her left hand remained in the pocket of the smock, tightly gripping a pair of pruning shears.

Harry took her hand, now limp and lifeless. Something's wrong, he realized. She's nervous. Her voice is quivering. She's not happy to see me. This is not a good time. Maybe I shouldn't be here.

"Good morning, Rosa," he said, turning on the charm with a big smile that he hoped would melt the ice. "I just happened to be in the neighborhood, so I thought I'd stop by and say hello." He knew he had to do more than just smile, and say something more than just "hello," to bridge the awkward chasm. "This is a beautiful shop you have here. It smells so fresh, and you have so many beautiful flowers. You must think you're working somewhere in the lavish garden of a country estate." A little corny, he realized, just like his first words to her on the bus, but it might work.

"Thank you," she said, forcing a smile. "Sometimes it does seem like I'm somewhere else. Now you can see why I love my job so much. This is like my second home.

"Right now we're very busy in the workroom," she continued in a formal, business-like voice, "preparing displays that I'll have to set up for a press conference this afternoon. The press conference will be in the Pemex headquarters ... at *two o'clock.*" She delivered these words slowly and clearly, pausing to emphasize the time of the press conference.

Harry got the message: our lunch date is off. She can't talk right now, that man with the clippers is listening. He must be Pedro, the owner she talked about on the bus, the guy she referred to as Uncle Pedro. He looks like an uncle. "Well, if you're busy, I don't want to take up any more of your time. Like I said, I just happened to be in the neighborhood."

"Oh, no, I'm glad you came in. It's so thoughtful of you." She smiled, but it was not the genuine smile she had shown spontaneously on the bus and during dinner last night.

The door bell tinkled again, and a man and woman walked in.

"Good morning," Rosa said. "Can I help you, perhaps show you something?"

"We'll look around a bit. We just want to get some ideas," the woman said.

Rosa moved toward a display of orchids near the far corner of the shop, and Harry followed her. "I'm glad you survived that long bus ride," she said, still with a smile. The voice was calm now, and that nervous tension seemed to be gone. "And I know you'll enjoy your brief time here in our country, and see all that you can. There's so much to see and so much to do. But perhaps you could come back here some other time, when you have a spare moment, when we're not so busy?" The inflection in her voice, and the expression on her face, underlined the question.

Harry picked up that message, too: she's being polite, and she wants me out of here now, but she wants to see me again. "Thanks. I'm sure I'll enjoy it here in Mexico. And thanks for those tourist tips you gave me on the bus. I want to see as much as I can while I'm here, just like all the other tourists, and I'll be sure to get down to Acapulco, like you suggested.

"But, hey, I don't want to keep you from your work," he said. "You have a deadline to meet, and I have a busy day ahead of me, too. Maybe we can see each other again sometime soon. How about this evening?"

"Yes, perhaps we can meet again sometime soon, but not this evening. I know where you're staying, and you know where I work, so I'm sure we can arrange it. Thank you for coming in."

The telephone rang, and Pedro went to the workroom to take the call. Harry spoke quickly, in a hushed tone. "Okay, now we can talk. I gotta know what the hell's going on. What happened last night? You sure got out of there in a hurry. You've got some explaining to do. Where can we meet tonight, and what time?"

"Oh, no, Harry, not tonight," Rosa said, her voice rising.

The recently-arrived shoppers looked at Harry, looked at Rosa, looked at each other, and walked quickly to the door "We'll be back," the woman said as they left.

"Harry, please leave now," Rosa said, once again in a whisper. "I can't see you tonight. I tried to call you this morning, but you already had left the hotel. I'll call you later tonight at your hotel. You'll be there, yes?"

"Okay, where are you going to be tonight? I'll meet you. Name the place, and I'll be there. Otherwise, I don't know where I'll be. I might go out and take in some night life. I might even go back to the Restaurante 33 for dinner. That was a pretty good meal."

"No, no, Harry. Don't go back there!"

"Why not?"

"Harry, keep your voice down, please. It's just that I don't think you should go back."

"But why not? What're you afraid of? You have to tell me what happened, Rosa, before one of us gets into trouble. Or both of us, before the police come looking for us. In fact, I think you're already in trouble. I saw that man in the back of the restaurant."

"Oh? Which man?" she asked with feigned innocence.

"Come on, Rosa, you know which man. The *dead* man. Did you kill him? Tell me what you know, and this time tell it straight."

"Yes, I'll tell you. I want to tell you, I have to tell you," Rosa said, leading Harry to the door. "I'll call you later at your hotel, but you must go now. Please, before Pedro comes back."

"What's your telephone number at home? I'll call you there."

"No, Harry, I'll call you at the Hotel Comé. Please go now."

Harry picked up a Florería Roma business card on his way out the door and stuck it in his pocket, wondering what his next move would be. He had planned to check out of the Comé, but now he realized he was stuck there for another night, waiting once again for a phone call that might not come.

Rosa walked slowly toward the back of the shop, pausing by a bougainvillea to snip a sagging branch, stopping at a dahlia to clip a fading blossom, as she tried to organize her thoughts. In the back, she joined Pedro at the worktable. María Elena had gone to the front to wait on a customer.

Pedro broke the silence. "He seemed like a nice young man. Handsome, well-dressed. I didn't mean to eavesdrop, but I couldn't help overhear. He was on the bus with you yesterday?"

"Yes," she replied, somewhat relieved that the subject had been broached. Little by little, the whole story will have to come out. The bus ride, Harry, Pachuca, supper at the Restaurante 33, even that horrendous incident after supper. But everything in its proper time. Not now. "He sat next to me on the bus," she said, "and we chatted quite a bit. He's here on vacation, but he doesn't know his way around."

"I assume from the conversation, and by his accent, that he's an American. It's nice that you were able to give him a few friendly tourist tips. We must be good hosts when strangers come to visit. But you must be careful, Rosita, with men you don't know."

That's what Harry said to me on the bus, she recalled. Pedro and Harry are both wise in the ways of the world. "Oh, I know, and I am careful. I'm always careful. He's such a nice man."

"But you didn't mention him, my Rosa Blanca, when you came here last night."

"No, it was so late, and you and María Elena were busy finishing the flowers for today's press conference."

"Yes, I understand," he said, nodding. "And tell me, Rosita, were you able to advise your new friend where he might have supper while he's visiting here in Mexico City?"

CHAPTER 12

The little bell on the front door jingled once again. "I'll wait on them," Rosa volunteered, jumping up from her stool.

Rosa rushed through the curtain toward the front of the shop. She left the workroom so hastily that she didn't have a chance to answer Pedro's question. When she got to the front, María Elena's customers were leaving, just as two new customers entered, and María Elena greeted the newcomers.

Troubled by Pedro's question, Rosa turned and walked slowly back to the workroom. He must know about my supper with Harry last night, she reasoned. What else does he know? I'll have to answer his question, but I must choose my words carefully.

"Oh, María Elena is taking care of the new customers," she said sheepishly. "The other people were leaving."

"Yes, I know," Pedro said. He was putting finishing touches on the floor baskets for the afternoon press conference, adding ribbons of bright red, green and white, the colors of the Mexican national flag.

Rosa noticed that Pedro was smiling again—and humming. This may not be so difficult after all, she decided.

"You were so eager to rush to serve those new customers," he continued, still smiling, "that you didn't have a chance to answer my question. As I was saying, I think it was very hospitable of you to help your new friend, the American tourist—what was his name?"

"He calls himself Harry. I don't know if that's the formal name, or just an abbreviated nickname. And I don't know his last name. We never got around to that."

"I was wondering if you were able to recommend a good place for him to dine last evening. You said you were hungry, and that you went out to get supper. I assume he must have been hungry, too, after such a long trip. Did you recommend a restaurant for him?"

Rosa swallowed, and immediately forgot her hastily-planned response. But she knew she couldn't conceal anything from Pedro any longer. "Yes," she began, "we both were very hungry. The food at the rest stops was not very appetizing."

"I know, you mentioned that. I've had the dubious pleasure, from time to time, of eating at those rural cantinas."

"So I recommended the Restaurante 33," Rosa said, "and we agreed to meet there. I went home to change, and he went to his hotel, and then we met for supper."

"A fine restaurant. I've dined there a few times. And where is he staying?"

"I suggested the Hotel Comé as an inexpensive place for him to stay. He doesn't have a job right now. We met at the Restaurante 33 and had an excellent supper. I had the trout. I didn't want to take the time to tell you about it last evening, Pedro, because you and María Elena were so busy arranging the flowers for today's press conference."

"Yes, I was busy, and I was excited about such an important assignment. Pemex has been a good customer for our little shop, and I want them to be pleased with the flowers today. And I'm sure you didn't want to bother María Elena with chatter about your new boyfriend."

Rosa blushed. "Oh, Pedro, he's not a boyfriend, he's just a man I met on the bus. A very nice man. We shared some conversation, and some disgusting *burritos* along the way, and when we arrived in Mexico City we met for supper."

"What is he doing here? What kind of work does he do? Does he have a job?"

"He came here on vacation. He's a newspaper reporter. No, he doesn't have a job. He's 'between assignments,' is the way he expressed it, but he said he might have to get a part-time job so he can stay longer."

"How does he expect to find a part-time job?"

"I don't know, Pedro. He said he might just 'knock on a few doors.'"

Pedro was still smiling, but his voice had dropped in volume and in pitch. "Rosita, my child, you hardly know the man. You don't even know is name. He's a stranger in a strange land. And you must be careful with strangers. What kind of man would come to a foreign country, without a job, and simply go knocking on doors to see if he can pick up a job? Is he so talented that he thinks he can find work simply by knocking on a few doors?"

Pedro laid his scissors on the table. His voice now was calm, but the smile was gone. "Tell me, Rosita, what kind of man can come down here to Mexico on vacation, on a whim, with no employment? Or is he so wealthy that he doesn't have to work? And what doors will he knock on? Where will he look for work? Does he know anyone here? And how can he get a job here if he's visiting on a tourist card? He cannot work if he's a tourist, you know. It's against the law. And who would hire him? You must be very careful, Rosita, with men you don't know."

Rosa was becoming agitated, the anger building. Why is this man questioning me so aggressively, she wondered, the way an overbearing father might interrogate his frivolous teen-age daughter? Doesn't he trust me? Pedro always has treated me kindly, and he has tried to help me ever since Mamá died. But he is not my father. He's not even my uncle, even though I call him Tío. He does not have the right to interfere in my personal life.

Rosa spoke up. "I'm always careful with men, Pedro. My mother, may God bless her, taught me to be careful. There was plenty of opportunity to get to know something about him during that long bus ride. We talked almost constantly, we talked about many things. I was helping him with his Spanish, although he speaks it very well, almost like a native. He's a newspaperman, a reporter.

"I like him, Pedro. He's so much a gentleman, and I intend to see him again."

"My Rosita, you say you got to know him. But how much did he learn about you? Does he know your background? Does he know about your family, your past? And did he learn things about you he shouldn't know? Does he understand what you do here? I want you to be very careful, my child. You should try to find out more about him if you're going to see him again. As a matter of fact, I would like to know more about him."

Pedro's voice dropped to a near-whisper. "Your father, before he died, asked me to look after you, to protect you. That's what I always have tried to do, even while your mother was still alive. After she died, I gave you this job in the flower shop to help you, so you would not be completely alone in the world, so you could have honest work and a steady income. I've always tried to protect you, Rosita, and that's what I want to do now."

"Yes, I know, Tío Pedro, and I understand. You've been kind to me, and I appreciate everything you've done for me. But my mother raised me very well. She was a wonderful person, God rest her soul. She was very strict with me, she guided me well, and she pointed me in the right direction, and she saw to it that I had a good education in good schools."

Rosa paused, but continued quickly. "She also taught me to be self-reliant, to take care of myself. My mother was a deeply religious woman, and she raised me in the strict traditions of the Church. She had high moral values, and I like to believe she passed those values on to me. I'm always careful."

"I agree," Pedro said, "she was indeed a wonderful person."

But he didn't really agree. He had always considered Rosa's mother a religious relic, clinging obstinately to the past, interfering in her husband's life and in Rosa's life and in his own life as well. And he took great pride that he had cast off, at an early age, the debilitating shackles of God and the Church. Religion had no place in his life.

Pedro hummed a familiar zarzuela air as he took several pages from the morning editions of *Excelsior* and *Novedades* and spread them on a large table. He placed six vases of flowers on the pages and sprinkled them with a small hose, watching as the water dripped like drops of rain onto the headlines and stories and pictures and advertisements, and he laughed as he finished his task.

"You know, the daily newspaper is a wonderful servant of mankind," Pedro said, his face bright with a broad smile. "First it informs us of all the news of the city and the nation and the world. The news of politics and war and the weather and, of course, baseball and the bulls. Then, after we've read all the news, we can use the newspaper to wrap our dead fish.

"And right now, we can use the newspaper to absorb the excess water draining from our flower pots and dripping from the leaves of our plants. As you know, Rosa, it's good to keep a supply of newspapers on hand for this purpose."

Rosa also laughed, relieved that Pedro had changed the subject and returned to a more jovial mood.

"And the daily newspaper also brings us all the news of crime." The smile disappeared from his face. "Oh, by the way, I saw in this morning's papers that a man was killed last night at the Bar Restaurante 33. Were you there when that happened?"

Rosa was prepared. She had rehearsed her answer in her mind a dozen times since last night, and she spoke up without hesitation. "Oh, good heavens. Is that what all the commotion was about? A man was killed? How horrible. Yes, I heard some kind of fuss in the back of the restaurant, back by the restrooms. We had finished our supper by then, and we were just leaving, and Harry went back to his hotel, and, as you know, I came here to the shop."

"Yes, I know, Rosita, my dear Rosa Blanca. You told me last night that you came here earlier in the evening to get fresh white roses to pin on your jacket. Your name badge. Remember, you said you 'feel almost naked' without those three little roses? Obviously, you wanted to look your best for your date with your new friend, yes?"

Rosa reached instinctively for the spot on her shoulder where the flowers should be. Then she laughed when she realized they were on her jacket hanging across the room. "Oh, yes, my name badge. Harry joked about that. He said he thought the three white roses are perfect for me."

Pedro continued, peering intently into Rosa's eyes, his voice even softer, "Rosita, my dear child, when you arrived here last night, you were wearing only two white roses on your lapel. What, in the name of God, happened to the third flower?"

CHAPTER 13

Outside the Florería Roma, Harry checked his map and decided to walk to the United Press office. Like Rosa said last night, it's important to know your way around the city, and walking is a good way to learn.

When he turned the corner onto Bucareli, Harry found himself absorbed in the main artery of Mexico's thriving newspaper world. If you want to know what's happening, this is where you could find out. *Excelsior, El Universal, Ultimas Noticias, Ovaciones, Novedades, The News*—all the daily, weekly and monthly periodicals were here, measuring and reporting the pulse of the city and the nation and the world. Sandwiched in were the offices for AP, INS, UP, Reuters, France Presse, *The New York Times*, and many other world-wide news-gathering organizations.

Trucks with rolls of newsprint jockeyed with vans carrying bundles of newspapers, the ink still fresh, all trying to avoid an army of eager boys dashing artfully in and out of traffic, hawking the latest editions of today's papers. Automobiles, vans, bicycles and pedestrians took their chances weaving through the mid-morning maze. The bustling traffic reminded Harry of his arrival in Mexico City last night.

The United Press office was busy with the clicking of typewriters and the babble of people talking to each other and talking to their telephones, in some cases almost shouting above the rhythmic rattling of the teletype machines. Harry looked around the room, recognized the familiar scene, and immediately felt right at home.

"Welcome to Mexico," the bureau chief greeted, wrapping his arms around Harry with a hearty Mexican-style *abrazo*. "It's good to see you again."

"I'll have to get used to this friendly bear hug thing," Harry said, after he caught his breath, "and remember to do it myself in the future, so I can fit right in."

"That's right, Harry, When in Rome... The abrazo and a firm hand shake are a must here in Mexico, even if you already shook hands with the same guy three times earlier in the day."

The bureau chief led Harry into his office, a small room formed by glass partitions that provided a modicum of quiet and a full view of the activity in the rest of the bureau's work space. The office was crowded by a desk, two chairs, an overstuffed leather sofa, several filing cabinets, two muffled teletype printers, and a Royal on a rolling stand. On the desk sat two black telephones, a tan telephone, a yellow legal pad, a gooseneck lamp, an ashtray, and a beer mug stuffed with pencils and markers.

"So tell me, how was your trip down?"

"Well, you know I came by bus. *On the Downhold*, as those UP bean-counters up in New York like to say, to hold down my expenses. The trip was long and the food was lousy. Those rest stops don't offer much in the way of gourmet fare."

"No, you're right about that, but you can make up for it now. There are plenty of good places to eat right here in Mexico City, and I'm sure you'll find them. Was there anything unusual on the trip?"

"Depends what you mean by unusual. There was a pretty girl sitting next to me."

"That's not unusual. If there's a good-looking dame around somewhere, you'll find her, and you'll sit next to her."

"No, it was the other way around. She found me, and she sat next to me."

"How did you arrange that?"

"She was the last one on the bus, and it was the only seat available." Harry smiled, recalling how he had arranged the situation by spreading his coat on the vacant seat.

"I assume she was a dark-haired Latin beauty?"

"She's a beauty, all right, but she has fair skin and blue eyes, and she has blond hair. She's about my age, mid-twenties. She's Mexican, although she doesn't look like what I thought a Mexican girl would be. She looks more like she could be Scandinavian, or German."

"Or maybe even Dutch?"

"Yeah," Harry replied, "maybe Dutch. I hadn't thought about Dutch."

"Looks can be deceiving, Harry, and names can be deceiving. Mexico has quite an ethnic blend, not just Spanish and native Indian. There are plenty of other nationalities mixed in here, and plenty of non-Hispanic names. Did she have a Spanish name?"

"All I know is her name is Rosa. We didn't get around to last names."

"You keep referring to her in the present tense. I assume you're going to see her again?"

Harry shuffled his feet, and reached for his pack of Camels. "Mind if I smoke?"

"No, not at all," Bob said, smiling and scribbling something on the yellow note pad. "Go right ahead. Everyone out there in the main room is smoking, you might as well, too."

"Yeah, I was thinking about meeting her for lunch sometime."

"I'm sure you will. I'm sure you don't want to pass up an opportunity with a pretty girl. Meanwhile, what do you say? Do you want to go to work?"

The question caught Harry off guard. "Geez, Bob, we talked on the phone, must be three or four times, about my coming down here on a pleasure trip, but you never said anything about a job, and I never asked. Are you offering me a job now?"

"Sure, but just a part-time job, more like a stringer, when I need extra help. I'm a little short-handed right now, with a man on vacation. I can't put you on the payroll full time. That's not in the budget. I wouldn't work you too hard, and you wouldn't have to punch a clock. Your time would be pretty much your own, just working on special assignments or digging up feature stories."

"Like maybe a few travel stories? Acapulco? Or Cuernavaca? I hear Cuernavaca is a nice little town."

"Sure, maybe something like that."

"I'm really not interested in rushing into this work thing, Bob. Like I told you on the phone, I'm looking forward to this trip as a vacation. Of course, if I get in a bind, a little extra walkin' around money would help."

Bob laughed, and held up his right hand with the thumb and forefinger barely touching. "That's what you'd get from me—a little money."

"Can I get back to you on that?"

"Okay, let me know when you're ready. Changing the subject, they had your registration okay at the Del Prado?"

"Yeah, and thanks again for setting that up for me. Say, that's a first-class place, and my room has a beautiful view of the Alameda."

"No problem. How did you sleep last night? Better than on the bus, I bet."

Harry coughed on a puff of smoke. "I slept fairly well, but not at Del Prado. I slept at the Hotel Comé."

"You what?" Bob dropped his pencil and pad on the desk, and made a futile grab for the pencil as it rolled to the floor. "I set you up at the Del Prado, one of the best places in town, and you stayed at the Comé? What's the matter, you don't appreciate my help? And Harry, if you're really On the Downhold, what're you doing with two hotel rooms?"

"Oh, sure, I appreciate what you're doing for me," Harry said sheepishly, "but I talked myself into a corner. You see, I told Rosa I was unemployed, just a tourist on a tight budget. She recommended the Hotel Comé as a good bargain-rate place, and I thought it would look better for an out-of-work tourist like me to be staying there." Harry chuckled. "So I checked in first at the Comé, and then I went over to the Del Prado and checked in there. That's when I got your message."

"Well, you must have thought that would be a good pick-up line. You figured she would take pity on the poor, impoverished, suffering, out-of-work, hungry, road-weary traveler, and offer to put you up for the night at her place, right?"

Harry laughed when he realized Bob's observation was right on target. "Yeah, maybe that idea did enter my mind, and you never know, it might have worked."

Bob grinned and shook his head slowly from side to side. "Well, Harry old boy, it sounds like you've really backed yourself into a corner. Now you have to get out of that corner, and get out of one of those rooms, and if you're really On the Downhold, you should give up the Del Prado."

"Or both of them," Harry said, trying to sound frugal.

A teletype operator knocked and entered the office, handing the bureau chief several sheets of copy paper. Harry looked around the room while Bob marked the sheets with a black grease pencil. On the back wall were maps of Mexico City, Mexico, and Central America. Colored thumbtacks indicated locations that must have some significance to Bob, trouble spots or a hot story in progress. A bright red tack on the Mexico City map sat just below the Alameda. Harry wondered if that red tack represented the dead man at the Restaurante 33.

CHAPTER 14

When the teletype operator left the cubicle Harry considered the risk, and decided to plow right into it. It's going to come up eventually anyway. "Say, to change the subject, you said there are plenty of good places to eat here. Are you familiar with the Bar Restaurante 33?"

"Sure, right down the street from the Del Prado. Good spot, but if you go there, be sure to get a table near the door."

"Oh? Why's that?"

"You never know what might happen. They've had a few incidents there from time to time. As a matter of fact, someone was killed there last night."

"Funny you should say that. Rosa and I went there last night for dinner. We had a pretty good meal, but there was some kind of disturbance in the back of the joint, just as we were getting ready to leave."

"You were there? Did you get caught up in it?"

"I had a glimpse of the body, but I didn't hang around. Rosa already had left by then. That's why I went back to the Comé, and that's why I stayed there last night. I thought she might call me there. Do you folks have anything on it?"

"We didn't do anything with it. It's just another killing in a local bar. The local papers played it big, but the police don't have much to go on. Good thing you got out of there."

"You want me to look in on it?"

"No, don't bother. There was a shooting the other night at the Waikiki, and there'll be another one somewhere tonight. That reporter who wrote the story for *Excelsior* is a tiger. He'll dig up whatever there is. If not, the story will fade away and be dropped.

"But I'll tell you what you can do, if you'd like to get your feet wet," Bob said. "Pemex is having a press conference at two o'clock this afternoon. Do you know who Pemex is?"

"Yeah, as a matter of fact, Rosa mentioned them on the bus. That's the government oil outfit, right?"

"Why don't you sit in on the press conference? You could meet a few of the local reporters, listen to what Pemex has to say, and soak up the atmosphere, but don't worry about writing anything. Their messenger will drop off a press release for us here at the Bureau, and we get carbon copies of significant local stories from the reporters at one of the daily papers."

"Hey, that sounds like it would be fun, strictly as an observer, of course. What do I need to get in?"

"Not much, really. Just tell them you're the new guy here, and show them this card if they ask. They're not too strict about that sort of thing. They welcome the publicity." He handed Harry a card with the Pemex address, and a UP identification card with his name already on it. Harry put the cards in his pocket.

"Geez, Bob, you took a lot for granted when you had this I.D. card printed up. You've got me working here already."

"Just being prepared. Say, speaking of downholding expenses, you do understand I would be paying you in pesos, not dollars. UP lets me hire stringers and pay for other special coverage out of my bureau funds. In a way, you'd be working like a stringer for me here. Off the books, you might say. Since this is not a full time job, you wouldn't really be on the payroll."

"You mean I'd be just another petty cash item?"

"Not in the least. I don't consider you petty."

"Yeah, I understand," Harry said. "It's just that my pay would be petty. Maybe I really would have to give up one of my hotel rooms."

"Get a room somewhere, Harry, or a small apartment. Save your money for the restaurants and cantinas. Save your money for travel, and see the country. But you're going to have to watch what you spend. The *sindicato*—that's the newspaper union—the sindicato scale for a reporter is less than two hundred pesos a week. I'm afraid that's more than I had in mind for you."

Harry did a quick mental tabulation. "You're kidding! That's barely twenty-three bucks a week. I don't think I could live on that."

"Listen, Harry, don't get caught in the usual tourist trap of trying to convert pesos to dollars. You're going to have to think like a Mexican, and think in terms of pesos, not dollars."

"But how do those reporters live on that kind of dough?"

"They don't. They all have some kind of extra income or outside jobs. A lot of them are on the take. Everybody has to hustle to get by. That fellow Duarte, who wrote this morning's story on the Restaurante 33, has an extra job at *Excelsior*, and some kind of public relations job on the outside. You might be able to do some free lance writing from time to time, if you want to pick up extra cash."

Bob spun his Rolodex, stopped on a name, and jotted a phone number on a card. "Here's one possibility. This man might be able to throw some work your way. Give him a call when you get pressed for beer money, after you settle into a cheap room or a cheap apartment." He handed the card to Harry.

"Jesus, Bob, I don't want to be living on the cheap down here. After all, this is supposed to be a vacation." Harry paused to glance at the card—no name, nothing but a phone number. "Who is he, anyway?"

"He's an American. He's been down here a few years now, doing some kind of agricultural research or something like that, but he told me he might need help sometime on a project. He knows about you. I told him you were coming down, and I told him you're a damn good reporter and a good writer. He says he might be able to hire you to do some writing if the need ever comes up."

"What kind of writing? I don't know much about agriculture. I'm a city boy at heart."

"I'm not sure. Call him any time you're interested in doing some extra writing—or any time you think you need the money. If you're interested, he can explain it when you meet him."

One of the many telephones on Bob's desk rang. "I'll have to take that, Harry—it should be our stringer in Acapulco. New York is pressing me for a story about the new airport there."

"Hey, maybe you could send me down to Acapulco on assignment sometime," Harry said.

"No need for that. Enjoy the press conference, then get yourself settled somewhere, and get a good night's sleep."

"Thanks for everything."

Harry left the UP office with cards in every pocket of his jacket.

CHAPTER 15

Harry realized it was too late in the day to check out of either hotel without paying for another night. God damn it, he thought, I'll be broke before I make it down to Acapulco. I'll have to watch the pesos, maybe do a little hustling, like Bob was talking about.

Harry considered going to the restaurant Rosa had picked for today, but he decided to save that one for another time. Instead, he headed for the cantina across the street, practically next door to *Excelsior*.

Printed in white chalk on a blackboard next to the swinging doors was the menu for today's comida corrida: chicken consomé, beef ragú, a roll, rice and refried beans on the side. Three pesos.

As he stepped through the doors, Harry stopped to look around. The place was noisy with people yakking and laughing, glasses and bottles clinking, and men slamming dominoes on the hard table tops. A juke box in the corner blared a spirited mariachi rendition of the Zacatecas march. Two ceiling fans slowly disturbed the air, which was heavy with the odor of cigarette smoke, stale beer and frying food. One man, sitting alone at a table, was nursing a beer and scribbling on a sheet of yellow copy paper. His tie was loose, his shirt collar was open, and his coat was draped on the back of a chair. Newspaper reporter, no doubt.

Harry ordered the comida corrida. Easy on the *cebollas* in the beef stew, he told them—he didn't want to arrive at the press conference, new kid on the block, with onion breath. In a further attempt to be non-offensive, he ordered Pepsi Cola instead of beer.

At ten minutes before two, Harry slipped into a vacant chair near the back of the meeting room and, as was his habit, studied the room and the people. At the front was a riser about twenty-four inches off the floor. On the riser was a rectangular table with four chairs and, to one side, a podium with a microphone attached. At each end of the riser stood a Mexican flag. On the wall behind the riser was a sign proclaiming "Petróleos Mexicanos," in case you forgot where you were. On the front of the podium was the Mexican national emblem. The whole scene gave the impression that the Pemex officials wanted to be able to look down on the reporters from a position of authority.

Bright, colorful flowers—small bowls on the table and planters in front of the podium and the table—softened this haughty display of power.

Harry turned his eye to the reporters waiting in chairs, the television cameras in position for their big opportunity, and the newspaper photographers clutching their Speed Graphics and sitting or sprawling on the floor in front of the podium. Then he spotted Rosa, half-hidden behind a curtain in a corner of the room, in earnest conversation with an important-looking man—dark blue pin-striped business suit, carnation on the lapel, red necktie, small brief case in his hand.

"Hello, and welcome," a man sitting next to Harry said, in English. "You're new here. Do you speak any Spanish?"

"Yes, a little, but I'd like to learn more, so I try to speak it whenever I can," Harry responded in Spanish.

"Okay, then Spanish it is. Welcome to the circus. My name is Alberto Duarte, and I'm with *Excelsior*. If there's anything I can do to help you, let me know." He handed Harry his card.

"Thanks," Harry replied, relaxed and pleased that someone had greeted him so cordially. He slipped the card into his coat pocket. "Yes, I'm new, all right. I just arrived in town last night. My name is Banister, Harry Banister. I, uh … I might be doing some part-time work at United Press. Feature stories and stuff like that."

"Banister? Like the *pasamano* you grab when you go up a flight of stairs?" Alberto asked, grasping thin air with his hand.

Harry laughed, duplicating the gesture. "Well, going up or going down. Take your pick, either way, but I prefer to think that I'm on my way up, not down. Say, I read your story in this morning's paper on the shooting at the Bar 33. Kind of a mystery?"

"Right now it is, and my story must have read like a mystery, without much in the way of facts. I went to police headquarters this morning to see if Detective Gonzalez could give me any more information, but he didn't have much. After I left him I stopped by the Bar 33 to see what I could find, but the place was closed, locked up tight. This is the kind of story that could die on the vine."

"Why's that?"

"Well, the police have a theory that if they can't solve a murder in the first twenty-four hours, they're not going to be able to crack it, and by then they'll have other homicides to worry about, and we'll have other homicides to write about. There was another one last night at another bar, but that was just a routine bar fight, just a couple of drunks fighting, one killed the other, and we buried the story. Right now, they can't identify the victim or the killer at the Bar 33, so that made it worth a headline. I'll have to talk to Gonzalez one more time before his twenty-four hours are up."

"How about the 'third man' Gonzalez hinted at in your story? Did he have anything more on that?"

"Not much. He wanted to talk about the movie *The Third Man*, and how he was able to solve that mystery before the cop in the movie."

"The cop never did solve it," Harry commented. "It was the American paperback writer, Holly Martins."

"Exactly," Alberto laughed. "Of course, it was the writer. Maybe you and I will have to solve this one for Gonzalez."

"Hey, that might work," Harry said. "Sometimes two reporters are better than one. Did he give any indication that his third man actually might have been a woman? Did he say anything more on the identity of the victim?"

"No, but he said they're going to keep working on it."

CHAPTER 16

Harry decided this would not be a good time to admit he was at the Bar 33 last night—why give this reporter the idea that I might have been the third man? Or the killer? Time to get off the subject. "Say, what's going to happen here today?"

"Well, you saw my story about the Bar 33 this morning, and you also might have seen the piece about the oil fires up north. One last night, one the night before last, and one a few weeks ago."

"No, I missed today's story, but I knew about the earlier ones. I take it Pemex must be on the hot seat."

Alberto laughed. "I like your little joke. Yes, they're on the hot seat for more reasons than one. They're always on the hot seat for something or other. We hope they can tell us what's going on, but probably they've cooked up a spin about something entirely different, something to take the heat off the fires."

Harry laughed. "Hey, I like your little joke, too. But let me tell you something. I came down here on the bus the night before last, and I saw that fire off in the distance. I didn't think anything about it at the time."

"Then you're an eye witness. When we do a follow-up piece we can quote you. Adds a little authenticity to the story."

"Not really. All I saw were balls of fire and clouds of smoke in the distance. But tell me, who are some of the other reporters here today? Any of them my fellow countrymen?"

"Well, that fellow over there in the front row is the correspondent for *The New York Times*, and the woman with him is his wife. They're sort of a team here, and they do a hell of a job."

"She works for the *Times* too?"

"No, they don't allow husband-and-wife teams, but she does free lance pieces for them. They have good connections in all the right places.

"Now, let's see, that fellow over there, the one with the mustache, is the editor at *The News*. He's Mexican, but he's completely bi-lingual. Are you familiar with *The News*?"

"I picked up a copy of yesterday's paper when I got in last night. A little bit of news plus a lot of comic strips and cartoons and syndicated columnists and other features from the States."

"You should meet Luis and a few of his people." Alberto pointed toward a girl at the end of the second row. "That girl over there is with *Novedades* which, incidentally, owns *The News*."

Alberto stopped as the buzz of conversation around the room dropped to a whisper. Four men in dark suits climbed up onto the riser, each man wearing a fresh carnation on his lapel. Rosa's been doing her job, Harry decided, pinning flowers on the dignitaries. Good public relations on her part. I'll catch her when this is over.

Three of the dark-suited men took chairs behind the table, and the fourth stepped to the podium. This was the one Rosa had been talking to, obviously the man in charge. He cleared his throat, adjusted the height of the microphone, cleared his throat again, smiled, and welcomed the ladies and gentlemen of the press to this very important conference. He introduced himself as Antonio Aguilar, with a title that sounded like he had something to do with press relations, and he introduced the other men on the dais, and, of course, he thanked everyone for taking time out of their busy schedules to attend.

When Harry heard that old "taking time out of your busy schedule" cliché, he decided this could turn out to be as dull and unproductive as many of the other press conferences he had covered.

Aguilar, the man in charge, promised there will be a very important announcement for them, a very important story, and the two pretty young ladies standing at the side of the stage will be distributing press releases in just a few minutes. He nodded to the girls and smiled, and they smiled back.

Then he droned on for three or four minutes about how fortunate Mexico was, and how fortunate Pemex in particular was, to have such a fine corps of talented reporters to carry the news to the people of Mexico.

He droned on about the excellent work Pemex was doing to provide the people of Mexico with the finest petroleum products for their cars and their homes and farms and factories.

About how Pemex was in the vanguard in the search for new techniques and new facilities and new products and new underground reserves.

And about how Pemex was bolstering the Mexican economy by providing employment for thousands of hard-working Mexican citizens and paying some of the highest wages in the nation

"They should throw some of those high wages in our direction," Alberto whispered, "to help those wonderful reporters that he loves so much. He's right, Pemex workers are among the best-paid in the country. Nothing new so far. Same old crap they talk about all the time."

"Who are those other men?" Harry asked.

"Nobody very important. They're mid-level management. One of them, the bald guy on the left, has something to do with field operations—laying pipelines or drilling wells or something like that. I don't know who the other two are. They're just up there to nod their heads at the right time. Pemex has an army of mid-level management people with fancy titles, and nobody is quite sure what any of them do."

And speaking of those vast underground reserves, Aguilar said he was pleased to introduce Engineer Humberto Velasco (who turned out to be the bald guy on the left), who will have a very important announcement to make.

Engineer Velasco also thanked everyone for taking time out of their busy day, and he said he was pleased to announce the discovery of a promising new oil field in the Southern Zone, in the State of

Campeche, where drilling would begin soon. The probable reserves in this new field, he said, could approach the ultimate recoverable oil in the rich Poza Rica field in eastern Mexico. The other three heads on the dais bobbled in approval.

Velasco smiled and nodded to the girls. "The details are in the press release the young ladies will now distribute. Are there any questions?"

CHAPTER 17

The correspondent from the *Times* raised his hand and called out. "Yes, I have a question. What can you tell us about these fires that are popping up all around the country, like the fire last night in the north of Mexico? And the one the night before last? Seems like they're getting out of hand. What's going on? Is Pemex going to burn up?"

Aguilar stepped up to the microphone and pushed Velasco aside. "I'll be happy to address that question for you, Sidney. Those minor fires are nothing to be concerned about. They're part of the everyday events in the petroleum business. Small, insignificant fires like these happen from time to time in our business. These were self-contained fires, easy to extinguish. From time to time fires happen, and we put them out, and they cause virtually no damage. It's part of the business."

The heads on the dais bobbled in agreement.

"But who do you think is behind these fires? Foreigners? And where is the next one going to be? Do you have any leads?"

"Who's behind them? You make it sound sinister. Perhaps it's just a careless workman, or a spark from a steel wrench that someone should not have been using, a faulty gasket in a pipeline joint. The fire several weeks ago, we determined, was nothing more than a ruptured seam in a pipeline. We replaced that section of pipe with new seamless pipe. Any number of things can happen to cause an accident. We investigate each time, and we take steps to correct any problems that might show up. It's just a coincidence that these particular accidents occurred in such a short time frame."

Another reporter raised his hand. "How much are these fires costing Pemex? Do you have a figure on the amount of the damages so far?"

"Our accountants have not tabulated the amount in pesos, but I can assure you that the total will not be crippling. Like I said, these have been minor fires, easy to control."

Once again the heads on the dais bobbled in unison.

"What about the reports that the first two fires were caused by sabotage? Is there any truth to that? Who would the saboteurs be?"

"No, there's no way anyone could do that. Our security is so tight that no saboteur could possibly gain access to any of our facilities."

The heads once again nodded in agreement. "Now, are there any questions about our new Campeche field? That new field really is the big news of the day. That's the reason we invited you here today."

There were a few questions about the new field—when would drilling begin? How many barrels would it produce? Would there be any off-shore drilling? How many new jobs will there be?

"I have a question about this new Campeche field," one of the reporters said. "Is this really new? One of the newspapers down there had something on that a month or two ago."

Engineer Velasco stepped to the microphone. "Well, yes, there have been rumors about it, but today we are happy to confirm those rumors and bring the news to all of you reporters, and to the people of Mexico. The press release gives you all the details."

Aguilar moved back to the podium. "If there are no more questions, I want to thank you all for taking time out of your busy schedules and coming here today. Please help yourselves to the refreshments on the tables at the rear of the room." Someone turned off the microphone, Aguilar wiped his brow with a handkerchief, and he and his colleagues stepped down from the dais and left the room by a rear door.

"Well, that was exciting," Alberto mocked as he and Harry left the meeting room. "Not a lot of meat. A press conference to confirm old rumors about a new oil field, and a stone wall on the current rash of fires."

"It sounds to me like the fires are worse than they want to admit," Harry said, "but they thought they'd better say something to try to stop the rumor mill."

The two reporters stopped at a table offering coffee, soft drinks and cookies, and picked up a few chocolate chip cookies. Harry stuffed a couple of cookies into a coat pocket, where they nestled among the various business cards and scraps of paper he had collected earlier in the day. He looked around for Rosa as he took a bite of cookie, but saw no sign of her. That girl is fast on her feet, he realized—she got out of here as quickly as she cleared out of the restaurant last night.

"Do you think you'll get a story out of this?"

"Actually I won't be writing this one," Alberto said. "There's another reporter here from *Excelsior*, and Pemex is her *fuente*, her fountain. Pemex pays her a small fee to write kind words about them. It's the system. It helps us reporters supplement our meager salaries, helps us buy the groceries."

"Do you have a fuente, too?"

Alberto laughed. "Like I say, it's the system. Margarita will really have to be creative with this story, to tell it straight and also be kind to Pemex. She and I are going back to *Excelsior* now—I still have to write my story on this morning's interview with Detective Gonzalez.

"Why don't you meet me at the cantina later?" Alberto asked. "Around six o'clock, and I'll take you to a couple of cocktail parties. We'll have a drink, meet a few people, maybe meet a couple of *muchachas*, have dinner for free—these cookies won't last long anyway."

Harry nibbled on another cookie. "Great. I can't pass up free food. I'll be there at six. Right now I've got a few things to do to get settled in."

CHAPTER 18

The Bar Restaurante 33 was open for business, and Harry settled on a bar stool with a clear view of the front door. Best to keep a path open to the door, he thought, in case I need to make a quick exit.

"Let me have a Carta Blanca, please, well-chilled."

"Sí, Señor. Carta Blanca is one of our best-selling beers, and we always keep a dozen bottles cold for our American customers."

Harry forced a feeble laugh. Great start. "That sounds good, but I don't think I'll need a dozen bottles or you'll have to carry me out of here in a basket." He remembered the body he saw last night. "Or a casket."

As he waited for his beer, Harry looked around the near-empty room. The only other customers were two men, deep in conversation, at the far end of the bar. Several waiters and busboys were busy setting up the dining room. Harry didn't recognize this bartender or any of the other staff. So far so good.

"Were you working last evening?" Harry asked. "I understand you had a little action here. Somebody got shot?" Like a lawyer in court, Harry thought, you want to start by asking a question you already know the answer to.

Harry paid for his beer with a one hundred-peso note, and left the change sitting on the bar. He began to fidget with the money, using a finger to draw little circles on the bar with a one-peso note.

The bartender noticed Harry's little circles. "I usually work nights," he said, "but last night was my night off, so I took my wife to the movies."

Harry laughed. "Yeah, you have to do that once in a while to keep peace in the family, but you missed out on the action here. Did your colleagues fill you in on the details? They probably wanted to share their experience with you."

"Oh, yes," the bartender said, "they've all been eager to tell me what they know. At least, what they think they know. But just like it said in the newspaper, a man was shot in the back of the restaurant. No one knows who he was, and nobody knows who the killer was. Apparently the police didn't find many worthwhile clues, making it a true mystery."

"Was there a fight, or some kind of argument? Or a robbery? Maybe the victim and the killer were fighting over a woman," Harry said, throwing out a few crumbs to coax the bartender. "Or maybe it was a real lovers' quarrel, and the woman shot the man."

Harry quickly realized that this might have been what actually happened. After all, he didn't really know much about Rosa, and she sure cleared out in one hell of a hurry. "Or maybe it was about money. You know, the root of all evil?" He switched his finger from the peso note to a five-peso bill.

"The manager of our restaurant, Señor Fernandez, says it's possible there were two killers. He says yes, there was a woman involved, but he doesn't know how she was involved. He says he thinks she might have been the killer."

"Really? Why does he say that? What do you think, Manolo?" Harry had noticed the bartender's name badge when he first sat down, and he decided now would be a good time to get a little friendlier.

Manolo glanced down the bar from time to time to see how his other customers were doing, but he kept one practiced eye on those bar-top circles Harry was drawing with his finger. Harry doubled the ante, and replaced the five-peso note with a ten-spot.

"I think Fernandez is only guessing." the bartender said. "I think Fernandez is caught in a dilemma. He wants to be discreet, he wants to keep the whole thing out of the papers, as if it never happened, to maintain the good reputation of his restaurant. But at the same time he would like to dramatize the killing for the publicity value. Personally, I think he's more interested in publicity than discretion."

"Well, maybe he can have it both ways, and have discreet publicity. A little notoriety never hurt any business. You know what the movie stars say—'I don't care what they say about me as long as they spell my name right.' Tell me, did they spell your boss's name right in the newspapers this morning?"

The bartender laughed as he set a dish of peanuts in front of Harry, right next to that dancing ten-peso note. "Yes, they spelled it right. He probably bought a copy of every morning paper, not just *Excelsior*, and he has the clippings mounted on the bulletin board in his office, along with all the other press mentions of the bar from the past few years."

"Any murders in those other clippings?" Harry asked.

"No, most of those are stories or pictures of famous people having supper or drinks here."

Apparently his guy Fernandez is the type who likes to revel in his celebrity, Harry decided, and he might turn out to be more help than hindrance. Manolo seems to enjoy the attention, too.

"Is your boss around now? It sounds like he's right on top of the situation."

"He was here earlier, and he was working hard with the porter to get the hallway and the men's room cleaned. There was a lot of blood, on the floor and on the wall. They removed a bullfight poster that had blood on it and put up another one. Fernandez says the police found a bullet in the poster they took down."

"And no one reported hearing a gunshot?"

The bartender laughed. "Señor, as you yourself should remember, the band can be so loud you're lucky to hear your companion talk. In fact, some of the waiters wear ear plugs so the band will not make them permanently deaf."

Harry laughed. "That must be the reason the waiter never comes when you call him."

The bartender lifted Harry's sweating beer bottle and wiped the moisture from the bar, careful not to disturb the money. "Would you like to talk to him? He should be back soon."

"Yeah, I think it would be interesting to hear if he knows any more about it now."

"And one other thing, Señor. I feel I should tell you this. Fernandez says there were two customers, a man and a woman, who were involved in one way or another."

"Really? Does he think this guy might have been the killer?"

"I don't think he knows for sure, but I think his vote goes to *la güera*."

"La güera?"

"Yes, the waiter said she was a güera, a blue-eyed blonde with fair skin. Fernandez says the two of them had supper together."

"Was she an American."

"No, the woman was Mexican. There are a lot of fair-skinned Mexicans, and a lot of blonds. We have a regular United Nations mixture of Mexicans here in Mexico—French, German, Spanish, Irish, Italian, Chinese, English, you name it. And of course," he added with a grin, "North Americans such as yourself. I'm one-eighth Irish myself. My great-grandfather was a *patricio*, an Irish migrant who came here from New York to avoid the draft during the American Civil War."

"And what does Fernandez say about the man?"

"He says the man definitely was a Yankee. He says the guy was acting very suspicious back there in the hallway, snooping around, asking a lot of questions. He actually pushed his way right into the men's room, where the body was lying. Fernandez says the guy tripped over the body and nearly fell."

"Maybe the guy just wanted to take a leak," Harry suggested, forcing a smile.

"Oh, I agree." Manolo smiled, too, and picked up three one-peso bills for Harry's second beer, carefully separating the remaining singles from the fifty and the tens. "That's only natural. I think the man was drinking cold beer."

"That's right," Harry said, "cold beer will do it."

THE FLOWER SHOP

Manolo put his elbows on the bar, leaned closer to Harry, looked him in the eye, and grinned. "You know, I'm telling you all this so that you know what Fernandez is thinking, in case he comes back soon and you have a chance to meet him. I think the American man was drinking cold Carta Blanca. I had to restock the cooler with Carta when I came in today."

Harry thought this might be a good opportunity to look things over again in the back of the place. "Say, I think this cold beer is beginning to work on my bladder, too," he said as he slid off the stool and slid the twenty-peso note off the edge of the bar into Manolo's waiting hand.

Manolo grinned. "Sí, Señor. I believe you already know where the men's room is."

Harry turned and stepped full-face into Enrique Fernandez as the manager approached from the back hall.

CHAPTER 19

"Yes, Manolo, this man certainly should know where the men's room is," Fernandez said. "He was there last night."

Harry would have preferred to talk to Fernandez right there at the bar, where he could keep a clear path to the door, but it was too late.

Fernandez escorted Harry to his office. He was not going to let Harry out of his sight. It was too good to be true, this nosy gringo showing up here today.

The floor in the long hallway, Harry noticed, had been scrubbed sparkling clean, and it reflected the bright overhead lights that seemed so dim last night. A burned out fluorescent tube had been replaced. The hallway reeked of fresh lemon and chlorine, nothing like the pleasant aroma at Rosa's Florería Roma earlier today.

"Come in, please, and close the door. Have a seat. When I saw you just now, sitting at my bar, I thought I should call the police. I thought of that old adage, 'the criminal always returns to the scene of the crime.' I thought you must be the killer, come back to inspect the scene of your handiwork.

"Then it occurred to me that you could not be the killer. You could not be guilty of anything, or you wouldn't be here now. The way you were snooping around last night, asking questions, you seemed as interested as I was in finding out what happened. No, Señor, you would not risk sitting at my bar today, calmly drinking beer, if you were guilty of anything. You would be far away, perhaps on your way out of the country."

As he spoke, Fernandez opened a humidor on his desk and pulled out two cigars. He offered one to Harry, and clipped the end from the other.

"No thanks," Harry said, "I'll pass." Unfortunately, the strong odor of lemon and chlorine never made it from the hallway into Fernandez's office to penetrate the cloud of stale cigar smoke. Harry lit one of his own Camels in self-defense.

"No, Señor, you are not the killer. So tell me, who are you? What were you doing here last night? And what are you doing here now, besides drinking beer at my bar?"

"Well, to answer your last question first, I came here hoping to see you, and talk to you. I'm a reporter, and I had dinner here last night with a friend."

"A blonde lady, correct? Your waiter said you were sitting near the front door. Steak and beer, he told me, and your friend had trout and vodka."

"Yes, that's correct. He has an excellent memory, and it was an excellent dinner, if I may say so, and excellent service as well. You have a very fine restaurant, Señor. After dinner, after she left, I came back here to use the men's room, and that's when you saw me. As you can imagine, I was shocked to see a body stretched out there on the floor."

"Yes, I was shocked, too. I don't like to see things like that in my restaurant. The waiter said your friend left in hurry. Why did she leave so quickly? Was she running away from something? Was she afraid of something? Was she involved in the crime? Was she the killer?"

"Señor, she's a young, sensitive female," Harry replied, thinking he was the one who should be asking the questions. "She's probably afraid of bats and spiders and mice, and I believe she left quickly because she saw the body when she came back to powder her nose, and of course, she naturally would've been quite shocked, and even frightened. You and I, Señor, being men, can handle these things, but it's natural for a woman, particularly a vulnerable young one, to be upset."

"Yes," Fernandez replied, nodding in agreement. "You're quite right about that. We men can handle such traumatic events. But I must say, you seemed to lose your composure. You almost tripped and fell when you encountered the corpse. In fact, it looked to me like you actually did fall."

Harry laughed. "Yes, that must have looked rather awkward. No, I didn't fall. I just lost my balance temporarily because I was trying to be so careful. I didn't want to step on the body, and I didn't want to step in the blood. And, of course, I didn't want to upset the crime scene in any manner."

"But why didn't you identify yourself as a reporter last night?"

"Because I had no press credentials at the time. I just arrived in Mexico last night, and I received my credentials this morning at the United Press office. Here, let me show you." Harry reached into his jacket pocket and pulled out the UP identity card. He flashed it just long enough for Fernandez to see **UNITED PRESS** and **PRENSA UNIDA** in large bold red letters, and get a quick glimpse of his name inscribed in smaller official-looking type. He returned the card to his pocket before Fernandez could study it too carefully. He wasn't sure if Fernandez was able to read his name. "I'm what you might call a rookie, the new man on the job. A *novillero*, you might say."

Fernandez laughed. "Yes, a novillero, stepping into the plaza for the first time, perhaps to be gored by your first bull. So that's why you came back here this afternoon, to be gored by a bull? Or to gather more information? You want to write a story for the wire service? The Mexico City newspapers already have carried stories on the crime."

"Yes, I know, but I hoped you might be able to give me some fresh information, something the reporter missed, something the police missed last night. What can you tell me?"

Fernandez laughed again. "Well, you certainly saw as much as the police. You were right in the middle of it, walking all around it, even stepping in it. Perhaps you know more than the police. You could write your story as a first-person eye-witness account."

"Oh, I didn't witness the killing. I only saw the aftermath."

"If you say so," Fernandez said, tapping ashes in an ashtray on his desk. "But your friend—I'm sorry, Señor, but I don't know her name. Your friend has been here before. I recognized her, and so did the waiter, but we know her only as an occasional customer. She ran out so quickly. Was there a problem with her trout?

"Or," he asked, pausing to relight his cigar, "did she do something she should not have done?"

"I only met her yesterday myself, and she suggested coming here for supper. She has good taste, I must say. Oh, it wasn't the trout, I think she enjoyed her dinner. Like I said, she must have been shocked to see a body back here. But is there anything more you can tell me? Did any of you recognize the dead man? Any idea who he was?"

"No, none of us recognized him, and like the story in the paper said, the police found no identification on his body."

"Was he a customer here last night?"

"No," Fernandez said with a laugh. "If he had been eating or drinking here, we would have known. We would have ended the evening with an unpaid bill, and we don't like that."

"Of course," Harry said. "Unless someone paid his bill for him. Or he paid his bill before he was shot. Maybe he was sitting at the bar, and paid cash when he was served. Or maybe he was eating at a table, and his dinner companion paid the bill."

"Yes, any of those situations could be possible."

"In fact, he could have been having dinner with the person who killed him."

Fernandez laughed again. "Yes, that could be true, and they got into an argument over who was going to pay the check, and they argued all the way back to the men's room, and the loser ended up dead on the floor. But still, there would have been an unpaid bill, because I don't think the killer would have taken the time to stop and pay it on his way out."

"The killer may have had an accomplice," Harry said. "In this morning's newspaper story, the detective mentioned clues pointing to the possibility of a third person. What did he mean by that?"

"Yes, he did say that," Fernandez said, laughing even louder this time. "Perhaps he was referring to you, Señor. Perhaps you were his third man. You certainly were at the scene of the crime."

"How about the back door?" Harry asked. "The screen was on the floor. Is that door locked all the time?"

"It's supposed to be locked, but sometimes a careless employee leaves it open during the evening. I don't know if it was locked or unlocked at the time of the killing, but the killer certainly could have escaped that way."

Yes, Harry thought, or the killer also might have come in that way. "One last question, Señor, and I'll be out of here. When the police returned here this morning, did they know anything new, anything that wasn't in the newspaper story?"

"If they discovered anything new, they weren't telling me." Fernandez laughed again. "But I did overhear them talking about the 'international angle' to the case."

Boy, this guy's getting a kick out of this. Biggest story ever for the Restaurante 33. Is Fernandez so jovial because he has nothing to hide, or is he laughing to cover up something? Maybe he's the killer.

Somebody knocked, and Fernandez got up to open the door. A man wearing soiled white pants and a mottled semi-white apron brought an important kitchen crisis for Fernandez to solve. While the two argued in the open doorway, Harry stood and took a careful look around the room, with particular attention to the top of the desk.

Fernandez turned and smiled at Harry. "Please pardon the interruption. It seems like there's always some little problem running a business like this. One day it's a homicide, the next day it's pork."

"I understand. I was just admiring your bulletin board. That's quite an array of celebrities you've hosted here."

"Ah, yes, they like to come here and be seen here. And, of course, we like to serve them, too. It's good publicity for us."

"Better than a murder?"

"Of course," Fernandez said, holding the door open so Harry could leave.

THE FLOWER SHOP

CHAPTER 20

"So tell me, Alberto, you've finished your work for the day?"

"Yes and no. I turned in the piece on my interview with Gonzalez, but I'll have to come back later tonight. I have another job here, proofreading the galleys for our English-language page. Those linotype operators are good, but they don't speak English, and their fingers work automatically, so they don't know when they make a mistake setting type in English."

"You're in demand for your language skills?"

"You could say that. It's the law of supply and demand. *Excelsior* demands and I supply. Of course, it doesn't always work that way. If I demand more money, they don't necessarily supply."

Alberto stepped into the street to flag a taxi. "Right now, let's check out the supply of parties we can attend tonight." He pulled out a scrap of note paper and glanced at it. "Look—we have two good possibilities, one at the Brazilian Embassy, the other at the Norwegian Embassy."

"Which one do you recommend?"

"I say we do both. It's the right way to spend the evening after a busy day. Let's start at the Brazilian Embassy. The music will be good, the food will be tasty, and there should be plenty of good-looking *meninas*. Then, if there aren't any girls available, or if they run out of food, we can go to the Norwegian reception. Of course, at the Norwegian Embassy, we can have codfish."

"That sounds good to me. You have invitations for both parties?"

"Not really. I stopped by the society editor's desk on my way out just now, and looked at her desk calendar, and I saw what she had penciled in for tonight. There's also an art gallery opening, and my guess is she'll be going there. She likes that kind of stuff, but you and I will have a better time."

"Without invitations?"

Alberto laughed. "Of course. We are the gentlemen of the press. Into the night we gallantly go, wherever a story is to be found, wherever our presence is required."

Alberto was right. This was the perfect way to put the cap on a busy day. A small combo in the corner of the main room was playing a soft samba, and several couples were dancing. Harry stopped by the edge of the dance floor and watched. I could do that, he decided, with a little help from the right partner.

The crowd was from the upper rung of the social ladder. Most of the men were in business suits and probably came right from their offices. Some were in military uniforms with decks of colorful campaign ribbons on their chests. Harry wondered what battles these ribbons could possibly represent. Several men were in dinner jackets, while three or four were coatless, wearing the traditional white guayabera and black bow tie. Most of the women were dressed in chic cocktail dresses, many of them strapless.

The women, Harry noted, were gorgeous. He glanced in a large gilt-framed mirror as he strolled along one side of the main room, and he nonchalantly straightened his tie.

The room was decorated with Brazilian banners and tourist posters, including scenes of the Amazon rain forest, Copacabana Beach, Sugar Loaf, and the beach at Ipanema. Harry wondered why a Mexican, with the Acapulco beach so close, would want to fly down to Brazil for a vacation.

The room was colorful with baskets and vases of bright flowers. Some of the baskets were decorated with ribbons and bows of green, yellow and blue, the colors of the Brazilian flag.

Harry accepted a drink offered by a white-gloved roving waiter, and continued on his circuit, with an occasional sip of the potent *caipirinha*. Along the way he picked up bits of conversation, mostly in Spanish and Portuguese, with English and several other languages scattered in.

As he continued to work the room, he nodded and smiled and felt right at home. He paused to exchange pleasantries with a few people, shaking hands and greeting them like old friends. He always felt at home at a party like this.

Alberto already was busy at the buffet in the next room. He was talking to a beautiful dark-haired girl while juggling a glass in one hand and a plate of *bolinhos de bacalhau* in the other. The girl laughed at something Alberto said as Harry approached.

"Harry, step over here and have some of these hors d'oeuvres direct from Rio," Alberto said. "Try the *camarão tempura*, they're delicious. Right now I'm having a codfish cake. And say hello to—I'm sorry, what's your name again?"

"Carolina," the girl said, smiling at Alberto and then at Harry.

"Yes, of course. Carolina's from Rio, and she works here at the embassy. She speaks four languages, but we're speaking Spanish now because I don't know much Portuguese. Carolina, say hello to my good friend Harry. He comes from north of the border, but he speaks Spanish. He's new to town." Alberto slowed down to catch his breath and restack his plate with cheese balls and shrimp.

"*Muito prazer*," Carolina said. Then, switching from Portuguese back to Spanish, she said "I have a cousin living in Chicago. Do you know Chicago?"

Harry smiled as he set two codfish cakes and several shrimp on a plate. That sounds familiar, he thought. I think I've used that corny opener a few times myself. "Yes, I've been to Chicago, but it's a very large city. I don't know many people there." Pretty girl, Harry decided, but I'll leave her to Alberto. He seems to be doing all right.

Carolina introduced a girl from São Paulo who was a secretary at the embassy. A pleasant girl, plump and not very attractive, probably the daughter or niece of someone important back home.

The four of them continued to sample the snacks and make cheerful cocktail chatter, but Harry's eyes wandered. Plenty of important people here, he decided, and a lot of folks who may not be very important at all. The usual hangers-on. Place is probably loaded with politicians. Lots of military brass. There's one famous face across the table. He's known as the 'Tenor of the Americas,' a title no doubt cooked up by his publicist.

There's another familiar face at the other end of the table, Harry noticed, loading his plate high—one of the reporters from today's press conference. I'm sure he makes all the embassy receptions to supplement his meager salary. Reporters are the same the world over.

Harry's eyes stopped wandering. There, across the dining room, was Rosa, laughing and talking with a group of men and women.

Harry realized that Rosa was as beautiful as any of the other women at the party, outstanding in her strapless cocktail dress, sort of a royal blue with soft white dots and a white sash around the waist. The blue dress brought out the blue in her eyes. Her silver charm bracelet, dangling from her right wrist, glistened in the light of the crystal chandelier. Around her neck was a choker of silver and rhinestones, or maybe even real diamonds. A matching barrette by her left temple clasped her otherwise-flowing blond hair.

And pinned to the left side of her dress, in full bloom on her bountiful bosom, was her name badge of three small white roses.

But what the hell is she doing here? She didn't have to get dressed up like that just to deliver the flowers.

"Excuse me for a moment," Harry said to Alberto, "I'm going to make the circuit."

"Don't be gone long. Remember, we have another stop to make tonight."

"Yeah, but you don't really want to leave this party, do you?" Harry asked, glancing at Carolina. "I mean, we're having a good time here, aren't we? And I think I've already had my fill of codfish cakes."

"Yes, that's right, we're having a good time right now, right here. Let's forget about Norway. You're right about the cod, too. I know I've had enough. Anyway, I'm sure we can find codfish somewhere tomorrow."

"What does your social secretary say about tomorrow?"

"I'm not sure, I'll have to check her calendar in the morning, but I believe it might be Russia."

"Vodka, boiled potatoes and borscht," Harry replied. "And cod. Hey, Alberto, keep an eye on that calendar. I could do this every night of the week. This is gonna be a great vacation."

"Vacation? You just started a job today, right?"

"Well, sort of, but I want to keep my priorities straight. Play first, work second."

Harry worked his way toward Rosa's group, hoping to make this a chance encounter. As he got closer he saw that one of the men was Pedro, her boss at the flower shop. Harry realized this could be awkward for everybody, so he decided to back off and try to catch Rosa alone later.

But it was too late.

CHAPTER 21

"Rosa, I believe your friend Harry is here tonight," Pedro said, loud enough for Rosa and a lot of other people to hear. He stepped out from the group, extending his hand and blocking Harry's escape route. "What a pleasant surprise, Señor. I saw you in our shop this morning, but I didn't have an opportunity to meet you formally."

Rosa was surprised and flustered, but she recovered quickly and moved in between the two men to make the introductions and prevent any sort of disaster. "Harry, it's so nice to see you. I didn't expect you to be here this evening."

"Hello, Rosa, I didn't expect I'd see you here either."

"Harry, I'd like you to meet the owner of the Florería Roma, Pedro Yzaguirre Mendoza. Pedro, this is the man I told you about, the man I met on the bus. But Harry, I don't know your last name."

Harry noticed a quick frown on Pedro's face and a flash in his eye. Apparently something Rosa said hit Pedro the wrong way, or maybe it was just the surprise of seeing me here, but she handled the introduction well. He extended his hand to Pedro for the obligatory shake. "I'm pleased to meet you, Señor Yzaguirre. My full name is Harry Banister. Rosa told me how much she enjoys working for you in your shop, and she's told me what a wonderful horticulturalist you are. She says you have a great passion for flowers, and that you have what we Americans would say is a green thumb."

Now Pedro seemed to blush as he laughed at the compliment, and Harry hoped he hadn't laid it on too thick. "I don't know about the green thumb, Señor Banister—"

"Please, call me Harry."

"Yes, Harry, I do enjoy working with flowers. I guess you could call it a passion. I believe I already know you very well from what Rosa has told me. She speaks highly of you, and I'm sure you must be every bit as nice as Rosa has portrayed you. A friend of Rosa's is a friend of mine."

Rosa bit her lip. Pedro didn't seem all that friendly this morning in his questions and his comments about Harry. This morning, he sounded like he was ready to run Harry out of the country on the next north-bound freight train.

Pedro introduced an army officer, General Horacio Something-or-Other. Harry didn't catch the full name, but he figured he could find out later if it was important. The General's chest was emblazoned with an array of medals, although not quite as many as some of the other military men at the party. But hell, he's young, so he still has time to earn more medals. Maybe he'll get another one tonight for braving the Battle of the Brazilian Buffet.

Pedro next introduced two of the men Harry had seen at the press conference: Antonio Aguilar and his wife Aurora, and Engineer Humberto Velasco and his wife Hortensia. "Antonio has a very important position with Pemex, in the publicity and press relations department," Pedro said, "and Humberto has a very important job in the engineering department."

Harry knew that. Bobbling heads. He could tell that Pedro was impressed by the importance of these two men. Obviously, Pedro liked to move in the right circles. Good for the flower business, no doubt.

"It's a pleasure to meet you," Aguilar said, smiling and taking Harry's hand in a firm, cordial shake.

"Yes, it's a pleasure," Velasco said. He shifted his drink from his right hand to his left, offering Harry a cold, wet hand for one single unenthusiastic shake.

Harry noticed immediately that Aguilar was not as pompous up close as he appeared to be at the press conference—the guy has a human side. Velasco appeared to be just the way he was at the press conference—arrogant and aloof.

"I'm pleased to meet you in person, gentlemen. I was at your press conference this afternoon, and I found it to be most informative."

"You were there today?" Aguilar asked.

Harry hesitated, and then replied. "Yes, I started working part-time today at United Press, and my first assignment was to attend your press conference."

Aguilar beamed. "Splendid. So today was your first day on the job. I'm happy to hear that, and I'm pleased you were able to learn something at our meeting. Did we answer all your questions satisfactorily?"

"Well, I have a lot to learn. But I was particularly interested in hearing about the new field in Campeche. I gather it will be very productive for you?"

"Yes, we're quite optimistic," Aguilar said. "Our geologists tell us this new field will prove to be very profitable, with probable reserves of several billions of barrels for years to come. Isn't that right, Humberto?"

"Yes, of course," Velasco replied, "very productive."

"I'd like to learn more about that field," Harry said, "and I'd like to learn more about the oil business. Perhaps you could educate me."

"I would be delighted," Aguilar replied, handing Harry his card. "Just call my office and arrange an appointment with my secretary. I would be delighted to talk with you anytime."

Harry stuck the card in his coat pocket. I'll have a regular phone book in there before the day is over, he thought. Engineer Velasco, the technical guy, the guy who really should be able to answer my questions, didn't offer me his card. He doesn't want to help me. I guess he doesn't like reporters, or else he's a real sourpuss, or both.

Harry turned to Rosa. "I saw you across the room at Pemex this afternoon, but you were busy talking and you got away before I had a chance to say hello."

"Oh, I didn't know you were there, Harry. You keep popping up everywhere—the flower shop, the press conference, and now here tonight. I wanted to be sure the flowers for the press conference looked just right, and then I had to leave quickly to call on Señora Velasco to discuss plans for her daughter's quinceañero the end of next month."

"Yes," Sra. Velasco said, "Our daughter will be turning fifteen, and Humberto and I are planning a gala celebration for her, and the Florería Roma will provide the flowers."

"This must be the season," Aguilar said. "Our daughter's quinceañero will be next month, and I've reserved a ballroom at the Hotel Del Prado for the occasion."

"I must congratulate you, Antonio, on selecting an excellent location," Gen. Something-or-Other said. "The Del Prado is a magnificent hotel with wonderful facilities. You were fortunate to be able to reserve a ballroom, considering all that's going on there."

"I made the reservation several months ago."

"Pedro, will you also be providing the flowers for the Aguilars' quinceañero?" the General asked.

"No, the hotel will provide the flowers as part of the total package—the food, the beverages, the music, the decorations, and so forth," Aguilar said. "The hotel's florist has a corner on all the in-house business, but I'm sure they'll do a good job. Not as good as Pedro and the Florería Roma, of course."

Everyone in the group laughed, and Pedro raised his glass and mumbled a mild "thank you."

"Aurora and I are looking forward to the evening," Aguilar said, "and so, of course, is our daughter. I can see her now descending that Grand Staircase in the dress she and Aurora have picked for the occasion."

Rosa nodded and smiled. "Yes, the dress is gorgeous. She'll be a charming quinceañera, and it should be a festive evening." Then she turned again to Harry. "I think it's wonderful that you were able to find a job so quickly. I'm so happy for you."

Pedro interrupted. He was not smiling. "And you were able to start work immediately?"

Rosa's happy for me, Harry realized, but Ol' Uncle Pedro is not ready to celebrate. He probably didn't want me to find a job at all. He would just as soon have me out of his hair, if he had any—and keep me out of Rosa's hair, too. Out of the country, for that matter. I'll have to be careful what I say.

"Rosa told me you came to Mexico as a tourist," Pedro continued, "and that you planned to 'knock on a few doors' as you put it, to see if you could find employment. Apparently you knocked on the right door without any hesitation. You must have known which door to choose."

Harry laughed as he took a fresh caipirinha from the tray of a passing waiter.

"Yes, but I'm still a tourist. I'll just be helping out part-time at United Press, on a free lance basis. The bureau chief is an old friend of mine. You're right, Pedro, that was the only door I knocked on, and I'm really not looking for a full-time job. I came down here for a vacation."

"You must be careful not to offend the people at Gobernación," the General warned with a stern tone. "They don't like it when tourists, especially North Americans, take jobs that Mexican citizens might be able to fill. They like to preserve Mexico for the Mexicans."

"Oh, they have bigger things to worry about," Aguilar said. "I don't think they worry too much if an English-speaking reporter is working at an English-language newspaper or wire service. They're concerned with more important affairs of state."

"One never knows," Horacio persisted. "They might consider an illegal immigrant working in the communications business to be a matter of some significance, a possible security risk. They have their own interpretations of what's important and what is not. They might be concerned that a foreigner, in a position to transmit unfavorable information about the government, or perhaps information about our military, could be a threat to national security."

Harry recalled what the doorman said last night at the restaurant: Article 33 of the Constitution empowers the government to throw out criminals and spies and other undesirables.

Rosa laughed, hoping to inject a little levity in the conversation. "Well, Harry certainly hasn't done anything wrong. After all, he just arrived yesterday, and he doesn't know anything important."

"You're right about that," Harry said with a chuckle. "I don't know anything about anything—or anybody."

"But Harry, you must know someone here at the Brazilian Embassy," Pedro said. "You were fortunate to get an invitation to this reception so quickly."

Harry laughed again. "Please don't tell anyone, but I really didn't have an invitation." He nodded in the direction of the food table. "I tagged along with my new friend over there. He's a reporter. I met him today at the press conference."

With the introductions and the formalities and birthday parties out of the way, and a few awkward moments for Harry, the little group settled into a round of typical cocktail party small talk. They talked about how charming the ladies look this evening, what a wonderful reception this is, how excellent the Brazilian food and music are, and, of course, how nice the flowers look. They talked about the inevitable afternoon thundershowers and the mounting traffic problems in the city. They argued about the bravery of last Sunday's bulls and the technique of next Sunday's matadors.

They talked about everything but politics and religion—those subjects did pop up a few times but were quickly sidetracked by timely bullfight speculation. From time to time, various members of the group said hello and shook hands with a strolling acquaintance or two.

At one point Pedro said he would like to have lunch or supper with Harry sometime to get to know him better. Sure thing, Harry replied, I would look forward to that, you name the time and the place, and I'll be there. We'll do it soon, Pedro said.

Eventually they all seemed to be running out of things to talk about, and the group was getting restless. Gen. What's-His-Name looked at his watch and took the lead. "I hate to be the one to break up this little party within a party, but I want to say hello to two or three friends who are here tonight, and then I'm afraid I must leave. I'm going to meet some fellow officers for supper at the Jena."

Antonio Aguilar took the cue. "An excellent choice," he said. "One of my favorite restaurants. Aurora and I dine there frequently. We also should be leaving soon."

"We have to get home now," Velasco said.

"Yes," Pedro said, "I've enjoyed this immensely, but it's time for me to get back to the shop. The flowers are continuing to flourish, right now, as we speak—time and flowers wait for no man." He laughed at his own little joke, and one or two of the others laughed with him. They all had heard it a few times before. "And you should not be too late, Rosita. Remember, I have a little project I would like you to take care of first thing in the morning."

Rosa frowned. "Yes, I'll be leaving soon. This has been such a busy day."

Harry took her hand. "Why don't you stay a little longer, and dance one little dance with me? That music is too good to waste."

"No, I really must leave, but it's been so nice seeing you here tonight, Harry." She gave his hand a gentle squeeze. "Please stop by the shop again sometime soon."

With that, the little group, which Harry mentally dubbed the "mutual admiration society," disbanded.

CHAPTER 22

Harry kept an eye on the group as it broke up. Horacio stopped to say hello to an army colonel. The Aguilars paid their respects to the ambassador on their way out the door. Pedro Yzaguirre Mendoza slipped out behind the ambassador and made a quick exit. Harry recalled what Pedro had said only a moment ago, "Time and flowers wait for no man." This guy is really wrapped up in his flowers.

Rosa, trailing behind the others, hesitated under the Ipanema poster and turned to look back at Harry. She smiled, did a little dance step in time with the samba music, and with a flick of her head she motioned for Harry to join her.

So Harry joined Rosa on the dance floor, the musicians segued from the samba to *Qué Rico el Mambo* and Rosa switched right along with the music.

"That's not my best step," Harry confessed. "I haven't learned the mambo yet. I'm still working on the delphoy."

"That's all right, I'll teach you. Follow me. The mambo is really just an upbeat version of the danzón."

"Great. What's a danzón?"

Rosa laughed. "It's Cuban. The mambo is everywhere now. It's the latest dance craze here in Mexico. You're doing fine. You're a good dancer, Harry. We should do this more often."

"Yeah, I'd like that. But it's hard to carry on a serious conversation and also do this Latin stuff, all at the same time."

It's good to see her in such a happy mood, Harry thought, as if she doesn't have a care in the world, but after last night, how can she not be worried? I sure as hell am. "I went back to the Bar Restaurante 33 this afternoon," he blurted, almost in time with the music.

Rosa nearly missed a beat, but kept right on dancing. "My God, Harry, that was a dangerous thing to do! Weren't you afraid? What did you see?"

Harry also kept right on dancing, smiling, trying to perfect his step. "No, it wasn't really dangerous. I kept my eyes and my ears open. Anyway, I don't have anything to be afraid of. I didn't kill anybody." He realized his remark carried a clear implication that Rosa was the killer, but he kept right on with his pseudo mambo. His remark triggered no discernible response from her. Maybe she didn't hear it.

"Let's dance one more," she said. "I saw Pedro leave, but we want to give him time to clear away from the front of the embassy, then we can get out of here and go somewhere quiet and talk by ourselves. There's something I want to tell you."

After another samba, Harry and Rosa offered a moment of polite applause and turned to leave the dance floor. "We'll thank the ambassador and his wife and get a taxi out front," she said.

"Hey, you two, not so fast," a voice called out. "Hold it! Stop right there! You're not going to get away that fast."

Harry and Rosa stopped in mid-step, frozen by a stern command bellowed from somewhere across the room. Instinctively, Harry tightened his grip on Rosa's hand. She winced. He released her hand, freeing his own hand for further use. He clenched his fist and turned, and there, sashaying onto the dance floor was a grinning Alberto Duarte, arm-in-arm with Carolina.

"You look like two long-time dance partners," Alberto said, "like you've been dancing together all your lives. Sort of like Fred Astaire and Ginger Rogers. We thought we'd join you for the next set."

"Oh, it's you," Harry said. "I wasn't sure who was barking at us like a traffic cop or an army drill sergeant. I didn't see you at the buffet just now, so I figured you'd left for another party, or maybe gone back to work."

"No, the English galley proofs will have to wait," Alberto said. He and Carolina got right into the swing of things, doing a mambo with rhythm and polish that Harry could never hope to achieve.

After one more samba, the musicians played the Brazilian national anthem and began to pack up their instruments. "It's time to move on to the next party," Alberto announced.

"Not another embassy," Harry said, "I've had enough cod for one evening."

"No, it's too late for the Norwegians anyway, but Carolina and I are going to Plaza Garibaldi to have a nightcap and hear some mariachi music. Why don't you two come along?"

"Yes, come with us. It'll be great fun." Carolina took Rosa's elbow and guided her toward the front door.

"Oh, Harry, I know it's late," Rosa said, "but let's go with them. You'll love it. Plaza Garibaldi is just like being in Jalisco, the state where mariachi music was born. The music is so exciting, the very soul of our Mexican spirit."

The four of them were in a taxi before Harry could protest. That mariachi music is so damned important to her, he thought. I guess if she has something to tell me, she'll find a way, and if she doesn't, I'll find a way to get it out of her.

CHAPTER 23

Plaza Garibaldi was everything Rosa said it would be. Two mariachi bands alternated out in the plaza while four or five others waited their turn to play. Still others roamed in and out of the cantinas that bordered the square. A few solitary musicians, instruments in hand, stood on the sidelines and smiled, hoping to join a needful group.

The men were dressed in the traditional charro outfit of the Mexican vaquero, but much fancier than a working cowboy would wear. Some of their outfits were black, some tan, some white, some red, and some sky blue. Their tight pants and short jackets were accented by the ruffled shirts, colorful cravats, pseudo silver or gold buttons and buckles and spangles. All wore riding boots, some with spurs. Some wore, or at least carried, the typical broad-brimmed sombrero. Many carried six-shooters (presumably empty) holstered on their hips.

Many of the female musicians wore similar outfits, with skirts rather than the tight riding pants. Some of the female singers wore the colorful *china poblana* costume, the voluminous national dress of the typical Mexican girl.

Harry and his friends found a table in the Salon Tenampa, and their party continued. The din on the inside was almost as boisterous as the music out on the plaza. Meaningful conversation was out of the question, so the four friends ordered more food and drinks, joined in the music and the celebration, and tried to sing along with the mariachis and the other patrons. Rosa knew the words to all the songs.

When he had finished his enchiladas, Alberto announced it was time for him to get back to *Excelsior*. "Duty calls," he said with a grin, as he and Carolina got up from the table. "You know how it is, Harry."

"Duty, hell," Harry replied, glancing at Carolina.

"Harry, can we stay a little longer?" Rosa asked. "I'd like to hear a few more songs. I don't get a chance to hear this mariachi music as much as I'd like."

"Sure, why not? It's still early." What the hell, he figured, a few minutes won't make any difference, might even help. Rosa looks like she's having a good time, but I think she's scared, and she's worried. She loves this music, and one or two lively songs should cheer her up and put her in a better mood.

Harry ordered another beer and Rosa asked the band to play a ranchera, but the song she asked for was anything but lively. Instead, it was a lament about love that somehow got away. Most rancheras, Harry already had learned, were mournful and melancholy. Sad songs like this were not going to make her very happy.

Then the band struck the opening chords of a plaintive song that immediately grabbed Rosa's attention and stopped her in the middle of a sentence. Just standard stuff, Harry decided, sentimental lyrics that pay tribute to Mexico's "volcanoes and prairies and flowers."

> *"... if I should die far from Mexico,*
> *tell them I'm just sleeping,*
> *tell them to bring me back,*
> *and bury me here in the mountains,*
> *and cover me with Mexican soil,*
> *at the foot of the maguey trees."*

Rosa sang along with the band, tears building in her eyes, her voice cracking and fading on the final phrase. When the song ended, Rosa bowed her head, sobbing softly. She pulled a handkerchief from her purse and dabbed at her eyes and her cheeks, fighting to forestall further tears. Her festive mood had abandoned her.

Harry nursed his beer, waiting for the right opportunity. He knew it was a long shot at this hour, with Rosa on the brink of a full-scale flow of tears, but damn it, time was running out.

Then the musicians moved to the next table and struck up *Ay Jalisco, no te rajes*, and Rosa perked up immediately, and sang along with the band. When the song ended, Harry wasted no time. "Rosita, you've got to tell me what happened last night in the back of the restaurant. What happened?"

"What do you mean? Nothing happened. I went back to the ladies' room, then I said good night to you, and I went home."

"Something happened back there, Rosita. Something happened, and you ran out fast, like you were running away, like you were scared." Harry reached into his coat pocket and pulled out a small white rose, by now crumpled, with the appearance of a rotten lemon flecked with chocolate cookie crumbs. "I went back there after you left, and I found this on the floor. I found it partly hidden under the body of the dead man. How did it get there? Tell me what happened. Did you kill him?"

Rosa tried to stifle a sudden tear. "Oh, Harry, I've wanted all day to tell you what happened, but I didn't know how to begin. I'm so worried, I'm so frightened. I couldn't tell you this morning at the flower shop, and I couldn't say anything tonight at the Embassy, and I certainly couldn't say anything here. It was all so noisy and confusing tonight, and there were too many people."

Harry pocketed the fading flower and put his arm around Rosa's shoulder and hugged her gently. "I know, Rosita, I understand. We've been having a lot of fun, so let's hold off for now. We can talk about it later. Let's get a taxi and go someplace where it's quiet, someplace where we can be alone. I know just the place"

When the cab pulled up in front of the Hotel Comé, Rosa sat up, her eyes still moist. She put one hand on the door handle and the other hand on Harry's knee. "I must go home now," she said in English, hoping the driver would not understand. "I am very sorry, Harry. I cannot go with you now. I want to, but I can't. I am too nervous. I must go home. Today has been such a long day, and I am still exhausted from the bus trip, and it is getting late now. You do understand, don't you, Harry? And tomorrow is going to be another busy day. You do understand?"

Harry clenched his teeth. God damn it, that's two times I've struck out in two nights, but I shouldn't be too surprised. With my luck, she would fall asleep anyway, as soon as we got up to the room.

"Yes, I understand," he said in English, and tomorrow's another day. Go home now and get a good night's sleep and we can talk tomorrow. Give me your phone number and I'll call you first thing in the morning. We could have breakfast together."

"No, it is better that I call you. I don't think we could have breakfast together anyway, because Pedro has something he wants me to do in the morning."

"Then I'll call you at the flower shop."

"Harry, I don't want you to call me. I'll call you here at your hotel, in the morning."

"Okay, you call me and we'll go from there. Let's have lunch at that little Spanish restaurant we missed out on today. Remember, you still have a lot of explaining to do. I want to know what happened."

"Yes. I'll call you, I promise, and I'll meet you there at two o'clock."

"And we're still on for Sunday, right?"

"Yes, we'll see the bulls on Sunday." She took her hand off the door handle, reached around Harry's neck, and kissed him, deeply and deliberately. "I've wanted to do this ever since last night, Harry. There is so much I've wanted to tell you, and I want to do so much more. But not tonight."

Harry hugged her tightly and kissed her. "I know, Rosita, I understand. Tomorrow is another day." He took a quick glance at the taxi driver's permit hanging on the dashboard, kissed her again, and got out of the cab. Then, switching back to Spanish, he gave the driver a ten-peso note and said "Abelardo, take the lady where she wants to go."

Harry watched as the taxi drove away. The poor girl is frightened, he thought. She wants to tell me what happened, but she's afraid. She's afraid of me, she doesn't really know who I am. She doesn't feel she can trust me. Not yet, anyway. Or she's afraid of what might happen to her. I'll go easy tomorrow, I won't press her. She'll tell me when she's ready.

CHAPTER 24

"Let me open a bottle of aguardiente," Pedro said, "and we can sit down for a moment here in my office, and enjoy *una copita*, one little cup."

"Yes, a little nip of brandy would taste good right now," Miguel agreed.

Pedro opened the antique armoire that served as his desk, his bookcase, and catch-all storage cabinet. He pulled out a bottle and poured a cup for Miguel and one for himself. He set the open bottle on the table, a sure sign that this would be more than just one little cup.

Miguel finished his brandy in one quick quaff. "Now tell me about the Brazilian reception tonight," he said, wiping his mouth with the back of his hand. "Was there a crowd? Who was there? All the blue-bloods?"

Pedro refilled Miguel's glass and took a sip from his own glass. "It was a typical embassy party, with plenty of politicians and glad-handers and climbers, everyone trying to get on the right side of the right person. People were eating and drinking, and laughing and dancing, as if they had no worries, as if there were no problems here in Mexico, or in Brazil or anywhere else in the world. Give them a drink and a little food, and people are oblivious to the cares of the world. Our flowers, of course, were the best part of it."

"Of course."

"Yes, there was a crowd, some familiar faces and some new ones. The Aguilars were there, and the Velascos, and a few other friends.

And I met that American fellow, Banister, Rosa's new friend, the one who came to the shop this morning."

"He was there? How the hell did he get in?"

"Yes, he was there. He took a job today as a reporter with United Press. Reporters can get in anywhere, it seems, whether they're invited or not. I had a brief chat with him. Nothing serious, all of us in a group, just the usual cocktail party conversation."

"Nothing serious?"

"No, nothing serious, just idle prattle." Pedro placed a hand on Miguel's shoulder. "But I do have something serious to discuss with you, Miguel. I have an important task I would like you to take care of."

"Tell me, Pedro, and it's done."

"I would like to know more about this Banister fellow. Rosa seems to be infatuated with him, and I don't know where it might lead. I don't want any harm to come to her. He's a stranger, he's a foreigner, and he strikes me as being a little pushy. Did you happen to see him this morning when he was here in the shop?"

"Yes, I saw him. I didn't know who he was at first, but then I saw him again at the press conference, sitting with the other reporters."

"He was chatting with Rosa tonight at the Embassy, very chummy, perhaps too chummy. He asked her to dance. After I left, I realized I had forgotten my *boina*, so I had to go back into the Embassy to pick it up, and I saw them dancing together. I thought Rosa left when I did, but obviously she stayed behind to dance with him."

Miguel snorted, then laughed. "Pedrito, you old goat. You're never without your beloved red beret. Sometimes I think you even sleep with it on. I think you left it behind intentionally."

Pedro laughed and set his empty glass on the table. "You're right. I wear by boina every time I go outside, and often I wear it here in the shop and around the house." He laughed again. "But I do take it off when I go to bed. You know me too well, Miguelito. Yes, I did leave it behind deliberately. I wanted to go back so I could see for myself, and there they were, the two of them, dancing and laughing and having a good time like old friends. I'm not sure I like the idea of Rosa getting involved with him."

"I don't blame you. He's a gringo."

Pedro paused to pour another aguardiente for himself and one for Miguel. "Yes, he's an American and he's a reporter. I don't know which is worse. And he was very aggressive, the way he was pursuing her."

"He could be trouble."

"La Rosa Blanca is a good girl, and I want to protect her. She's still a child, and she's alone in the world, now that her mother's gone. I promised her father that I would look after her. I gave her the job here at the flower shop so she would have a steady income, so she would have security—"

Miguel grinned. "And so you can keep an eye on her?"

"Well, that, too, but I don't want that gringo causing Rosa any grief. I don't want him to do anything that would hurt her. She's young and she's good-looking and she's vulnerable. She's not experienced with men and the ways of the world. It's my duty to protect her."

Pedro took a sip of aguardiente. "And I don't want him snooping around here, either. He's a reporter, and a reporter's job is to be inquisitive. I want you to be the grand inquisitor, Miguel. See what you can learn about him."

"Of course, Pedrito, I'll see what he's up to."

"You've seen him, so you know what he looks like. He's staying at the Hotel Comé. It should be easy for you to find him and track him."

Pedro set his glass on the table and reached into the pocket of his suit coat, which was hanging conveniently over the back of his chair. "I took a photo this morning with my Polaroid Land camera, when he was talking with Rosa here in the shop. It's not a great picture, but it should help you. I covered the flowers in the background with masking tape and I made a copy for you."

Miguel smiled when he examined the photo. "It's a good likeness of him. Thank you, Pedro, this'll be a great help. He might have seen me today at the press conference, and he would be able to recognize me, so I'll remain in the shadows. I'll get one of my friends to help me. I know just the man for the job." He raised his glass in a salute. "I'll take care of everything."

Pedro laughed. "That's funny. You say you'll remain in the shadows, but what I know about your friends, Miguel, they all live in the shadows anyway. They're creatures of the night, lurking behind lamp posts."

"That may be, but they have night vision, and they can see everything. Nothing escapes them. They get things done."

"But don't be too hasty, Miguel. We must walk a fine line. First we must learn more about him, find out what kind of man he is, if he's an honorable man, and if his intentions are honorable. I don't want you to do anything that would cause any pain for Rosita."

Pedro was silent for a moment, slowly swirling the brandy in his glass. He took a small sip and spoke. "But there may be an opportunity for us. Remember what I said just a moment ago—reporters can go anywhere they want, they can get in anywhere, whether they're invited or not. Just like tonight, at the Brazilian Embassy. Perhaps he could be useful to us. He appears to be a footloose type, a man with no roots. He strikes me as a man who has no strong convictions about anything. He has no ties here in Mexico, coming down here without a job on the slim chance of finding one, and I gather from the conversation tonight, he has no particular ties back in the United States."

"Perhaps he's running away from something, or he's running from someone," Miguel suggested. "Perhaps he's running away from the law."

"Yes, that's possible. If that's the case, I would like to know. I don't want Rosa to get mixed up with a criminal. From what he said tonight, he enjoys having a good time, and I'm sure he needs money to feed his taste for the good life. Perhaps he could be persuaded to help us. With his press credentials he might be very helpful. I don't know how, I have to think about it."

"Yes, it's possible he could be helpful," Miguel said, although he didn't understand how, either.

"I think I'll invite him to join us for supper tomorrow. And Rosa, of course."

"You want him to dine with us?"

"Precisely. That'll be a good way to get to know him better. I don't want him to think I'm his enemy just because I appear to be protective of Rosa. I want him to think of me as a friend. I'll call him in the morning and invite him."

Pedro laughed and set his glass on the table. "Rosita calls me Tio Pedro. Perhaps someday he might think of me as his uncle, too."

Miguel drained his glass and set it in front of the bottle. He slipped the Polaroid picture into his pocket and laughed. "Yes. He might end up calling you Tio Pedro. That's very funny—you, his kindly, beloved uncle."

Pedro paused and replaced the cork on the bottle. "But depending on what you learn, Miguelito, at some point you may have to take precautionary steps, whatever needs to be done. I don't want him snooping around here. I don't want him interfering. And I don't want him causing any pain or disappointment to Rosa. Do whatever you have to do, but be careful you don't upset Rosa. Her happiness is paramount. Do you understand?"

"I understand. I'll take care of everything."

CHAPTER 25

Harry didn't want to hang around the Hotel Comé all morning waiting for a call that might not come, so by nine o'clock he was back at the Del Prado, having breakfast in Sanborn's. Just like yesterday, it was an American-style breakfast of ham and eggs with toast on the side and a background of scattered bits of conversation in Spanish, English, German, French and a couple of languages he couldn't identify.

Up in his room, Harry flopped into the lounge chair by the window with the view of Avenida Juárez and the Alameda. I should check out of the Hotel Comé, he thought, and bring the rest of my stuff over here. I deserve a place like this, even if I can't afford it. But I'm stuck at the Comé for another day in case she does try to call.

Avenida Juárez was bustling with the same frantic procession he had seen yesterday, all in some kind of a hurry. A cabbie cursed a trucker who had just cut him off. A bus driver honked at a big black Buick. A motorcycle messenger weaved in and out of traffic. A boy on a bicycle balanced a basket of bread on his head. The hotel doorman helped an elderly guest into a taxi.

Across the street, the park was alive. Impatient people pushed into line at the bus stop. An artist set up an easel and a folding stool. Two nannies in matching grey uniforms pushed baby buggies. A young man on a bench sat reading a newspaper. Next to him, an old man tossed bread crumbs to a gathering of hungry pigeons. An organ-grinder with a monkey on a leash played an out-of-tune song. What a great day to be alive.

Except for the headache.

Is Rosa feeling pain this morning? Probably not. She didn't drink that much, but she sure seemed to be having a good time. She danced a little bit of the Mexican Hat Dance when the trumpet player tossed his sombrero on the floor next to the table. She knew the lyrics to all the songs. She's cute and she's sexy, and she's full of life and lots of fun, but God damn it, she's all kinds of trouble, and I sure don't need trouble.

Harry picked up the copy of *Excelsior* he bought in the lobby. The single sheet of English-language stories and ads slipped out and landed on his lap. In a quick scan of the page he counted ten typos and misspelled words. He smiled as he confirmed that Alberto never made it back to his proofreading job last night.

As usual, Harry checked the sports section first. Soccer, golf, tennis, baseball and the bulls. The Yankees lost to the Senators.

On an inside page in the main news section Harry found Alberto's brief story about the continuing investigation of the *Mysterious Madrileño Murdered in Bowels of Bar 33*, and he smiled at the headline. The story came out the way Alberto said it would, although it did include a couple of points not mentioned in yesterday's story.

On another inside page the word "Pemex" popped up in three headlines. One story was Margarita Villarreal's report on the press conference, with Aguilar's statement brushing off the recent fires as "routine, insignificant, everyday occurrences … a cost of doing business, part of the everyday events in the petroleum business." Another piece, also with her byline, was a word-for-word reprint of the press release about the new Campeche oil field. How the hell does this woman get away with that, he wondered. She puts her byline on a press agent's handout?

The phone rang before Harry could read the third Pemex story.

"I'm glad I caught you. I thought I'd better let you know. We just got a visit from a policeman, Detective Gonzalez Moreno. He wanted to know if you work here."

"A cop? What did you tell him?"

"I told him you just arrived in Mexico, but you don't really work here, you're going to be a part-timer, sort of like a stringer. I told him you don't have a regular schedule, so I didn't know when you'd be in. I was a little edgy at first, but then I felt better when I learned he was just a homicide detective."

"What do you mean, just a homicide detective?"

Bob chuckled. "I didn't want anyone from Gobernación snooping around here."

"And what the hell is Gobernación?" Harry recalled that Gen. Something-or-Other mentioned Gobernación last night at the embassy party.

"They're the government people who keep an eye on foreigners working here illegally, among other affairs of state. You don't want to mess with Gobernación. You're just a tourist, remember, here on a six-month tourist card, and you're not supposed to be working, so you're going to have to be careful. You don't want to be deported just yet."

Now Harry remembered what the doorman at the restaurant told him about Article 33 of the Constitution. The government can deport undesirables such as criminals or spies or foreign agents. I guess that also includes tourists working here illegally. "God, no. Let me see a little of the country first. Acapulco, at least. I'd like to hit the beach in Acapulco, and do some fishing, and I'd like to play a little golf. But I'm not even a stringer."

"I know, I was just trying to put him off."

"Did he say what he wants?"

"Well, he said he wanted to verify that you're working here. Of course, he could have done that by telephone. But he said he wants to talk to you. He wanted to know where you're staying. I didn't know which one of your many hotels to tell him, so I told him the Hotel Comé. I had to tell him something, he's going to find you anyway."

"Was he alone?"

"No, there was another man with him. They're both in plain clothes."

"You picked the right hotel," Harry said. "They'll go to the Comé and they won't find me there, but when I left this morning, I told the guy at the desk I was going to Sanborn's to get some breakfast, so they might come here next."

"Did you tell him which Sanborn's? There's more than one."

"I didn't know that. How long ago did they leave?"

"They just walked out the door."

"Okay, if they're coming here I've got ten, maybe twenty minutes."

"He's the detective investigating that shooting at the Restaurante 33, isn't he? Why is he looking for you? Are you clean on that deal?"

"I'm clean. I just caught a glimpse of the body when I went back to take a leak. A lot of people were milling around, some employees and customers. The police hadn't arrived yet. I looked around, and I asked a few questions. The manager was back there, trying to keep order. I talked with him briefly, and then I cleared out."

"How did Gonzalez know about you?"

Harry could tell that the Bureau Chief was not happy. He obviously did not want his office dragged into a messy murder investigation. "You said the killing at the Bar 33 wasn't much of a story for you, so I thought I'd look into it myself, since I did sort of stumble on it, so to speak. I stopped by the restaurant yesterday afternoon, after the press conference. I talked with the manager again, and of course, he wanted to know who I was, and I showed him the UP card you gave me. I planned to tell you about it today, to bring you up to date."

"Well, you sure caught me off guard, the police coming in here looking for one of our people. Doesn't look good, Harry. You put me on the spot. I don't like to have the police coming around here."

"I'm sorry, Bob."

"What did you learn?"

"Not much, except that Fernandez, the manager, likes the publicity. And they got the hallway and the men's room cleaned up pretty good. Everything else was pretty much in the newspaper stories. Fernandez said the police think they have some kind of a lead on the identity of the dead man."

"How about the killer? Is that why the detective wants to talk to you? Does he think you did it?"

"Jesus, I hope not. I think he's just covering all the bases. Obviously Fernandez told him about me, and I suppose he just wants to ask me a few questions."

"Were you planning to come over here this morning?"

"I haven't figured out my schedule yet."

"I think what you should do today is stay out of sight. Be a tourist, see the sights. Keep in touch by phone, but don't come around here till you get yourself cleared with the police. This is not a very good way to start, Harry."

"Okay. I've got a couple of things to take care of here at the hotel. Like get the hell out before someone comes knocking on my door."

CHAPTER 26

The elevator door opened and Harry stepped out into a crowd of convention delegates. A quick glance at a few name badges told him he was in the midst of a group of bankers. Perfect, he thought. They don't know me and I don't know them, and Gonzalez doesn't know what I look like, so I'm safe for a while, blending in with these people here in the lobby. A fresh pack of Camels, a couple of phone calls, and I'm outta here.

At the row of public telephones, Harry reached into his coat pocket and dug through his collection of cards and scribbled notes, and he realized he had dressed in a hurry and put on the same clothes he had worn all day yesterday and the night before. Half his clothes were still at the Comé.

María Elena answered when Harry called the Florería Roma. "I'm sorry, Señor, but Rosa is not here today."

"She's not feeling well?"

"Oh, it's nothing like that. She was here earlier and then she had to leave. Pedro said she'll be busy all day today, planning a special event. Pedro said she won't be in the rest of the day. He's out right now, too."

"Okay, please tell her I called."

Harry slipped the flower shop's card back into his pocket. She's on her own now. She has her own troubles, and she'll have to take care of herself. I just want to be sure she doesn't drag me down with her. Plenty of good-looking girls in Mexico City. Matter of fact, there are plenty of them right here in this lobby.

Next, a call to the Hotel Comé.

"Yes, Sir, you haven't been gone that long, but already you have two telephone messages. The first call was from a young lady who did not leave her name. I believe it might have been the same young lady who called yesterday. The connection was not very good. I had difficulty understanding her. Perhaps she was calling from an Ericsson telephone."

"An Ericsson phone?"

"Yes, Sir. Those Swedish phones don't always connect well with our Mexican equipment. Or perhaps it was a long distance call. Sometimes the connection is bad when the call originates outside the Valley of Mexico. She said she would contact you later today.

"The second call was from Señor Pedro Yzaguirre Mendoza. He would like you to join him for supper at eight o'clock tonight at La Gran Tasca. He said to tell you he'll reserve a table, and he said to be sure to tell you that Rosa will be there. He said you could call him at the Florería Roma to confirm, or he will call back here later to verify that you can make it."

"La Gran Tasca?"

"Yes, Sir. It's not far, just off the Reforma. Any taxi driver will be able to take you there."

"Okay, thanks. I'll try to reach him, but if he calls back, tell him I'll be happy to join his party. Eight o'clock. Any other calls?"

"No sir, no other telephone calls, but two men were here asking for you just a few minutes ago. I told them you had gone to breakfast, and they asked if I knew where, and I told them you said you were going to Sanborn's. They didn't give their names."

"Okay. Any idea who they were? Tourists like me, maybe?"

"No, Sir, I don't believe they were tourists. They weren't dressed like tourists. They were wearing dark suits and fedoras. Wrinkled suits, I might add."

"Probably just a couple of salesmen," Harry said.

Harry searched in his pocket and found Alberto Duarte's card, now crusty with chocolate cookie crumbs. As he started to dial, he heard a voice call out in English, "Good morning, Yank."

Slowly, Harry hung up the phone and weighed the situation. This could be a problem, he thought. They got here quicker than I expected. Obviously, the cop speaks English. Bob said there were two of them, and they must be carrying guns, so I'm outnumbered, and I'm trapped here in this lobby. God damn it, I should've left the hotel to make my calls.

CHAPTER 27

Harry smiled and reached out to shake hands, relieved this was not an English-speaking cop.

"I saw you in the lounge the other night," the man said, "and I pegged you for an American. I was going to invite you to join us, but you left before I had a chance."

"Oh, yes, I remember you," Harry said. "You were the lucky guy with two girls. You looked like you were having a good time."

"Right, and you were alone, and we thought you looked kind of forlorn, like maybe your best friend had just died, and we thought you needed some company to cheer you up."

Harry laughed at the suggestion. It wasn't my best friend who had just died, he thought, just some guy in the back of a bar. "Well, it wasn't quite that bad, but maybe it looked that way. I just arrived in town a few hours before you saw me, and I guess I was worn out from the trip. My name's Harry, and your name is Ed. I wasn't really eavesdropping, but when your friends called you by name, I couldn't help overhear."

"That's only natural. We might've been making a lot of noise. They're old friends from the States. Are you staying here at the Del Prado? You'll like it here, and I should know because I live here. It's just like home. Say, how about a quick cup of coffee? Do you have time?"

Harry glanced at his watch. He didn't want to take the time for another coffee, but sometimes you have to make your breaks, and take whatever comes along. This guy could be helpful, in more ways than one, and maybe I can help him handle his harem. "I'll take a rain check on the coffee," Harry said, "but sure, let's sit down and chat, over there, out of the traffic."

Harry guided his new-found friend to a bench in a corner of the lower lobby, where he could keep an eye on the front door and also on the elevators and the Grand Staircase coming down from the mezzanine. "I'm just making a few phone calls in the lobby while they clean my room, then I have to get moving. So you live right here in the hotel. Nice place, but doesn't it get to be a little expensive?"

"No, not at all. With the favorable exchange rate, it turns out to be quite affordable, and anyway, I get a housing allowance from my company."

"Favorable exchange rate? Seems like I've been shelling out a lot of pesos ever since I got here."

"But the exchange rate means those are cheap pesos. You pay about eleven-and-a-half cents for each peso, so your dollar goes a long way."

"I hadn't thought of it that way. But what do you do, that you can afford to live in a luxury hotel, even at the favorable exchange rate?"

"I sell cars. How about you? Are you here on business? You don't look like a tourist, so you must be a businessman."

Harry laughed, and gestured toward a group of three or four men walking through the lobby. "I didn't think I look like a businessman, like these bankers in their sincere suits. No, I'm here on vacation, but I'm going to be working part-time for United Press, the wire service, and yesterday was my first day on the job. I'm still getting my feet wet, finding my way around the city. The bureau chief at UP tells me I should find myself a cheap room or apartment, but I kind of like it here in the Del Prado. It's sort of like a palace."

Ed laughed and waved his hand in a sweeping gesture. "Funny you should mention a palace. They promote this as the 'palatial acme of gracious living.'"

"That's quite a mouthful."

"Yes, it is rather corny, but there's always a lot going on here, and I'll bet you could always find a good story here. There's always a party or a meeting or a convention of some kind."

"Like this group of somber-looking bankers, for instance, or those architects over there?"

"Right. You never know what story might be hidden behind their name badges and their dour expressions."

"Yeah, I'm sure of that," Harry said, glancing around the lobby. He spotted plenty of men with expensive, neatly-pressed business suits and polished shoes, but no plainclothes cops. "I'll have to find out more about these fellows, and where they come from."

"I've always thought it would be exciting to be a reporter. You're always right in the middle of the action, just as things happen."

Harry laughed. "Mostly it's routine stuff, and sometimes it can be pretty dull. After all, I don't make the news, I just write about it. So where do you sell your cars? It looks like there are too many cars on the streets here already."

"Oh, we just want to get our fair share of the market. I'm the regional manager for Nash. I'm based here in Mexico City, but I cover Mexico and all of Central America and the Caribbean, so it makes sense for me to live in a hotel since I'm gone so much of the time. Do you have a car, Harry? Maybe I can sell you a car."

"No, I don't have one, but right now I think I'd be afraid to drive a car in this crazy city. I don't know my way around yet."

"You'll get used to it. It's really not that bad. But if you're in a bind for transportation sometime, I can fix you up with one of my courtesy cars. I've got a couple of Nash Ambassadors right here in the hotel garage. Four-door sedans, lots of room."

"You mean you'd let me drive one of your cars?"

"Sure, that's what they're for. It's good public relations. Putting those cars out on the streets where people can see them gives them great visibility. It's like free advertising. I'll give your name to the garage attendants and tell them you might be coming in to borrow a car. They'll have a car all gassed and ready to go. What's your last name, Harry?"

"Banister. I don't know when it might be, but I sure do appreciate the opportunity."

"You won't have any trouble driving here. Just keep your eye on the traffic police in the brown uniforms, directing traffic in all the major intersections."

"I'll remember that. Sounds like you have an exciting job," Harry said. "You must travel a lot. Where're you off to next?"

"Well, I just got back a few days ago from a meeting in Detroit, and I'm leaving for the airport in a few minutes for a trip to Central America—Guatemala, Nicaragua and Panama."

"Do you sell many cars down there?"

"Oh yes, we sell a few. Not as many as we'd like, of course. Politics are a little hectic in Central America right now, but we like to keep our oar in the water. Let's get together when I get back, and maybe I can show you around. I'll be back in about ten days. Here's my card."

"Hey, that would be great. And thanks for the offer of a car to drive. I'll take you up on that."

Harry added another card to his collection, checked his watch again, and disappeared. Ten minutes later he was back in the lobby, dressed in dirty white bucks, lavender slacks, a Hawaiian shirt landscaped with green palm trees and yellow pineapples, and a straw hat with a brim covering half his face. He checked his image and smiled as he passed a mirror. You can't say I look like a somber businessman now.

Fortunately, when he made the quick change up in his room, he remembered to transfer the stuff from his sport coat to his lavender pants pockets. Back at the bank of telephones, he fished in a pocket, pulled out Alberto's card and dialed the number.

"How're you feeling this morning?" Harry asked.

"Never better. I had a great evening. Of course, my head's killing me, but I don't let that bother me. The rest of me feels great. How about you?"

"Never better. I got a good night's sleep. Three aspirins and a good breakfast help. Can you break away for a few minutes?"

"I have a call in for Detective Gonzalez, but they tell me he's out on the street somewhere, chasing down leads. I'll try him again in an hour or so. How about the cantina over here on Bucareli? We can get a cup of black coffee. I'll see you there in twenty minutes."

Harry hung up the phone and shoved Alberto's card back into his pocket. Behind him, at another telephone, he heard someone mention his name. Harry had seen enough cops in cities around the world to recognize one or two when he saw them, even without the uniform or the shield. In seven minutes flat he was at the cantina, pouring a cold Carta Blanca into a glass.

CHAPTER 28

Harry figured he was safe in the cantina, at least for now. With only four tables occupied, the place was much quieter than at lunch time yesterday. Sometimes reporters are slow to get started on their day.

Alberto laughed as he sat down at the table. "Where the hell did you get that shirt? And that crazy jipijapa?"

"I've had this old straw hat for a while. Picked it up in Panama. It travels well. Look, I can roll it up and stick it in my hip pocket if I want to." Harry crushed the hat into a tight roll to demonstrate.

"You look like a real gringo tourist in that outfit."

"Well, that's what I am, and I decided that's what I'm going to be today, a tourist. A gringo tourist, as you put it. That's really why I came down here. I might take a tour of the city and see some sights. After all, I can't write about Mexico City if I don't know my way around."

"Well, you saw a bit of the city last night, you and Rosa. How did you make out with her after Carolina and I left?"

"Yeah, how about that? She turned up at the embassy party. Quite a coincidence in this big city. By the way, you had fresh information in your Bar 33 story today."

"That's right. I didn't get a chance to tell you last night. There was too much going on at the Embassy." Alberto laughed and rubbed his forehead. "And way too much after the Embassy.

"Say, you just reminded me of something, Harry. Remember when we first met yesterday, we joked that you and I might have to solve the murder ourselves? Like the writer in that movie, *The Third Man*? You said two reporters are better than one. Maybe we can put our heads together and do it."

"That's right. That's what I want to talk to you about. I might know something about that case." Not too fast, Harry told himself. Don't talk yourself into a corner. Don't give him too much detail. He's bound to find out eventually, but it's better that he hears it now, rather than from the police.

"Of course you do," Alberto said, lifting his coffee cup in a salute to his own prowess. "You've been reading my stories in *Excelsior*."

"Yeah, but I mean more than that. I was there when it happened."

Alberto gulped, and spewed hot coffee on the table. "You were there? What the hell were you doing there?"

"Well, after we arrived in Mexico City, Rosa and I had dinner at the Restaurante 33. I didn't actually see what happened, but after dinner she left and caught a cab to go home. I paid the check and then I went to use the can, and there was a body on the floor, half in and half out of the men's room. I damned near tripped over the body. The manager was there, and he thought I was getting in the way so he told me to get the hell out."

"What did you learn?"

"Not much, just looking around. I went back after the press conference yesterday and I talked with the day bartender, but he didn't know much. Then I talked with the manager. He recognized me, of course. He remembered that I was the guy who almost tripped over the body. He wanted to know why I was so interested. I told him I was a reporter with United Press. Now, this morning, Bob told me the police came looking for me at the UP office."

"That didn't take long."

"No, and I don't want to stay here in this cantina much longer. It's too close to the UP office."

"Does Rosa know anything about what happened?"

"I don't know. She left before I went back to the men's room. She didn't say anything last night, and I've been trying to get in touch with her so she can tell me if she knows anything, but she's like a clam. If she knows anything, she's not telling me."

"Well, we'll have to get it out of her."

"Later. She's not in the flower shop now anyway. Pedro's got her working on some kind of special project, so it'll have to be later, maybe this evening. I'm going to get the hell out of here now, and just be a tourist today, do some sight-seeing. I'm dressed for the occasion. I might go out to the race track this afternoon."

"That's a good place to be a tourist. Just don't lose everything you've got."

Harry finished his beer and got up to leave. "Maybe just one or two easy bets. Our murder investigation will have to go on the back burner for a while. I just wanted to bring you up to date on my involvement, such as it is, so you're not in the dark when you talk to Gonzalez. You and I might have to solve the case, but we'll let him do a little work on the case himself."

"I understand."

"Good. What's on for tonight?"

"I already checked the society editor's calendar. Like I mentioned last night, it's the Russian Embassy."

"Good God, more cod."

"And caviar, don't forget the caviar. Meet me here at six o'clock if you can, otherwise meet me at the embassy."

"How do I get in?"

"Just like last night. Remember, my good man, we are the gentlemen of the press." Alberto broke into a loud laugh and pointed at Harry's shirt. "But I think you'll have to change your clothes first."

CHAPTER 29

Alberto drank the last of his coffee, trying to evaluate what he had just heard. This guy didn't waste any time finding a girl and getting himself in trouble. I don't know much about him, except that he likes to have a good time. Maybe I should stay away from him until he gets himself straightened around. I don't want to get dragged into something messy.

A familiar voice called out as Alberto stood up to leave "Good morning, Duarte, I thought I might find you here. I'm told this is where you reporters hang out when you're not working."

"Ah, Captain Gonzalez, good morning," Alberto replied, laughing to mask his surprise. "At last you've caught me in my hideout, but who says we're not working? Look around. Look at these hard-working journalists. Yes, our secret's out. This is where all the great news stories are generated. This is our informal, unofficial press club. Would you care to join me and have a beer or a coffee?"

"You look like you were just ready to leave, but yes, we'll join you. My sergeant and I will have coffee. After all, we're on duty, you know." Gonzalez looked around the room and made a broad sweep of the air with his hand. "Yes, I can see how hard you journalists are working, drinking beer and playing cards and dominoes this early in the day." He clipped a fresh cigar and lit it with a flourish.

"But see that fellow over there," Alberto said, pointing to a colleague sitting alone at a table. "The man with the yellow note pad? See, he's writing something in his notebook. He's working on a story right now, trying to perfect the grammar, trying to pick the right words."

"Ha," the detective said with a gruff laugh. "He's probably trying to pick today's winners out at the Hipódromo de las Américas."

"No, I don't think so," Alberto said with a straight face. "He'd be wasting his time doing that, because he knows it's already been decided who's going to win today." All three men laughed.

"I called earlier this morning," Alberto said, "and your office told me you were out. Do you have anything more on our case of the Mysterious Man from Madrid?"

Gonzalez blew a cloud of smoke and frowned. "Those are your words, Duarte. I never told you that we were certain the victim was from Madrid, I only said we believed the jacket came from Madrid. Your headline was premature."

Alberto knew the captain was not happy with the choice of words in this morning's headline. When things were running smoothly, he and Gonzalez communicated informally, on a first name basis. When there was a problem, Gonzalez called him Duarte.

"The victim still is a mystery man," Gonzalez said, "because we haven't been able to identify him. But we're working on it."

"So what do you have that's new?"

"Our forensic experts are studying the bullets that were taken from the wall and from the dead man's body, and we expect to learn something from the ballistics report. And we hope to learn something from his fingerprints."

"So what brings you to Bucareli Street this morning, into this evil lion's den of journalists?"

Gonzalez laughed. "Why, to see you, Alberto, of course. I just naturally expected to find you in a cantina this time of day."

Alberto laughed, too. "Of course, I always come here for my second breakfast."

"Seriously, we just happened to be in the neighborhood. And it's good to sit down with you and have a cup of coffee, because it feels like we've been on a wild goose chase."

"How so?"

"We're looking for a reporter."

"Well, like you said, you found me."

"We're looking for a North American."

"A North American? Really?"

"Yes. A reporter named Banister. He's new in town. He just started working yesterday at United Press. We came to this place, thinking he might be here, and we found you instead."

"Sorry to disappoint you," Alberto said. "But why are you looking for him?"

"We want to question him. He was at the Restaurante 33 the night before last. He had supper with a blonde woman who left very quickly, and then he went to the back of the restaurant."

"So you think he was involved?"

"Perhaps." Gonzalez took a moment to relight his cigar. "Someone gave me this cheap cigar. The damned thing won't stay lit. We don't know if he was involved or not, but we want to talk to him. Right now he's at the top of our list. We believe he knows something about it. The restaurant manager—"

"Fernandez."

"Yes, Fernandez said Banister was snooping around, asking questions. Fernandez said Banister nearly fell when he tripped over the body. Then Banister came back to the restaurant yesterday afternoon, asking more questions."

"Ah, the guilty man returns to the scene of the crime?"

"Perhaps. I think he was trying to find out as much as he could, so he could know as much as we know, and rehearse a story to tell us when we do catch up with him."

"But if he reads my stories in *Excelsior*, he'll know all there is to know."

"Perhaps. That assumes that you know as much as I do, which assumes that I tell you everything I know." Gonzalez laughed. He enjoyed playing this little game with Alberto. "But we'll find him, and we'll bring him in."

"Then he's a suspect in the case?"

"Perhaps. We want to talk to him, ask him a few questions."

"And you say he's at the top of your list of suspects?"

"Well, it's a list of the people we're interested in talking to. And we want to know more about his companion, too."

"Is she a suspect?"

"Perhaps. Let's just say we believe there might be something suspicious about the way she ran out so quickly. By the way, do you know this Banister fellow? I realize he just arrived in Mexico two days ago, but I thought you might have run across him already."

"Yes, as a matter of fact, I met him yesterday. He was at the Pemex press conference. Seems like a nice enough guy, although I don't know what kind of a reporter he is. He didn't take any notes, and he didn't ask any questions. He strikes me as being rather timid, not too aggressive, the kind that will just stand around with his hands in his pockets while the rest of us do all the work."

"Do you know anything about his background? Do you know what brought him to Mexico?"

"He's on vacation, and his job at UP is just a part-time thing. I don't know where he worked before, if that's what you mean about his background. We never got around to that. He said the UP bureau chief was an old friend, so I assume he might have worked for UP somewhere, either in the United States or some other country."

"Some other country?"

"He speaks Spanish pretty well, so perhaps he worked in Spain or somewhere in South America or Central America."

"Well, we'll apprehend him. Like I say, he's up there near the top of our list." Gonzalez knocked his cigar ashes into the ashtray in the center of the table. "Now, Alberto, if you believe you have enough new information for a story for tomorrow's paper, just remember my full name and title when you write it."

"But you really haven't told me anything new today. Can I assume you don't have any new leads? Is the case turning cold?"

"The case is very much alive. We're still working diligently, of course. We always are diligent in the pursuit of justice. We're always diligent in our efforts to solve a case."

CHAPTER 30

Harry got back to the Del Prado just as the afternoon thundershower hit. He asked the taxi driver to drop him at the garage entrance. Fewer people here, he figured, with fewer eyes watching and fewer ears listening. This morning in the hotel lobby, and this afternoon at the race track, there was safety in numbers, but right now there's security in solitude.

As he passed through the garage Harry noticed a shiny blue Nash Ambassador parked against one wall, close to the door and close to the service elevator. The other Nash must be out on loan, he thought, or maybe Ed drove it to the airport. Geez, driving one of those things in Mexico City would be like pushing a Sherman tank in a war zone. Driving one on the open highway would be better. Maybe I could drive one down to Cuernavaca or Acapulco.

In his room, the air conditioning was on full blast, and it made the room a little cooler than the hallway and a lot cooler than the stands out at the race track. Everything seemed to be in place. The valet had hung the freshly-pressed suit in the closet.

Harry took a shower, shaved, and got dressed. He pulled forty dollars from his fast-dwindling reserves, left the room and left the hotel.

The rain had stopped, and Harry strolled as leisurely as the bustle of pedestrians would permit, and as he walked, his mind wandered from his original plan for a fun-filled vacation to his present predicament—the possibility of a part-time job with piddling pay from petty cash. Hardly enough to support an afternoon at the track. And how the hell did I get mixed up in a murder, and mixed up with a girl I don't really know?

"*¿Bolero, Señor?*" A small boy, perhaps ten or eleven years old, with a shoeshine box slung over his wisp of a shoulder, waved a boney little hand. "You like shine, Mister?" he repeated, this time in English.

Harry stopped, looked down at his dusty loafers, and smiled. At the boy's direction Harry leaned against a storefront and placed his left foot on the box. Might as well look my best, he reasoned, for the Russian embassy and for my supper date with Pedro. And Rosa.

"*Un millon de pesos,*" another boy called out, running up to Harry hawking tickets for the National Lottery.

This kid's even younger than the little boleador working so hard on my shoes, Harry realized. It's like Bob said, everybody has to hustle to make a living here in the big city.

So Harry bought a piece of a lottery ticket, partly to help the kid, partly with a vague hope of winning a few pesos.

Harry was leaning next to an open window that displayed cigarettes, candy, chewing gum and other incidentals for sale. On the windowsill was a telephone. While his shoes were being shined, a woman walked up to the window, picked up the phone, and placed a call. When she finished her call she dropped a *veinte*, a twenty-centavo coin, in a dish next to the phone.

Harry thought about what Bob said: everybody hustles. I think I'm going to have to hustle up a little extra money, or I'll be on my way back to the States pretty quick.

This is a long shot, just like a couple of those nags I bet on this afternoon. I don't know who this guy is or where he works, but when you're hustling there's no time like the present, so what the hell.

When his shoes were ready, Harry gave the boy a peso, picked up the phone, and dialed the number the bureau chief had given him.

"*Bueno, ¿quién habla?*" the female voice asked. She repeated her question in English, "Who's calling?"

"This is Harry Banister. A mutual friend gave me this number to call."

"Oh, yes, Mr. Banister, good afternoon. Could you hold for one moment? He's on the phone right now." New England accent, Harry decided. Boston?

"Yes, I'm back. I slipped him a message. We've been expecting your call. He's tied up right now, but he asked me to tell you he would like to meet with you Monday morning, if that would be possible for you."

"Monday?"

"Yes, Sir, and he would like you to call room service at your hotel and order breakfast for two persons, at eight o'clock, in your room. And he asked me to tell you that he likes huevos rancheros with a side of ham."

"At my hotel?"

"Yes, Sir, at the Del Prado."

"Well, I'll have to check my schedule. Hold on a moment ... you did say Monday?"

"If that would be convenient."

"Let me check my schedule." Harry paused for eight or ten seconds and cleared his throat. "Yes, it looks like I'm available. He likes huevos rancheros, you say?"

"Yes, Sir, ranch style eggs, with a side of ham. At eight o'clock, Monday morning. In your room at the Del Prado."

"Eight o'clock. Okay."

The line went dead before Harry could ask any more questions. God damn it, he thought, I didn't even have a chance to get the guy's name.

Harry hung up the phone and dropped a coin in the dish. She was expecting my call? Son of a bitch.

CHAPTER 31

At six-fifteen Alberto left the cantina and headed for the Russian Embassy. On his way he swung by the Brazilian Embassy and picked up Carolina. "Banister's late," he said. "He didn't show up at the cantina. He got tied up on a story, or tied up at the race track, and he's running behind schedule, but he's a big boy, and he'll find his way. Meanwhile, you and I don't want to miss out on a good party."

Carolina tweaked Alberto's ear and smiled. "That's okay, we don't need him to have a good time."

"You're right. I do feel a little sorry for him, though. He could miss out on all the good food."

Carolina laughed. "Yes, he surely will, if you eat it all before he arrives."

"Oh, I'll probably have a little something, but mainly I want to see who's there tonight. I want to see who's on the Russians' invitation list. You can learn a lot just looking around the room. And I want to see if I can pick up a story."

"But how will I get in? Will there be a name badge for me? They don't know me."

"Don't worry," Alberto said. "I don't know if they're going to have name badges, but if they do, there won't be one for me either, because they don't know I'm coming. You're with me. Tonight you'll be my editorial assistant, or my photographer."

"I don't have a camera."

"Don't worry about that either. Tell them it's in the car. They probably wouldn't let you take pictures anyway. Just be sure to give the guards at the door your sexiest smile."

Inside the embassy, Alberto and Carolina made a leisurely swing through the main room, smiling, shaking hands and reading name badges, relentlessly heading in the direction of the buffet table. Sure enough, there was codfish, along with borscht, cold potato soup and, of course, caviar. But there also was plenty of Mexican food. The Russian party planners didn't forget where they were and who their guests were. And the music at the moment was Mexican—the planners didn't slip up on that detail, either.

"This is a big crowd," Carolina said, "but I think we had a more sophisticated group at our reception last night. A lot of these people look like they're very bored, like they're not having a good time."

"Many of them are bored," Alberto said, his eyes sweeping the room. "They're here because they have to be, because they were ordered to be here, or they're here for political reasons or business reasons. Some of the guests are here just to see what the inside of the embassy looks like."

Alberto noticed a small army of men dressed in dark suits. Some were wearing dark glasses, so you couldn't be sure where they were looking or who they were looking at. "And a lot of these people are not guests, they're security people. I think there are more Ministry for State Security agents here than guests. It looks like they might be expecting some sort of trouble tonight."

"But aren't those MGB agents always on their toes, on the lookout?"

"Sure, but it seems like there are more than usual. Maybe that's because of the size of the crowd."

"Or the party crashers like us. But will they bother us?"

"We are not party crashers, we're legitimate members of the working press. They won't bother us if we don't cause trouble." Alberto refilled his plate, and he smiled as he nodded toward a pair of Russian agents he had seen a couple of times before. "They won't bother us unless we eat all their food. Those guys have to eat, too."

Alberto recognized familiar faces among the guests—government people, movie stars, and freeloading reporters, including several from his own paper. He also saw a couple of the people Harry had been talking to last night at the Brazilian reception. "Harry should be here to see this," he said.

"See what? I should see what?"

Alberto turned his head when he recognized Harry's voice. "Ah, you're here. I didn't know if you were going to make it tonight. And I can see you've just arrived—your hands are empty, no food yet, and no drink."

"Yeah, I had a busy day. I didn't know if I'd make it either. It's tough being a tourist. And you're right, I could use a little of each," Harry said, setting three codfish balls and three little taquitos on a plate. He took a glass of Russian beer from a passing waiter. "What did I hear you saying just now? I should see what?"

"That florist, Pedro Yzaguirre Mendoza, the one you were talking to last night, is here." Alberto turned to point across the room. "Well, I don't see him now, but he was here a few minutes ago."

"Who was he with?"

"He was talking with three or four Russians. I don't know who they were. I think one might have been the man in charge of arrangements for this party." Alberto chuckled. "I don't know his name, but you could say he's the Party's party planner."

"That makes sense. Pedro supplied the flowers for this reception. He mentioned it last night. He's a shrewd salesman, and he's probably trying to drum up more business." Harry set his still-full glass on the tray of another passing waiter and asked if he could get a Carta Blanca.

"Our Brazilian party planner did a better job with the decorations for our party last night," Carolina said. "It's too somber here, like a funeral parlor. I get the feeling we're at a wake. I get the feeling someone has died."

Alberto uttered a low, sinister chuckle. "Or someone is about to die. This could be the night."

Ignoring Alberto's joke, Carolina turned to Harry and asked, "Where's Rosa? She's not with you? You're alone tonight?"

"Yeah, I'm alone. I don't know where she is." Harry's eyes made a fast sweep around the room. "Pedro had some kind of an important assignment for her. I haven't talked to her all day."

"You two were having a good time when we left you last night," Alberto said. "Rosa was singing right along with the mariachis. Come to think of it, so were you."

"Me? I didn't know any of those songs."

Alberto and Carolina laughed. "You sure did," he said. "You knew all the lyrics for *Coronelas*, and you sang right along."

Harry laughed. "Yeah, that's right. *Coronelas*. I guess I was singing that one. I must be a fast learner. Or else it was the beer."

Harry stopped laughing when he recalled Rosa's distant mood at the end of the evening. Things had been going well up to then. Rosa seemed to be having a good time, laughing and singing and even dancing, but after that last ranchera, the one about how beautiful Mexico is, her whole mood crashed.

"Hey," Harry said suddenly, "I had a great day today. I took a Gray Line tour of Mexico City, with a bunch of American and British tourists, and I saw the Cathedral and the Zócalo and Chapultepec Castle and the Palacio de Bellas Artes. Did you know that the Palace of Fine Arts is slowly sinking into the soft soil of an ancient lake bed? Steps that used to go up now go down. A hundred years from now the Palacio won't even be here."

"You're right," Alberto said, "and neither will we, and nobody will miss us."

"Yeah, but it would be a shame to lose that classic old building with its beautiful Tiffany glass curtain. People would really miss that place."

Now Alberto laughed. "It sounds like you got the usual spiel from the tour guide. Did he also tell you that the "classic old building" was completed just a few years ago?"

"Yeah, come to think of it, he did say that. He said they started building it in 1904 but didn't finish until 1934. Anyway, it's a beautiful building, and I'd hate to see anything happen to it."

"You must have fit in with all those tourists, dressed the way you were. You should have seen him, Carolina. He was a picture right out of a Thomas Cook four-color magazine ad."

"You have to go along with the group. After all, that's what I am, just a typical gringo tourist. Bus tour this morning, race track in the afternoon, party in the evening. I want to see everything, get my money's worth. And I'd like to play some golf tomorrow. Do you think you could set me up for golf somewhere Alberto?'

"Did you bring your clubs?"

"You bet. I'm ready to play."

"Tomorrow might be difficult on such short notice. Next week would be easier. But tell me, how did you do out at the Hipódromo today?"

"I broke even," Harry lied. "You know how it is—win a few, lose a few. Actually, I dropped more than I planned. I did have one good winner, though, in the seventh race."

"How were you able to pick that one? You don't know anything about those nags."

"I had a tip from a guy in the stands."

"A tout?" Alberto looked surprised. "You're a stranger here, and you took a tip from a tout at a strange track in a strange city?"

"Hey, I'm not a stranger anymore. After the tour this morning, I know this city inside out, I feel like I'm a native. And he wasn't exactly a stranger. You pointed him out yesterday at the press conference, the correspondent from *The New York Times*."

"Sydney was at the track today?"

"Right. I got talking to him after the second race—hey, that guy's a fountain of information."

"That's what I told you. He has a lot of good contacts."

"So I asked him if he had any good tips, and he said I should bet the number four horse in the seventh race. 'That's my horse,' he said, 'and he's ready to run.' So I bet the four horse to win, and sure enough, he won and he paid pretty good. I picked up a few pesos on that one, but not enough to cover my losses in the first six races."

"Lucky break," Alberto said. "I knew he had a couple of horses at the Hipódromo, but I didn't know any of them were capable of running that fast. Did he have anything else to say, or was it all horse talk?"

"We talked about a lot of things. He sounds like he really knows what's going on, not just here in Mexico, but also in Central America. He said there's some kind of trouble brewing in Guatemala, and it could blow up into something big. Something about bananas."

"That's right. United Fruit Company grows a lot of bananas there, and they own a lot of land. They also own the only port on the Gulf, so Guatemala's new president, Arbenz, decided to build a new port. Arbenz also wants to distribute land to the peasants, and a lot of United Fruit's uncultivated land is marked for redistribution. There's a lot of unrest down there, and opposition from United Fruit and from your government up in Washington."

"Yeah, he mentioned something about that, something about the two Dulles brothers, John Foster and Allen."

"Right. They're close to United Fruit. Like I said, Sydney has solid contacts. Say, Harry, I'm glad you made it here tonight. Did you have any trouble getting in?"

Harry laughed. "No problem at all. As a matter of fact, I had an invitation. Sydney gave me one. He had a couple extras."

"Sydney's here right now," Alberto said. "I saw him a few minutes ago. He's probably over in a corner with one or two Russians, digging up a good story. Maybe he's trying to get a story out of Diego."

"Diego?"

"Diego Rivera, the artist. He's here, too. I saw him earlier in the other room, surrounded by a group of admirers. He always attracts a crowd."

"Yeah, he's a big man," Harry said, "in more ways than one. He draws a crowd, but he also attracts controversy. I remember he made a big hit up in New York a few years ago with the mural he painted in Rockefeller Center, the one with Lenin's face in the crowd. Nelson Rockefeller wanted him to remove the face, but he refused, so Rockefeller fired him and had the mural removed."

"He loves the controversy, the crowds," Alberto said. "Say, speaking of crowds, it's too crowded here for Carolina and me, so we're going to leave in a little while and find another party. Would you like to join us?"

"No, you two go ahead and have a good time. I'm going to look around and see who's here, and I want to talk to Sydney for a few minutes. I've got a couple of questions for him. Then I'm going to have supper. Pedro invited me to join him and some of his friends at a restaurant called La Gran Tasca."

"That's a good spot—you'll like it there. Will Rosa be there?"

"Yeah, that's what he told me."

"You sly fox. That's one way to get next to her."

"Hey, it's his idea, not mine. He invited me, and anyway, I never want to pass up a free meal.

CHAPTER 32

La Gran Tasca reminded Harry of a tavern in a small mountain village in northern Spain. The façade featured pock-marked granite walls accented by solid oak columns and beams. The entrance was a fourteen-foot oak door with black wrought iron hinges and iron rings for pullers.

The interior carried out the mountain theme, with oak tables and tall ladder-backed chairs, red-and-white checkered tablecloths, and candles on the tables. Sconces with candles mounted on the oak pillars and ornate wrought iron chandeliers helped create an atmosphere of warmth and camaraderie.

"I'm joining Señor Yzaguirre Mendoza at his table," Harry said to the headwaiter.

"Of course, Señor, they're expecting you. Please follow me."

Waiters in soft-soled white slippers reminded Harry of the waiters at the Hungarian Village in Detroit, gypsies dressed in tuxedos and white tennis shoes, gliding silently around the room. Tonight's waiters wore white stockings, black knee-length britches, white shirts with red sashes around the waist, and open black vests that looked like they were too small. Some were wearing red berets, others bright green or blue plaid kerchiefs wrapped into tight skullcaps. Waitresses wore the same soft-soled slippers and full skirts of red, green or blue with colorful shawls over their shoulders.

The headwaiter led Harry to a round table set for five. Harry saw Pedro and Rosa and another man at the table. Pedro and the other man already had been served wine and small plates of tapas, and a server was just now delivering a glass of dry sherry and a plate of tapas to Rosa. She looks beautiful tonight, Harry told himself. Sad, and a bit haggard, but beautiful.

"Good evening, Harry, I'm glad you could join us," Pedro said, smiling and gesturing to the vacant chair next to Rosa. "This is one of my favorite restaurants, and I'm sure you'll enjoy it too. The food is outstanding, and I promise you, this will be a wonderful, festive evening for all of us. Miguel will be joining us. Did you meet Miguel yesterday?"

Harry slipped into the vacant chair. "No, I saw him but I didn't meet him formally. Hello, Rosa, looks like you got here just ahead of me. I missed you today. I called the shop this morning, but María Elena said you were—"

"Here's someone else you haven't met," Pedro broke in abruptly. "This is my good friend and colleague, José."

Rosa didn't have a chance to say anything, and Harry got the message. He wasn't going to get any information out of her now. He gave her leg a nudge with his knee.

"Hello, Harry," she said with a quiet smile. "It's good to see you." She pressed her knee against his. Sometimes gentle nudges are better than words.

A waiter set a plate of northern pintxos in front of Harry and asked him if he would like something to drink. Harry ordered a beer and sampled a clam. A server set a large bowl of paella in the center of the table for everyone to share, and the head waiter set menus at each place. The conversation now turned to those spicy tapas and tonight's menu of seafood specialties.

Miguel hurried up to the table and dropped into the vacant chair. "Sorry I'm late," he said. "Something came up at the last minute." He looked around the table, his eyes pausing briefly but intently on each face.

"If it's a problem, I don't want to hear it now," Pedro said, lifting his wine glass to make his point. "We don't need any problems. We're here to have a good time."

When they had placed their orders, Pedro went right to the heart of the matter. "Harry, I thought this would be a good opportunity for us to get together and get to know each other and, of course, to relax and enjoy a good meal. Like I said, this is one of my favorite restaurants. But I feel that I already know you, from our brief conversation last night and from what Rosa has told me, and like I said last evening, a friend of Rosa's is a friend of mine."

"I always enjoy a good meal, Pedro, and I always enjoy good company," Harry said, smiling and once again pressing his knee against Rosa's leg. "And I like your choice of a place to meet—this tavern has authentic atmosphere, and this Spanish beer is great."

Harry turned to face Rosa. "Tell me, Rosa, how do you like those—"

"I'm glad you like the beer," Pedro interrupted. "Yes, it does feel good to relax. José and I—in fact, all of us—have had a strenuous day. How about you, Harry? Were you busy in your new job?"

Harry was about to answer, but he was cut short when a waiter standing near their table picked up a tambourine and shook it. In the back of the room another waiter strummed a chord on a guitar. Someone across the room picked out a melody on a small guitar. A man wearing a white apron came out of the kitchen and began to sing, and the entire staff joined in playing and singing a rousing Aragonese jota. A young waiter and a pretty waitress moved to the center of the room, arched their arms over their heads, clicked their castanets, and began to dance.

Harry relaxed and watched the show and sipped his beer. Better than that Russian stuff at the last stop, he thought. Last night it was the samba and the mambo and then the mariachis, earlier tonight it was the balalaika, and now it's the jota. But that son of a bitch Pedro won't let me talk to Rosa. Why am I here?

CHAPTER 33

Dinner was served when the entertainment ended, and Pedro picked up the conversation where he left off before the show. "You were going to tell us about your new job, Harry. I know you went to the Pemex press conference yesterday. Were you busy again today?"

"Well actually, no. The UP bureau chief and I agreed I should take it easy today and get acclimated. He said he didn't want the thin mountain air to lay me low." The three men laughed. Rosa, straight-faced, took a bite of trout. She's consistent, Harry decided. She also had trout at the Restaurante 33. But she's quiet tonight. Rough day?

"You'll get used to it soon enough," Pedro said. "Thin air doesn't bother any of us. We all grew up with it. We're all mountain men. So how did you pass the day?"

"I took a sightseeing tour of the city this morning and I went out to the Hipódromo in the afternoon."

"And what did you think of our city?"

"Big, energetic, with a lot of people and a lot of traffic, and a trove of fascinating history."

"And how did our thin mountain air affect the horses at the Hipódromo?" José asked. "Were they laid low by it?"

"Apparently the ones I picked were. They seemed to be struggling when they came down the home stretch. Maybe that's because the horses in front of them used up all the good air." This time everyone laughed.

"Do you bet the favorites to win?"

"No, I like to bet the long shot. I like to bet on the little guy—the scrawniest horse, the skinniest jockey. I like to bet on the underdog. If I don't have a bet riding in a particular race, I yell like hell for the horse that's running dead last coming 'round the clubhouse turn."

Pedro raised his wine glass in a salute. "Ah, you demonstrate a wonderful egalitarian spirit. Excellent. Does that noble philosophy carry beyond the race track?"

"Of course. When I go out to the Plaza México next Sunday afternoon, I'll probably bet on the bull, even though I know the bull is going to lose." Once again the three men laughed. Rosa forced a timid smile.

"And how about life away from the sporting world?" Pedro asked. "Do you have that same spirit of equality when it comes to, say, the working man? Do you still support the underdog?"

Harry took a drink of his beer. He wasn't sure where this conversation was heading, but he figured he might as well get on board. "Absolutely. I'm a working stiff myself, a union man."

José raised his glass in a salute. "Excellent, a union man."

"Yes, I'm a card-carrying member of the Newspaper Guild. I've never identified with the upper echelons of the corporate world, or the blue bloods of Park Avenue, or the country club set. I guess I'm just a peasant at heart. I fully support the working man's struggle for equality in this dog-eat-dog world."

A little white lie every now and then won't hurt, Harry thought. Sure, I'm still a Guild member, but these people don't have to know I'm behind in my dues. And they don't have to know my life history.

Pedro's eyes sparkled, and his face lit up in a broad smile. "So when you write your news stories, you're writing for the working man."

Harry had never thought of it that way. He always figured he was writing for the general public, whoever they might be, just writing the best way he knew how. "I guess you could say that. When I studied journalism in college, I studied the great writers of the English language—Shakespeare, Chaucer, Dickens, Poe, Mark Twain from the past, for example, and of course Twentieth Century writers like Maugham, Hemingway—"

"Ah, Ernest Hemingway," Pedro interrupted. "A great writer indeed. *For Whom the Bell Tolls*. I know that book well. A truly great story of the conflict in Spain, the brave war against the perils of Fascism. A brave war, but a sad war in its outcome. Thousands of valiant lives were sacrificed."

"Well, yes," Harry said, caught off guard by Pedro's exuberant reference to the Spanish Civil War. "He was able to convey the pathos of the Spanish tragedy with that novel, with his superb writing style. But when I got out of college, and went to work for United Press, we were taught to write in the everyday language that everyone understands. We were taught to write for the Kansas City Milkman."

Pedro reacted with a hearty *"¡Olé!* The Kansas City Milkman. I like that." He raised his glass. "¡Salud! Here's a toast to your Kansas City Milkman, a toast to the working man. ¡Salud!"

"And to the milkman of Mérida," José joined in, "and the plumber of Pachuca, the tailor of Taxco—"

Miguel cleared his throat and interrupted. "But now you go to the race track your second day on the job? Sounds to me like it's not much of a job. Sounds to me like your boss is not working you very hard."

Harry laughed. "Well, he wants me to get settled in, get my feet on the ground, and get used to the mountain air. And, like I said last night, it wouldn't really be a full time job. I'd be just a part-time employee, sort of a stringer, pretty much on my own. I'd have some special assignments, and I'd write the occasional feature story, maybe a travel story, maybe something about history—hey, I learned a lot about the history of the country, and the history of Mexico City, on my bus tour."

"And I suppose he's paying you accordingly?" José asked.

"I'm afraid so. Since it's not a full time job, it wouldn't be a full time salary. But tell me, José, what is it that you do?"

José glanced at Pedro, drained his wine glass and wiped his lips dramatically with his napkin. "Well, Pedro and I, uh … we're in the same business, but at different ends of the chain. I work in the fields, and he works in the comfort of a store here in the city. I plant the seeds and grow the flowers. I cultivate them and nurture them and help them grow. I do all the work, and then Pedro sells them and gets all the credit."

"But it's much more than that," Pedro said. "We're members of a group, a floral trade association, you might say. It's called the, uh … it's called the *Asociación Mexicana del Fomento de Flores*, The Mexican Association for the Promotion of Flowers. We call it AsMexFomFlor."

"Yes, we're dedicated to … well, we're dedicated to improving the lives of the Mexican people," José said, "and we believe flowers are just one way to accomplish this."

"We believe flowers can bring beauty and pleasure to the lives of the working people," Pedro said, "the downtrodden, the people who toil so hard to scratch out a living, the people in the factories and in the fields, the people who can appreciate the pure beauty of a dahlia or an orchid or a red rose—or a white rose," he added, laughing and patting Rosa on the shoulder.

It occurred to Harry that Rosa hadn't said much more than a subdued 'hello' since he sat down next to her. Pedro and José were doing all the talking, their spirited repartee bouncing back and forth like a ping pong ball. Miguel hadn't said much, either. And Rosa acted like she doesn't want to be here. Maybe she had a bad day. Maybe it's because she's the only woman in a group of noisy men.

Almost as if he had read Harry's mind, José signaled the waiter for another bottle of rioja and another bottle of beer.

"Yes," Pedro continued, "we believe that flowers are for the people, and it occurred to me earlier today that perhaps you could help us. You're a writer, perhaps you could do some writing for us. Perhaps a brochure, maybe a press release, or a pamphlet. We would pay you, of course."

"Well, I don't know much about flowers. I don't know an azalea from an aster, although I do know something about white roses." He looked at Rosa and smiled, and he gave her leg another gentle nudge with his knee. She pressed back with hers.

Pedro laughed. "We could teach you. Perhaps Rosa could teach you. She knows just about all there is to know about flowers."

Harry looked again at Rosa and thought he saw a faint smile. "Gee, that would be nice. She'd be the prettiest teacher I've ever had."

This time everyone laughed.

"But seriously, I have a question. I guess I speak Spanish reasonably well—"

"You speak it very well," Pedro said. "You speak it almost like a native."

"—but I don't know if I could write a sensible pamphlet or a press release in Spanish. I've never really tried to do any serious writing in Spanish."

"Don't worry about that. José is a university graduate, and he'll be able to correct any mistakes you make. He'll even be happy to suggest the right words for you to use, the right phrases, and guide you in the right direction."

"Yes, we can help you," José added. "We can tell you what to write—"

"But we don't need to go into a lot of detail right now," Pedro interrupted, giving Harry a friendly slap on the shoulder. "We can talk more about it later. This is just an informal supper, getting to know each other better, exploring our common interests—and I wanted to give you and Rosa, you two young people, an opportunity to get together and chat. Tonight it's just good food, lively music, and friendly camaraderie."

Perplexed, Harry took a slow sip of beer, and set the glass on the table. An opportunity to chat? We haven't been able to say one word together.

The conversation during the rest of the meal bounced around from the music to the dancers, the weather, baseball and the bulls, from horses to flowers and the poverty of the people, and of course, the wine and the food. And Miguel occasionally agreed or disagreed with someone or other on something or other.

When Pedro finished his flan, he placed his hand on Harry's shoulder. "This has been a most enjoyable evening," he said, "and I'd like you to understand, any friend of Rosa's is a friend of mine. I know

Rosa thinks highly of you, and now that I know you better, I think of you as a true friend."

Harry thought he saw a momentary flash of red on Rosa's pale cheeks.

"I want you to feel free to drop by and visit Rosa at the flower shop," Pedro said, "any time you're in the neighborhood."

"Well, thank you, Pedro, I'll be sure to do that."

Draining his wine glass, Harry reflected on Pedro's offer. For Christ's sake, I need an invitation to see Rosa? I'd like to believe I can see her any God-damned time I want to, without ol' Uncle Pedro's permission. "That's very kind of you, Pedro. I'll do that."

Pedro folded his napkin, placed it next to his plate, and paid the check. He took Harry's hand and shook it vigorously. "Now, my good friends, I must call it an evening. I have things to do back at the flower shop."

"Yeah, I know," Harry said with a laugh, "time and flowers wait for no man."

Harry slipped in front of Rosa as the group left La Gran Tasca, hoping he could pull her away and pick up where they left off last night, but Pedro took her by the arm and said, "Come along, Rosita, it's getting late. I'll drive you home. You've had a long day, and tomorrow's going to be another busy day. Good night, Harry, I've enjoyed our time together this evening. Like I said, I consider you a good friend now."

Pedro and the others drove away, leaving Harry alone on the sidewalk in front of the restaurant. God damn it, he mumbled. Shot down again, before I could even get off the ground.

Harry stepped out into the traffic and signaled a taxi.

CHAPTER 34

Pedro parked by the curb and waited until Rosa was safely in her front door, then drove away. "Well, gentlemen, what do you think about Banister? Is he worthy of La Rosa Blanca?"

"Who knows? He's pleasant," José said, "but he didn't have much to say. She didn't say much this evening either, but—"

Pedro burst out laughing. "How could she? She didn't have a chance, with you doing all the talking."

José laughed right along with Pedro. "Me? No more than you. You're the one who was ranting about the great 'floral trade association.' Tell me, where did you get that crazy idea for a trade association? And how did you come up with that name? AsFomFlor."

"Ah, yes, AsMexFomFlor. Don't forget the 'México' part of it. You like that? I made that up while we were eating. A stroke of genius, no?"

"A creative gem," José agreed, "although it doesn't exactly roll off the tongue. How about we just call it FomFlor?"

"Call it whatever you wish, amigo. The name probably won't get a lot of use anyway, and I'm sure it'll never make it into print."

"I know what you mean—but you ask what I think of Banister. It strikes me he's nothing more than a hedonistic loafer. He has an opportunity for a good job, but he's not interested in working. I think he fancies himself the Playboy of the Western World."

"Right. That's what I told Miguel last night. He appears to be footloose, with no roots, a man with no strong convictions about anything. But he's a working man when he does work, and he is a union member. He seems to be sympathetic to the plight of the common man. Rosa, poor thing, certainly does have an eye for him, and I want only the best for her."

"Of course. I understand."

Pedro slowed for a crowded intersection. "That could be a problem. Yes, I want to protect her, but I have an idea, just the germ of an idea, and it would be worth a try. It could be an opportunity. I have to think about it."

"Pedro, you were full of ideas back there at La Gran Tasca. That trade association, and also your idea that he might be able to write something for us? Where did that come from? Was that the rioja talking?"

Pedro laughed. "No, it wasn't the wine. It's simply a matter of working with the tools you're given. If he were an electrician, for example, I would ask him to fix that faulty lamp in the back of the flower shop. If he were a mechanic, I could ask him to fix the *camioneta*, but Miguel does a good job of keeping the delivery van in good running condition. And if he were a munitions expert, we could ask him to build us a bomb. But he happens to be a writer."

Miguel, slouching in the back seat, grumbled. "Yeah, well, I don't trust him. What's he doing here in Mexico anyway?"

"I think he's here just to have a good time," José said, "but he's taken a job as a reporter."

"Exactly, and as a reporter he could go places we can't go," Pedro said. "Doors will open for him, and for us."

"As a reporter he also could write things we don't want to see in print," Miguel said. "A good bi-lingual Mexican reporter would serve us just as well, someone who could write a proper press release in Spanish or in English, if that's what you want. Someone who could write what we want him to write. Someone who wouldn't be so God-damned conspicuous. Someone we know."

"Perhaps," Pedro said. "Let me think about it. What I have in mind, it shouldn't make any difference."

"But I don't trust him," Miguel continued. "What do we really know about him?"

"Miguel is right," José said. "He tells us he's a reporter, but what do we really know?"

"Of course he's a reporter," Pedro replied, peeved that they were challenging his judgment and his plan.

"Don't let him get too close to Rosa," Miguel said. "He could be trouble. Remember, he's a gringo, and he's a stranger in our land."

"Yes, that's true."

"And how the hell did he get a job so fast? What kind of a job is it? The *cabrón* works one day and then goes to the race track the next day? What kind of a job is that?"

Pedro blew a cloud of smoke, wondering why he had to defend a man he hardly knew. "He explained it. The UP bureau chief is an old friend."

"Well, I still don't trust him. You say you have an idea, but what if he doesn't work out?"

"If he doesn't work out, Miguelito, I'm sure you can handle it. I leave that to you."

CHAPTER 35

At seven o'clock Monday morning, Harry checked out of the Hotel Comé. "I'm not expecting any mail," he told the desk clerk, "but I might get a phone call."

"How can I reach you if that young lady calls?"

Harry gave the desk clerk a ten-peso note. "If she calls, you can tell her I'm at the Del Prado, but nobody else needs to know."

"Yes, Sir. And what about those two men who were looking for you last week, if they should come back again?"

"I think they're just salesmen. Whatever they're selling, I'm not buying."

The desk clerk nodded his head and smiled. "But I don't believe they're salesmen, Sir. They don't look like salesmen, not the way they're dressed."

"Well, whoever they are, I don't need them following me around."

"I understand."

"How long are you on duty today?"

"I'm here until five o'clock."

"That's a long day." Harry slipped him another ten-peso note. "Nobody else has to know I checked out, just the girl."

"Yes, Sir. I understand completely."

By seven-thirty Harry was unpacking in his room at the Del Prado. He put his bags in the closet, pulled down the bed spread, and rumpled the pillows. Next he ran water in the shower and the wash basin and splashed water on a bath towel. That should give the place a lived-in look, in case anyone is curious.

Harry stretched out in the lounge chair by the window and lit a cigarette. He was ready to face the day, whatever it might bring, and happy to have only one hotel room to worry about.

The taste of the tacos he had for dinner at the cantina across from the bull ring still lingered in his mouth. He smiled when he recalled what the waiter told him: "These tacos will make you very strong and very courageous, Señor, because you are eating the balls of one of the brave bulls killed this afternoon at the Plaza México."

Harry ate one of the pillow-top mints, hoping it might kill the pungent taste of the tacos and the salsa picante. He pulled Rosa's note from his coat pocket and read it again, for the third or fourth time:

> **Dear Harry –**
>
> *I'm sorry, but something has come up, and I won't be able to see you tomorrow, but you should go by yourself to the Palacio de Bellas Artes in the morning and the bullfight in the afternoon (Be sure you buy a ticket in the shade at the Plaza México — it's only three pesos.)*
>
> *And let's be sure to meet Monday for lunch at that little restaurant on Morelos. Two o'clock. And let's plan on going to the bullfight next Sunday. Sorry about the mix-up, but I'm looking forward to seeing you for lunch Monday*
>
> *-- R.*

Obviously, she wrote the note Saturday night before she got to La Gran Tasca, Harry realized. She wouldn't have been able to write such a long note at the dinner table, even when the lights went down for the entertainment. She barely was able to slip it into my coat pocket. I don't know what was so damned important yesterday, but she missed a good show at the Palace of Fine Arts, and she missed a great afternoon at the bullfight. Six brave bulls, one in particular.

Harry smiled as he ate the other mint ... she might not have liked the tacos anyway.

But what kind of a mess am I getting into now? I'm going to buy breakfast for a total stranger. I don't know who he is or what he does, I don't know what he wants, and I don't even know his name.

At eight o'clock a waiter wheeled a cart into the room. Harry lifted the lids from the hot trays to see what huevos rancheros looked like. Not bad, he decided, smells good, maybe a little on the spicy side, but nothing like last night's tacos. Might be worth trying next time.

At two minutes past eight, Harry opened the door and greeted his guest with a friendly "good morning" and a firm handshake. The visitor returned the handshake and introduced himself. "Corbett's the name," he said.

Harry was stunned when he heard the introduction. This was not what he expected. "Of course, I've heard of your outfit," Harry said. "Who hasn't? But Bob didn't give me any details. All he gave me was a telephone number. He didn't tell me your name or your title or who you work for. He said you're in Mexico on some kind agricultural research project."

The visitor smiled. "Well, I guess the 'research' part of it is accurate. We do a hell of a lot of research, always looking for information, searching for the truth. The title is irrelevant. You can just call me Stephen, or Steve, if you prefer."

"Obviously you already know my name."

"I know all about you. He gave me some of the basics and I had our people check you out."

"Did I pass?" Harry asked, half joking.

"Yes, you passed."

With a few more of these awkward pleasantries out of the way—the beautiful morning, the view of the park, how good the breakfast smelled—the two men sat down and dug right in, Harry on his scrambled eggs and bacon, his visitor on his huevos rancheros with a side of ham. Then Harry decided to beat this guy to the punch. "So tell me, what can I do for you? I understand you might want me to do some writing?"

"That's right, if you want to make a little extra money, and I assume you do, or you wouldn't have called."

"Well, I can always use a little extra walkin' around money. Bob said I could call you if I wanted to do some free lance writing. Based on what he offered to pay me for being a part-time employee, I figured I would have to call you sooner or later, so I called, and here I am."

Harry paused and took a bite of food, waiting for a response. His visitor nodded and smiled but said nothing, just concentrating on his breakfast, letting Harry do the talking.

So Harry continued. "Your secretary said you were expecting my call. She told me to order breakfast, and what time, and she told me what to order for you. She even knew where I'm staying. For Christ's sake, you guys really set me up. What's going on?"

"Well, it's not quite that dramatic. Let's just say we did some planning. Bob told me about you, and he said you were coming down here, and I asked him if we could borrow you, so to speak, to help us on a project."

"Obviously he agreed."

"Yes, he did. But you must be curious about what I have to say. You sure didn't waste much time calling." He laughed as he took another bite of his spicy eggs. "You called sooner rather than later."

"Yeah, I had a bad day at the track Saturday. But when I called your office, that was supposed to be just an exploratory call. I didn't think things would move this fast. So what gives? What's this all about?"

"Harry, I want you to work for us. You're a reporter, that's why I want you. Not so much for your writing. I want to use your reporting skills, your nose for news. We need information, Harry, we thrive on good information, and you can help us get what we need. The armed forces have their weapons. The Army has its tanks and its artillery, the Air Force has its planes, and the Navy has its ships. Information is our weapon, Harry. Intelligence is our weapon."

Harry smiled, thinking his guest sounded a bit melodramatic. Maybe that's part of the game. Role-playing. Maybe it's the melodrama that inspires these guys to do whatever the hell it is they do.

CHAPTER 36

"Like I said, we want to hire you. We want you to be another pair of eyes for us, and another pair of ears."

Harry chased a piece of bacon around his plate and pushed it into a pile of scrambled eggs. I'm here only a few days, Harry thought, and already and I'm offered a job with UP, those guys Saturday night want to pay me to write about flowers, and now this guy wants to give me another job. Maybe I'd be biting off more than I could chew.

"But I already told you, I came down here to have some fun, and I sure as hell don't want work interfere with my fun."

"You'll still have plenty of time to enjoy the pleasures of Mexico. And you can help your country in a time of crisis. You can help us, Harry. With your UP press credentials, you'll be able to go places I can't go and ask questions I can't ask. You'll be able to ferret out the information we need."

"What kind of places? What kind of questions? And what kind of information?"

"We like to keep up to date on whatever's going on here in Mexico. We read the newspapers, of course, but often there's more information behind the stories, information that never makes it into the papers. We like to know what the Mexican government is doing, particularly if it might have anything to do with the United States. We like to know what's going on with Mexican companies, what they're doing that might have a bearing on business back in the States. Manufacturing, for example. Imports and exports. Cotton, corn, sugar. And, of course, oil. And we like to know what the military is up to."

"In other words, you guys are just plain nosy."

"Let's say we just like to keep abreast of things. We have good sources here, of course, but it never hurts to have another pair of eyes and another pair of ears."

"So what's got your ears buzzing today?"

"Well, I see they brought you a copy of *Excelsior* with the breakfast cart. Have you had a chance to read about last night's refinery fire?"

"There was another fire last night?"

"Yes. That's just an example of the kind of thing we like to keep an eye on."

Harry laughed. "That's the hot story right now?"

"One of them. You can read about it later, after I've left. But I don't want you to think your job here will be to fight fires. As a matter of fact, when I first talked to Bob about you, the fires were not an issue. I figured the first fire was just a minor flare-up. Now I think they might be significant. What do you know about the fires?"

"I saw one the other night coming down on the bus. Tell me, why is the U.S. government interested in these local fires? Aren't these a matter for the Mexican officials? For the local police, if not the Federales? Why are you interested?"

"I'm interested in everything that goes on down here, anything that might involve us, anything that might involve the security of the United States. I'm interested in anything that might impact our trade relations with Mexico or with any other country, for that matter. Right now, the fires are in the news, and I like to keep abreast of the news. I have some theories, but I need better information. What did the people on your bus say about the fire you saw?"

"Sounded to me like they were all guessing. Someone near the front of the bus said it was probably just a crop burn. Someone said they were burning bagasse in the sugar fields. One man said it was a fire at a well in the oil fields, or perhaps at a storage tank. They all said it was just one isolated fire, a small one at that. They seemed to agree it was no big deal. But I don't think anybody knew anything for certain."

"What did the driver say? He was right up front. He must have had a good view."

"That wise-ass said they must be burning gringos again. The son of a bitch was looking right at me, and grinning, when he said that."

"Welcome to Mexico. Let me take a minute to give you a little background. Our position here is precarious, to say the least. It's like walking on egg shells. The Mexicans are very good hosts, and they want us to feel welcome as tourists, because they want our tourist dollars. But they're a very proud, patriotic, nationalistic people, and a lot of Mexicans resent us Americans, for a variety of reasons, and a lot of them resent us being here now."

"Yeah, so I've noticed."

"Right. Like your bus driver. It might seem like paranoia, but they're only trying to protect their sovereignty and safeguard their borders. That's exactly what I want to do, Harry. I want to protect our borders, and one way to do that is to help them protect theirs.

"You know, we've stuck our nose in Mexico's affairs many times in the past. We've invaded this country, and our troops have occupied parts of the country, as recently as 1914. We've invaded by land, and we've invaded by sea. We even fought the Mexicans right here in Mexico City."

Harry's visitor slowed down for a bite of his eggs, and then continued, "We've taken a lot of their land. That hackneyed battle cry, 'Remember the Alamo,' might get a Texan's xenophobia cranked up, but to a Mexican it's a different kind of battle cry. They would just as soon forget the Alamo.

"A few years later they lost the war they fought against us, and that was barely a hundred years ago. All in all, they lost more than a third of their land to the United States—land that now runs from Texas and New Mexico and California and Arizona all the way up into Utah and Wyoming."

Corbett poured hot milk into his thick coffee and stirred it. "We remember the Alamo, but the Mexicans still remember the Yankee land grab, and a lot of them would like to get that land back."

"So we Americans have to be careful where we step," Harry said, recalling what the manager told him at the Bar 33. "We don't want to step in anything we shouldn't step in."

"Right. One of our first rules here is 'do the job right, do whatever it takes to get it done, but don't step on too many toes.' It looks like we could have a big job facing us right now, but I don't want them to think we're intervening again. Help is one thing, intervention is another."

"So how would I fit in?"

"I want information. Like I said, we thrive on information. Let's start with the fires. The people on your bus were right. These fires haven't caused any real damage, and they haven't had a lot of coverage in the newspapers here in the Capital, but they are creating a stir out in the country. I want to find out what's going on, and why, and where it's leading. I want to know who's behind it. What's their ultimate plan and what's their goal? That's what I want from you."

"So you think someone is setting the fires? They're not accidental?"

"I don't know, that's what I want to find out."

"Who do you think it might be?"

"There are a lot of theories. One of my sources here in the government thinks it might be somebody with a grudge, someone who has an ax to grind with Pemex. A disgruntled employee or former employee. It could be Communists, or it could be Nazis on the run. It could be Mexican revolutionaries, or vandals, or it could be agents of foreign oil companies—that's a strong supposition in some quarters. Hell, it could be anybody. I tend to lean toward foreign involvement, the foreign oil companies.

"Or maybe it's nothing at all, just a string of accidents. That's what I want to find out, Harry. You're a reporter, you know how to dig out the information. That's what I want from you. I want names, I want information."

Harry couldn't resist a minor chortle. "I'll bet you vote for the Communists, right? I mean, isn't that what everybody up there in Washington thinks when something goes wrong? Commies in the closet, Reds under the bed, Bolsheviks in the basement? The old Red Scare, back to scare us again?"

The man was not amused. "You're right, we do tend to be cautious, but when we really have to get tough, we can get tough, and we take risks, and we get things done."

"So what do you know so far?"

"Not much. That's why I need your help."

Harry buttered another piece of pan dulce, trying to act nonchalant. He wasn't sure his churning stomach would accept this extra bite of sweet roll. This guy's a slick professional, part of the Ivy League Eastern Elite, and I'm just a kid jumping into water that's over my head. Best thing to do when you're in deep water is get the hell out.

"But I already told you, I'm not interested. "

"I know, but I don't think you'll turn me down. For one thing, it's a challenge, and I think you like to take on a good fight. From what I know about you, you're a scrapper, a fighter. And perhaps most important, I'm going to pay you, and I think the money will appeal to you. I think you're going to need the extra money to support your wannabe lifestyle. And who knows? When it's all over, you might get a good story out of it."

"Yeah, that's what I thought we'd be talking about here this morning—some kind of a writing job."

"Well, there you have it. You can work for me, and you still can write for UP. But most important, Harry, you'll be doing a great service to your country in a time of crisis."

Something struck a chord with Harry, but it wasn't that flag-waving bit about service to our country. It was what the man said about money.

CHAPTER 37

Harry stood up and walked over to the window. He looked down at a motorcycle messenger cutting in and out of heavy traffic on Avenida Juárez, nearly hitting a lanky pedestrian who was darting across the street mid-block. The guy on the motorcycle is traveling too damned fast, and the skinny man is taking a stupid chance running out into traffic. They both think they're doing the right thing. They both think they're in control. They're both trying to get somewhere in a hurry, trying to reach a very important goal. And who knows, they might make it, but in the process somebody could get hurt. Jesus, somebody could get killed.

"So if I decide to join you, when would you want me to start?" Harry asked as he returned to his breakfast chair.

"You start right now, today. Here's what I'd like you to—"

"Hey, hold on there, not so fast. I didn't say I'm going to join you. Give me a little time to figure out what the hell you're talking about."

"How much time do you want?"

"I'll have to think about it. I'll have to know more about it. For instance, do you have any leads? Not just speculation, but solid leads?"

"I'll tell you what I know. I'm sure the Mexican authorities are investigating the fires. Pemex is their crown jewel, their cash cow. Pemex oil revenues are a major source of income for the Mexican government. Pemex expects to gross about two-hundred and thirty million dollars this year, Harry. That's U.S. dollars, not pesos."

"That's big money."

"Damned right it is. Two-hundred and thirty million dollars. The government will wind up with about seventy million dollars as its share." He took a bite of huevos rancheros, and waved the empty fork in the air for Harry to inspect. "The Mexican government probably has multiple investigations under way right now, using what I'll call the 'breakfast fork' technique."

"The breakfast fork?"

"Right. One tine of the fork could point to an accident, a second tine might point to an inside job. A third tine could lead to careless workmen or faulty equipment. A fourth tine could point to vandalism. A fifth tine—"

"A fork doesn't have that many tines."

Corbett laughed, and he gave his fork a few more mid-air twirls for emphasis. "I know, but this hypothetical fork does. Those first four tines I'll call the domestic tines, and they all point to matters for Pemex and the Mexican authorities to track, but a fifth tine could point to foreign involvement, and that's the tine I want you to follow."

"Me?"

"Yes, you. And when you think about it, vandalism and sabotage are basically the same thing. It's the motive that separates them. If it's vandalism, it could be someone who has a grudge against Pemex, someone who got fired from his job, or something like that. Vandalism might be just for the hell of it, or maybe it's some weirdo who gets a kick out of seeing flames light up the sky. Lots of laughs.

"But with sabotage, there are no laughs. They don't do it just for the hell of it. Sabotage, one way or another, has a clear motive. And that's where we come in."

"Wait a minute," Harry interrupted. "When you say 'sabotage,' I think of the war in Europe. I think of the resistance forces, and what they did in France, and Norway, and Holland and Poland and the other occupied countries—blowing up bridges and trains and killing Nazis and things like that."

"Right. Those guys had motive. Their motive was to screw up the German occupation, to create havoc for the Germans, to drive the Germans out of their homelands. So the motive depends on who's doing it, and which side of the trench they're sitting on. What the French maquis and the other underground fighters did—and what our OSS did—helped us win the war. That particular sabotage had a patriotic motive, a positive motive. From the German point of view, of course, those saboteurs were terrorists, but from our point of view, they were heroes."

Corbett paused for a swallow of coffee. "But that's only part of the story. There were plenty of resistance fighters in the Eastern European countries, too. Countries like Yugoslavia and Czechoslovakia and Hungary and Rumania. And their motives were slightly different. Sure, they wanted the Nazis out, but they wanted the Communists in. And those Communist Partisans paved the way for the Soviet takeover in Eastern Europe after the War."

"But there were Communists everywhere in Europe before the war," Harry said.

"Sure there were, and like I said, they helped us win the war. Unfortunately, those bastards are still there. The Russians control Eastern Europe. Germany is split, and the Communists control half the country. And the Reds are causing problems all over Europe.

"But right now, here in Mexico, there's another possibility."

Harry laughed. "Another tine?"

"Well, yes, you could say that. If it really is sabotage, there's a chance the saboteurs are employees, or maybe paid agents, of the foreign oil companies that got kicked out when Mexico took over the oil industry back in '38. These companies would like to get their business back. And the Mexicans also might be looking at the possibility that the saboteurs are agents of the governments of one or two of those countries, like England or Holland."

"Holland?"

"Oh, yes. Royal Dutch Shell was a big operator here before the expropriation. And the English controlled one of the biggest oil companies here."

"What about us? Weren't there a few American oil companies here back in the Thirties?"

"Sure, American companies like Standard Oil and Sinclair were very big, along with quite a few others. And they fought the expropriation, even took it to court, and they lost in court."

"Okay, so what you're telling me is that the Mexican police might think the saboteurs are Americans?"

"Well, why not? After all, we Americans are experienced at that kind of thing. Remember, the OSS was right there alongside the resistance fighters in Europe, blowing up bridges and doing all the other stuff. So the Mexicans would be looking at all the possibilities. If they didn't, they wouldn't be doing their job."

"You haven't told me what I would be doing if I join you. Wouldn't I get some sort of instructions? Some training? Where would I start?"

"You've had good training and good experience as a reporter. Start with the fires and see where they take you. You already took your first step when you went to the press conference. Follow up on that. You're a reporter, do some digging. You'll be pretty much on your own. You've got a good cover at UP, and we don't want to blow that. We can talk on the phone. You called me Saturday. That number's good anytime. If I'm not there, Helen knows how to reach me, day or night. If she's not there, the call will patch through automatically to my mobile phone.

"And be sure to let us know how we can contact you when you get settled in somewhere. I suggest you find yourself a quiet room, or maybe a small apartment, and give up this luxury living. Try to blend into the background. You'll be able to operate better that way."

"Wait a minute. You're talking like I'm already in. I haven't said yes."

"Well, I'm assuming your better judgment will prevail."

"Who else knows you're talking to me?"

"Only a couple of people on E Street up in Washington, and only Bob here in Mexico. Let's keep it that way. To keep your cover, you're going to have to continue writing for UP. And you should know you're not alone here. I have a staff, and I have a few contract people working for me on special assignment, and you'll meet some of them later."

Harry smiled. This guy assumes I'm already on board. I'll humor him a little. "You mean I would have two jobs? Two bosses? Wouldn't there be a conflict of interest?"

"No, there won't be any conflict. You'll have just one boss, and that's me, but you'll have two assignments. You can work it out."

Harry broke out a broad grin and laughed. "Hey, I have a question. If I do decide to work for you and your agency, will I be packin' iron? You know, like all those spies in the movies and on TV?"

"No, you would not be required to carry a gun. Our business, as I told you, is gathering information. Intelligence. Just like our name says. All I expect from you is information."

"Aw, gee, I was hoping I could carry a rod. Maybe a Beretta in a shoulder holster, or a pistol in a pocket, or some kinda piece in an ankle holster?"

"Don't be so damned dramatic. Nothing like that. You won't be using a gun. Use your brain. Your brain is your weapon. Information is what we want."

"We haven't discussed what you'd be paying me. I think you and I should come to some kind of an understanding now. It could help me make a decision."

"Don't worry about that. None of our people ever complained about being underpaid. You'll have a good stream of money coming in, and we'll be paying you in cash."

Corbett reached into his coat pocket and pulled out an envelope. "Here, this will help you get started. Spend whatever you need to spend to do whatever you need to do. When you need more, call Helen. You've got the number. We can't afford to be chintzy. You may have to buy a meal or two, or you may have to buy a lot more than just a meal. You may have to buy information, grease a few palms. You may need to do a little traveling. Just don't waste it. Remember, Washington expects us to do a good job."

Harry didn't want to appear greedy, so he tossed the envelope on the table without opening it, and he nonchalantly buttered another piece of pan dulce.

Corbett looked at his watch and pushed his chair back from the table. "I have an appointment in a few minutes. It's good to meet you, Harry, and thanks for the breakfast. Charge it up to the agency. I think you're going to be a big help to us. See what you can find out. Follow your nose, and follow the smoke. See if you can follow up on that Pemex press conference you attended on Friday. Call me when you've got something, or I'll be back in touch with you."

"Hold on a minute," Harry said, jumping up from his chair. "I haven't said yes. I'm here on vacation, not to get caught up in a fancy web of international intrigue. Anyway, you're asking me to do something I'm not prepared to do. I'm a reporter, not a God-damned spook. I'm not cut out for that kind of work."

"We're in the same business, Harry, the information business. You're the reporter, and I'm the editor. You bring me the information and I'll sift through it and decide what's important. That's what this is all about, just gathering a little information. And Harry, if you have any more questions, just take a look in that envelope."

CHAPTER 38

With a cup of black coffee and a Camel, Harry collapsed again into his favorite lounge chair, overwhelmed by this prospect of a sudden career change. How the hell did I manage to land in this mess? I know damned well there would be some sort of conflict. This is supposed to be a vacation—have a little fun, see the sights—and all of a sudden I'm caught in the middle of something I don't understand. What about the golf and the deep sea fishing? And the beach in Acapulco?

Harry finished the last of the orange juice and picked up the newspaper again. "Holy Christ," he muttered when he saw a front page headline proclaiming a "devastating explosion and fire" last night at a Pemex refinery in Veracruz. Three men were killed and twelve others hospitalized with various injuries and burns, some critical. The explosion occurred just before midnight.

Excelsior played it big. A correspondent in Veracruz filed the lead story with a quote from a Pemex workman who described how "frightening and horrible and disastrous" the fire was, and how terrifying it was to see one of his fellow workmen engulfed in flames. The story quoted Veracruz police and fire officials who said the cause of the explosion and fire had not been determined.

Two AP wire photos showed dramatic flames and smoke as firemen fought the blaze.

Margarita Villarreal's story, with a byline and a Mexico City dateline, was a straight-forward recap of all the fires of the past four weeks. A map next to her story pinpointed the locations of all the recent fires.

Her story quoted a Pemex official who said those earlier fires were still under investigation. Harry chuckled when he saw Antonio Aguilar's remarks from the press conference. This Veracruz thing contradicts his claim of "insignificant fires of little consequence."

Villarreal's story also included a Pemex statement expressing sympathy for the families of the deceased. The statement said that "at this point, Pemex believes the explosion in Veracruz was a tragic accident, but Pemex will investigate thoroughly the cause of this disaster, and if the investigation uncovers any hint of arson or sabotage, Pemex and the police will round up and prosecute the perpetrators, with stiff penalties for anyone found guilty of criminal activity."

Harry dropped the newspaper to the floor and sat motionless for several minutes, watching the traffic below on Avenida Juárez. Buses, taxis, vans, cars, motorcycles, trucks—all going somewhere, all in a hell of a hurry. The steady flow of vehicles that keeps the city humming. Some of those drivers are angry about last night's fire, some are worried, more are frightened, many are just curious, and some are quietly unaware. Right now, all of them just want to get where they're going. Tragedy strikes, but life goes on.

If I decide to join Corbett and his agency, Harry realized, it could turn out to be dangerous. This thing is bigger than the fire I saw on the bus. A guy could get burned when a gas line explodes. Or lose an arm or a leg when an oil tank blows up. Or get killed. I don't need that kind of trouble.

CHAPTER 39

Harry smiled as he dialed the number for the United Press. Two jobs but only one boss, he thought, just ain't going to work out.

"Morning, Bob. I just read about that refinery fire in Veracruz. That was quite a blast."

"Right. We've got people working on it here in the bureau, and we're picking up more details from our stringer down there. I think we've got it covered. By the way, how was your breakfast with Corbett? You sure didn't waste any time calling him."

Harry swallowed, tasting once again the orange juice and the bacon. "For Christ's sake, isn't anything sacred around here? You know about the breakfast already? How the hell can I be a secret agent if I can't keep anything secret?"

Bob laughed. "Is that what he had in mind? I thought maybe he wanted you to write something about the corn harvest, or maybe hoof-and-mouth disease."

"Come on, Bob, you knew damn well what it was all about. Why didn't you warn me?"

"Well, we cooperate when we can, and I wanted to help him, and I also want to help you. Remember, I'm the one who recommended you for the job. I'm the one who gave you his phone number."

"I'll remember that when I get blown up. Breakfast was fine—by the way, that's going to end up on my hotel bill."

"Don't worry about it, I'll reimburse you."

"It's not the money, it's the idea of it. I called him because I was curious, after I did a little mental tabulation of my bleak financial outlook. You didn't tell me who he is. Caught me by surprise. Yeah, he wants me to join him. He wants me to check into the fires, see what I can find."

"So you're going to work for him?"

"I told him I'm not interested. Besides, I'm not trained for that kind of work."

"So you turned him down?"

"Yeah, I turned him down. It's not the kind of free lance writing I had in mind."

"If you do join him, you'll still be able to work for me, and if you dig up anything you think I can use, without compromising what you're doing for him, just give me a couple hundred words or so."

"I think there would be a conflict. I asked him if this means I would have two jobs and two bosses, and he said, no, I would have only one boss, and he's the boss."

"He might think so, but as far as I'm concerned I'm your boss here at UP, and you're going to have to produce some copy for me to earn the money I'll be paying you. What you do for him is strictly between the two of you. Anyway, he'll want you to keep your cover as a reporter.

"But remember, do it all by telephone for the time being. I don't want you to come around here till you're clear with that homicide detective. I don't want him snooping around here looking for you."

"Okay. By the way, I checked out of the Hotel Comé and I'm at the Del Prado full time now. I'll save a few bucks with only one hotel room. But do me a favor, keep a lid on that, in case that cop Gonzalez comes back looking for me."

CHAPTER 40

Harry looked at his watch. Time for one more quick call.

"I'm sorry, Señor Aguilar is not available at the moment. Who's calling?"

"This is Harry Banister with United Press. I was at the press conference on Friday, and I met Señor Aguilar at the Brazilian Embassy reception Friday evening."

"Oh, yes, Señor Banister, good morning. Señor Aguilar told me he met you at the Embassy, and he said he had a very pleasant conversation with you. He said you're a recent arrival here in Mexico. He asked me to add your name to our contact list, and he asked me to extend every courtesy to you if you should call."

"Well thank you, I appreciate that. Yes, I'm new here, and I'm still trying to find my way around. I think it'll take me a while to get used to the heavy traffic. I think I'm going to need help. A guide dog, maybe." Harry chuckled. She laughed too. Good sign.

"Oh, that heavy traffic is not such a problem, Señor Banister. As a matter of fact, it's important. We love it here at Pemex. Those cars and trucks and buses are good customers. We like to see traffic like that. How can I help you this morning?"

"Señor Aguilar told me that since I'm new in town, he would give me a quick introduction to Pemex and the oil industry. I thought maybe I could see him this morning."

"He's in a meeting right now, and he'll be very busy all morning. Perhaps you heard about the fire last night in Veracruz?"

"Yes, I read about it in the morning paper. Some kind of an accident?" Nice voice, he decided. Young, about my age. Easy to talk to. Good public relations for Pemex. She could be a good source for me, an important door-opener. Maybe even my personal guide dog.

"We don't know yet, that's what he's trying to find out right now. Things are in somewhat of a turmoil here this morning. He and other members of our department are in a meeting with Señor Bermúdez and the other top management people. We're about to release an official statement to the press. If you would like, I could read it to you now. It's very brief."

"Yes, if you would, please."

She read him the statement, only four paragraphs. It said something to the effect that Petróleos Mexicanos is investigating the cause of the explosion and fire last night in Veracruz, and Pemex is deeply saddened by the tragic loss of life resulting from this unfortunate accident, and we offer our sincere condolences to the families of the victims.

"Thank you very much, Señorita—tell me please, what is your name?"

"You're quite welcome, I'm happy to be of service. My name is Isabel."

"Isabel, that's a pretty name. Like Queen Isabel of Spain. Royalty."

She laughed. "I don't know about the royalty part, but yes, the name's the same."

"Well, you sound like you must be royalty. Now, if you could do one small favor for me, Isabel, I would appreciate it. I'm not in the office right now—I wonder if you could call the bureau chief at United Press and read him the statement. You could tell him that I asked you to call, so he could handle it quickly."

"I'd be happy to do that for you. I have the number right here."

Harry smiled as he thought about this little gambit. Bob will know I'm on top of the Veracruz story, even though he says he won't need my help. "Thanks, Isabel. I'll check back later to talk with Señor Aguilar, when things have calmed down. And to chat with you, too, of course. Maybe you can give me some advice on how to navigate the traffic here in Mexico City."

Isabel laughed. "Oh, it's not as bad as all that, Señor Banister."

"Harry. Call me Harry."

"Okay, Harry it is. The traffic is not so bad once you know a few little tricks. For example, how to drive around the glorietas, our traffic circles, without getting hit."

Go for it, Harry thought—there's plenty to gain, and nothing to lose. "Hey, if you could show me how to do that I would appreciate it. I don't have a car right now, but I'm planning to buy one soon."

"Well," she said, lowering her voice, "perhaps I could help you. I have a car, and I would be happy to give you a lesson."

"Hey, that would be great. Maybe later today, after work? And maybe we could have a bite to eat, or a cocktail?"

"Oh, I would like that, and I could answer any questions you might have about Mexico City."

"Great. I'll call you this afternoon. What time do you get out of work?"

"That depends on what happens with this Veracruz incident. I may have to work late, but if it's not too late, I'd look forward to meeting you, and helping you. Where are you staying, Harry? Since you don't have a car, perhaps I could pick you up."

"I'm at the Del Prado. I'll call back later and we'll set a time, and when I drive your car, Isabel, I promise I won't wreck it. Now, since Señor Aguilar is tied up, would it be all right if I spoke with Humberto Velasco to ask him a few questions? He might be able to give me a little technical background information, but I want to clear it with you first."

"Of course, if he's available. He might be in that same meeting with Señor Bermudez and the others, but if you'll hold for a moment, I'll transfer you. And please call later, Harry. I'm happy to help you."

After a couple of clicks and a brief pause, Harry recognized Velasco's voice. "What can I do for you? Isabel says you want to talk to me. I don't have much time. I'll be leaving here very soon."

"I don't want to take too much of your time, but I'm wondering if I could have a moment this morning. I can stop by your office right now if it's convenient."

"Nothing's convenient this morning. We're very busy here, I just came out of a meeting, and I'm leaving for Veracruz in a few minutes. I have to survey the damage at our facilities there. I'm afraid I won't be able to see you."

"How about if I tag along with you? We could talk on the plane, and you could bring me up to date on what's happening."

"That's not possible. It's a full plane. There'll be other Pemex engineers and technicians on the plane. There's a lot of information we'll need to discuss, and you'd just be in the way. We don't want a reporter on the plane, asking a lot of questions, getting in our way, and I certainly would not have any time for you."

"I understand. One quick question—you believe all these recent fires were caused by sabotage, right?" Dangle the bait, Harry thought. You never know what it might catch. "That's what happened last night?"

"Damn it, Banister, I never said that. Where the hell did you get that crazy idea? At this point, I don't have anything to tell you. At this point, our people in Veracruz tell us it was just an accident. That's why I'm going down there, to find out what happened. But I would caution you to go slow, Banister. I don't think you want to write something you might regret later on."

"No, Sir, of course not, but I just want to ask you one thing about—"

"And I don't want you to write anything that I'll regret, understand? Do you know what I mean? I'm leaving now for the airport. You can check back with Aguilar later for more information, if you want to. Maybe he'll be able to help you, but I sure as hell don't have any time for you."

Harry laughed when the phone went dead. Chalk that up as a fifty-fifty call. Made a few points with her, got zilch from him.

Time for one more quick call, this one to the Hotel Comé.

"Yes, Sir, a young lady called. She didn't leave her name, but I believe it was the same girl who has been trying to reach you."

"Okay. You told her I checked out?"

"Yes, Sir."

"If she calls again, tell her I'll see her at the restaurant at two o'clock, and you can tell her I've moved to the Del Prado. But please, don't tell anyone else."

"I understand."

"Okay. I'll check back with you later."

One more quick phone call and I'm gone.

"How about the cantina over here on Bucareli?" Alberto suggested. "We can get a cup of black coffee there."

"I've had enough coffee. Make mine a beer. I'm on my way out the door now."

Almost as an afterthought, Harry opened the envelope that was lying on the table and counted the money. "Holy Christ," he muttered. Corbett must think I'm going to say yes, and those people up there on E Street must think I'm going to do one hell of a job for them.

Harry closed the bulging envelope and stuck it in the laundry bag in the corner of his closet. He pulled several bills from his own cache. As an after-thought, he took another hundred-dollar bill and three more hundred-peso notes. He put the American money in his wallet, folded the pesos in with the other Mexican money in his pants pocket, and zipped what was left in the ball pocket of his golf bag.

CHAPTER 41

"So what have you got planned?" Alberto asked. "The ponies aren't running today, and you're not going to play golf."

"I think I might do more sight-seeing, maybe go out to see the Pyramids."

"Good idea. You'll enjoy that. Were you a tourist yesterday, too?"

"Oh, you bet. I saw the Ballet Folklórico at the Palace of Fine Arts in the morning—hey, that place is impressive—and then I just wandered around a little bit, sort of a walking tour through the Alameda. Then I went to the bullfight in the afternoon. Finished with dinner in a cantina across the street from the bull ring."

"How was that?"

"It must have been good because I can still taste it."

"Do you have any assignments from UP?"

"No, and I don't want to push it, either. Today I just—"

A tall, dark-haired girl hurried into the cantina, interrupting Harry as she approached the table. Alberto made the necessary introductions and signaled the waiter, but the girl remained standing.

"Nothing for me," Margarita said. "I can only stay a minute. Welcome to Mexico, Harry, and welcome to the Bucareli Brigade. Alberto tells me you're new in town, and you've already started working at UP."

"Sort of, part time, but I'm still getting settled in. I read your stories in this morning's paper. That was quite a disaster."

"Yes, I'm leaving for Veracruz in a few minutes to do a follow-up on the fire. I want to see what it looks like there and I want to talk to the Pemex people on the scene."

"Good idea," Harry said. "You say you're going there now? How're you going to get there?"

"I'm going on a Pemex plane. Humberto Velasco invited me to fly with him."

"Velasco? He spoke at the press conference, right? The guy with thin hair? They must have a big plane, like a DC-3?"

"They have several planes, and some of the other Pemex people will be using a DC-3, but he prefers to go by himself. He flies his own Piper four-seater. His job requires him to travel so much, working in the oil fields. Some of the places he visits don't have airports, just an unpaved landing strip or a clearing in the jungle. Sometimes he has to land in the highway and taxi off the road onto a clearing."

"He must have an important job at Pemex."

"He does. I'm sorry to rush off like this, but I have to get out to the airport. Nice to meet you Harry, and good luck in your new job—and Alberto, I'll see you later, back in the office."

"Isn't that something," Alberto said when she was gone. "She gets to fly with the man who has all the right answers. That's one reason she gets such good stories, she has excellent contacts."

Harry was silent for a moment, brooding. Then he slammed his fist on the table. "God damn it, that son of a bitch Velasco has the right answers, all right, including that bullshit about a full plane. I talked to him on the phone just a few minutes ago, and I asked him if I could go with him to Veracruz. He said he was going on a plane full of Pemex engineers and technicians."

"I thought you weren't interested in doing any work today."

"Well, I'm not, really, but I asked him for a ride because it seemed like a good opportunity. I smelled a story."

Alberto laughed. "You smelled smoke."

"Something like that. He said they would have to discuss the fire on the plane and there wouldn't be any room for me. He said I'd just be in the way. That son of a bitch."

THE FLOWER SHOP

"Can you blame him, Harry? After all, Margarita is a hell of a lot better-looking than you. I guess she can't help you very much now."

"Something's fishy. There's a bunch of Pemex technical people going to Veracruz, but Velasco's flying down there alone? On his own plane? Why doesn't he want to fly on the DC-3 with the other engineers, and talk shop with them and compare notes?"

"Because he wants to take a girl with him."

"No, it's not that. Does he know something he doesn't want to share with them?"

Alberto offered a suggestion: "Maybe they don't like him. Maybe they don't want him on their plane."

Harry fumed as he took a slow sip of beer. His face lit up in a broad grin. "Yeah, you're right. She is better-looking—but God damn it, she already has helped me. She gave me an idea. I'm going to Veracruz, too!"

"*¡Olé!*" Alberto exclaimed. "Now you're talking! But what about the Pyramids?"

"The Pyramids have been there for fifteen hundred years or whatever, and they'll still be there tomorrow. I'll see them tomorrow."

"UP must have a stringer in Veracruz. Can't he handle it?"

"Sure, but I want to see what I can turn up myself."

"How are you going to get there?"

"I don't know. How far is it? I'll borrow a car, or I'll rent one. How long would it take me to drive?"

"You're going to borrow a car? Who are you going to borrow a car from? Anyway, you'd better fly. It'll be a lot faster. Check the airline schedule, or maybe you can charter a plane."

"Good idea, I'll charter a plane. I'll track down a plane out there at the airport."

Harry finished his beer in two gulps and jumped up from the table. "I'll worry about the cost later," he said as he ran toward the door. "See if you can set me up for golf sometime tomorrow. Right now, I'm going to Veracruz. I'm outta here!"

Alberto shook his head and laughed. "If you fly like that, you won't need an airplane."

CHAPTER 42

At the airport, Harry decided against a commercial flight. He didn't want to be bound by a fixed timetable. A small-plane charter would give him the flexibility to leave right away and return whenever he wanted, or perhaps go somewhere else if necessary.

Out on the tarmac, Harry spotted a scruffy Cessna C-170A. The plane looked like it was well-traveled. One wing showed a rectangle of fresh red paint that must be hiding a patch. Two or three other spots on the fuselage were badly scarred. In fact, the whole damned plane looked like it could use a fresh paint job. Paint can cover a multitude of sins. The balding tires looked like they had slammed a few rough landings. The windshield showed a network of scratches, and a strip of silver duct tape covered a crack in an upper corner. A piece of twisted wire hung from the door where a handle used to be. A stenciled sign on the nose identified the plane as *Alas de Libertad*.

Sitting in the shade under a wing, reading a copy of *Novedades*, was a man who looked almost as disheveled as the plane. Harry decided the guy, dressed in an old U.S. Army Air Corps bomber jacket and a cap with a fifty-mission crush, must be the owner.

"Are you the owner?" Harry asked, in English.

The man stood up and offered his hand to greet Harry. "At your service. Name's Armstrong. Arnold Armstrong. Call me Arnie."

"Good morning. I'm Harry. Nice looking plane."

"Thanks. My pride and joy, my bread and butter."

"Will these Wings of Liberty, as you call them, really fly?"

"You bet. Don't let the pretty face deceive you. A-One condition."

"You think it would make it to Veracruz and back?"

"No problem."

"How long a trip would it be?'

"Not long. Right now, we're about a mile and a half above sea level. We'll have to climb even higher, of course, to clear the rim of the Valley of Mexico." He raised one hand up next to his ear and, with a graceful sweeping motion, brought it down next to his knee, "Then, it's downhill all the way. Couple hours, give or take."

"That'll work," Harry said. "Tell me, how did you wind up in Mexico?"

"Just lucky. Came from Florida seven years ago, when I got out of service. Enrolled in college on the GI Bill, learned Spanish, got married, started a family, bought a house, bought this plane."

"Okay, Arnie, if you've got a good strong rubber band in that thing, I think we can make a deal."

"Got two rubber bands, one to get us there and a spare to get us back."

Harry gave Arnie a cash deposit and Arnie topped off the tanks with fuel, "just in case the rubber band breaks." Inside the terminal Arnie bought a jug of coffee and Harry bought a small package of aspirin, a pack of Camels, a copy of the Veracruz morning paper, and a cold beer.

Back outside, the two men climbed into the plane. A bright Indian serape covered God-only-knows-what-kind-of foul stains on the rear passenger seat. The cockpit, with its St. Christopher medal and statuette of the Virgin of Guadalupe over the instrument panel, reminded Harry of the bus from the border and every taxi he had been in since he arrived in Mexico.

Harry had learned in the past few days that the Mexicans, predominantly Roman Catholic, are a deeply religious people. They share a heritage brought from Spain centuries ago by the Franciscan and Dominican monks. You see the ardent faith of the Mexican people every day, everywhere. You see it in the medals and crosses they wear around their necks. You see it in the cars and trucks and buses and taxicabs—and now the airplanes—where the drivers face veritable shrines to the Virgin of Guadalupe or to their favorite saints, mounted on the dashboards and sun visors or hanging from the rear view mirrors. You see it in the penitent pilgrims approaching the Cathedral on their knees, taking one deliberate, painful knee-step at a time.

And you see it in the ubiquitous sign of the cross Mexicans make as they bless themselves at every possible opportunity, countless times each day. When they enter a church, when they pass by the front of a church, when they pass by a cemetery. When they speak of a deceased family member or close friend. Cabbies and other motorists do it when they undertake a dangerous venture, like driving around a crowded glorieta or trying to zip through a yellow light. Pedestrians do it before they dash across a busy street. Matadors make the sign of the cross and ask God's protection when they step into the bull ring. Baseball players bless themselves when they step up to the plate to bat. Boxers, even with their bulky boxing gloves, bless themselves when they hear the bell to start the next round.

Arnie taxied to the head of the runway, revved the Wings of Liberty's engine, made the sign of the cross three times, and took off. Harry relaxed and enjoyed the scenery, putting the decrepit appearance of the airplane out of his mind. *This guy has a wife, two kids, a dog and a parrot at home. He doesn't want to die either.*

The air in Veracruz was heavy with haze. Harry boarded a taxi and told the driver to take him straight out to the refinery.

"I don't know if I can, Señor. I don't know how close I can get. The police will have barricades. There will be soldiers everywhere. The gate will be closed."

"Well, let's see how close we can get."

As they approached, Harry could see uniformed police and soldiers everywhere. The main gate was blocked by a dozen soldiers. Two TV camionetas were parked near the gate, with a couple of cameramen leaning against the shady side of one of the vans. A dozen reporters, men and women, some with note pads in their hands, sat on benches near the gate. "I see what you mean. I could probably get in this way, but it's going to be crowded with reporters. Can you take me someplace where the workmen hang out?"

"Sí, Señor, I could take you to a cantina up the road a bit, close to an employee gate, but I don't think you will want to go there."

"Why not?"

"You would not be comfortable, Señor. It's not a very nice place, not very clean. The men are in a bad mood today, and they might not be pleased to have a stranger in their midst, especially a foreigner dressed in a business suit."

"That's okay, let's go there. I need a beer anyway." Harry took off his necktie, folded it a few times, and stuffed it into the inside breast pocket of his coat. Should have left the coat and tie on the Alas de Libertad, he realized.

"Do you want me to wait for you, Señor? Or you could call me when you're ready to leave, and I'll take you back to the airport." The driver grinned as he handed Harry a card. "Or I could take you to the hospital, whichever seems more appropriate at the time."

Harry laughed and added the card to his collection, "I'll watch my back, and I'll be careful what I eat. And I'll call you when I'm ready, if they have a telephone in this place. We'll decide where to go when you pick me up."

Let Margarita talk to her Pemex cronies from Mexico City, he thought, and let her get the official story. I'll learn more from the guys in this joint, with the aid of some well-placed pesos and a few shots of tequila.

A stifling smell smacked Harry in the face when he stepped out of the taxi. The regular reek of the refinery reminded him of Whiting or East Chicago back in Indiana. Blended in was the smell of smoke from last night's fire, and the odor of stale beer and fried foods that flowed from the cantina.

The fractured sign over the front door welcomed Harry:

Ca tina Pozo Hondo

Harry treated himself to a silent laugh, figuring 'Deep Well' was a good name for a cantina that must be pumping a constant flow of beer and tequila and pulque to satisfy its patrons from the refinery across the road.

A sign next to the doorway laid down the house rules:

*No Women, Dogs, or Men
in Uniform Allowed*

Harry decided women wouldn't want to come in here anyway, and the dogs could come and go as they pleased under the swinging café style half-doors. The owner probably didn't worry about the men-in-uniform rule as long as they paid for their drinks and didn't shoot any of the other customers.

The Pozo Hondo, however, featured a new element not noticeable in the other four or five cantinas Harry had visited during his short stay in Mexico: the pungent smell of urine. As soon as he pushed through the doors he spotted what must be the primary source of the odor. A rectangular metal pan, roughly seven feet long and two feet wide, was mounted knee-high off the floor in the corner between the front entrance and the side door.

Over the metal pan was a long wooden crate with several holes drilled in the bottom. In the box sat a shrinking block of ice. As the ice melted, water dripped into the pan, providing an erratic flush of fresh water. The rate of flush depended on the heat of the day. The effluence drained through a pipe that led to a hole in the floor and from there, only God knows where.

The location of this improvised sanitary solution, in the triangle between the two open doors, provided a bit of cross-ventilation which, depending on the direction of the breeze, carried the odor either out to the street or back into the cantina.

Harry chuckled when he read a piece of graffiti on the sheet metal that served as a backsplash. Someone had printed **Cantina Pozo Negro** with a heavy black marker, thus changing the cantina's name from 'Deep Well' to 'Cesspool.' He decided the other cantinas he had seen in his short visit to Mexico were The Ritz compared to this joint. He knew right away he was in the right place.

The noise in the Pozo Hondo was almost as penetrating as the smell. The place was crowded with men in work clothes. A few were laughing, perhaps happy to have a day without work. Most were serious, some were half-drunk, a few were all the way there.

Harry took in as much of the chatter as he could as he crossed the room, working his way up to the bar. Most of the talk was about last night's big event—what might have caused it, who was at fault, when do we get back to work, who was killed or injured. Three men at a table near the bar were arguing about a soccer match, and two men standing in the middle of the room were laughing at something one of them said about a girl they knew.

At the bar Harry greeted the bartender with a warm *buenos días*, and ordered a cold Carta Blanca. The bartender's response was as cold as the bottle of beer he delivered.

The man on Harry's left gave him a stare as cold as the beer and the bartender's glare. "I don't think you work around here, Gringo," he growled. "I don't think you belong here. We don't like strangers coming in here to our private club, like tourists on a sight-seeing bus. What are you doing here? Aren't you afraid you'll get your suit dirty? Aren't you afraid you'll get mud, or dog shit, on those fancy shoes?"

This may not be easy, Harry thought. There's more ice right here at the bar than there is in that crate in the corner.

Harry looked straight ahead at the label on his beer bottle, pretending he didn't hear or understand the questions.

"What's the matter, Gringo, you don't speak Spanish?"

A silver-haired man on Harry's right interrupted. "Calm down, Panchito, we must be polite to our guest. We must make him feel welcome." Turning to Harry he said, in English, "You must forgive my son. He's been here too long today with nothing more than tequila and a burrito for breakfast."

"Yes, I speak Spanish," Harry replied in Spanish, trying to sneak a peek at his shoes.

"Then let's continue in Spanish," the older man said, switching back to his native tongue, "since Pancho does not speak English. Pancho's in a foul mood today because of what happened last night. When he's worked here as long as I have he'll be able to take these things in stride. I don't think he means to be rude, he was not brought up that way."

Harry turned to Pancho and gave him a friendly smile. "That's all right, I can understand. That was a horrible fire, and you must be under a lot of pressure."

Straight-faced, Pancho nodded. "Welcome to the Cantina Pozo Negro, stranger. As usual, my father's right. We should be polite to our guests."

Harry relaxed a bit, feeling he was on safer ground. To break the ice, and change the subject, he turned to the older man and said, "You say you've worked here for a while, so you must really know your way around the refinery. How long have you been here?"

"Twenty years, since before the expropriation, before there even was a Pemex, when this was *El Águila*, the *Compañía Mexicana del Petróleo El Águila*. Pancho is working here barely one year, but he's a clever boy, a fast learner."

Harry said to the silver-haired man, "My name is Harry. Your son's name is Pancho, so what should I call you?"

"My name is Mario. But tell me, what are you doing in this disreputable dive? Surely you didn't come here just for Cantina Pozo Hondo's celebrated gourmet food?"

"I'm a reporter with United Press, the wire service. I came down from Mexico City this morning to do a story on last night's fire."

"But doesn't United Press have someone here in Veracruz to do that? I saw stories on the fire in two of the morning papers from Mexico City. And why are you here in this palatial pub, of all places?"

"Oh, yes, we have someone here to do the basic news coverage, but I came to see if there's a story with a human interest angle. Something about the people and the tragedy. This explosion and fire surely will have an effect on the lives of many people here."

"Many people. Not just the ones who were killed, may God bless them." Mario made a quick sign of the cross. "But also the survivors."

"Yes, the survivors," Harry said. "Say, I notice you're out—can I buy you a drink? And how about you, Pancho? You ready for another?"

Both men accepted the offer and the bartender brought refills for all three men—tequila for Pancho, beer for Harry and Mario. Harry reached into his pocket to pull out a few pesos, but the bartender smiled and said "later" as he rubbed out the chalk mark on the bar top in front of Harry and wrote a new number.

I'm in, Harry thought. Two new friends—three, counting the bartender—and the bartender lets me run a tab. The ice has melted.

CHAPTER 43

Harry laughed and patted his stomach. "Mario, you mentioned the Pozo Hondo's gourmet food. I don't know about you, but I'm hungry, and whatever's cooking back there sure smells good." A little white lie now and then won't hurt, he thought.

"Yes, it's time to eat. As a matter of fact, that's why I'm here. I came to have lunch with my son. I arrived just before you did. I don't know about gourmet, Harry, but we're safe with today's comida corrida, for only two-fifty."

Mario led the others to a vacant table. As they crossed the room Harry noticed Pancho's grimy steel-toed work boots and soiled dungarees. Mario's shoes, in surprising contrast, were freshly-polished ox blood tasseled loafers, and his slacks were crisply-pressed gabardines.

The three men dug into their chicken burritos. They talked briefly about the food and then turned to the events of last night. Harry held his questions to a minimum, letting the father-and-son team do most of the talking.

Pancho said one of the workmen killed last night was a close friend.

"You worked with him?"

"Yes, we worked in different departments, but we played baseball together, on the same team."

"How old was he?"

"Only eighteen. He was going to get married in a month or so, and he wanted to go to the university next year. He hoped to become a doctor. His mother's a widow, but she's been working two jobs to save enough money to send him to school."

"It's a terrible thing for someone to die so young, before he's had a chance to live a life,"

Harry said. He made a mental note: possible human interest story for UP. "And how old are you, Pancho?"

"I'm nineteen."

"Are you also planning to go on to school?"

"No, my life is right here, in the oil fields. I have a wife and a baby, I have a good job, and I'm well-paid."

"What's your job with Pemex?"

"Right now I'm just a laborer, a roustabout, but next month I'll begin training for a new job driving a tank truck, bringing crude oil in from the well site."

"Did you also know the other victim?"

"I knew him," Mario said. "He was another young one, only 18 years old. This was his first job. He was just a roustabout, and he was burned almost beyond recognition in the fire that followed the initial explosion. I've known his father for some time. He's been working with the company since the days of El Águila, almost as long as I have. He and I have been through some rough times and some good times together. This will be hard on him."

"And what is your job with the company, Mario?"

"Oh, I've done just about everything over the years. You name it, I've done it. I started as a roustabout, and worked my way into a variety of other jobs, here and in other places up and down the Gulf Coast. Now it seems the *Consejo Local* takes up most of my time."

"What's the Consejo Local?" Harry asked.

"That's the Local Council of the STPRM."

"The STP...? Boy, that's a mouthful."

Mario laughed. "Yes, that stands for *Sindicato de Trabajadores Petroleros de la República Mexicana*, the national petroleum workers' union. I'm a member of the Local Council."

"What do you think might have caused the explosion," Harry asked, looking back and forth at both men.

"I heard some men talking about it this morning," Pancho replied. "They said it was an accident, a blown gasket on a feeder pipeline."

Mario shook his head. "The official word is 'accident.' and that's the story that was given to the press, but I think it was something else. I think there was an explosion. At one-thirty I'll be in a meeting with members of the Local Council. We're conducting our own investigation. I should know more then."

"So you don't think it was an accident?"

"You know, many so-called accidents are not accidents at all. When two cars collide at an intersection, it's a safe bet that one of the drivers was at fault. He was speeding, or he was making an improper turn or running through the red light. Yet it's generally called an accident, even though it was caused by one of the drivers."

"Then you're telling me that someone intentionally caused the explosion last night?"

"That's what we're trying to find out."

"This meeting of the Local Council, is it a closed meeting?" Harry asked. "I'd like to go with you."

Mario took a forkful of refried beans and hesitated before answering. "I don't think so. This is an emergency meeting. Two of our investigators will be making preliminary reports, and at this point I don't know what their findings will be. Some of the other members of the Council won't want you there. They're always afraid of outsiders."

"Especially gringos," Pancho interrupted with an abrupt laugh.

"But I can talk to them about it," Mario continued. "If they decide you can attend, you would have to agree not to write anything without clearing it with the Council. And, of course, there might not be anything worthwhile for you."

"I wouldn't want to write anything that would be harmful to your investigation, and I certainly wouldn't want to report anything that's inaccurate." First things first, Harry thought. Just get me into the meeting, and I'll take it from there. I don't like to agree to prior censorship, but this could be a good break.

"The other Council members, of course, will want to know who you are, and I'll have to vouch for you."

Harry got the message, and pulled out his new UP identification card for Mario and Pancho to admire. Mario's eyebrows arched when he saw it. The power of the press, Harry mused. Works every time.

"You two fellows were hit personally by this fire," Harry said. "It's an unfortunate coincidence that two of the three men killed last night were your friends. A double blow."

"Yes," Mario said. "It hits close to home. Two good friends."

"Did you know the third victim?"

Pancho looked at his father, and Mario took a long pull on his beer before answering. "I don't know who he was. As a matter of fact, the third victim had not been identified when I left my office this morning. The police and the Army and the Pemex security people all have been combing the rubble, searching for some trace of identification."

"I'm sure the Pemex *paracaidistas* are here today," Pancho said.

"The paratroopers?"

"Yes, the bureaucrats from the Capital. They sit in their fancy offices in Mexico City, or they go to the race track, or sit in saloons all day, and from time to time they fly down here and drop in like invading paratroopers and act important," Pancho explained.

"And most of them never worked on a pipe line or a derrick or in a refinery," Mario added. "Pancho's right. They're here today, poking around and asking questions, because something like this doesn't look good in the newspapers. They'll say something kind to the families of the men who were killed, and of course they'll want to find out who the third unfortunate man was."

"Did the third victim work here?"

"That's part of our investigation," Mario said. "At this point, we don't know anything about him."

As he ate, Harry asked a few more questions about the personal lives of his lunch companions and their two friends who had been killed, and he jotted a few notes on a scratch sheet. Should make a pretty good story for the UP wire.

Harry was half-way through his enchilada when he noticed a pair of soulful eyes staring at him. A skinny, bedraggled mutt with long ears and ribs that looked like railroad ties was sitting by his elbow.

Pancho laughed and broke off a corner of bread for her. "You have a new friend, Harry. She's here everyday. We call her La Flaquita."

"So much for that sign by the door," Harry said, "the one that says 'No Dogs Allowed.'"

"Rules are meant to be broken," Pancho replied with a laugh. "Those poor dogs practically live here. And as for that 'No Women' rule, that's laughable, too. A few women do come in here, but most of them are ugly whores, no more attractive than this skinny bitch at our table."

Mario raised his hand and spoke out in a dramatic tone much like an elder statesman. "No, my son, rules are meant to be followed. Rules are established for a reason, generally for a valid reason. The Pozo Hondo has rules, the government has rules and regulations—we generally call them laws. Pemex has rules, the union has rules, and we abide by them as best we can."

"That's right," Pancho said with a little laugh, "We don't want to get a speeding ticket."

"But sometimes it's necessary to break the rules," Mario said, "in order to achieve a better end. I agree with you, however, that most of the women who come in here are ugly whores, but now and then the wife of one of the men comes in and grabs him by the ear and drags him home for supper."

Pancho roared with laughter. "That's right, like what happened last week to poor old Ordóñez. He didn't even have a chance to finish his beer."

"And remember the güera who was in here Saturday, the one at the table over in the corner?" Mario asked. "She looked like she was a real lady, and she was good-looking."

Pancho laughed again. "Yeah, she was good-looking, for sure, nothing like the old hags we usually see in here. But who was she, and who was that guy with her? I didn't recognize either one of them."

"Neither did I," Mario said. "They were strangers."

"And how can you say she was a güera, Papá, with that mop of black hair?"

"By the face, my son, by the face. And the eyes, those bright blue eyes. When you get to be my age, and you've had the experience I've had, you'll know these things. That mop of black hair, as you call it, was a wig. You must look in the eyes, my son, you must look in the eyes."

CHAPTER 44

Harry and Mario left the cantina by the side door. The smell of the smoke still hung in the air, but otherwise the atmosphere was fresher and the sunlight was brighter than the rancid pall inside the cantina. Harry stepped carefully on his way to Mario's car, trying to avoid the mud puddles, the dozing dogs, the dog droppings, and numerous other obstacles. He noticed Mario doing the same. One must respect one's shoes, especially if they're expensive Italian loafers.

Mario's car was a late-model black Buick Roadmaster, a four-door sedan big enough, Harry figured, to carry the entire Local Council. Mario flipped a peso coin to a boy who was wiping traces of mud from the rear fender. "Thanks, Chico, you'll have it looking like new. Any news?"

"One little bit of news, Señor Mario. There's a stranger down at the union hall."

"A stranger?"

"A paratrooper, Señor, from Mexico City."

"Keep your eyes and ears open, Chico." Mario flipped the boy another coin. "And catch that spot on the right front fender."

"It's only a few minutes over to the hall," Mario said as he slipped behind the steering wheel. "This Pemex guy, I'm curious why he's at the union hall. Either he knows something we don't know or he wants to find out what we know."

"He probably spent the morning at the refinery or at the local Pemex office and didn't learn anything there," Harry suggested.

"That could be, but he won't learn much here, either. The Local Council is not going to share anything with him. We're in control here, and we deal only with the Veracruz management people, not with those big shots who drop in here from Mexico City from time to time.

"Incidentally, before we get there, I should tell you again that some of the members of the Council will not want to have you sitting in on our meeting, but I'll do what I can to get you in. I think it could be helpful for us to see a favorable newspaper story on the good work the Local Council is doing for our members and for Pemex."

"I understand, let's just take it as it comes." Harry couldn't recall saying he was going to write a favorable story.

Mario slowed his car to a crawl as he approached the union hall. Ten or twelve gawkers had gathered on the sidewalk next to a sleek black limousine. "That must be the guy from Mexico City, the bald guy in the black suit," Mario said. "I'm going to park up ahead and wait in the car. He's talking with Pablo and a couple members of our Council, and I don't want to interrupt them. I'll let Pablo handle this."

Harry smiled when he recognized the man. "Hey, I know that guy—he was at the press conference last Friday. He's some kind of field engineer with Pemex, name is Velasco. I'm going to ask him a few questions, find out what he learned today."

Harry opened the car door and hopped out just as the sidewalk conference broke up.

"Señor Velasco, can you give me a minute? What's the situation here? What did you find out? Do you know what caused it?"

Velasco turned and glared at Harry. "Who the hell are you?"

"I'm Harry Banister with United Press. We spoke this morning on the telephone, remember?"

"Oh, yeah, I remember, you're that pushy son of bitch who called this morning and invited yourself to ride on my plane. And you were at the Brazilian party the other night. Pushed yourself into that, too, eh? You've got one hell of a lot of nerve, Banister. I see you got here all right. Well, I have nothing to say to you. Talk to Aguilar. He's our official flack."

Velasco opened the limo door and Margarita slipped into the back seat. He tossed his brief case on the seat next to her and started to climb in, but Harry stopped him with a quick question. "Was it sabotage? You believe it was sabotage, right? You're the man right here on the scene now, and you've seen all the evidence. Who was it? Foreigners maybe? Do you think it might have been the English?"

Velasco turned and faced Harry with a scowl. "You asked me that question this morning. Where'd you get the crazy idea this was sabotage? What are you insinuating, Banister? Where do you get the idea somebody set it?"

"Do you think it might have been the third man? The victim they haven't identified yet?"

"The third man? You God-damned reporters are all alike, pushy bastards, always trying to stir things up, trying to make something out of nothing. This was an accident. Get that idea of sabotage out of your head. I don't have time for you, Banister. Now get out of my way, I've got a plane to catch."

Keep pushing, Harry thought. This guy knows something, he's afraid to talk. "So you say it was some sort of an accident?"

"That's right, Banister. It was an accident, pure and simple."

"But did you see any signs of sabotage? Any indicators?"

"That's it, Banister! I don't have time for you. Get the fuck out of my way." Velasco climbed in and slammed the door, and the limo drove away.

"Nasty son of a bitch," Harry mumbled.

"Nice try," Mario said, "you were pushing him pretty good, but I guess he doesn't like you. Here comes Pablo. Maybe he'll like you, and maybe he's learned something."

"You just missed him," Pablo called out. "He was a stuffed-shirt from Mexico City. He wanted to know what we found out about the fire."

"What did you tell him?"

The man looked at Harry and hesitated. Mario gave him a reassuring smile and said, "It's all right, Pablo, this is my friend, Harry Banister. You can talk."

"We told him only a few things that he already knew," Pablo continued, "things that were in the papers this morning. Anything else we learn we'll pass on up to the managers here in Veracruz, and they can pass the information along to Mexico City."

"Of course. What did he have to offer?"

"Nothing much. He said he thinks it was a terrible accident. He said he talked to some of the technical people at the refinery, and he talked to the police and the security people, but they didn't know anything new that was helpful. He didn't seem to be interested in how it started, he was more interested in knowing the extent of the damage."

Mario laughed. "It's like a chess game."

"Oh, there is one thing of interest," Pablo said, pulling several photographs from a manila envelope. "These are pictures of the third victim's face. A friend of mine is a nurse at the infirmary, and she took several Polaroid photos of the cadaver this morning after it had been washed. She gave one to her supervisor, of course, and she saved a few for me."

Mario smiled as he took the photos. "It's always nice to have friends in high places."

"No one in the managing director's office or the personnel office has been able to identify him," Pablo said, "and none of us here at the union hall recognize him."

"Didn't he have any identification?" Harry asked.

"Nothing. No wallet, just some cash in his pocket, but nothing that would tell us anything about him. The people in personnel are still checking to see if they can learn anything."

"Did the paratrooper see these?"

"I didn't show them to him. Maybe someone showed him a copy, but I didn't show him anything."

Mario studied the pictures. Although the body had been cleansed, the pictures showed a deep gash on the top of the skull, a laceration on the chest, and signs of severe burns on the face, neck, and arms. "Is that the face of peaceful innocence, or the face of a hardened criminal?" Mario asked of no one in particular.

"It's the face of a dead man now," Harry replied.

"I don't recognize him either," Mario continued, "but if we all agree he didn't work here, that leads us to a simple conclusion: he's an outsider, and it's logical to assume he's the man who set the explosion. Trapped by his own evil mischief. But who the hell was he?"

"Well, at least we know he was not one us, not one of our members here in Veracruz," Pablo said.

"I've seen him before," Mario said. "He was in the Pozo Hondo Saturday, sitting at a table in the corner."

"What the hell was he doing there?" Pablo asked. "Who was he with? One of our members?"

"He was having lunch. I don't know who he was with. Just a girl, a güera. He didn't look dangerous then."

'Well, he doesn't look very dangerous now either," Pablo said with a laugh. "Come on, Mario. We should get inside and get started with our meeting."

"Of course. I'd like my friend Harry to join us. He's a reporter from Mexico City, and he's here to do a story on the fire."

"My God, no," Pablo said, "Absolutely not. There've been reporters and photographers and TV cameras all over the place this morning. We don't need another one in our meeting now. And why are you out here at our union hall, Harry? Why aren't you at the refinery with the rest of the pack?"

"He's interested in the human angle," Mario answered. "You know, the drama, the people. What this means to the people of Veracruz, the survivors, the victims and their families."

"No way. We've got enough to worry about, without a God-damned reporter hanging around. A gringo, at that." Pablo turned and headed for the hall. "You coming, Mario?"

Mario lingered to say goodbye to Harry. "Sorry about that. He never has liked the press."

"He's not alone. Thanks anyway, it was worth a try."

"Here, take my card, and call me if you have any questions," Mario said. "Perhaps I'll have something for you later today or tomorrow. And take these photos. I can get more copies later."

Harry put the two pictures and Mario's card in his coat pocket.

THE FLOWER SHOP

CHAPTER 45

"I want to see a little bit of Veracruz on the way back to the airport. Can you show me around?"

"Of course, Señor. I would like you to feel welcome in our city. I'll give you my special ten-peso tour. Some of the streets are closed to traffic now, but we can go down to the center of the city, to the Plaza de Armas, and also you can see our port facilities. Our port is very busy today, with many ships coming and going."

"Okay, drop me off and give me a few minutes to walk around, and then we'll continue to the airport."

The air downtown was scrubbed clean of smoke by a strong breeze off the Gulf of Mexico. Harry strolled around the Plaza, intent on collecting casual comments on the catastrophe. He talked to two local citizens, and they both said the fire was terrible, but neither wanted to discuss it in detail.

Harry sat down on a bench by the fountain. "Say, that was quite an explosion last night," he said to a man sitting next to him. "What do you think might have caused it? An accident?"

"The story in this paper says it might have been an accident, but personally, I don't believe it could have been. I believe someone set it off intentionally. There is a good deal of unrest at Pemex. I'm gravely concerned. I'm afraid this disaster points to the probability of more explosions and fires, with more damage and more death, along with serious economic hardships for our city. You're a stranger here in our city, no?"

"Yes. I'm a reporter, from Mexico City. I'm with the United Press. UP has a correspondent here, so I'm just getting a little background information. Sort of an education, you might say, learning something about the oil business. Do you live here in Veracruz?"

"Yes, I live here. I'm a professor in economics at the Universidad Veracruzana. I was born and raised here, but I've lived in a few other places, including your fine country, during my years of study."

"Where did you study?"

"I began my studies at the National University in Mexico City, and then I did post-graduate work at the University of Michigan and Stanford. I've been with Veracruzana since 1944, both here and at the Xalapa campus, but my heart is right here in Veracruz. This is my home."

"Well, I can see one reason you feel at home here. This plaza is beautiful."

"Yes, beautiful and peaceful. I like to come down here now and then, whenever I have spare time away from the classroom. I can relax here and catch up on my reading."

"So as a native of Veracruz, you have a personal interest in this calamity. Who do you think could have done it?"

"I don't know. One of the rumors circulating here in the Plaza says it was caused by an agent of one of the foreign oil companies, or perhaps it was some kind of anti-government conspiracy. Another rumor says it was the Communists. I don't think anyone knows for sure yet, but I worry that whoever did this could be planning a repeat performance, either here in Veracruz or somewhere nearby."

"But why would it be an anti-government thing? Isn't Pemex popular here, a good employer, a good citizen?"

"Pemex is not always held in high regard. A good employer, yes, in that they pay excellent wages, but there's always conflict between Pemex management and the oil workers' union. The union has a lot of power, and they would like to call all the shots."

"But wasn't the nationalization of the oil industry popular with the people of Mexico?"

"With some people, such as the union leaders and the Marxists, yes. There are many Mexicans now who would like to see everything run by the government—not just Pemex, but also the banks, the airlines, the railroads, everything that is productive. On the other hand, many people believe in the competitive power of a free and unfettered economy, with no government interference."

"A difference of opinion is always a healthy thing," Harry commented, trying to sound academic.

"Yes, and we have plenty of that. Even though the outcome of the presidential election is a foregone conclusion, for example, there's always a wide range of opinion. The leaders of the petroleum workers' union made out well with the expropriation, nailing down good-paying jobs and job security for themselves within the union, and, of course, the union has placed several members on the Pemex board of directors. Pemex workers are well-paid. Pemex workers and also the railroad worker, but naturally, workers in other industries resent the pay differential.

"Nationalization, of course, was not an easy transition. At the time, in 1938, Mexico had virtually no trained engineers or technicians or scientists in the oil industry, and it was like starting from scratch. Even now, there are many foreign companies working here under contract. Foreign companies, for example, do much of the drilling."

"They're hired by Pemex?"

"Yes, they work with risk contacts—if they hit a dry hole, they absorb the cost and move on to another location. And, of course, not all of the foreign companies were taken over by the government, only the biggest, the ones that were having labor problems at the time, the ones that resisted the union demands."

"You're saying the union had a lot to do with it?"

"They made demands the foreign oil companies couldn't meet, or didn't want to meet, and President Cárdenas sided with the union."

"So the union has a lot of power?"

"The union has several seats on the Pemex board of directors, so yes, the union does have power. But it's also to the union's benefit to see Pemex remain strong and successful, now and in the future. It's not always the confrontational "us versus them" situation that you seem to have with your unions in the United States."

"What does the future hold for Pemex? And for Mexico?"

"Ah, that is a dilemma. Pemex is doing better now, but it's still top-heavy with bureaucrats and weighed down by overstaffing. And, of course, the unions have a strong voice in how the company is run. But tell me, what have you learned in your visit here today?"

"Well, I had lunch at a place called the Cantina Pozo Hondo, and I talked with a couple of Pemex workers."

The Professor laughed. "You went to the oil workers' private club? That's like going right into the lion's den. I hope you got a good story to go with your heartburn."

"The fellows I talked to weren't actually in the fire, but two of the men killed were friends of theirs. They believe the third victim was the guy who set the fire, but they don't have any idea who he was. That's where the real story is, and I don't know if the local UP correspondent got anything on it."

"You have a challenging job. You're always right in the middle of the excitement, you're part of the news as it happens."

Harry laughed. "Well, I'm not always in the middle. It's more like I'm on the sidelines, maybe watching it as it happens. Or after it happens, like today. I don't make the news, I just write about it. In fact, many times I don't even write about it, I just report it by telephone and somebody else does the actual writing."

"Well, your continuing story right now, Señor, will be much more than just last night's fire. I'm afraid there could be more deaths before this is over, and I'm sure you'll want to know the identity of that third victim. It seems the third man could hold the key. Are you going to remain here and pursue that lead?"

"No, I have to get back to Mexico City, but I can follow up by telephone. What would you suggest for a follow-up?"

"Well, I think you will want to try to find a contact at Pemex itself, if you know anyone there. And I think you'll want to keep in touch with your luncheon partners from the Cantina Pozo Hondo."

"Yes, and I'd like to call you tomorrow with a few questions, if I could," Harry said.

"Of course, feel free to call." The professor pulled a card from his pocket and gave it to Harry. "If I'm not in class or in my office, I'm probably down here. I can relax, and think clearly here, watching the water and watching the ships come and go. Just don't write anything that will get me in hot water with the university."

"No, I wouldn't do that. Your help is most appreciated, but your identity will be secure." Harry read from the card. "Professor Gilberto Gomez. Pleased to meet you, Professor. My name is Harry Banister."

"How would I reach you in Mexico City, Harry? At the UP office?"

"Yes. I don't have a card yet, I'm here just a couple of days now, but I'll jot the number on this slip of paper. Or you could reach me at the Del Prado. Say, I notice you have binoculars."

"Oh, yes. Some days I like to walk along the malecón that borders the harbor, or relax on a bench and watch the ships. This harbor is very important to us here in Veracruz, not only for the petroleum exports but also for general commerce. We receive a lot of shipments here from the U.S. and also from Europe, and we also have a lot of trade with Caribbean nations."

"And how is the traffic today?"

"I'd say the traffic today is about average, mostly the regular vessels coming and going, but there are a few strange ships anchored out there, waiting to tie up."

"What kind of cargo would they be bringing in? Or taking out?"

"Those are general cargo ships. It's hard to tell from here what their cargo might be."

Harry thanked the professor, stuffed the card in his pocket, and bid him a pleasant day.

CHAPTER 46

Across the plaza, a man on another bench had a different theory. "You know, there've been several oil fires in Mexico recently, and there's little doubt that the Martians are responsible. They're here now, you know. They landed last month up in the mountains, you know, up in the Sierra Madre."

"Last month? In the Sierra Madre? I did not know that."

"Yes. Their saucers were flying all across the skies of North America last month. They were spotted here in Mexico, and there were something like fifty sightings in more than twenty American states last month, and they were spotted in Washington D.C., you know, flying over the White House and the Washington National Airport. They even were seen flying over Andrews Air Force Base."

Harry tried not to smile. "Yes, I read about that."

"And the saucers landed right here in Mexico, up in the mountains, you know, and now the Martians have worked their way down here to the Coast. They're the ones who caused the explosion last night, you know, and the blaze that followed. No doubt about it. Who knows what they might do next? They might try something even worse, right here in the harbor."

"I suppose that would be entirely possible," Harry said, still trying to hold back the smile. "Did you happen to see what they looked like?"

"No, I haven't actually seen any of them myself, but my brother-in-law saw one last night, just an hour or so before the explosion."

"Really? Just before the explosion? Where did your brother-in-law see him?"

"Hernando saw him behind a cantina over there on Avenida Miguel Lerda. He said the Martian was carrying a package under his arm, and he looked very suspicious."

"Could Hernando see what the package looked like? I mean, does he have any idea what was in the package?"

"Like I said, it was dark, and of course the package was wrapped in plain brown paper, so Hernando couldn't really see it too well. But plain brown paper is always suspicious, you know."

"Yes, I know. Did your brother-in-law get a good look at his face?"

"Well, Hernando was just coming out of the cantina, and he said it was too dark to see the creature clearly. He didn't get a good look at the face. He said the creature was short, very short, with spindly legs. The Martians probably send short people on these exploratory missions, you know, because those space ships are so cramped on the inside and the short people fit better."

"Yes, I'm sure you're right about that. Short people always fit better in tight spaces. Perhaps the police will have to pick him up," Harry said, thinking of Hernando, not the Martian.

Harry moved down the walk and sat down next to a man on another bench. "I can tell you what happened last night," the man said, tossing bits of tortilla chips to a cluster of seagulls waiting nearby. "The fire was part of a Communist plot to take over the government of Mexico and ultimately the entire world."

"Communists?"

"Yes, they're everywhere now, infiltrating Pemex and even working their way into our labor unions and our schools and our government. Those dirty rotten Commies are everywhere."

"I take it you don't like the Communists."

"I don't like them. They cause trouble everywhere. Look at Europe now, and Russia, and China, and Korea. Nothing but trouble. We don't need that here."

"That fellow back there thinks it was the Martians," Harry said, gesturing to the previous bench.

"No, no," the man's companion frowned and shook her head. "It wasn't the Martians. My husband believes it was the Communists, but I don't agree. I don't think it was the Commies. I'm convinced last night's disaster, like so many other evil events, was caused by that greedy nation up north, beyond the border. You gringos are the cause of so many of our problems here in Mexico."

"Hey, I didn't do anything," Harry said.

"Oh, I don't mean you, Señor. I mean your government in Washington and all those avaricious capitalists on Wall Street. Those rich people in Washington and on Wall Street are part of an evil conspiracy of wealthy nations who want to control the world's money supply, and struggling countries like Mexico, at the other end of the spectrum, will continue to suffer. Wealthy bankers want to control the money supply so that eventually there will be just one government ruling the entire world."

"That's a good possibility," Harry said.

"Yes," she continued, "it's a law of nature. The rich get richer, and the poor get poorer."

"I don't know much about the laws of nature," Harry said, trying to sidestep the issue so he could move on. "I guess those are all good possibilities for last night's disaster, the Martians or the Communists or the Yankee capitalists."

Harry's taxi followed him as he walked down to the harbor and strolled along the malecón. Harry counted three tankers tied up in the harbor, but he couldn't be certain if the dockside pumps were operating. Probably not.

In another section of the harbor Harry saw the yachts and sailboats of the Veracruz wealthy, and nearby, the docks of commercial fishing vessels. Several foreign-flag package freighters were waiting at anchor for space to open at the commercial docks. Harry recognized a couple of flags, but three or four he couldn't identify.

The taxi driver honked at Harry. "It's time to move on to the airport," he called out, "or I'll have to charge you more for the sightseeing tour."

"Busy place," Harry remarked as he closed the door. "A few foreign ships in port today."

"Yes, perhaps it's another invasion. Throughout history, our city has been the target of many hostile incursions by foreign powers. In 1519, Cortez and the Spanish Conquistadors landed here. In the Seventeenth and Eighteenth centuries, European pirates continually occupied and ravaged the city. French armies invaded in 1838 and again in 1862. In 1847 the Americans bombarded and occupied our city. The Yankees bombarded and invaded again just thirty-eight years ago, killing many people and occupying our city for seven months.

"We hope and pray, Señor, that we will never again be cursed by such avaricious aggression."

Harry absorbed the driver's story in silence. Just like Bob and Steve said, and just like Mario said back at the Cantina Pozo Hondo, the Mexicans want to make us feel welcome, but sometimes they like to add a little twist of the knife while they're at it.

CHAPTER 47

"Arnie, I sure hope you take care of your engine as well as you do that windshield," Harry said as he approached.

"Even better. This thing is my pride and joy. Checked over the plane, topped off the tanks, bought another rubber band just in case. But I like to keep a clean windshield so I can see where we're going, and if we're going to crash I like to see where we're going to hit."

"That extra rubber band sounds like a good idea. What else have you been doing while I was gone?"

"Figured you'd be gone a while, so I grabbed some lunch. Ready to go whenever you are, soon as the weather is clear."

"What's with the weather?"

"Brisk breeze coming in off the Gulf. More wind than I want. Looks like it's bringing rain, typical tropical cloudburst. When we get up, the wind could bounce us around a bit. Anyway, we'll have to wait till that Mexicana DC-3 over there finishes boarding its passengers and takes off. Have to wait till we get clearance."

Harry looked to his left and saw what Arnie meant. The passengers boarding the DC-3 were battling the breeze, clutching their hats, coats, newspapers and packages. "That's all right, a few minutes won't matter. I want to make a call to Mexico City before we leave. I want to phone in my story."

In the terminal Harry called the UP office and dictated a real tearjerker about the human tragedy of the two young fire victims: their jobs, their lives, their families, their youthful energy, their dreams and their early deaths. He spiced up the story with tributes from their friends and co-workers, Mario and Pancho.

Then he dictated a separate story with some of the speculation from "several Pemex workers" that the unidentified third victim was responsible for the calamity. He included the quotes he picked up from citizens at the Plaza de Armas, including the man who said the "Communists are everywhere now, infiltrating Pemex and even working their way into our labor unions and our schools and our government."

For added punch, he included the quotes suggesting that Martians or Americans were responsible. "That might give the story extra play in the American newspapers," Harry commented to the rewrite man.

Harry smiled when he got off the phone. That should be enough to convince Bob to pay for the plane and the taxis. Lunch, at two-and-a-half pesos, I can handle myself.

Twenty minutes and a Carta Blanca later Harry felt a tap on his shoulder. "Clear to go. The wind coming in off the Gulf is still blowing pretty good, could make the trip a little rough. Might even help us, give us a tailwind." Arnie laughed, and swept his hand into the air, from below his hip up over his head. "But you realize, it's uphill all the way back."

"Okay, let's go. A little bouncing won't bother me. By the way, Arnie, do you know any of the other planes out here on the tarmac? Like that Piper over there, for instance?"

""What's the matter, you don't like my Wings of Liberty? Looking for a better ride next time?"

"No, no," Harry laughed. "I love your plane. I was just wondering if you're familiar with some of the other planes around here. I know that most of the Pemex people came on a company DC-3, but one of their top brass came on his own plane, and I was wondering what kind of a plane he has."

"It's that red-and-white Piper PA-22 Tri-Pacer sitting at the end of the runway, ready to take off."

Arnie jockeyed the Wings of Liberty around a couple of clouds that were left over from the afternoon storms, and landed in Mexico City just as the sun dipped behind the western rim of the Valley of Mexico.

Harry paid Arnie the balance of his fee, and Arnie gave him a glossy four-color, eight-page, eight-by-ten inch brochure that featured Arnie's picture (three times), a glowing autobiography, a description of the Wings of Liberty, several retouched pictures of a freshly-painted plane, plus shots of the Cathedral in Guadalajara and the Caleta Beach in Acapulco. A highlight was a checklist of ten compelling reasons why you should call Alas de Arnoldo when you want to fly for business or pleasure. Included were two telephone numbers.

"That's pretty fancy."

"My wife helped me plan it. She suggested the heavy glossy magazine stock for durability. I had more pictures in mind, but she said three shots of me were enough."

"Well, I guess when you're in business you have to put your best foot forward. In this case, your best wings. But calling your business Alas de Arnoldo? Isn't that a little corny?"

"Arnoldo's Wings? No worse than naming my plane the Wings of Liberty. Played around with a couple other names for the company, like 'Come Fly with Arnie, or maybe 'Arnoldo's Air Service,' but my wife liked this one best. My wings are at your service, Harry, any time you need them."

Harry laughed. "Thanks. I think my next flight will be down to Acapulco, so I can lie on the beach and soak up some sun. How long would it take us to get to Acapulco?"

"Couple hours. All downhill from here, you know."

"That might be my next trip." Harry folded the brochure and crammed it into the crowded breast pocket of his suit coat. "I'll give you a call."

CHAPTER 48

Harry couldn't remember half the stuff he learned in journalism school, but one thing he never forgot: the three essential tools for a good reporter are a No. 2 pencil, a blank piece of paper, and a telephone.

The pencil and paper are for jotting significant statements during a press conference or an interview, or for recording important data such as dollar amounts, sports scores, dates, addresses and phone numbers. The telephone is for probing your secret sources for information, for dictating your story to the rewrite man, or for calling one of those promising phone numbers scribbled on the note paper. The pencil and paper you carry with you at all times. In an emergency, such as a broken pencil, you can use a typewriter.

The telephone—thank God for the telephone—is anywhere you find it.

Inside the terminal Harry found a telephone and placed a call to the Hotel Comé.

"Yes Sir, that young lady called this morning. I told her you had checked out and moved to the Del Prado, just as you asked."

"Okay, that's good. Many thanks. I don't think there'll be any more calls."

Next, Harry called the Del Prado.

"Yes Sir, there have been four calls for you, all in the last few minutes. And those two men were back, asking for you at the reception desk."

"Salesmen?"

"It's possible. They didn't leave their names. Also, there was another man inquiring for you at the desk. He was alone."

"Another salesman?"

"He didn't leave his name, and he didn't say what he wanted. He spoke with the rural dialect of a campesino, perhaps a cowboy, from Jalisco or Nayarit or one of the other western states. You're a very popular man, Señor Banister. Everybody wants to talk to you, but no one wants to leave a message."

"Yeah, I think they're all salesmen, either that or bill collectors."

"Yes Sir, but I don't think the man who came looking for you was a salesman."

"Oh? Why not?"

"He wasn't dressed like a salesman. He was dressed more like a cowboy."

"Maybe he's selling horses, or manure or hay. Whatever it is, I'm not buying. Who were the phone calls?"

"There was a call from a young lady named Isabel. She just now hung up, so perhaps you can still catch her if you call right away."

"Okay, I have her number."

"The first message is from Señor Prescott. It says, 'Veracruz stories good. Call me.' Your second message says, 'The Chief wants to talk to you. Call immediately.' The lady who placed the call said to tell you it's urgent. She didn't leave her name, but she sounded like she was a North American."

What the hell is that all about, Harry wondered? The Chief? Urgent? I never told him I was going to work for him. He's taking a lot for granted.

"The third call, ten minutes ago, was from Alberto. He said 'Call me for location of tonight's party.' And the fourth message, as I said, was from the young lady named Isabel."

Harry ranked the messages in the order of immediate importance and dialed Isabel's number. The two jefes can wait a few minutes. Urgency is a relative matter.

"I'm so glad you called, Harry. What a day this has been. We've been deluged here with calls from the press."

"I can believe it, but I didn't know if you'd still be in the office at this hour."

"Oh, yes, we're just now cleaning up. Did you talk with Señor Velasco this morning?"

"Sort of. He said hello, but that's about all. He said he didn't have time for me. He was in a hurry, on his way out the door to catch a plane to Veracruz. I asked him if I could go with him, and he said there was no room for me on his plane."

"Yes, he went down there to inspect the damage, and he returned just a little while ago. He stuck his head in our office to check on a press release he wants us to send out. Something about all the recent fires, not just Veracruz. I read your Veracruz stories on our UP printer, Harry. A touching story about the two boys who were killed, and how their young lives were cut short so tragically. A sad story, and a sad day."

"Yes, it was sad. And it was a mess."

"And your story about the people you met down at the Plaza de Armas."

Harry laughed. "Yeah, how about that? People sure do get some strange ideas. Sometimes you wonder, though, how strange those ideas really are. Sometimes they seem to make sense."

"Yes, I know what you mean. When you called this morning, I didn't know you were going to Veracruz."

"Neither did I. It was a quick decision. I went because I wanted to see for myself what it was all about."

"How did you get there?"

"I flew, and I'm back in Mexico City now."

"You flew?"

"Yes, I chartered a plane."

"Oh, my, you're really a man of action. I admire a man of action. That's the way to get things done, and I guess it's important in your job. You must like to get right into the middle of the story."

"Well, Velasco gave me the brush-off. He said he didn't have time to talk to me, so I figured I might as well go down there and see for myself. I ran into him in Veracruz, but he still didn't want to talk to me."

"That sounds just like him. He's not very cooperative with the press. Harry, I could tell from your stories that you were deeply moved by what you saw in Veracruz, and what you learned while you were there, especially the unfortunate deaths of those two young fellows. You must be a warm, compassionate man."

"I'll tell you more about Veracruz when I see you. How about tonight?"

"Well, I'm not ready to leave the office. It'll be a little while yet, and I'm afraid it'll be too late for the driving lesson."

"We could have a quick drink."

"I know just the place. I can pick you up in front of the Del Prado in an hour. I'll be driving a green Morris Minor. It's small, but there's room for the two of us if you're not too tall."

"Is six-feet-two okay?"

Isabel laughed, forming an image of a tall good-looking Yankee in her mind. "Oh, you are tall, but I think you'll fit. We'll have a drink today and maybe you can learn to drive the glorietas tomorrow."

"Good. I'm still at the airport, but I think I can make it back to the hotel in time. I'll be looking for your car out front. One hour. A green Morris Minor."

Harry reconsidered as he hung up. Slow down a minute. A drink or two would be all right now, but I'm not sure I want to get tied down with a driving lesson tomorrow. Besides, Isabel might turn out to be an ugly old bruja.

Nah, she couldn't be a witch. At least, she doesn't sound like a witch. I'll bet she's a real Latin doll.

CHAPTER 49

"You get around," Alberto said. "I called the Comé and they told me you'd moved to the Del Prado."

"That's right, I didn't have a chance to tell you. I moved over there this morning. Say, the Del Prado is a classy place. There's a lot going on there."

"It's the best hotel in town. All the important people hang out there. You might even run into Diego in the lobby."

"Diego?"

"Diego Rivera. He painted a mural for the hotel when it opened a few years ago, all about the plight of the working man."

"Jesus, the plight of the working man," Harry said. "That's all I heard Saturday night at dinner. I guess that's me, the working man. I'll have to look for his mural and check it out."

"You won't be able to see it. It's been covered over. He included a banner that says *Dios no existe*, and it caused a lot of controversy."

"God does not exist?"

"Yeah, Diego's an atheist, a very public atheist. He likes to stir things up. There was a big protest after he did the mural, and some people came in and painted over the 'no', then Diego came in with a bunch of his friends and painted it back in, and then the hotel people covered the whole damned mural."

"I'll have to see if I can track it down."

"You must be making good dough at UP to be able to afford the Del Prado, and to rent a plane to fly to Veracruz. Tell me, how was Veracruz? Where are you now?"

"I'm back in Mexico City, at the airport. I just got back a few minutes ago. My stories were pretty routine stuff. The city was mostly smoky, except down by the harbor. The breeze off the Gulf kept the air clear there. I'd like to go back again sometime, when I can see more of the city."

"I'll go with you, and get some of that fresh sea air. Say, did you happen to run into our girl Margarita while you were there?"

"She and I were on different tracks, but I did catch a glimpse of her getting into a car with her friend Velasco. How was her story?"

"I don't know, I haven't seen it yet. By the way, Detective Gonzalez is still looking for you. He came into the cantina just after you left this morning."

"For Christ's sake, doesn't he know where to find me? What kind of detective is he? Everyone else in the Federal District seems to know I moved to the Del Prado."

"Now that you mention it, I think he knows, too. He said he'd catch up with you later."

"Did he have anything new to say?"

"He says he's close to wrapping up that Bar 33 killing. He says he still has a few details to pin down. But he's eager to talk to you. I think maybe he suspects you. Did you do it?"

Harry laughed. "Well, I guess that's his job, to suspect everybody, including the butler and the chauffer and the upstairs maid, until he finds his killer. Are you sure you didn't do it, Alberto?"

Now Alberto laughed. "At this point, I'm not sure, but I'm pretty sure I was working Thursday night. Say, I know it's getting late now, but I'm just leaving for an evening of poetry reading at a rich lady's penthouse on the Paseo de la Reforma. There'll be cocktails, plenty of good food, and I'm sure there'll be a few pretty girls, too. Do you want to come along?"

Harry looked at his watch and thought about Isabel and her little green Morris Minor. "Poetry? No thanks. The food and the drinks and the girls sound interesting, but I'm not into poetry. Right now, I just want to get back to the hotel and get cleaned up. By the way, you were going to try to set up a golf game for me for tomorrow. Any luck?"

"Yeah, you're all set for two o'clock."

"Great, then I'll be able to go out to the Pyramids in the morning. What do I have to do?"

"Just take your clubs out to Churubusco and introduce yourself to the pro. He'll be expecting you and he'll introduce you to our ad salesman. But what about Veracruz? Don't you want to follow up on that?"

"No, I think UP has it wrapped up by now, and I've already done enough work today to last me for a week or two. I need a little diversion now, a little recreation."

Next, Harry called the UP office. "We got the lead story from our stringer," Prescott said, "but your two stories were good stuff, especially the piece on the two young victims. I put your byline on it and moved it on the trunk here in Mexico and also on the main trunk back to the States. I like the other piece, too. A Martian in a flying saucer? Tell me, how did you get to Veracruz?"

"Well, I can tell you it wasn't a UFO. At least, I don't think it was. I chartered a plane, more like a flying orange crate. It was a little Cessna four-seater owned by an American ex-pat named Armstrong."

"Yeah, I know him. I'm glad you made it there and back in that plane of his, and I hope he didn't charge us too much."

When Bob said "us" Harry knew UP was going to cover the cost of the plane. "No, it wasn't much. I'll bring you the receipt in the morning."

"Hang onto it for now, and we'll settle later. What are you planning for tomorrow?"

Harry hesitated, trying to sort out his growing list of things to do. Top of the list, of course, was golf. "I might make a couple follow-up calls to Veracruz first thing in the morning," he said. "See what I can pick up. Then I'm going out to the Pyramids, and I'm going to play golf in the afternoon."

"Good. Make those phone calls from your hotel. I don't want you coming around here until you're clear with Detective Gonzalez. He's been asking about you again. He really wants to talk to you. Are you sure you're in the clear on that Bar 33 thing?"

Harry swallowed. "Absolutely, I'm clear."

"Okay, call me in the morning, just don't come around here."

Harry took a deep breath and dialed Corbett's anytime phone number. Corbett answered on the first ring and didn't bother to say hello when Harry identified himself. "I read your stuff from Veracruz," he barked. "Pure crap."

Harry ignored the remark about 'pure crap.' One man's opinion, he decided. Anyway, the rewrite man at UP liked it, and Bob liked it. And Isabel liked it. "You saw it already? I just phoned it in a little while ago."

"I have a UP printer in my office. Keeps me up to date on what's happening up in Washington, some of the news that's not on my internal teletype. What the hell were you doing in Veracruz? I'm looking for hard information, and you come up with that schmaltz about a couple of poor kids who got caught in the wrong place at the wrong time. I need better stuff than that."

"Hold on a minute, Steve. I don't work for you. I never said I was going to work for you, and I didn't go to Veracruz for you. I went there because I smelled a story, and I got a couple of pretty good stories, if I do say so myself. Somebody else did the main piece, and I was looking for a backgrounder, a feature story, a human interest piece, and that story on the victims had plenty of real human interest."

"Not much useful information," Corbett grunted. "Where are you now?"

"I'm at the airport."

"You didn't tell us you were going to Veracruz. How'd you get there?"

"I made a quick decision, so I had to move fast. I chartered a plane. And no, I didn't tell you. It never occurred to me that I had to clear my movements with you."

"How were you able to charter a plane?"

"Easy. I just walked up to a guy who was sitting in a chair under the wing of a Cessna and I said, 'You wanna take me to Veracruz?' And he said 'Sure' and away we went. Listen, Steve, I got a couple good stories down there—"

"You chartered a plane? I hope he didn't charge us too much."

Harry frowned. "What do you mean 'us'?"

"I mean you and me and the agency."

"The Agency? There you go again, Steve. I don't work for you. I went to Veracruz on my own, and I think UP will cover the expense. Anyway, I had enough money in my pocket. I paid him cash. And I picked up a lot of good stuff in Veracruz."

"Well, how about sharing some of that good stuff with me. That's what I'm paying you for. I need—"

Harry held the telephone handset at arm's length out the open window. A DC-6 revved its four big piston engines for a minute or two, taxied into position, revved the engines again, and took off with an ear-splitting roar. When the plane was up, Harry pulled the handset back into the terminal and resumed speaking into the mouthpiece, "Sorry about that. What was that you were saying? I couldn't hear you. It's pretty noisy here."

Corbett's voice was calm now. "I was telling you to get me something with some real meat on it. I want to know what's going on. Do some digging. Follow up with the contacts you made at the Pemex press conference. Get inside Pemex. That's where you'll find something."

Harry looked at the clock on the wall by the ticket counter. "Listen, right now I just want to get back to the hotel. I'll call you first thing in the morning and we can talk about it. We could have an early breakfast. Where do you want to—?"

"God damn it, Banister! Forget about breakfast. I'm tied up right now, but I'll pick you up in an hour in front of the Del Prado. I want to know what you learned in Veracruz."

"I've had a long day. I just want to get back to the hotel and get cleaned up, and anyway, I've got a date to meet a girl back at the Del Prado."

"Forget about your God-damned social life. Get laid on your own time. Be on the sidewalk in front of the hotel in one hour. Look for a blue Ford station wagon. I'm paying you good money, Banister."

"Wait a minute, Steve, I don't work for you. I never said I would join your secret club and I'm not interested in your damned money. I haven't spent any of your money. Anyway, this is not exactly a social date. I'm going to meet—"

"One hour, Banister. Be there."

Corbett hung up before Harry could say anything more. Harry dialed again and waited while it rang seven times, then he slammed the phone down and stuck the pencil and the note paper into his pocket.

For Christ's sake, Harry prayed, give me a little peace. I'm in town four days, and already I'm caught in crossfire. I'm supposed to be having a good time here. Maybe I should forget about Acapulco. Maybe I should go to Cuba or Guatemala, or someplace where there aren't any telephones, where I can lie in the sun on the beach and drink beer and make out with a beautiful girl.

But Harry's innate curiosity took hold as he hopped into a taxi outside the terminal. "I want to go to the Del Prado," he told the driver, "but let's drive by the Florería Roma on the way. It's on Calle Londres."

"I know where it is, but I'm not sure the flower shop would be open now. It's just past the closing hour, but if you're late, and you need to bring flowers to pacify your wife or your girl friend, you can buy flowers right there in the Del Prado."

"I know it's getting late, but let's drive by and find out."

And, of course, the driver was right. The steel shutters were down and the sign on the door said *Cerrado*. The shop was closed, but Harry could see bits of light filtering through the shutters. The lights are on, and Pedro's in the back—like he said, time and flowers wait for no man. Maybe Rosa's back there, too.

"You're right, the shop is closed. Pull up behind that car at the curb, and I'll get out here anyway. I'd like to get some fresh air."

CHAPTER 50

The woman laid the telephone handset in its cradle. Leaning back in her chair, she removed a cigarette from a polished silver case, placed it in the end of an elongated cigarette holder, and lit the tip. She blew a perfect smoke ring into the air, and dramatically stabbed the center of the circle of smoke with her cigarette.

"We have a problem," the woman said. "Semyon Denisovich reminds us the target date is fast approaching, and he's under the gun. That, of course, means you and I are under the gun."

"But we're on schedule, are we not? Everything is moving in an orderly fashion. All the players are in position. All the pieces are fitting together neatly, is that not true?"

"Not entirely. I don't know if we're on schedule. The calendar dictates the schedule, and it's our responsibility to keep pace with the calendar. As the lawyers like to say, 'time is of the essence.' Certain things take place on certain dates, and we have no control over those dates. We can control our own actions, of course, and we also can control the actions of others when necessary, but I'm not certain that all the pieces are fitting together so neatly. There are problems."

"So what are the problems?"

The woman blew another smoke ring and smiled. "Imagine, if you will, that we have a large jigsaw puzzle sitting here on the table in front of us. A beautiful picture is taking shape, let's say it's a picture of a bear, but several key pieces have yet to be put in place, and one of the key pieces is missing. Let's say the missing piece is the nose of the bear.

To further complicate matters, there is a piece on the table that does not belong in the picture, and that piece is getting in our way.

"But we cannot complete the picture if the bear's nose has gone into hiding somewhere in another room or another city. We need all the proper pieces in their proper places. Yes, Semyon Denisovich is concerned."

The woman's companion grinned. "I assumed as much, Yelena, watching your face and your reactions during the telephone conversation. But I believe his concern might be premature. The incident last night in Veracruz was a success, particularly with the deaths of three men."

"Last night was not a success, Vlad. No one was supposed to die. Not yet."

"I disagree. Those deaths were a good thing. Those deaths will heighten the public awareness and curiosity and, more important, create fear in the hearts of the public. Death is a necessary ingredient. Death is a primary ingredient."

The woman once again pierced a drifting smoke ring. "Yes, death is necessary, at the proper time. Right now, Semyon Denisovich is concerned about the plan, but he's also concerned about the missing nose."

"Ah yes, the nose. You're so graphic. You're almost poetic, Yelena, conjuring a portrait of a bear. But you've heard nothing from the missing nose?"

"Nothing. Not a telephone call, not a word. No reports. Of course, this is not unusual. He's disappeared like this several times in the past. It seems he has a habit of disappearing for a day or two with one of his female friends. He's shirking his responsibilities, and he's become a threat to the stability of our presence here."

"Pedro could know something about his whereabouts."

Yelena spat. "Pedro? He knows nothing. Pedro's a sentimental old fool. He's engrossed in his damned flowers. His nose is in his flowers, and I think his head is in the clouds. Sometimes I think his head is up his ass."

Vladimir laughed. "He reminds me of Ferdinand the Bull, who would prefer to sit all day under a cork tree and smell the flowers rather than fight. Pedro could miss a Red Army parade, with full military band, marching down Londres street, right past his flower shop."

"Yes, you're right. I'm sure Pedro is hoping the missing nose will materialize, as if by magic, and saunter into the flower shop and say '*privyet*', and Pedro would smile and say 'hello' right back, as if nothing's wrong."

"Does Pedro know anything at all about what else is happening?"

"He knows only his specific assignment, which is the way it should be."

"But what does he know about other phases of the operation? Does he know about you?"

"I'm sure he doesn't know about me, Vlad. He may pick up dribs and drabs, but I don't believe he knows anything concrete, anything important. When the final fire has turned to ashes, he'll be of little value. He'll be useless, just like the ashes, nothing but a pile of smoldering dust, ready to blow away in the breeze."

"Yes, a good breeze from the mountains should do it. But where is this elusive nose now?"

"I wish I knew, but I'm going to find out. I have my sources."

"And what about the other pieces?"

"They're all on the table, ready to slide into place."

"Lena Masha, you said there's a piece on the table that doesn't belong in your picture."

"Yes, there appears to be an extra nose, but it's the nose of a different animal, not a bear. Let's call it a tiger—"

"An American tiger?"

"Yes, an American tiger, and this nose of a tiger is sniffing around where it shouldn't be sniffing, where it might smell something it should not discover. Any piece that does not belong in this picture, cluttering our table, will have to be removed."

"Absolutely. And what will you do now?"

"I can wait no longer. I'll have to take steps. I may have to patch the picture with a piece of masking tape, so to speak, where the bear's nose should be. I may have to step in and fill the void myself. Actually, I believe I would be a better fit. I believe I would do a better job.

"And you, my dear Vlad, may have to take care of that obtrusive nose of a curious tiger. Keep it out of our picture, get it off the table. Get rid of it altogether."

"I can handle that, with no problem."

"And what about your assignment?" she asked.

"My assignment is right on schedule. As you said, the calendar dictates my schedule, and everything is ready."

"Excellent." Yelena jabbed her cigarette into another circle of smoke. She rose from the chair and loosened the sash on her dressing gown, letting the open gown hang carelessly from her shoulders. "Tell me, Vlad, when do you have to leave?"

Vladimir looked at her and grinned. "As you said, Lena, time is of the essence. I have an hour or so, and it would be a shame for us to let this hour slip away."

CHAPTER 51

Pedro had no problem with people who smoked. In fact, he himself was one of them. He liked to light up a Cuban cigar, especially after a good meal or at a bullfight or a soccer game. Smoking was a universal habit, he realized, and he was just one of the millions of people around the world who enjoyed it.

But Pedro did not want anyone to smoke in the Florería Roma. He didn't want cigar and cigarette smoke contaminating the sweet aroma of his flowers, so he tried to maintain a strict "no smoking" policy in the front section of the store, where customers mingled with the fresh flowers and admired the floral displays. And he also tried to maintain a smoking ban in the workroom, where the baskets and bouquets and displays were assembled.

Pedro also knew he would have a hard time enforcing his rule when outsiders gathered in his office, the special room in back of the workroom that he sometimes used as a meeting room, so he had a pair of facing doors installed to connect the two rooms, with one door opening into his office, the other into the workroom. When the two doors were closed against each other, the workroom and the rest of the shop had an extra wall of protection against smoke that might try to drift from the back room.

As a bonus, in case any of his meetings became too raucous, the double-facing doors also provided an extra sound barrier between the two rooms.

Pedro, however, was a realist. He knew that someone would want to smoke tonight, so he taped a "No Smoking" sign on the side of the door facing into his office, and he placed a small sign on the circular table in the middle of the room. For added protection, he jammed a rolled-up scatter rug along the bottom of the connecting door to prevent smoke from creeping through and poisoning the air in the workroom and the front of the shop.

But no matter how much I might plead and cuss, he told himself, some son of a whore is going to light up tonight.

Softly humming an air from an old Spanish zarzuela, Pedro arranged six chairs around the circular table and placed an array of glasses in the center of the table. He knew he wouldn't need the extra seating tonight, but he straightened up the day bed, removing a pile of old magazines and newspapers and a pair of moth-eaten slippers.

From the refrigerator he pulled out a roll of spicy chorizo picante and a roll of mild sausage, plus three wedges of cheese, two loaves of bread, a jar of salsa and a plate of green grapes. He sliced three lemons into bite-size pieces and set a salt shaker next to the lemon. Then he opened the multi-purpose antique armoire and retrieved a bottle of vodka, a bottle of scotch, two bottles of his best tequila, a bottle of reasonable scotch, and a bottle of cheap Mexican aguardiente. A truly international selection, he mused, and there's plenty more in the cabinet.

From a drawer in the lower part of the armoire, Pedro removed a pocket-size notebook and sat down at the table. After a few moments of scrutiny, he jotted a few notations in the notebook and then closed it.

Satisfied that everything was in order, Pedro poured himself a glass of aguardiente. The rough brandy warmed his tongue and his palate, and carried him back to his youth in Spain. He sat silently and sipped slowly, recalling some of the battles he had fought side by side with Miguel and the other members of his brigade.

Those were glorious days—brutal days, to be sure—when they all were younger, filled with the fervor of youth, eager to fight the fascist forces of Francisco Franco's Falange.

Pedro and Miguel had been childhood friends and schoolmates in Spain. In school, Pedro excelled in his studies and Miguel struggled. Pedro wanted to continue his studies at the university, but family finances would not permit it, so he took a job as an apprentice in a local florist. Miguel, with a knack for things mechanical, took a job at an automobile repair shop.

As young men, they played on the same local soccer team. Pedro was the keeper (the coach thought Pedro's girth might provide extra protective coverage for the goal). Miguel, the fastest member of the team, was the striker, scoring most of the goals, and his speedy play earned him a once-in-a-lifetime opportunity to try out with the pros at Athletic Bilbao.

When the Civil War broke out in Spain, Pedro and Miguel joined a brigade fighting for the Loyalist cause. Pedro came though the fighting with only a minor scratch. In one skirmish, a bullet ripped through his shirt sleeve, leaving a superficial flesh wound in his arm. Another time, when he climbed high in a tree on a reconnaissance mission, searching the distant hills for Nationalist troop movement, the tree branch snapped, throwing him to the ground. His binoculars were smashed and his pants and his jacket were ripped, but he bounced up, dusty and unhurt.

And during a fierce battle near the Río Ebro, a grenade landed at Pedro's feet and he quickly picked it up and lobbed it back at the approaching troops before it could explode.

No wonder his comrades called him *El Dichoso*, the Lucky One.

Miguel was not so lucky. The plucky little fellow lost a foot in the fighting. "But it wasn't the whole leg," he later would joke, "it was only a part of a leg, just the bottom part." The medicos were able to fit him with an artificial foot that he could now wear strapped to the stump of his leg. Since then, Miguel liked to joke about his foot, and he boasted that he sacrificed it for a noble cause, but he was bitter that he never again would be able to play football.

When the war ended in 1939, the two friends went separate ways. Pedro joined thousands of Loyalist refugees in their flight north to France. After a brief visit in Russia, he settled in Mexico in 1940 and, with the help of a friend from Spain, he opened the Florería Roma.

Miguel also fled from Spain, traveling first to Portugal, then to Argentina and Uruguay. After brief stops in Nicaragua and Guatemala he arrived in Mexico with barely a peso in his pocket. With a few well-placed phone calls, he tracked Pedro to Mexico City, where Pedro hired him to drive the Florería Roma's camioneta and deliver the flowers.

But poor Juan Pablo. Pedro smiled as he recalled how Ivan Pavlovich had adopted the Spanish version of his name when he arrived in Spain, so he could mingle better with the peasants. Juan Pablo never tried to hide his Russian heritage—he was proud of it. He was proud of the wonderful things the Revolution was doing to rebuild Mother Russia, and he was excited about his mission in Spain.

Juan Pablo came to Spain well ahead of the Civil War, and when the war broke out he was eager to help the Loyalists in their struggle against Fascism. He wanted to fit in with the rest of his brigade, but his thick Russian accent gave him away when he spoke Spanish. Pedro and the others joked about his splintered Spanish. "Please," they would say, "please do not slaughter our language—save your bullets for the Fascists."

Pedro sipped his drink and smiled when he recalled those moments. Some of his colleagues in the brigade would laugh, and protest that the language he and Miguel spoke wasn't even Spanish, and he would remind them that it was their heritage and their commitment to the cause that held them all together as comrades, regardless of whether they spoke pure Castilian or Catalan or Basque or Russian or even English.

Now Pedro missed his good friend and trusted comrade Juan Pablo, and he wished he could be with him here tonight. Pedro's eyes clouded as he recalled how poor Juan Pablo had died in his arms, coughing blood and struggling to speak, a bullet lodged deep in his chest. Juan Pablo, with all the strength he could muster, had pulled himself closer to Pedro and whispered, "Compadre Pedro, take care of my little girl. Watch over her. *Protégela.*"

Pedro took another sip of aguardiente, and muttered his comrade's last words. Watch over her ... protect her. Pedro felt honored that Juan Pablo had called him compadre with his dying breath, clearly implying that he wanted him to watch over his little girl as a true godfather. Pobre de Juan.

CHAPTER 52

The sound of the doorbell shook Pedro from his reverie, and he returned quickly to the present. He wiped his eyes with a sleeve of his shirt and jumped up.

"Ah, Professor, welcome," Pedro said. "Come in and have a seat and I'll pour you a drink. What can I get you? The usual?"

Jorge Bustamente, a tall, thin man with horn-rimmed glasses, corduroy jacket and the neatly trimmed beard required of a university professor, burst into the room and threw his arms around Pedro in a warm abrazo. *"Hola* Pedro. I was afraid I was going to be late. I was tied up with one of my students after class. Yes, let me have the usual. "

The Professor ignored the salt and downed his shot of tequila in one quick gulp. "I needed that. It's been a long day. What's this meeting all about? You didn't leave any details in your message."

"No, I couldn't say much. Sergio asked me to call the meeting. He'll explain when he gets here."

"Ah, the elusive Sergio. So, in effect, it's his meeting. Who else is coming?"

"Horacio, Miguel and José. They should be here any minute. Miguel's out making a delivery now."

The bell rang again and Pedro opened the door for José.

"Come in, take a seat. I'll pour you a scotch. Sergio and Horacio will be here any minute."

"Sergio's not here yet?"

"Apparently he's been delayed." Pedro capped the aguardiente bottle, set it on the sideboard, and pulled out a bottle of Cardenal Mendoza. He poured scotch for his newcomer, brandy for himself and another shot of tequila for the Professor, then moved the three bottles to the middle of the table.

"There, I've performed my bartender duties. From now on, you can get your own refills. Meanwhile, my friends, fix yourselves a *bocadillo*. The bread and the cheese are fresh, the sausage on the blue plate is picante, but the sausage on the other plate is mild."

"Your table, as always, is well provisioned," the Professor said, "as well it should be. I mean, how could we have an important meeting without good food and drink?"

"That's right," José said. "Engines like ours don't run on empty. We require plenty of fuel, good fuel like this scotch. But where the hell is Sergio?"

"He'll be here, don't worry."

"Yes, the body and the soul require fuel," the Professor continued, answering his own question. "But even with Sergio and Horacio, what about the others? Shouldn't there be more than six?"

Pedro took a sip from his snifter and laughed. "Well, for one thing, six bodies are just about all we can fit around this table. And for another thing, you four are the ones Sergio asked me to invite. This is his meeting.

"But in the meantime, let me tell you a little story, a bit of horticultural history, while we're waiting for the others. Years ago, when I was much younger, I learned my trade from *La Maestra de las Flores,* a wise old florist in Bilbao. She taught me an important lesson, a lesson for flower arranging and a lesson for life. When you want to make a beautiful arrangement in a vase, she said, you must first fill the vase with healthy flowers and buds and greens. Fill it up, she said. Fill it with as many as it will take, and the brighter the color the better.

"Then, with great care," he continued, pleased that he had the attention of the others, "you remove one-third and set them aside, and you rearrange the ones that are left. Then once again, you remove one-third. Now you can create a truly glorious display with the flowers and buds and greens that remain in the vase, because you've saved the best, and you've given them the space they need to breathe and flourish even more."

"What the hell are you talking about," José asked, not bothering to hide his irritation.

The bell rang before Pedro could answer, and this time the door opened without his help. "Ah, good evening, General," Pedro said. Come right in. I see you're wearing a suit and tie tonight."

"There's a time and place for everything," Horacio said, "but I didn't think your flower shop would be the right place tonight for my uniform. More to the point, I have another commitment this evening that won't require the uniform."

"Of course. We don't stand on formality here at the Florería Roma. You'll have plenty of time for that later on, and plenty of time to wear your uniform and your medals with great pride."

"That may be true, but right now I'm pressed for time. I can stay only a few minutes, so I hope this won't take too long. My driver's waiting for me by the curb out in front."

"Well, Sergio asked me to call this meeting. I'm not sure why, and he's not here yet, but let's make the most of your time here with us. This won't be a lengthy meeting. I think of this as a tertulia, just a friendly social gathering. Let me pour you a drink."

"Tequila would be good," Horacio said. "I see you have six chairs at the table. Who else is coming, and who's not coming?"

"Miguel will be here, of course. He's making a delivery. And Sergio will be joining us any moment."

"But where the hell is he?" José asked again.

"Apparently he's been delayed," Pedro replied, vexation in his voice. "He's a busy man."

"When did you talk to him?"

"Actually, it was last week. He had to go out of town for the week end, but he wanted this meeting set up for today.

"Meanwhile, I was just explaining why we're a small group tonight. Let me continue. When you remove the extra flowers and buds from your first bouquet, you don't throw them in the trash, you set them aside for further use. They still have value and they still have a purpose. At the proper time, they will be placed in another vase, another basket, for another display, ready to flourish when their time comes."

José scowled as he carved another piece of *chorizo* and a slab of cheese and laid them on a slice of bread. "What the hell are you talking about? Are you saying that flowers are people? And how will they know when it's their time to 'blossom,' as you put it?"

"Sergio will tell them, just as he'll tell us."

"So everything is up to Sergio? He's the key to everything?"

"No, not entirely," Pedro said. "We all know what our roles are, and we all know the timetable. We're not dependent on Sergio. We're all capable of acting on our own, but I believe he has information he wants to share."

"And what happens to your bouquet when a flower wilts?" José asked. "Surely you don't want to leave a faded flower in there with all your fresh blossoms."

"Certainly not," Pedro replied, grinning, and making a snipping gesture with the first two fingers of his right hand, "you must get rid of the withering flower. There's no room for a fading flower in a bouquet."

"So it's a case of the survival of the fittest?"

"Absolutely, whether it's flowers or people." Pedro laughed. "But that's a strange question coming from you, José, a question about flowers. You're in the flower business yourself, remember? At least that's what you told Banister Saturday night at dinner. But the truth is you don't know a damned thing about flowers, do you?"

"I guess I did say that, didn't I? That was just a convenient answer to his question. He asked me, 'what do you do, José?' and I sure as hell was not going to give him any details about what I do. I withdraw into a shell when Banister asks a question. I'm not certain if he's playing his role as a newspaper reporter, or if he's just curious, or making polite conversation, or sticking his nose in where it doesn't belong, probing for information I don't want him to have."

"Now, let me continue," Pedro said. "There's another important lesson I learned from La Maestra—"

"For Christ's sake, Pedro, forget about La Maestra, and come to the point," Horacio interrupted. "Your God-damned flowers can wait, but I can't. I have things to do."

"The General's right," José said. "Enough with the flowers. Come to the point, Pedro, in plain Spanish that we all can understand—if you can speak plain Spanish."

"Okay, I'll bring you up to date on my activities. You're all aware of the recent fires at Pemex facilities in several locations around the country. There've been a few small fires, all carefully planned, all carefully executed. These are the vanguard fires, I call them. You might say they're lighting the way to our future."

"*¡Ay, carajo!*" the Professor muttered. "Sure, the fires are spectacular, but the flames die down and the smoke blows away, and in the end only the ashes remain, and eventually the ashes blow away. I believe it's time for something concrete to happen, something that won't drift off with the breeze, something with lasting results."

"Patience, my friend," Pedro replied. "Remember, we're just a few flowers in a much larger bouquet. Yes, the flames die out and the smoke blows away, but the fires are doing their job, creating headlines, causing worry and concern and anxiety and even terror. And Pemex is feeling the heat."

José cursed. "But how long will we have to smell the smoke of your God-damned fires, and listen to you babble about flowers, while we sit around here and twiddle our thumbs?"

Pedro sighed and wiped his brow with a napkin. He could sense he was on the verge of losing control, and José was on the verge of exploding. "Patience," he repeated. "We're not twiddling our thumbs. By the way, José, I notice you're not twiddling your thumbs. You're putting them to good use, stuffing all the food you can into that cavernous mouth of yours.

"Believe me, my friends, things are happening," he continued. "You want action? We're getting action right now. These fires are an important part of the action."

José jumped up and shouted. "God damn it, we're wasting too much time on these fires."

Pedro's face flushed red with rage, and he slammed his fist on the table top. "Sit down and shut up! We are moving ahead. These are not piddling fires. Everyone has a role to play, a job to do. The fires are my job, and I intend to carry out my assignment, just as I know you all will do whatever you're assigned to do."

Pedro leaned back in his chair and lowered his voice, shifting into a diplomatic mode. "We all have to work together, work as a team. As I told you, Sergio will have further information for us when he gets here."

"But where the hell is he?"

Pedro struggled to contain his anger. "He'll be here. Now, like I said, we've hit Pemex with small fires, controlled fires, easy to set and easy to handle, and none of these fires has caused any real damage. Except last night. Three men died. Most unfortunate."

"Unfortunate for the men who died," the General said, "but in the greater scheme of progress, such things happen. War is inevitable, my friends, and in war, death is necessary. A few deaths here and there are insignificant when you consider the universal scope of our struggle. It's the outcome that's important."

"Comrades, our next step will be to carry the battle directly to the people," the Professor said, "right here in the Capital, and in Monterrey and Guadalajara and Tampico and all the other cities, and in every small village and all across the countryside."

"Soon there will be more fires," Pedro said, "even more spectacular than the ones Pemex refers to as 'routine.' Soon, all of Mexico will be ablaze, all our blossoms will be in full bloom. Soon everything will come together in one glorious battle."

"Yes," the Professor chimed in, "people will be rioting in the streets, people will be demonstrating in the Zócalo here in the Capital and in the plazas of every city and town in Mexico. Soon all the people of Mexico will rise up in anger. They'll rise up in protest against the incompetence of Pemex, against the injustice of capitalism, against the corruption of the PRI and the ruling class. The government will be crippled!"

The General jumped to his feet, slammed his empty glass on the table and strode over to the door. "But right now, Pedro, I can't delay any longer." With his feet set wide apart, he placed one hand on the doorknob and one hand on his hip. "My driver's waiting for me. I leave the details of the fires in your hands, Pedro. You know where to contact me." He swung open the door and left.

An eerie silence enveloped the room when the door slammed shut. "Horacio's a good man," Pedro said after a moment or two. "He knows his business."

"And he's enthusiastic," the Professor commented. "Enthusiastic, and dramatic. He stormed out of here like a pompous thespian in a Shakespeare tragedy."

"He's also ambitious, which is good. He sees this as a great opportunity for power and advancement. But we'll have to keep an eye on him. Sometimes ambition can be dangerous. Sometimes Mexico has been blessed, or cursed, with ambitious military men who—"

The sound of the front doorbell stopped Pedro in mid-sentence. "*¡Olé!* That will be Sergio now," he said. A broad grin swept over his face as he jumped up from the table, kicked the barrier rug out of the way, opened the double doors and hurried to the front of the shop.

CHAPTER 53

Pedro's shoulders slumped and his grin melted to a nervous frown when he opened the front door. "Oh … it's you."

"Hello, Pedro. I was just passing by and I saw the light through the shutters," Harry said, "so I thought I'd stop in and say hello to Rosa."

"Rosa's not here, but, uh … come in. This is a surprise. I didn't expect you tonight. A few of my friends are with me in the back room. We're having a little meeting, but we're about to wrap it up."

"I don't want to interrupt anything, I could come back another time."

"Oh, no, that's all right. Come in and join us. I closed the shop early today. I didn't realize the light in the front of the shop was still on."

Pedro took Harry by the arm and led him back through the workroom and through the anti-smoke doors to the meeting room. "Have a seat, and let me get you a beer. You remember José, of course, from our dinner Saturday night. We had a good time, no? One of my favorite restaurants. Good food and great entertainment, eh? Say hello to Professor Jorge Bustamente, the, uh … the academic anchor of our little group."

Pedro motioned to the empty chair next to his own spot at the table. "Let me clear a little space for you. I wasn't expecting you tonight." He removed the General's plate and glass, and he laughed a nervous laugh as he opened a bottle of beer and set it in front of

Harry. "I'm sorry, but it appears these starving vultures have finished most of the food."

Harry took a quick glance around the room, and his eyes paused at the clutter of empty and half-empty bottles and crumb-splattered plates on the table. "That's all right, Pedro. I'm not very hungry."

"No, Rosa's not here, just a bunch of old men enjoying a drink and a snack and a bit of idle men-talk. Macho kind of stuff, you know. Soccer and baseball."

"And bulls," Professor Bustamente added.

"Yes, soccer and baseball and bulls," Pedro said. "Are you a baseball fan, Harry?"

"Sure, we're all baseball fans up there, but baseball is popular here in Mexico, isn't it?" Harry recalled seeing a billboard just a few hours ago saluting the Veracruz Águila, champions of the Mexican League.

"Oh, yes," Pedro replied. "We're great aficionados of the game, and we have quite a few Americans playing here in the Mexican League."

For Christ's sake, Harry thought, I sure arrived at the wrong time. Pedro was all shook up when he saw me at the door. He was expecting someone else. He still has two more seats open at the table. I'm interrupting something, and these guys are on the edge of their chairs. They don't want me here, I'm not welcome. They're not here to talk about baseball or bulls, and they don't give a damn about the World Series.

The Professor jumped back in. "Tell us, Harry, who'll be playing in the World Series?"

"That's right, it's just about a month away, and it looks like it'll be another subway series, the Yankees against the Dodgers. The Yankees are hot. They beat up on the Washington Senators again yesterday. I believe—"

The alley door opened and Miguel pushed his way into the room carrying two empty flower pots. "I hope I'm not late."

"Not at all," Pedro said. You're just in time Your timing is perfect. Help yourself to a brandy and a little food, if you can find any scraps on those platters. You made all your deliveries with no trouble?"

Miguel hesitated, unsure of what to say. "Oh, the deliveries? Yes, the deliveries went well, but we have a problem with … well, we have a problem with one of the orders."

Miguel grabbed Pedro's elbow and pulled him over toward the door. "I just saw Orozco," he whispered, glancing at Harry and the others, "and he told me—"

"Later, Miguelito. Later. Problems can wait. I don't need any more problems right now."

Pedro turned and called across the room. "Harry, I'm sorry, but I'm afraid I don't know where Rosa is. We were just about ready to break up when you rang the bell. As you can see, the food is almost gone. There's still a little bit of bread, but not much to put on it. I knew you would want to stop by some time to say hello to Rosa, but I didn't think it would be today."

"That's right," José said. "We weren't expecting you."

Miguel slipped into the vacant chair across from Harry, poured himself a brandy and downed it fast. "I didn't think you'd show up at all," he said as he poured himself another.

"I guess Miguel doesn't trust you," Pedro grinned.

It occurred to Harry that he didn't trust Miguel either.

"I thought maybe you'd been attacked in a dark alley somewhere," Miguel continued. "You don't know your way around our city. You could get lost, you could get hurt, you could run into foul play."

Harry laughed. "Oh, I'm getting acquainted with your city pretty fast."

Miguel started to speak again, but Pedro cut in before he had a chance. "Miguel, you arrived just in time. Harry was just going to tell us who's going to win the World Series."

"I think the Yankees will repeat," Harry said. "They have all the big guns, like Mantle and Mize and Rizzuto."

José laughed. "You're right about that, the Yankees have the big guns, all right, and the big ships and the big planes."

Harry ignored the joke, wondering of it really was meant as a joke. "Say, Pedro" he said, quick to change the subject, "I think I just saw your friend the General out in front, the man I met the other night at the Brazilian embassy. I didn't recognize him at first. He was in civilian clothes. He seemed to be in a hurry."

"Yes, he was here, but he had to leave. He said something about an important commitment. You know how it is with the military brass. Always on duty, always on the alert. Did you get a chance to say hello?"

"No, he was standing next to a car, talking with another man. I don't think he saw me, and I didn't want to interrupt. I won't be able to stay long either. I need my beauty sleep."

"So you had a busy day today?" Pedro asked. "I know the horses weren't running today, so what did you do? Did you take another sightseeing tour?"

Harry hadn't planned on mentioning his Veracruz trip, but what the hell, he thought, they'll probably see my stories in the morning papers anyway.

"No, I had thought about going out to the Pyramids in the morning, and maybe playing a round of golf, but I had to do a little work today. I can't be a tourist all the time, much as I'd like to, so I went down to Veracruz and poked around at the scene of the fire, and I filed a couple of stories from there. I guess you could say it was sort of a sight-seeing tour. I saw a bit of Veracruz, and I just got back a little while ago."

Pedro drained his brandy snifter and set it on the table with a wave of his hand. "Ay, carajo, this Cardenal Mendoza is the best there is. It warms the gullet and the heart. You miss out on a good thing when you drink beer, Harry. So what did you find when you got to Veracruz?"

"Kind of a messy scene. Actually, I didn't write about the fire itself. The UP stringer handled that. I wrote about the two victims and their shattered lives. A human interest story."

"Two victims? I thought there were three people killed in that fire," the Professor said.

"Well, yes, three men were killed," Harry said, "but only two could be called victims. The third was the guy who set the fire, or caused the explosion, or whatever he did."

"So, he died, too," Pedro said, "but you might say he also was a victim—a victim of his own carelessness, his own ineptitude and stupidity, his own sloppy work. I'm afraid he won't be setting any more fires."

"Yeah, you're right, I guess you could say that. So tell me, what else have you men been talking about besides baseball and bulls? No serious conversation? Politics, maybe?"

José cleared his throat. "Well, we were just reviewing some of the things we talked about Saturday night at dinner—"

"Yes, we were just reviewing some of the things we talked about Saturday night," Pedro repeated. "You told us you were taught to write for the Kansas City Milkman when you joined United Press. Well, we would like to help the milkmen of Mexico—"

"And the plumbers and the farmers and the field workers and laborers all across the country," José cut in.

"Yes, we want to be sure they receive what they justly deserve—"

"Article 27 of the Mexican Constitution of 1917 says the land and its subsoil belong to the people," the Professor said, "and we believe that whatever comes from the land belongs to the people—"

"That's right," Pedro cut in. "Whether it's flowers or food or oil, everything that comes from the earth belongs to the people, and everything we do is for the people—"

"And for Mexico" José said, his voice rising. "Everything we do is for Mexico, and for the people of Mexico." He raised his glass in a toast. "To Mexico, and the people of Mexico, ¡Salud!"

Pedro, Miguel and the Professor joined in the toast, and Harry found himself raising his beer glass and clinking right along with the others. Pedro and José are going at it again, he realized, just like Saturday night, knocking that ping pong ball back and forth, finishing each other's thoughts and repeating their rant like mimicking mynahs. Are they both leaders, or are they both sheep, each one following blindly after the other? Who's really in charge here?

CHAPTER 54

José spoke with a subdued, almost sinister, voice. "Right now, we don't like what we see happening here in Mexico. There's too much hunger, and such terrible poverty. The wealthy have too much money, and too much land and too much power. And the poor have nothing. The poverty is horrendous."

Pedro cleared his throat and interrupted. "Harry, you said you saw signs of poverty during your Gray Line tour of our city?"

Harry thought about it as he lubricated his throat with a swallow of beer. They want signs of poverty? Okay, I'll give them some. "That's right. The tour guide didn't have to point it out. It was right there in front of me, right there for me to see. I saw one young mother, wrapped in a tattered shawl, sitting barefoot on the sidewalk, nursing her baby. She was holding the poor little thing up to her breast with one arm, and reaching her other hand out to people as they passed by, pleading for a coin or two.

"And I saw scenes of poverty last week during the bus ride down from the border. I saw it on the streets of Monterrey, and in every little village we passed through, and out in the countryside. Poverty. Nothing but poverty."

"There are millions of people here in Mexico," José said. "Some are rich, very rich, but most of them, I'm sorry to say, are poor. They have nothing. The poverty in Mexico is excruciating."

Pedro wiped his brow with his handkerchief. "It's tragic, the poor have nothing. The peasants come here to the Capital because there's nothing for them out in the country. They have no land, they have no jobs, they have no money, and they have no hope."

"And when they arrive in the city," José said, "there's nothing for them here either. The homeless and the hungry are helpless. They have no hope, and we want to help them, we want to give them hope."

"The government is corrupt," the Professor joined in. "Pemex is bulging with bureaucrats, the military is in turmoil. The peasants in the countryside are hungry and the students in the cities are restless. Wages are low and prices are too damned high. The economy needs help. The nation needs help."

"The country's heading down the wrong path," José said, "with too many things going wrong, and it's our mission to put the country on the right track. We're planting the seeds that will produce beautiful flowers for the people of Mexico, and ultimately, for the people of the entire world."

"Flowers?" Harry asked.

"Yes," Pedro said. "Flowers are the answer, flowers for the people. Flowers to make Mexico a better place, to make the world a better place." He paused, and the group fell silent.

In the silence, Harry took a long, slow pull on his beer, and thought about what he was hearing. They're planting flowers to help the down-trodden people of Mexico? And the world? What the hell are they talking about? How are flowers going to help the poor? How are flowers going to build a roof, or buy a pair of shoes, or pay for a liter of milk? What kind of crazy talk is this? These guys are really fired up, so I might as well toss a little fuel on their fire, and give them a little more of the stuff they want to hear. Let's see where it takes us.

"But the poor need more than flowers," Harry said. "They need real help. They need jobs. They need a roof over their heads. They need food in their stomachs and shoes on their feet and clothes on their backs. They need medical care. They need education. They need hope. I think of that barefoot young mother sitting on the sidewalk, plaintively pleading for a few centavos so she can buy an ear of corn and a couple of tortillas. The poor need a lot more than just flowers."

"Harry, I can see that you're a man of great compassion," Pedro said. "You understand the problem. Perhaps there are some things you might be able to do to help. You're a writer, perhaps you could write something for us, for example. You could write a press release, or maybe a tract or a pamphlet, promoting our project, explaining our mission to the public. You certainly must have a real talent for writing. Perhaps we could even pay you a small stipend for your work. I know you would like to travel and see more of our country, and I'm sure you might need the extra money."

José rose from his chair, wobbled, and lifted his glass to make a toast. A splash of scotch landed on the table next to Harry, with a couple of drops landing on Harry's cheek. "Yes," José cried out, "from each according to his ability, to each according to his needs."

Harry almost choked when he heard that hackneyed rhetoric. "You mentioned your trade association at dinner Saturday night," he said when he recovered his breath. "This is something new? How will your trade association help?"

"Well, yes, it is new," Pedro replied. "You might say it's still in the formative stage."

"What does your group do? I mean, why do you have to promote flowers? Everybody likes flowers. And how can flowers help the poor people of Mexico?"

"I'm glad you ask. We speak of flowers as symbols. We're talking about the miracle of nature that begins below the surface of the earth and, with help from the sun and the rain, blossoms into flowers that represent the peace and security of the people. Flowers are like oil, Harry, bursting through the rigid confines of the earth's crust and bringing peace and prosperity and enjoyment for all the people."

"Flowers are like oil?"

"Yes. Oil brings prosperity and security. Oil brings industry and jobs and progress, while flowers bring peace and pleasure and contentment. We want to do whatever it takes to bring that peace and contentment to the people of Mexico, and ultimately to the entire world. Simply put, we want to improve the lives of the people so they can appreciate the beauty of life."

"Sounds like a worthy cause, but how do you expect to accomplish this?"

No one hurried to answer Harry's question. Then the Professor broke the silence. "We want to break the debilitating stranglehold the capitalists have on the economy. We want to see a more equitable distribution of the products of the earth. We want to see a representative government, where the people have a voice in the important decisions that need to be made."

"In this way," Pedro said, "the people would be able to appreciate the beauty of the flowers that we offer."

"But you already have a representative government. You had an election just last month, and you have a new president taking over in December. Won't he be able to change things? Won't he be able to help the poor? Won't he bring economic reform for the country?"

José grunted. "The election was fixed. Ruiz Cortines has been Miguel Alemán's shadow for the past twelve or thirteen years. He followed Alemán as governor of Veracruz State, and then as federal Minister of Gobernación, and now he'll be following him in as president. And, of course, it's the same political party, the same group of thieving bureaucrats. It'll be more of the same capitalistic corruption."

"How are you going to accomplish that? How are you going to change the government? There's what, only four of you guys here how? How are you going to pull it off? What kind of support do you have?"

"We are not alone," Pedro said. "There's plenty of support for our movement. Those of us in this room tonight may be a small group, but we're part of a much larger group. We're a few small buds in a much larger, flourishing bouquet—"

"That's right," José interrupted, quick to steer the conversation away from Pedro's redundant rambling about flowers. "We're not just a bunch of football fans talking about next Sunday's big game. We're part of a well-organized movement of the people, on the threshold of a bold new venture, a glorious new era."

The Professor spoke out with an air of boastful confidence. "We're going to install Lombardo Toledano as our new president."

Harry bit his lip. Are these guys for real, or are they just plain crazy? Or is the booze doing all the talking?

"Lombardo Toledano? I read that he finished at the bottom of the ballot in the election last month. The people didn't vote for him then, why will the people accept him now?"

"Of course the people will accept him," the Professor said. "He's a man of the people. He's a great leader, a progressive, a humanitarian. We'll do like the PRI, we'll help the people decide. Sometimes the people need a little help in matters such as this, and we're only too happy to assist them. That's the way it should be, because we, after all, are the people."

"But Lombardo Toledano got barely two percent of the vote."

"And who was counting the votes? The PRI, of course, the party in power. They already had decided who was going to win. Anyway, I'm sure his vote tally was much higher than two percent, but we'll never know, will we?"

Harry recalled a tip he picked up from a grizzled old reporter his first week out of college: If you want to know the answer, you'd better ask the question. "How about these fires that are popping up all over Mexico? Are they part of your plan? Like that disaster last night in Veracruz?"

"We believe Pemex is a logical place to start," José said. "Pemex is an industrial giant, with claws that control the daily lives of the Mexican people in so many ways. We believe Pemex is sucking much of the lifeblood from the country."

"Let's not get into too much detail," Pedro said, "You and I can talk about it tomorrow, Harry, when we're rested and our minds are clear of the brandy and the beer."

Pedro pushed back his chair and rose to his feet. He tossed an empty bottle into a trash can and slipped his green notebook into the middle drawer of the armoire. He removed a salsa-splattered platter from the middle of the table and set it in the sink.

"You must be exhausted from your trip to Veracruz," Pedro said, "and, frankly, I believe some of us are a little tired, too."

Harry wanted to dig a little deeper, but he decided against it. The party's over, the food's gone, Miguel's half-drunk, Pedro wants to put an end to the discussion, and José sounds like a broken record spouting that tired old Marxist mantra. It's time to clear out.

Pedro moved toward the rear door. "Like I said, Harry, we were just about to break up our meeting when you arrived. We were expecting another member of our group to be with us tonight, but apparently he was sidetracked."

"Yes, I think he took the wrong train," José said, forcing a feeble chuckle. "He was sidetracked."

"I'm sorry there's no more food," Pedro said. "Tomorrow is another day, and tomorrow we can talk about what you can do for us."

"You're right, tomorrow's another day. I'll stop by here and you can explain what you would like me to do. Thanks for the beer and the hospitality. Right now, I'm heading back to the hotel to get something to eat and catch up on my sleep."

CHAPTER 55

The Professor gave Harry a scant sixty seconds to get out the door before he was on his feet and ready to leave. "I have a big day ahead of me," he laughed. "A very heavy class schedule."

José was right behind him. "I know," he said, "I also have to get ready for tomorrow. It's going to be a big day. Goodnight, Pedro. Good night Miguel."

In the sudden quiet that followed, Miguel poured another brandy for himself and one for Pedro. "This has been a long evening," he said.

"Much longer than I anticipated, made all the longer by the drinking, and you've had more than your fair share tonight, Miguelito. You should taper off now."

"Nonsense, and what the hell is my 'fair share' anyway? José said something about 'to each according to his needs,' and tonight I think I really needed it."

"And I think you've dipped into someone else's share as well. Mine, maybe. Why do you think you really needed so much, tonight of all nights?"

"For one thing, it was that gringo bastard, Banister. He dropped in here unannounced and pushed his way into our meeting. He doesn't belong here with us. He heard too much tonight. You and José and the Professor were revealing too much. He heard too much about our plans. He could be trouble."

"Yes, that was a surprise. I knew he would come sometime. I didn't expect it would be tonight."

"He heard too much," Miguel repeated, suppressing a belch.

"But he did add a spark to our gathering, a little spice to the conversation."

"This brandy added a bit of spark as well. It's the spark that lights up one's life. It's a worthy companion."

Pedro nodded. "Cardenal Mendoza is the only member of the clergy I care to spend any time with, but yes, he certainly is a worthy companion."

"You know, Pedro, I always figured you prefer Cardenal Mendoza brandy because of the name. Was the cardinal a relative? Was he your great-grandfather many times back? A distant uncle, or maybe a cousin?"

Pedro laughed "Well, we do share the name, and my family used to joke about it all the time at home, sitting around the dinner table. We joked that we might be descended from one of the prolific cardinal's bastard sons. But I doubt it. The cardinal came from Castile. My family, as our name reveals, came from somewhere high on a cold mountain in our *ama lur*, our Basque homeland. No, the reason I prefer Cardenal Mendoza brandy is because it's the best there is."

"I'll drink to that," Miguel said, draining his glass and quickly refilling it. "A toast to our ama lur… and a toast to the venerable Mendoza family."

Miguel downed his brandy, nodded, and continued. "This takes me back to our days together in the War, when we celebrated our little victories with a toast. But we never had the good fortune to taste brandy as excellent as this. Ours was mostly rot-gut."

"Yes, our little victories," Pedro said quietly. "We had many small triumphs, but we also had a few significant victories. We lost the final battle in Spain, but perhaps we are now on the verge of a much bigger victory."

The smile disappeared from Pedro's face as he capped the bottle and pushed it to one side. Miguel thought he detected a tear in Pedro's eye.

"But tell me Miguelito, now that the others have left us alone, what news did you bring when you arrived tonight? You said something about a problem? You can tell me now."

"Ay, yes, Pedro, I didn't want to tell you while the others were here, especially Banister and José. I don't trust José, or the Professor, either. I'm not sure I trust any of those bastards. Yes, we do have a problem. Sergio is dead. I don't know—"

Pedro slammed his fist on the table, shock and fear clouding his face. "*¡Ay, caray!* Sergio dead? How can this be? Why didn't you tell me? Sergio was supposed to be here tonight. He's the one who wanted this meeting. He asked me to call the meeting."

"I know. I wanted to tell you when I first arrived, but there were too many people here, especially that gringo Banister. I ran into Orozco earlier and he told me, but all he could say was that Sergio is dead. He didn't have any details. He didn't know when or where he died. He didn't know how he died, although he thought it might have been natural causes."

"Death by natural causes. That could be. Sergio's health was not good. He didn't take very good care of himself, leading a life of debauchery." Pedro chuckled. "You know they called him *El Mucho Mujeriego*."

"The great womanizer. That's what he was, all right. Always on the prowl."

"And yes, Sergio did have a bad heart. As a matter of fact he was hospitalized for a short time, two or three years ago. He was taking some kind of medication for his heart, nitro glycerin or something like that. But that's all Orozco said?"

"He didn't know any details, but he said he'd try to learn more before the night is out."

"Your friend Orozco moves in shadowy circles. He seems to know all the dark secrets of the city. But Sergio, dead? And Orozco doesn't know when? It must have been yesterday. I expected to hear from him yesterday, but he didn't call. Yes, it must have been yesterday. Or perhaps it was Saturday."

"Orozco said he'll call when he gets more information." Miguel finished his drink in one bold gulp, and he uncapped the bottle and poured himself another. "Sergio would be late for his own funeral. I didn't trust him. He was sneaky. You never knew what he was up to."

Pedro sat staring at his snifter, brooding. Miguel's right, he thought, Sergio was a devious question mark, sneaking around in the murky shadows, much like Miguel's friend Orozco. You never knew what he was thinking, and you never knew what he might do next. I'm not surprised that someone wanted him out of the way, for whatever reason.

In the silence of Pedro's contemplation, Miguel's eyes closed and his head nodded.

"I'm concerned about José," Pedro said after a moment or two. "He was on the muscle, talking like an angry man."

Miguel jerked his head up when Pedro spoke. "What did you say? You mentioned José?"

Pedro laughed. "You dozed off, Miguel. You've had a long day, and too much brandy."

"Just a momentary lapse. Yes, we'll have to keep an eye on José. He talks like a proud Mexican, but I'm not convinced. He wears his *mexicanismo* on his sleeve, like a badge of honor, but I'm always suspicious of someone who flaunts his patriotism and waves the flag like that. You're never certain where his loyalties lie."

"I agree, patriotism can be confusing. You and I are Spaniards, Miguelito, born and raised, but by blood and at heart we're Basques, and since the Civil War we've lived in a few other countries, you more than I. Now here we are, living in Mexico, yet we're members of a worldwide political organization that was started a hundred-or-so years ago by some radical old atheist descended from a long line of Jewish rabbis from Holland and Prussia. And we're working with the Russians on some sort of a convoluted international scheme I'm not sure I comprehend. Sometimes I wonder who I am, and what I'm doing here."

"I know what you mean. Many times, when the traffic is heavy and the noise is deafening here in Mexico City, I miss the fresh mountain air and the tranquility of our Basque Country. But tell me, Pedrito, what about Banister? Who is he? What is he?"

"Banister is a man of the people. He thinks like we do, he cheers for the underdog. He's a working man, a union man. He could be a great help to us, and I have a plan for him."

"I'm not sure about him. I wouldn't let him get too close. I don't trust him. He's smart, maybe too clever. He was asking too many questions, and you and the others gave him too much information tonight, too many details."

"He's a reporter, he was just asking questions. That's what reporters do. Perhaps he did hear too much tonight, but he'll be fine."

Miguel reached for the brandy bottle and poured himself another drink.

"Save a little of that for another day," Pedro said. "You've had enough."

"Don't worry, I haven't had all that much. I, like you, favor this Mendoza because it's the best. I don't think Banister will be around much longer anyway."

"Why do you say that? You think he'll leave? He just got here a few days ago."

"Strange things sometimes happen to tourists." Miguel paused, and then continued. "One never knows. He's a stranger in a strange land, a stranger in our city. Anyway, Rosa deserves better. She's a good girl."

"Yes, you're right about that, my friend, she deserves better."

"What about the Professor? Can we trust him?"

"Of course, the Professor is one of our stalwarts. He's ready to deliver. But I'm like you. I'm not sure about José. His motives are not the same as ours, Miguel. His patriotism, shall we call it, might blind him to the universal goals of our struggle."

"You're right," Miguel agreed. "I think he overdoes that patriotism talk. I'm always suspicious of someone who waves the flag that much. It's like he's trying too hard to convince us, like he's hiding something. He could be a bomb with a short fuse, just waiting to explode."

"But you, Miguelito, you're on edge tonight. You're restless. It seems you don't trust anyone. And you've had too much to drink."

"Yeah, perhaps I am restless, but I'm just being cautious."

"You know," Pedro said, speaking slowly and deliberately, "someone will take Sergio's place. Perhaps someone already has stepped in, and he'll make himself known to us very soon. The world doesn't stop with the death of one man."

"You're right about that."

Pedro slowly swilled his brandy in his snifter. "I was thinking earlier tonight, Miguelito, while I was alone here. I was recalling some of our battles in Spain. I remember what Colonel Gutierrez told us. He told us to keep ours eyes focused on the enemy we face, but also to keep an extra eye to our flanks and an extra eye to the rear, in case another enemy should surprise us."

Pedro stood up and set a dirty plate in the sink. "Come on, Miguel, let's get out of here. I want to go home and get a few hours' sleep. You should, too. You're half-way there already. We have a big day ahead of us tomorrow."

"That's okay, Pedro, you go ahead, I'll stay here a while longer. I want to talk to Orozco. I'll stay here and wait for his call. Anyway, there's someone else I have to call right now."

"Another call? At this hour? Your friends keep late hours."

Miguel poured himself another cup and picked up the telephone. "The city never sleeps, Pedrito."

CHAPTER 56

Harry settled into the back seat of the taxi and grinned as he recalled what Pedro said about oil and flowers. Prosperity and security … peace and pleasure. What kind of bullshit is that? Sure, flowers bring beauty, but flowers wither and die. Oil might bring some measure of prosperity, but oil also brings greed, and aggression, and war … and death. Ol' Uncle Pedro is a dreamer. Or he's some kind of nutcase. Or he's flat-out dangerous, and so are his friends.

"Drop me around in back when we get to the Del Prado," Harry said to the driver.

"Wouldn't you prefer the main entrance on Avenida Juárez? It's starting to get dark in back, but the main entrance is bright, and alive with people and music and excitement this time of the evening."

For Christ's sake, Harry thought, I've got another bartender moonlighting as a taxi driver. "I know, but I want to get out on Independencia."

"As you wish, but it could be dangerous back there."

The cabbie, of course, was right. Independencia was dim and nearly deserted, not the kind of place Harry wanted to be at night in a strange city. Saturday, coming back from the race track, it was still daylight and a lot of people were strolling along the sidewalk, and the back door was okay. "Yeah, take me around to the front. I'm basically a front door type of guy anyway."

And of course, the cabbie was right about the front door. Taxis and cars and limos hugged the curb in front of the hotel. The hotel doorman scurried up and down along the curbside, opening car doors, tipping his hat and smiling. The cabbie had to use his best aggressive driving skills to get close enough to drop Harry. Pedestrians, strolling or simply standing around chatting, filled the sidewalk in front of the hotel. A gutsy little boy, no more than nine or ten years old, flitted around in the crowd hawking Chiclets.

The lower lobby was alive with music, laughter and babble. Flags of various nations were draped over the mezzanine railings. Bankers Harry had seen during the last few days dressed in business suits now were decked out in tuxedos, escorting their wives or daughters or girl friends to cocktail parties before a formal dinner. Even the tourists, back from their Gray Line tours, had changed into respectable clothing. Over by the Grand Staircase, a guitar trio was singing a lively ranchera, adding to the party atmosphere.

I should've been staying here all along, Harry realized. This is my kind of place, my kind of action. As long as I'm on vacation, I might as well enjoy a little luxury while I'm at it.

Harry went to the men's room to make himself half-way presentable for Isabel. He splashed cold water on his face, combed his hair, and wiped the Veracruz grime off his shoes with a paper towel.

Out on the sidewalk again, Harry blended in with the crowd near the curb. Immediately, he was accosted by the Chiclets boy. Harry bought a pack of gum and stuck it in his pocket, somewhere near the cigarettes and his wad of business cards and notes.

This is the place to be, he decided. From this vantage point I can see all the cars as they approach. Isabel and Corbett may not realize it, but this is a race, a contest. I'm the prize, and I'm ready. Whoever gets here first wins me, and I'm betting on Isabel.

Harry kept his eye out for the little green Morris Minor or the blue Ford station wagon, hoping he would see the little green car first. What he was not expecting, however, was the black Ford Custom Fordor.

The doorman ran over and held the passenger door open as a man in a rumpled black suit stepped out. The man's fedora was pulled so low on his head that Harry could barely see his ears and his mustache, but he recognized him immediately as a plain clothes cop. Harry slid back deeper into the crowd.

The man in the fedora signaled his driver to pull ahead and park by the curb. Harry smiled a smile of relief when the two plainclothes officers walked into the hotel lobby.

"*Banister!*"

Harry turned quickly when he heard his name over the din of the traffic and the buzz of conversation.

CHAPTER 57

"*Banister!* Over here. Get in the car."

Tonight's sweepstakes winner had arrived driving a blue Ford Custom Deluxe station wagon. Damn it, Isabel and her little green car didn't make it in time.

The doorman opened the passenger door. "I tried to call you back," Harry said as he climbed into the car. "I wanted to tell you my date tonight is with a girl from Pemex. She was going to pick me up right here in front of the hotel, but you beat her to it."

"Sorry about that. I heard the phone ringing but I couldn't get to it. I figured it was you." He squeezed the car into the flow of traffic heading down toward the Zócalo. "I want to get us away from the Del Prado for now. Too much going on there, too many people. That's good you got yourself inside the Pemex organization so quickly, Harry. Who's the lucky girl?"

"I'm not inside the organization. I talked with her on the phone, but I don't really know her. Like I said, you got here first, and now I don't know when I'll get a chance to meet her."

"I'll get you back to the hotel in just a couple of minutes. Who is she?"

"A secretary. I talked to her on the phone this morning, and I called her from the airport when I got back from Veracruz and set up the date."

"Stick with her. She could be valuable."

Harry smiled. "That's what I thought. Say, what's going on here? You didn't say anything at breakfast about people getting killed in Veracruz. I had to read it myself in the morning paper."

"I didn't want to scare you away. I believe it's those God-damned Communists." He gave the accelerator an extra kick when he said that.

"This morning I thought you suspected foreign oil companies, the ones who lost out when the government took over back in '38."

Corbett cursed as he turned onto Calle Lopez. "Crazy people here don't know how to drive. That was one theory, and it's still a good theory. Especially the Brits. They're always bad losers. They're still fighting it.

"But I also think it could be the Reds. Our country is in danger, Harry, and you can help us get the information we need to defend it. Those God-damned Commies are everywhere."

Corbett leaned on the horn when a taxi cut in front of him. "Damned crazy drivers. And they're making a hell of a lot of noise back home in the States, and when I say Communists, I'm thinking about Russians. They're the quarterbacks, Harry. They're the ones calling the plays, or calling the shots, or barking out the marching orders, or whatever-the-hell mixed metaphor you want to use. I want to stop them here in Mexico, so they won't be able to get into our country by the back door."

"Cut 'em off at the pass, eh pahdner." Harry said, trying to keep the conversation light, but realizing immediately that he might have made a slip of the tongue.

"Partner? Does that mean you're coming in? You've decided to join us?"

"No, I didn't say partner, I said *pahdner*. That was a joke, a bad joke. I was just thinking of some old cowboy movie, and I'm still not interested in joining your club. But if the Communists are causing trouble here, isn't it up to the Mexicans to take care of it? Why should you have to deal with it?"

Corbett slowed for a pedestrian crossing the street mid-block, then slowed again to make a right turn onto Victoria. "Sure, I'd like the Mexicans to handle their own God-damned problems," he continued, "but I don't mind giving them a little help on this one, because this could turn out to be our problem, too. I want to find out who's coming at us from across the pond. I want to know about foreign intervention here in Mexico before it goes any farther. If there's a problem here, I want to know about it. I don't want it sneaking across the border like some God-damned wetback."

Harry smiled in the semi-darkness. Corbett was on a roll, caught up in his favorite topic.

"We're at war, Harry, and I'm not just talking about Korea. Sure, Korea's part of the problem, but Russia's our big enemy. Hell, they've got Russian pilots flying those MiG fighter planes in Korea.

"But I'll let Washington take care of Korea. I'm talking about the Cold War, and the Cold War is heating up. Russia wants to take over the world. The whole God-damned world."

Corbett hit the horn again. "But I don't want Russia to expand its foothold here in Mexico. It's too close to home. The Monroe Doctrine says a foreign power, meaning a European power, cannot stick its nose into affairs on this side of the ocean. Same with the Truman Doctrine. Like I said, Harry, we're at war now, and Russia is our enemy. Communism is our enemy."

Harry smiled again when Corbett made the turn onto Humboldt. "Are there many Communists in Mexico now?" Harry asked.

"Sure, plenty of them. The Party has a long and stormy history here, dating back to 1919. The Mexican government banned the party in 1930 and many members just went underground.

"A few years later, President Cárdenas rescinded the embargo and Party membership vaulted to forty thousand or so. The Reds were instrumental in the formation of the labor unions during that period, particularly the oil workers' union.

"The number of active party members has dwindled in recent years," Corbett continued. "According to our best information, there's only about five thousand members here now. Some of the Commies are home-grown, native Mexicans, while others are transplants from other countries, like the ones who came here from Spain after the Spanish Civil War."

"Did some of them come directly from Russia?"

"Of course, and there are thousands of sympathizers who are not active party members."

"The fellow travelers."

"Right. And the party has close ties to Moscow. From what we can tell, the Russian embassy here is crawling with MGB operatives—and believe me, we keep a close eye on their embassy. We know who comes and goes. For instance, we know you were at their party Saturday night. We know what time you arrived and what time you left."

"I suppose you know what I had to eat."

"Not quite, but I can guess you probably had codfish and borscht."

"Geez, I guess I'll have to be more careful what I do around here if you guys have a tail on me."

"We weren't really tailing you, Harry. We were simply monitoring the door from an apartment across the street. We like to keep an eye on the comings and goings at the embassy. You just happened to pop up. What did you learn while you were there?"

"Well, the codfish cakes were pretty good, but the beer was lousy. Beyond that, not much. I didn't stay very long, but I guess you know that, too."

"We keep tabs, Harry. Remember what I said at breakfast. Information is our weapon. Russia has agents living here and operating here right now—and has had, for a long time, thirty-five years or so. They've burrowed into Mexican life, living here as Mexicans, working in all sorts of peaceful occupations.

"They're everywhere, Harry. They're working here as bartenders, factory workers, farmers, engineers, secretaries, shopkeepers, clerks—you name it. They even have jobs in the government.

"They're hiding in broad daylight, Harry. They could be anywhere, and you never know who they are or where they'll turn up or when you'll run into them."

Corbett made the turn back onto Avenida Juárez, putting the Del Prado in view straight ahead. "I'll drop you in front of the hotel and you'll still have time to meet the girl—but tell me, what else did you learn in Veracruz?"

"Well, just about everything worthwhile was in the stories I filed with the UP. Mario—that's the union honcho I met at lunch—he said the third victim probably was the guy who set the fire, or the explosion, whichever came first. He said nobody recognized the body, so they figured the guy didn't work in Veracruz, but he apparently knew just what to do."

"So they know who did it, but they don't know who he was. Do they think he was working alone, or was there someone else involved?"

"I don't think those guys at the union hall know that much about it. The police would have better information. I'm sure they're working on it."

"But I want to know, too. This could involve us. See what you can find out. What else did you dig up?"

"Like I said, the good stuff was all in the stories I filed."

Harry groped in his coat pocket for one of the pictures of the dead man, pulled it out, and waved it in the semi-darkness. What the hell, he thought, I only need one of these things. "But you say your agency thrives on information. How's this for a piece of information?"

"What do you have there?"

"It's a picture of a corpse stretched out on a marble slab. Mario said they think it's the guy who set the fire."

Corbett pulled his station wagon up to the curb. "That's great, Harry. Good work. Let me have it." He reached over to grab the picture out of Harry's hand, but by then the photo was back in Harry's pocket.

"I'll hang onto this for now," Harry said. "I'll ask around and see if I can identify him. Might make a good follow-up story for me."

"For Christ's sake, who're you going to ask? You don't know anyone here. Let the pros handle this, Banister. You bring us the information and we'll process it. That's the way it works."

Harry decided Corbett was right. These guys are the pros. I don't really want to get involved in this. "Hey, I never said I was going to work for you. But I guess you're right, who am I going to ask? I don't know very many people here yet." Harry reached back into his pocket and pulled out the picture again. "Here, you can have it. This one's on me. See what you can do with it. Like you said, you guys are the pros."

"That's more like it. Now you're thinking. By the way—did you happen to look in that envelope I gave you this morning?"

"Yeah, I looked. I was curious"

"Did you count it?"

"No, I didn't count it, but it was a pretty hefty bundle. Geez, you guys sure have a lot of money to throw around. They're still printing that stuff up there in Washington?"

"Don't be a smart ass, Banister. How did you pay for the airplane to get to Veracruz? How the hell do you expect to charter another plane when you need one, without that money? That cash can help you enjoy your time here in Mexico, buy your beer when you're thirsty, buy something for your girl friends."

"Don't worry, your money's intact. I brought cash with me, and anyway, UP is going to cover my flight to Veracruz. They liked the stories I filed."

"You still say you don't want to work for us, after what you saw today in Veracruz?"

"That's right. Not interested."

"I know, you're just interested in having a good time. People like you could be the downfall of our country, Banister, always thinking of yourself. We need to be united, just like our name says, United States and united people. We worked together during the war, and God damn it, we won."

"Yeah, I know, we all did our part, and I did my part, too, and now I want to relax. I'm just not interested in going to work right now."

"What do you mean? You were working in Veracruz, weren't you, filing two stories from there? You're working now for the UP, aren't you?"

Harry laughed. "That wasn't really work. I went don't there on a whim because I smelled a story, and I picked up one story from the guys I happened to have lunch with and another story from a few strangers sitting on a park bench. That's what I call 'fun 'n' games.' And I did some sight-seeing while I was there, just like any other tourist."

"You're a tough man, Banister. Well, good luck with your date tonight. Have a good time, and while you're at it, find out if the girl knows anything. We'll be in touch."

The doorman approached as Corbett drove away. "Señor Banister, someone was looking for you earlier this evening."

Harry glanced at the spot where the black Ford was parked when Corbett arrived.

"Yes sir, the men who came in that black car asked about you."

"Really? They were asking about me?"

"Yes, Sir. They went inside the hotel. They probably inquired at the reception desk, or looked in the lounges. They asked me if I knew you and I said, 'no, I don't really know him.' Tonight was the first time I've really seen you in person, Señor, when you got into that blue car, and this is the first time I've talked with you, so it is true, isn't it? I don't really know you?"

Harry smiled as he glanced at the doorman's name badge. "Yes, it's true, Roberto, but I feel like we're good friends already." He slipped the doorman a ten-peso note.

"Perhaps more important, Señor Banister, a young lady in a little green car drove up just a few minutes ago and asked for you. I told her you had just gone off with someone and she said she was sorry she missed you, but she said she couldn't wait."

CHAPTER 58

Harry was still hungry. His first thought was to go directly to the lounge for a sandwich, but the parade of tuxedos and formal gowns in the lobby convinced him he should freshen up and change out of his grungy clothes. There was a crowd waiting by the elevators, so he headed for the service elevator he had used Saturday when he returned from the race track.

The dimly-lit service hallway was deserted and eerily quiet after the bustle of the lobby. Harry stepped into the elevator and pushed the button for his floor. Just as the doors were about to close, a man rushed out of the shadows, grabbed the doors to hold them open, and forced his way into the elevator.

"*Muy buena' tarde'* Señor Banister. Welcome, to my country."

The man shoved his hands into the pockets of his black leather jacket and grinned, with a shiny gold tooth reflecting the light from the elevator's overhead fluorescents. "I hope, you are having, a very pleasant visit, here in my country, Señor Banister, but I'm afraid, it will be a very brief visit. I have been asked to deliver, an important message to you …"

Harry recognized the lilting rural dialect of a Mexican vaquero or campesino, just like he heard Friday night in the Plaza Garibaldi. His muscles tensed and the hair on the back of his neck bristled.

Something's wrong here. "Who the hell are you? How do you know my name? *What's the message? Who sent you?*"

"*Ay, carajo*, that is not important, Señor Banister. Let me show you, what is important… *This* is what is important, *pendejo*." He pulled his hands out of his jacket pockets and lunged at Harry like a charging bull, aiming his head at Harry's midsection. With a knife in his right hand, he made an uppercut thrust at Harry's chest. Harry jumped backward and pivoted slightly to his left in a quick reflexive action. At the same time he brought his right fist down in a crunching chop on the side of the man's neck. He felt a sudden sharp pain in his left side where the knife point penetrated, just below his rib cage. The head-butt missed its primary target but caught Harry on the side of his stomach and left him momentarily gasping for air. Harry felt a throbbing pain in his right hand from the blow he delivered to the man's neck.

Momentum carried the cowboy crashing into the wall of the elevator cabin. He muttered a muffled guttural gurgle and crumpled at Harry's feet, blood gushing from his ear and his nose and his mouth. His knife dropped to the floor by his side.

His head reeling, Harry staggered when the elevator stopped at his floor and the doors started to open. He leaned against the control panel, partly to catch his balance and his breath and partly to collect his thoughts, and he pushed the *Close* button with one hand. When the doors closed he flicked the *Off* switch, reached down, picked up a piece of paper that had fallen from the cowboy's left hand, and shoved it into the side pocket of his own suit coat. Then he quickly rifled the cowboy's pockets. Nothing but a key ring, a roll of pesos and some loose change in the pants pockets. Nothing but a pistol, a glossy black-and-white photograph, a pack of cigarettes, and a scrap of yellow paper in the jacket pockets. He left the cigarettes, the money and the keys where he found them.

Harry flicked the toggle switch and let the elevator doors open and, as he stepped out, he pushed the button for the garage level. The doors closed and he walked calmly down the deserted hallway, as calmly as his shattered nerves and trembling legs, and the pain in his side, would permit.

In the safety of his room, Harry stripped out of his clothes and took a quick cold shower, carefully washing the small puncture on his side and getting the Veracruz dust off his body. Out of the shower, he sprinkled a little sulfa powder from his toilet kit on the wound and covered it with two Band-Aids. He started to shave, but gave it up when he realized the razor in his shaking hand might do more damage than the cowboy's knife.

Harry spread his dusty clothing out on the bed. He pulled Arnie's brochure from the inside breast pocket of the coat. The glossy brochure, folded twice, had formed a valuable piece of body armor sixteen sheets thick. The brochure, along with Harry's folded necktie, his notepad, a Veracruz street map and his quick evasive action, had prevented the cowboy's knife from doing any real damage, although the knife point did put a small hole in the fuselage of Arnie's plane.

I never did like that necktie, Harry decided, but it served a good purpose, and that was an old shirt anyway. I should be able to get the coat fixed, maybe re-woven.

Then, from the other pockets, Harry rescued the day's collection of business cards, photographs, and odd scraps of note paper, and laid them on the table next to his favorite chair by the window. He eased his aching body into the chair. With a shaking hand, he lit a cigarette and took a long, slow draw to settle his nerves.

Harry stacked the gallery of photographs on his lap. On top was the other Polaroid print Mario had given him in Veracruz. Harry felt a sudden sting in his side when he saw the dead man's face. That guy must have felt a hell of a lot more pain than I feel right now, but he also caused mountains of pain and anguish for a lot of people.

Harry set the Veracruz photo aside and picked up the crumpled picture his assailant had dropped from his left hand. It's a grainy copy of a Polaroid photo, Harry decided. Somebody had plastered the original with masking tape so that only my face would be seen in this copy.

Pretty good image of me, but it's a sloppy job of taping. A lot of the background shows up, even in black and white.

But who took the picture, and who wrote my name on the back, and who gave it to the cowboy? And why? Somebody sure as hell wants me out of the way.

Next, Harry looked at the photograph that came from the cowboy's jacket pocket. This looks like the kind of glossy black-and-white you might send out with a press release, Harry thought. A publicity shot, taken by a professional photographer. On the back, someone had scrawled a man's name, plus a single word and a number, with a black grease pencil:

Ivan Booth — negro — 39 —

Harry took another long pull on his cigarette. The guy who attacked me was carrying my picture, with my name on the back, so he could pick me out as his target. He had this picture of a man named Booth. Is he supposed to kill Booth too? And who the hell is Booth?

On a hunch, Harry picked up the phone and called down to the reception desk. "Do you have a Señor Ivan Booth registered in the hotel?" he asked. "That's 'B' as in Bravo." He waited for an answer. "No? Do you have a reservation for someone with that name?" Again he waited. "Nothing? Okay, thank you."

Next, Harry unfolded the scrap of yellow note paper he had pulled from the cowboy's jacket pocket. Three six-digit numbers, which Harry recognized as telephone numbers. He picked up the phone, asked for an outside line, and dialed the first number. He hung up after twelve rings. Nobody home, or maybe this is a daytime number, like a business or a shop or an office.

Harry dialed the second number. After just one ring, a loud, rasping female voice screamed at him. "Where the hell are you, *chinga'o hijo de puta*?"

Harry hung up in a hurry. The cowboy's wife? Or his girlfriend? Whoever it is, she's one angry bitch. I sure as hell don't want to meet up with her.

A knock on the door startled Harry as he dialed the third number. Don't tell me that guy is back for more action? I thought I laid him out pretty good.

Harry put the phone back in its cradle and cautiously moved toward the door. He hesitated by the night stand and picked up a heavy glass ash tray. He stopped at the door, listening, hoping to hear any telltale sounds. Nothing, just another knock.

"Who is it?"

"The bellhop, Señor Banister. I have an envelope for you."

"Slide it under the door."

"I cannot do that, Señor, it's too thick to fit under the door. Besides, the messenger said it had to be delivered to you in person, as soon as possible."

"You didn't have to bring it up to the room. You could've phoned me and I'd pick it up later down at the desk. Who's it from?"

"I don't know, Señor. A messenger delivered it. He said it must be delivered to you as soon as possible."

Harry opened the door a crack and took the envelope. He returned to his chair by the window and opened the envelope. Inside were three mimeographed pages. He read the pages carefully, read them again, and put them back into the envelope. He slipped the envelope, along with his collection of photos, cards and miscellaneous notes, under his shirts in a dresser drawer.

A sandwich and a beer would taste good, Harry thought, right now and right here, in the solitude and comfort of this room. I could call room service, but I can't hide here forever. That guy might be on his feet, and coming after me. He knew my name and he knew my face, and he'll know where to find me. A sandwich will taste a lot better downstairs, when I'm wrapped in a crowd of people in the wide-open lounge. There's safety in numbers. No more dark streets and no more dingy service elevators.

Harry put on a sport coat, buttoned it, and checked his image in the full-length mirror. Satisfied that he looked half-way presentable, with no unsightly bulges, he left the room.

CHAPTER 59

The Salón de los Candiles was nearly full, but Harry found a small table against the wall, where he could see most of the room and keep an eye on the entrance. He looked around the room, checking faces at the other tables. A room full of strangers, all having a good time. He flagged down a waiter and ordered a beer.

Jesus, he thought, that was close. Too close. I was lucky, landed a lucky blow. Maybe I should check out of here and try a smaller hotel. Better yet, maybe I should clear out of Mexico and get on over to Cuba, or down to South America, or even Guatemala. Yeah, that's it. Guatemala's closer. I could check out right now and catch—

A soft, melodic voice interrupted his escape plans. "Pardon me, sir. Is this seat occupied?"

Harry looked up, and there she was, just like on the bus last Wednesday, as beautiful as ever, her blond hair falling loosely over one shoulder.

"No, no it's not," he replied, smiling and jumping to his feet, "but it's your seat now. I've been saving it just for you. Sit down and let me buy you a drink. How about something to eat? I was just about to order something, maybe a chicken sandwich?"

Rosa smiled, and forced a timid laugh. "No thanks, I'm not hungry, but I couldn't resist asking you if the chair was occupied. That question worked so well on the bus, and I was hoping it would work again."

"No problem. Hey, no matter what you said it would've worked. When you asked me that question on the bus, it reminded me of what the Frenchman said to Bogey at the end of *Casablanca*, 'this could be the beginning of a beautiful friendship.'"

"Or maybe the beginning of a beautiful romance?" Rosa replied, her voice rising as she posed the question. Then she blushed. "Oh, Harry, I hope that didn't sound silly. How can I mention romance? A true romance, I should think, would take time, and closeness, in order to mature, and we haven't had a chance to be close. We've hardly had a chance even to be together. We've only known each other a few days, and it seems like I've been running away from you most of that time."

"Yeah, it does seem like it. I guess you've been kinda busy—I haven't seen you since dinner Saturday night."

"I know. I'm sorry, Harry, and it seemed like Pedro was trying to keep us apart. Every time I tried to say something to you, he cut me off. He can be so domineering. I wanted to see you yesterday, Harry, and I wanted to see you last night, and I've been thinking of you every moment."

A bright smile momentarily lit up Rosa's face, but her sad blue eyes revealed the anguish of a long and troubling day. The three white roses on her lapel had taken on a pallid yellow tint. "I tried to call your room just now, and then I looked here in the lounge on a hunch. I'm so happy I found you."

Harry shifted his chair and took a quick glance around the room. If she could find me that easily, he thought, so could anyone else. I'm a God-damned sitting duck. "Well, I'm glad you found me, too. Sure you don't want something to eat? Maybe we could go into the Versalles, have supper and catch the show."

"No, I'm not dressed for the night club. Let's stay right here, and you order a sandwich."

"Okay, and let's see if we can pick up where we left off Saturday night."

"Yes, that was so frustrating. Pedro and José monopolized the evening, talking about sports and talking about the poor people of Mexico. That's all they ever want to talk about. Then Pedro pulled me away from you and took me home. I wanted to talk to you, Harry. I wanted to be with you."

"I know. Those guys sure were wound up. They were going at it again a little while ago, over at the Florería Roma."

"What are you saying? You went to the flower shop?"

"Sure, I stopped by. Pedro invited me, remember? He said I could drop in any time. I was hoping you'd be there, but it was just Pedro and a few of his cronies. They'd finished most of the food by the time I got there. They'd polished off a lot of booze, too"

Harry wondered if Rosa knew what was going on in the back room of the flower shop, so he decided to test her reaction. "They sounded like a bunch of crazies, ready to save Mexico, ready to save the world. They sounded like a bunch of Communists, ready to overthrow the government."

"Yes, I think his friends are a little crazy. They're like wild-eyed fanatics, and when they get together in the back room they do a lot of drinking. It seems like there's a constant flow of traffic at the flower shop, in and out through that alley door. Sometimes it's one, sometimes two or three together. They frighten me, and sometimes Pedro frightens me, too."

Rosa chuckled softly. Her voice dropped to a near whisper. "Dear old Uncle Pedro. He loves his flowers, and he's such a gentle old teddy bear when he's working with his flowers. He's been so good to me since my mother died, but he can sound so cold, even ruthless, when he's with his little group. They bring out the worst in him. And they were talking about overthrowing the government? You can't be serious."

"Yeah, but it might have been the booze that was doing all the talking. If they're really serious, why would they be talking like that with me in the room? They're an odd group. Who are they? What are they up to?"

"I'm not sure. Pedro truly is an enigma, Harry. When he's taking care of his flowers at the Florería Roma, he's all business. He loves his flowers. Sometimes he's even like the capitalists he berates so virulently. Then, he is a capitalist, determined to do a good job and make a profit for his flower shop. It certainly is ironic that he can arrange such beautiful floral displays with one hand, and engineer such horrible events with the other. He's like two different persons."

"Horrible events? What horrible events?"

Harry's question caught Rosa by surprise. She raised her head and sat up straight. "Oh, I don't know, Harry, I guess my mind was wandering. Pedro's been so kind to me since my mother's accident, and he's taught me so much about flowers. He lets me do whatever I want in the shop, designing floral arrangements and making baskets for customers. He trusts me with flowers. He won't let Miguel do any of that."

"Why not?"

"Miguel is color blind. He can't tell one flower from another by the color. Everything is gray to him. He can judge only by the shapes of the blossoms and the leaves, or perhaps by the smell, and he doesn't do very well with that either. Even more important, he doesn't have the passion for flowers that Pedro has."

"Or the passion you have," Harry said, smiling.

Rosa blushed. "Yes, I guess I do love flowers. They bring so much beauty to life."

Harry smiled, recalling something Pedro said earlier. "But a flower shop is an odd place for Miguel to be working."

"Yes, it is. Pedro always tells him, 'I'll fill the baskets, and you deliver them.' But Pedro is loyal. He and Miguel are old friends, from their childhood days in Spain. Pedro has been good to him, providing him with a job when others might have turned him away. Miguel looks up to Pedro as his mentor. Miguel will do anything Pedro asks him to do, and sometimes Pedro asks him to do things outside the normal routine of the flower shop."

Rosa looked down at her hands folded in front of her on the table. "And sometimes Pedro asks me to do some strange things, too, and usually I do what he asks because I feel compelled by gratitude, or maybe it's loyalty, or maybe I'm just afraid to say 'no.' But lately, since my mother died, he tries to interfere too much in my personal life."

"You mentioned your mother's accident. I didn't know she had an accident."

"Oh, I guess I didn't tell you. She was killed in a car crash, God rest her soul." Rosa touched her forehead, as if to make the sign of cross, and then pulled her hand away.

"I'm sorry to hear that, Rosa. What happened?"

"Her car went off the road one night near the Tres Marías pass, when she was driving home from Cuernavaca. She was alone in the car. She was always such a good driver, a careful driver. I never knew for sure how it happened." Rosa paused, and took a sip of her drink.

"When did this happen?"

"Just a few months ago. The police investigated, but they said they couldn't determine what caused her to go over the side. Perhaps she was driving too fast, in a hurry to get home. Perhaps she fell asleep, but I never believed that. Tres Marías is not that far. Maybe she was trying to avoid something in front of her on the road. A cow, maybe, or a dog or a boulder. Or perhaps another car. I don't know. The road is so treacherous, with so many hairpin turns, but she was always such a good driver."

"Yeah, those mountain roads are dangerous. You say the police investigated?"

"Yes, but they said they couldn't be certain. Perhaps the brakes failed, they said, or the steering gear, but the car was mangled so badly they couldn't be certain. Their report said it was 'careless driving,' but I never wanted to believe that. She was always such a careful driver. I'm not certain how carefully they investigated."

"And then Pedro gave you this job?"

"Yes. I had been working part time, learning a few of the basics of floral arrangements, learning something about the business. Pedro is a good teacher—he certainly knows everything there is to know about flowers. Then, right after she died, he offered me a permanent full time job. I guess he felt sorry for me."

"Or he needed you, Rosita. I think you know enough about flowers and the flower business to run the shop by yourself anyway."

Rosa sat silent for a brief moment. "Or he wanted to control me, wanted to run my life, now that she was gone. Pedro and my mother were friends for a long time, but it seems they were always fighting about something. They argued about politics, they argued about religion, and they argued about soccer. They even argued about how to run the flower shop. And often they argued about me, about what I should do or should not do." Rosa laughed. "They argued like an old married couple. You know, the kind you see in the movies. Sometimes he was so kind to me, but he also could be so overbearing."

Rosa paused, and took a sip of her vodka. "Who was there tonight?"

"Well, Miguel, of course, and Horacio the General. I don't know his last name."

"Oh, yes, that would be General Horacio Suárez de la Garza. I think he might be from somewhere up north, perhaps from Monterrey. He comes to the shop from time to time to visit with Pedro. He always comes in the alley door and they meet in the back room."

"He was leaving when I arrived. I didn't recognize him at first, dressed in mufti. I saw him getting into a car, but I didn't get a chance to talk to him. He was talking to his driver, and he looked like he was in a hurry."

"He was in civilian clothes? That's strange. I don't know him very well, but every time I've seen him he's always been in uniform. I think he loves his uniform so much he wears it to bed. He's such a pompous popinjay."

"Yeah, I got that same impression the other night at the Brazilian embassy party. He likes to strut and show his medals."

"Oh, I think half those medals are phony, but they do look impressive. I think he bought them at the Monte de Piedad."

"The Monte de Piedad?"

Rosa laughed. "Yes, that's the national pawn shop. You can find all sorts of things there—jewelry and luggage and clothing, or watches and clocks, you name it, and they've got it. And military medals, too, I suppose. Who else was at the flower shop?"

"José, the guy from the dinner party at La Gran Tasca."

"I don't know much about him, either. I don't even know his full name, and I don't know what he does for a living. He said he's in the flower business, but I don't believe him. He doesn't know that much about flowers. He said he grows flowers, but he's not one of our suppliers. I don't know why he said that. Maybe to impress you."

"Or maybe to mislead me."

"Yes, that could be. He's a mystery man. Like the others, he always comes to the back door. Maybe he's afraid the flowers in the front of the shop will bite him. Who else was there?"

"Well, there was a professor from the National University."

"Oh, yes, that would be Professor Bustamente, Jorge Bustamente. He's an odd one. You know, the typical college professor, with his nose always in his books."

"What does he teach?"

"Economics, I believe. He usually comes alone to the shop, but sometimes he comes with one or two of the others."

"Yes, tonight he was part of the group."

"All those friends of Pedro's are a scary group—Harry, I want to talk to you. There's so much I have to tell you."

"Okay, you can start by telling me where you've been, what you've been up to. We keep missing each other. I followed your instructions yesterday, and I splurged on a three-peso seat in the shade, and the matadors were brave and the bulls were brave." Harry grinned, "One in particular, but it would've been a lot more fun if you had been there with me."

"I know, I'm sorry about that, Harry, but let's plan on going to see the bulls next Sunday. I tried to call you this morning at the Hotel Comé. You already had left, but they told me you had moved here to the Del Prado."

"Yeah, it's a lot livelier here—in more ways than one." Harry laughed when he said that, and he felt a twinge in his side. "So where've you been? Running around all over Mexico?"

"Oh, Harry, there's something I have to tell you." She paused, and looked down at her hands, now clinched into two tight fists. "Saturday morning Pedro asked me to do something for him. I didn't want to, I didn't want to do it, but he told me I had to—"

A bustle of boisterous bankers burst into the bar and interrupted Rosa in mid-sentence, while a half dozen uniformed and plain clothes police gathered just outside the door. Harry recognized the two detectives he had seen earlier in front of the hotel. He grabbed a passing waiter by the arm. "What's going on?"

"Oh, there's been a slight problem."

"What happened?"

"It seems a man has died. They found his body in an elevator."

Harry put on his best expression of shock and surprise. "A man died? In an elevator. That's terrible. What happened?"

"I'm not sure, Señor. Someone said he had a heart attack, but one of the bellhops said he heard that the man had been murdered."

The waiter turned to move to another table, but Harry grabbed his arm again. "Murdered? Who was he? A hotel guest?"

"I don't know, Señor, but it's possible. He could have been a high-ranking government official from right here in Mexico, or from anywhere in the world. A lot of important people from countries all around the world are in the hotel this week."

"You say he died on an elevator?"

"Yes, sir. A service elevator. That's where they found him, just a short time ago."

"And they think it might have been a heart attack?"

"The bellhop said he had been murdered, and bellhops always seem to know what's going on around here. The police are still down in the garage. Just think, he could have been having a cocktail right here in this lounge, Señor, sitting right here at one of these tables, maybe that table right next to you."

"You mean right here in this lounge?"

The waiter grinned, his face lighting with the excitement of the event. "Yes sir. It's possible. He could have been sitting right there where you're sitting now, or he could have been sitting at the table next to you, having a drink, and now he's dead. Murdered. Excuse me, Señor, I must see to those people over there."

"*Oh my God*," Rosa gasped. "How *horrible*. The poor man, murdered, and he might have been sitting right here at that table next to us." Instinctively, she brought her right hand to her forehead and made the sign of the cross. As she finished, the silver charm bracelet dangling from her wrist snagged the roses on the lapel of her jacket and pulled them away. She caught the flowers and quickly pinned them back on.

Holy Christ! It struck Harry like a bolt of lightning. Old habits never die. She used her thumb and first two fingers to touch her forehead. Then she touched her stomach, then her right shoulder… and she ended by touching her left shoulder. That's the Orthodox way of making the sign of the cross. The Russian way of doing it. My God, *Rosa is Russian!*

Rosa recovered quickly. "How horrible! A man died while we were sitting here chatting. What a terrible shock."

What a shock is right, Harry thought. La Rosa Blanca, the essence of everything Mexican, is Russian. The girl who loves Xochimilco and Taxco, and the Alameda and the Plaza Garibaldi. The girl who knows the words to all the mariachi songs. The girl with all those little Mexican charms on her bracelet. The china poblana, the typical Mexican girl … *Russian.* Son of a bitch, she sure had me fooled.

Something flashed into Harry's memory: They've burrowed into Mexican life … they're hiding in broad daylight … they could be anywhere … you never know where they'll turn up.

Harry took a gulp of his beer. "No, Rosita, I don't think so. I'm sure he must have died earlier, but the news is just now spreading through the hotel. A lot of things can happen in a hotel as big and as busy as this, with so many people coming and going. You sure you're not hungry?"

Before she could answer, the guitar trio strolled over next to their table and struck the opening chords of *México lindo y querido.* Rosa leaned over and clutched Harry's arm. "Harry, let's get out of here," she whispered. "I don't want to hear that song. Not right now. Let's go somewhere else. *Please.*"

"I know just the place."

CHAPTER 60

Harry had counted six candles in the dresser drawer at the Hotel Comé when he checked in last Thursday. Later that evening, in his room in the Del Prado, he counted ten candles in the drawers. He since learned that the rooms in every hotel in Mexico City, even rooms in every private home, are stocked with candles to light the inevitable darkness during the frequent power outages. The city's power grid had been unable to keep up with the frenzied growth of the sprawling Federal District, and summer thunder showers made the problem even worse.

But tonight there had been no outage, and the power was on at the Del Prado. Harry closed the window blinds, switched off the bedside lamps, and lit four candles. He thought candlelight would be more appropriate for the occasion. Candlelight is soothing, he reasoned, and brings tranquility. Candlelight has a way of subduing inhibitions, untying the tongue and encouraging a free flow of whispered words, much like a beachside bonfire inspires scary ghost stories.

And, perhaps most important, candlelight casts a romantic spell.

The room was quiet now, and the candles were burning down. Two already had gone out, but the two remaining stubs continued to cast mesmerizing shadows on the walls of the room. The only other light was the soft glow of Harry's Camel. When he drew on his cigarette the ember momentarily brightened, and he could see tears on Rosa's cheek. He gently kissed away a tear. A second tear dropped softly on his chest.

"You're crying."

"This wasn't supposed to happen," she whispered. "Not yet, anyway."

Rosa sat up, pulling the top sheet loosely over her bare breasts, and the words began to flow. "Oh, Harry, of course this was supposed to happen. I knew it, and you knew it. I just didn't know when. How wonderful everything is with you tonight, *mi vida*. This is our special moment." She eased back into the crook of Harry's arm, resting her head gently on his shoulder.

"I was afraid, Harry. I was afraid I would never see you again after I left the Restaurante 33, but what a wonderful surprise it was to see you at the flower shop, and then at the Brazilian embassy. Those people wanted to talk about nothing but politics and sports, and I was so bored. Then you joined us, and you brightened my evening.

"I was afraid Pedro would say something to spoil it, but thank God he didn't. Sometimes he can be so possessive, so domineering, as if he thinks he's my father.

"And I was afraid you wouldn't see me across the dance floor, and I would have to leave without you because Pedro was in such a hurry and I thought he would tell me to go with him and I wanted to talk to you in private, just the two of us, without all those people.

"And when we left the Plaza Garibaldi, I wanted to tell you what happened at the restaurant, but by the time the taxi got to the Hotel Comé I guess I just lost my nerve."

Harry pulled on his cigarette, and he could see more tears on Rosa's cheeks. She's rambling, he thought, but that's good. Let her talk.

"And here we are now, just the two of us, just as God meant it to be. I knew this was going to happen, I just didn't know when. Oh Harry, *mi amor*, this has been so wonderful… just like I knew it would be. You're so tender, and so thoughtful … but you're so strong … you're *muy macho*."

She paused, and in the fading light of the remaining candles, Harry could see that her smile had disappeared. He pulled her closer and kissed her eyelids and her cheek.

"Then Pedro asked me to join him for supper at La Gran Tasca, and he said you would be there, too, and when he said that I was elated, but I didn't have much chance to talk to you, with Pedro and José carrying on the way they did.

"But I want to tell you now what happened. I was going to tell you when we left La Gran Tasca, and I wanted to go with you then, and I wanted to be with you, mi amor, and hold you, and kiss you, and love you, but Pedro wouldn't let it happen. And I wanted to tell you yesterday, but Pedro had other plans for me. He's so controlling."

Harry knew she couldn't keep it bottled up much longer.

Rosa hesitated, unsure of how to begin, and then she told him what happened last Thursday night in the back of the Bar Restaurante 33.

CHAPTER 61

When Rosa finished her brief tale she looked at Harry and asked, almost pleading, "You do understand, don't you Harry?"

"Yes. I understand."

"It all happened so fast. It was like a horrible nightmare. I was so frightened. He tried to force me to go with him. He was going to take me out the back door, and he was hurting me. I told him last week, and I told him again in Pachuca, that I would never go with him, but he was so persistent, so strong ... and so forceful. I had to protect myself, Harry. I was so afraid of what he would do. I didn't want to go with him. He was such a horrible man. He was hurting me, his grip was so strong, and he had a gun in his other hand. I was afraid he was going to kill me, and when he raised his gun I reached in my purse and I did what I had to do, as quickly as I could. And then I left. I didn't want to come back to the table because I didn't want to involve you."

"Where did he want to take you?"

"He wanted to take me out of the country, but Mexico is my home, Harry, and I don't want to leave Mexico."

Harry gave her a little tug on the shoulder, and he kissed her forehead. "I understand, Rosita. I don't blame you."

Rosa paused to catch her breath. "But now I'm afraid what will happen next. Will someone come looking for me? I'm afraid the police will arrest me. Oh Harry, I'm so frightened. What will I tell Pedro? Sometimes I'm so afraid of him, too."

"Don't worry, Rosita. Everything will be all right." Harry kissed her on the cheek and gently squeezed her shoulder. "Where did you get the gun?"

Rosa leaned back and retreated once again to the crook of Harry's arm. "My mother gave it to me. She gave it to me for protection. She said every girl needs protection. I had it in my purse."

Harry remembered Rosa at dinner Thursday night, bottom-fishing in that over-sized purse, trying to find a scrap of paper to jot the name and address of the restaurant on Morelos. "So you had the gun with you all evening. Did you think you'd need it when you were having dinner with me?"

"Oh no, Harry, of course not. I was never afraid of you, but I didn't know what he would do after we left Pachuca. I was afraid he'd follow me again."

"And obviously he did," Harry said. "I understand, Rosita. I saw what he was like, how rough he was. You had the gun with you on the bus?"

"Yes, I had it the entire trip."

"Great. I'm glad I didn't know. When you slugged him in Pachuca, you could've shot him right then and there."

"Oh, no. I never did intend to shoot him. He had me by the arm, and he was pulling me, and I slapped him just to make him let go. Then those men grabbed him and threw him out the back door."

"Yeah, that sure helped. Do you always carry it?"

"No, I've kept it hidden in my closet ever since my mother gave it to me. I've always been afraid of guns, ever since I was a little girl, and I've certainly been afraid to carry a gun. At first, when she gave it to me, I didn't think I would need it, and I put it away, but lately, since she died, I've been carrying it in my purse all the time."

"Good thing you have a big purse. How did your mother happen to have a gun?"

"It was my father's. When he died, she kept it. Then she gave it to me."

"Did she give you the bullets for the gun?"

"Oh, yes, she gave me three boxes. I've kept them hidden in the closet, too."

"And where's the gun now?"

"In my purse."

Harry looked over at the chair in the corner of the room, barely visible in the fading candle light. He felt a sudden jab of pain in his stomach when he saw the purse on the chair, partially hidden under her clothes.

"Of course, I didn't have it Friday evening at the embassy party. It wouldn't fit in that little clutch purse I was carrying, but the next morning I got it out again. I worry that Sergio was not alone. I know he's not alone."

"Sergio?"

Rosa hesitated. "Yes. That's his name. Even now, I'm afraid someone else will come after me. I'm afraid the police might stop me and discover the gun."

"And this guy—Sergio?—just showed up, unannounced, in the hallway at the restaurant? You didn't know he was coming?"

"No, I didn't know he was there. I thought I was through with him. I hoped I was through with him."

"Well, you're sure as hell through with him now."

"Yes, I'm through with him now, but am I? I mean, what about the police?"

"We'll worry about them later. It's been four days, and they haven't come after you yet."

"But what a shock it was when I saw him in the back of the restaurant. I thought I made it clear to him in Pachuca. He must have followed me to the restaurant. He must've been sitting at the bar, watching us all the time we were having supper. He must've seen me get up from the table and he hurried back into the hallway and he was waiting for me when I got there."

Rosa gently touched the Band-Aids on Harry's side and squeezed his hand. She turned to look in his eyes. Her voice dropped to a near-whisper as she repeated the question she had asked before. "You do believe me, don't you, Harry?"

"Sometimes I find it hard to believe you, Rosita. For one thing, I never did believe he was your ex-husband."

"Oh? Why do you say that?"

"Because I didn't think you'd ever been married. You said you lived with your mother until she died, just the two of you, and that you still live in the same house. Also, I didn't think any man in his right mind would drive up to Pachuca, in the middle of the night, just to make an alimony payment that he didn't want to make in the first place. It didn't make sense."

"You're right, I've never been married. That was the first thing that came to mind when you asked me about him on the bus. It was all I could think of. Harry, I was so afraid when I saw him in the back of the restaurant."

"Rosita, there's another thing. On the bus you said you'd been visiting your sister in Nuevo Laredo. You don't have a sister, do you?"

"Oh, Harry, I'll explain all that to you, but not now. I've already told you more than I should have. I don't want to spoil our wonderful moment. This has been so delightful with you this evening. This is an evening I'll cherish forever."

"You're right. I'll hold off the questions." Harry kissed her on the forehead and gave her hand a gentle squeeze. And he glanced at her purse, barely visible in the flickering shadows.

CHAPTER 62

After a few moments of silence, broken only by the muffled sounds of traffic in the street below, Rosa said softly, "Harry, I've been doing all the talking, and you haven't said very much, just asking me questions. Now it's my turn to ask you. What did you do today?"

"I went to Veracruz. I looked around, and I talked with a few people, and I filed a couple of stories with United Press on the refinery fire."

Rosa sat up with a start. "You went to Veracruz? But that's so far. How did you get there? What did you see? Who did you talk to? What did you write?"

"Well, I chartered a small plane. It really isn't that far, just a couple hours." Harry chuckled. "It's downhill all the way, you know. I couldn't get close enough to see the real damage, but I did see a lot of commotion in the streets, and I talked to a lot of people. I had lunch with a couple of Pemex workers in a cantina across from the refinery, and they gave me a lot of information. Two of the men killed in the explosion—just boys, really—were friends of theirs. Then I went out to the oil workers' union hall and talked with a couple of men there. I talked to some people at the Plaza de Armas, down by the harbor. Just casual conversations, but I did get some good information from them. And then I flew back."

Harry paused and took a slow puff on his cigarette. "Have you ever been to Veracruz, Rosa?"

Rosa put her head back down on Harry's chest. "Oh, yes, I've been there. It's a lovely town, a historic town, but it's such a long way to go and then come back, all in one day. I mean, it certainly was a long way for you to go today." She lifted her head again. "Harry, what's this bandage on your side?"

"Oh, I had a fight with some guy. Nothing serious, just a scratch. But who was this Sergio, the man you shot?"

"Where? You had a fight in Veracruz?"

"No, it was here, in Mexico City. He came at me with a knife, so I slugged him. Just a mugger, I guess."

"Does it hurt? You must be careful in the dark streets of the city."

Harry winced. "No, it doesn't really hurt. Not much, anyway. But who was Sergio? How did you happen to know him?"

"He was a friend of Pedro's. An acquaintance, really. They weren't really close friends. He would visit Pedro at the flower shop from time to time, and they would talk in that meeting room in the back of the shop. He was someone Pedro met years ago in Spain, and he's been living here in Mexico for a long time. I really didn't know him very well. I spoke with him a few times when he came to the shop."

"That room in the back of the shop is like a train station, with all that traffic. Has Pedro said anything about him since Friday?"

"No, he hasn't said a word. He may not know he's dead."

"Geez, he's been dead for four days. Pedro must wonder where his friend is."

"He hasn't said anything to me."

"Why did you take the time to empty his pockets?"

"It was a sudden impulse, and it didn't take very long at all. I was scared, and I wanted to confuse the police. I wanted them to think it was a robbery, so I took his wallet and his money."

"Good thinking. What else did you take?"

Rosa shifted her head on Harry's shoulder. "I took his watch. I didn't really want his watch, Harry. It's not like I was stealing it. I didn't want his wallet either, but I thought I should take all those things so they couldn't identify him. I was afraid that if they identified him they would connect him to Pedro and the flower shop."

She paused, as if she was trying to recall what else she might have taken. "And I took his gun. He had the gun in one hand, and he was pulling me with his other hand. He was twisting my arm and pulling me toward the back door. I thought he was going to shoot me if I didn't go with him. Why else would he have a gun? I was so afraid, Harry. He said he would have to shoot me if I didn't go with him. He dropped the gun when I shot him and I picked it up and I put it in my purse. Thank God he didn't use it."

Harry felt a sudden twinge in the wound in his side. "Thank God is right. But weren't you concerned about the noise?"

"Harry, at that point I was only concerned about stopping him, afraid for my life."

"Yeah, I can understand that. So now you have two guns?"

Rosa hesitated. "Yes. Now I have two guns."

Harry leaned over and lit another cigarette from the flickering flame of a candle stub. Smart girl. "Where's Sergio's gun now?"

"It's home, in my closet."

"And where are the other things you took?"

"Everything's at home, in the closet."

Harry chuckled. "You must have a pretty big closet. What do you plan to do with all that stuff?"

"I don't know, I haven't really thought about it."

"Hang on to everything for now. I suppose you could donate the money to charity, but you might want to keep his gun handy in case one of his friends comes looking for you."

"Oh, Harry, don't say that—that's what I'm afraid of."

"I'm sorry, Rosita, I didn't mean to alarm you. Nobody's going to bother you. Sounds to me you did everything right. It's been four days already, and nobody's come after you, because no one knows you shot him. I just meant it might be a good idea to have another gun available, just in case. Two guns are better than one. You never know what might happen next."

"You're right about that. What could happen next?"

"Now, does Pedro know you have your mother's gun?"

"Oh, heavens, no! He wouldn't understand, he wouldn't approve. He didn't approve of anything my mother did. He and my mother were always fighting, always at each other's throats. He liked to think he was responsible for my care, and they never could agree on what I should do. She wanted me to continue my studies here in Mexico City. She wanted me to continue my music studies, but Pedro seemed to have other plans for me."

"Why does he have that much to say? I mean, what was his hold over your mother?"

"He really didn't have any authority over either one of us. He just wants to assert himself. He seems to think he has some kind of mandate from my father, and he just wants to play the role of Uncle Pedro."

"Good ol' Tío Pedro," Harry said with a chuckle. "But aren't you afraid the police will be able to trace the bullets that killed Sergio?"

"Harry, I'm afraid of everything, but I believe they'll have trouble identifying my mother's gun. It's so old, and there's no record of it. I don't think they'll be able to trace it to me. I wasn't even sure it would work when I pulled the trigger. I pray to God they won't be able to trace it. And I pray to God that I did the right thing in my panic."

"Well, under the circumstances, I'd say you did the right thing. Sounds like you didn't have much choice." Harry kissed her on the cheek, and gave her shoulder a reassuring hug. "That was quick thinking."

Now Rosa kissed Harry, not just a quick kiss on the cheek but a long, passionate kiss on the lips. "Harry, I feel so comfortable here with you. This was meant to happen. God wanted us to be together. I feel like I've known you all my life. You have such a soothing effect on me, calming my fears."

"Be calm now, Rosita, and don't worry about a thing. Nobody's chasing you now. And don't worry about Pedro. Everything will be all right. You're safe here with me. I'll protect you." He kissed her once more and smiled. "As a matter of fact, I think I'd better protect you again tomorrow night."

Rosa smiled, nestling even closer to Harry. "Yes, *mi vida*, I think I'll need your protection again tomorrow night … and every night, from now on, for rest of my life."

The fading flicker of the final candle disappeared, and in the darkness Rosa fell asleep on Harry's arm. Whatever anxiety she might have felt about being alone with him in his room had melted in the comfort of the crook of his arm, and disappeared in the shadows of the candlelight. And whatever anxiety she might have felt about telling her story had vanished in the soft glow of that same candlelight.

In the silence, Corbett's words flashed back into Harry's memory. They're hiding in broad daylight … they could be anywhere … you never know where they'll turn up.

The jangle of the telephone interrupted the silence.

CHAPTER 63

Rosa jumped up, grabbed her clothes from the chair, and ran into the bathroom. Harry let the telephone ring. Who the hell would be calling at this hour?

After the tenth or twelfth ring Harry picked up the receiver and answered with a sleepy-sounding Hello.

"Hello, Harry, did I wake you?"

"Sort of, but that's all right."

"Did you receive the envelope?"

"Yes."

"Have you read the information?"

"Yes."

"Did you understand it?"

"Not entirely."

"I'll explain it. Meet me at one o'clock at Indianilla?"

"Where?"

"Indianilla. Take a taxi."

"Okay."

"The driver will know. It's not far from the Del Prado?"

"Okay."

"One o'clock."

"Okay."

Rosa came out of the bathroom buttoning her blouse. "Who would call you at this hour? I hope it's not a problem."

"No, it's nothing. The overnight man at the UP office had a couple of questions."

Rosa put her arms around his neck and kissed him. "You need a shave, and you need some clothes if you're going to get something to eat. And I need to go home. It's getting late, and I have to go to work in the morning." She kissed him again. "But the evening here with you, mi cariño, has been so wonderful. Better than I ever dreamed it would be. I'm so glad I found you tonight. I want to see you every night, Harry. I want to love you every night … and I want you to love me every night … every night and every day."

"Sounds good to me, every night and every day. And you're right, I should put on some clothes."

"I just hope I didn't bore you with my rambling tale. It wasn't easy to tell you."

"Bore me? Are you kidding? I wanted to know, and you wanted to tell me. And I'm sure it wasn't easy to tell me. I can sympathize with you, Rosita. Killing is not a very pleasant thing, but sometimes it has to happen. You were forced to do what you did. You had no choice. In a court of law, I'm sure they would say it was justifiable. I'm sure they would say it was self-defense, so don't you worry about it. Now, you say you're going to go to work tomorrow?"

"Yes, I'll have to, and Pedro's expecting me. There's so much to do. I'll go in, but not too early. I'd like to have more people around when I get there, like María Elena for instance, and a few customers."

"That's good. I told Pedro I might stop by and see him. He wants me to write something for his trade association—a press release, or something like that. I'm not interested in taking on another job, but I'd like to find out what he has in mind, and what the hell they're up to."

"Oh, be careful, Harry. That trade association of his is a charade. It doesn't really exist. It's something he and his friend José cooked up. Don't let them trap you."

"Yeah, I thought it sounded kind of fishy. Now, young lady, I have one more question before you leave, then I'll take you downstairs and get you a taxi. You said Sergio wanted to take you out of the country. Where did he want to take you? To Russia?"

Rosa was standing by the door, her purse slung over her shoulder, one hand on the doorknob. Harry's question caught her by surprise. She laid her purse on the bed and sat down next to it. "Russia? Why do you say Russia?"

"Rosita, I know you're Mexican in your heart. I know you're a regular china poblana, the typical Mexican girl. You love Mexico and everything Mexican. You speak the language, you know the history, and you love the mariachi music. You love the people, the flowers, the food, the ambiance. You love everything about Mexico. But somewhere deep inside your soul, you're also Russian, and Russian blood still flows in your veins.

"I believe he wanted to take you to Russia, Rosa. I don't know why, perhaps you'll tell me. You're afraid you might die far from Mexico, like that song says, the song you didn't want to hear tonight down in the lounge. You don't want to die in Russia—or anywhere else for that matter. You don't want to go to Russia. So, in the frenzy and the struggle, you shot him."

Rosa looked up at Harry and caught her breath. Once again, tears were trickling down her cheeks. Harry buckled his belt, sat down next to her, and kissed away one of the tears.

"Oh, Harry, you're right. Sometimes I get so confused. It's like I'm leading a double life. I was so afraid. Yes, he wanted to take me to Russia. And yes, I am Russian, but I'm also Mexican. I was born in Russia, but I don't remember anything about it. We left Russia when I was barely two years old, and we went to Spain. But how did you know?"

"In the lounge tonight, when the waiter told us about the dead man on the elevator, you made the sign of the cross."

Rosa smiled. "Of course, I remember. The sign of the cross. My charm bracelet snagged the flowers on my shoulder. And, of course, you saw that happen."

"Yes, I saw."

"My mother instilled in me the tenets and traditions of the Russian Orthodox Church, and our way of making the sign of the cross is not like the Roman Catholics do it. It's not the way they do it here in Mexico. Some things are part of you forever, and you never forget. What you said is true, Harry. My blood is Russian blood."

Rosa sighed, as if a heavy burden had been lifted from her shoulders. "We left Russia early in 1932, just a month or so after Stalin and his secret police destroyed the Cathedral of Christ the Savior in Moscow. Mother was afraid, and she wanted to get out. She wanted to go somewhere peaceful, and I guess she talked my father into going to Spain. Spain was so beautiful, but it was anything but peaceful.

"My parents spoke Russian to each other, and from birth I learned the Russian language from them, but I also learned Spanish while we were living in Spain. We had a Spanish maid, and I had a Spanish nursemaid and Spanish playmates. I started school in Spain and, of course, my teachers and classmates were Spanish. So as a child, I learned both languages, and I grew up speaking both languages."

Rosa smiled, and laughed a little laugh. "My English, such as it is, came later."

"Your English is very good, Rosita, but you had me fooled. You don't seem to have the Castilian accent. Come to think of it, neither do Pedro and Miguel."

Rosa frowned. "Oh, they don't speak true Spanish. Their mother tongue is Euskara, the language of the Basque people in the north of Spain, and when they speak Spanish they speak with the accent of Euskara. When my family came from Russia, we settled in Seville, where the pronunciation of Spanish is much like it is here in Mexico, so people here never suspected that I was anything but Mexican.

"When the Civil War started in Spain, Russia supported the Republican Loyalists, and my father went up north to fight on the side of the Loyalists. He was in the same brigade as Pedro and Miguel. Mother and I remained in Seville, which was difficult for us, because the Nationalists controlled Seville right from the start, and we could not tell anyone where my father was. I missed him so much during those times when he was gone."

Rosa closed her eyes for a moment. "My mother brought me to Mexico after he was killed. She was never a Communist. Her family had been wealthy, and they lost just about everything when the Bolsheviks took over in Russia, but my grandmother managed to hide some valuables that the looters never found. When Mother left Russia, she was able to bring money—English pounds and French francs. She also brought my grandmother's jewels and her own jewels and some gold and a few other valuable items. When she and I came to Mexico she made wise investments here. We were always comfortable.

"I remember nothing of Russia," Rosa continued. "I was barely two years old when we left, but Mother told me many pleasant things about the Russia she knew in the old days, before the Communist take-over. She loved my father, but she hated the Communists. That's one reason she and Pedro argued so much. That and religion. They argued right up to the night she was killed."

Rosa paused, and bowed her head for a nanosecond. Harry smiled a mental smile. *She's rambling again. That's good.* He took her hand and squeezed it, but he said nothing. He had learned, early in his life as a reporter, that the best way to do an interview is to let the water flow freely once the dam has been breached.

"In Mexico City my mother found solace in a small parish of the IORFR—that's the *Iglesia Ortodoxa Rusa Fuera de Rusia*. Perhaps you've heard of it in English as the ROCOR, the Russian Orthodox Church Outside Russia. She taught me the Russian Orthodox catechism. She wanted to preserve our Russian heritage. She wanted to raise me as a Mexican, but she also wanted me to remember my Russian roots."

"Well, Sergio's not going to take you to Russia," Harry said, "or anywhere else for that matter. You won't have to worry about him anymore. But why did he want to take you to Russia?"

"Oh, at first he tried to make it sound exciting and pleasant. He told me he had arranged a scholarship for me to study music at the Conservatory in Moscow. He said I would enjoy visiting Moscow and the land of my birth. I told him I had no interest in seeing Moscow, I told him I had no memories of Russia, and I told him I didn't like what's going on in Russia now. And I also told him I didn't want to go to school so far from home, so far from Mexico."

"Yeah, I know, so far from Mexico's 'volcanoes and prairies and flowers,' right?"

Rosa smiled, and softly sang that phrase. "Yes, just like the song says. My blood may be Russian, Harry, but I'm a Mexican now. I'm a citizen. My life is here in Mexico. My home is here, my heart is here. You do understand, don't you, Harry?"

"Yes, Rosita, I understand."

"I told him I would not go. I told him I wanted to continue my studies at the *Conservatorio Nacional* here, but he said everything had been arranged. He even had a plane ticket for me."

"What did you mother think of all this."

"Oh, she was furious when I told her about it. She said there was absolutely no way that she would she let me go."

"Did Pedro know about the scholarship?"

"He never mentioned it to me, and I'm not sure he knew. He and Sergio were always talking in whispers, as if they shared dark secrets. Sergio was a mystery man. He never came through the front of the Florería when he visited Pedro. He used the back door, just like all those friends of Pedro's. I don't know if they're afraid of the flowers, or what their problem is. And I never knew for sure what Sergio was doing here in Mexico. I never knew where he lived or where he worked."

"You said Sergio might not have been alone?"

"Yes, I'm sure there are others."

"Well, we'll have to be careful now, Rosa. We'll have to figure out what to do next. For now, we'll have to assume Pedro doesn't know Sergio is dead. You and I will go about our business as if nothing out of the ordinary has happened. Now, there's one more thing—"

Rosa stood up and headed for the door. "It's getting late, *mi vida*. Please, no more questions."

"I have to know. Where were you Saturday?"

CHAPTER 64

Rosa dropped her purse on the bed again. Her eyes closed, and slowly she sighed and sat down next to the purse. "Harry, I started to tell you in the lounge, and then the crowd came in making so much noise, and then the waiter told us about that poor man on the elevator. I was going to tell you, Harry, but I didn't have a chance."

Harry smiled. "I know. You had a lot on your mind."

"I was in Veracruz. Pedro called me early Saturday morning and told me he wanted me to take a quick trip to Veracruz to meet a man and deliver a package. I flew down there on an early Mexicana flight."

"Did you ask him what was in the package?"

"Yes, and he told me it was material for a publicity program called 'flowers for the people,' or something like that. I asked him if the package could be mailed or delivered by courier or in some other way, and he said no, it was urgent and I had to deliver it personally, right away."

"Tell me this, Rosita, when you were in Veracruz, did you have lunch at a cantina called the Pozo Hondo?"

Rosa looked up, a mixture of surprise and relief in her eyes and on her face. "How did you know?"

"I was there today, Rosita. I had lunch there. The two men I was with told me they saw a girl Saturday with fair skin and blue eyes, trying to hide her blond hair under a black wig."

Rosa didn't know whether to laugh or cry. "Yes, I was there, but I couldn't eat anything in that filthy place, the flies were so thick, and it smelled so bad, and a poor, emaciated dog kept staring at me, and that silly wig was so hot and uncomfortable, and it kept sliding out of place. I took the wig with me because I didn't want anyone to recognize me. I had a feeling, when I left home Saturday morning, that what I was doing was not right. Yes, that's where I met the man. That's where I gave him the package."

Harry reached into the side pocket of the coat lying next to him on the bed and pulled out a wrinkled photograph. "Is this the man?"

Rosa gasped, choking for air, and made a quick sign of the cross. "*Oh, my God!* He looks … he looks like … he's …"

"That's right, Rosita, he's dead. He was the third victim of the fire. No one I talked to could identify him, no one knew his name, but they all agreed he didn't work there at the refinery, and they agreed that he's the guy who set the fire. I'm sorry to do this, Rosita, but I have to know. Who was he?"

"Pedro didn't tell me who I was going to meet in Veracruz, he only told me I should go to that Pozo Hondo cantina. When I got there I recognized the man immediately. He was the same man I had delivered a package to last week in Nuevo Laredo. He called himself Paco. He recognized me, of course, even with that crazy wig."

Harry laughed. "I can understand that, and I'm sure you didn't look like any of the regular customers in that joint."

Rosa was crying. "No. I was the only woman there. I was uncomfortable the entire trip, Harry. I didn't know what was in the package I delivered to that man, but now I realize I was responsible for that horrible explosion in Veracruz. I realize I was also responsible for the fire you and I saw last week, and I was responsible for the deaths of those men in Veracruz."

Rosa paused for a moment, and then she jumped to her feet and exploded with rage, blood rushing to her tear-stained cheeks. "Tío Pedro! That bastard! That horrible man! Yes, I call him Tío Pedro, but he's not my uncle. He deceived me. He lied to me with that 'flowers for the people' story. He's an evil killer, and now he's turned me into a killer. I should have known, but I was blind. Those two men in Veracruz—the ones you wrote about—they were innocent victims of my foolishness. I was responsible for their deaths. I was responsible for the deaths of all three of those men."

"No, Rosita, you were not responsible. You were just a pawn. Pedro used you. He wanted you to do his dirty work."

Harry stood up and took Rosa's hand, squeezing it gently. "Don't worry about it, you were not responsible, you were a victim too. And don't worry about the guy you shot, either. Everything will be all right."

"Oh, I hope so, I hope so." Rosa put her head on Harry's shoulder and sobbed. Harry stroked her hair and let her cry for a brief moment.

"Now, there's one more thing—"

"Please, *mi amor*, no more questions tonight. It's getting late." She smiled, and gave Harry a gentle kiss.

Rosa brushed her hair back over her shoulder. "I really must leave. You're not dressed, so I'll go down and get a taxi. I suppose you'll have to go to the United Press in the morning?"

Harry had a bundle of questions he wanted to ask, but he knew it was time to change course. "Okay, no more questions, and no, I'm not going to the UP office. I'd like to forget about work, but there is one thing I don't want to forget—Alberto set me up for a round of golf at Churubusco."

Rosa put her arms around Harry's waist and pulled him close, pressing her body tight against his. "Here's something else you don't want to forget," she whispered. She reached up and pulled his head down till their lips met in a long, deep, passionate kiss.

"How could I forget?" he murmured. "Maybe I'll have to forget about the golf game, and spend the afternoon right here with you."

When Rosa was gone, Harry went down to the street and slipped into the thinning crowd of late-nighters in front of the hotel, careful to keep his back close to the building.

A stranger standing next to Harry tapped him on the shoulder. "I say, old man, that was a bloody awful thing, what?"

"What's that?"

"Some poor bloke got himself knocked off right here in the Del Prado."

Harry reacted with his best display of shock. "Really? You don't say. Right here in the Del Prado? What happened?"

"No one knows for sure. The hotel top brass are mum."

"Well, I suppose they want to preserve their good name."

"Right-o. They'll want to keep it out of the press."

"How'd it happen?"

"Poor bloke got coshed on the head, he did. They found him dead in a bloody lift."

Harry tried to think of a clever response, but he froze when he felt a vise-like grip on his arm.

"Good evening, Señor Banister. Fancy meeting you here."

CHAPTER 65

Harry's heart was thumping as he slipped into the back seat of the black Ford Fordor. The laceration in his side was throbbing, and his right hand hurt like hell. His mind was racing: think, Banister, think. Listen carefully, be sure you understand his questions, choose your words carefully. Don't tip your hand. Don't say anything to get him pissed off.

The plain clothes cop with the cigar and the big fedora climbed in next to Harry and closed the door. "At last we meet, Señor Banister. You're a hard man to pin down. Allow me to introduce myself. I am Detective Captain Victor Gonzalez Moreno of the Federal District police, and I want to take this opportunity to ask you a few questions."

This is it. He's going to lock me up. He's going to throw me in a dark cell and grill me. He knows about the Bar 33. He's got me cold on the cowboy in the elevator. There goes the golf. There goes Acapulco. There goes everything.

"You know my name?"

"Yes, I know all about you. I know, for example, that you moved this morning from the Hotel Comé to the Del Prado—Sergeant, turn onto Lopez —I know you arrived in town Thursday evening and you're working as a reporter at United Press. I know you entered Mexico on a tourist card. You realize, of course, that a tourist is not permitted to work here? You realize that a tourist is not permitted to have gainful employment? You are aware of that? You're aware that you're breaking the law?"

Harry struggled for a breath of fresh air in this iron cigar box on wheels, but he managed a quiet sigh of relief. If that's all this guy's worried about, the worst they can do is throw me out of the country, just like the doorman at the Bar Restaurante 33 said.

"Well, yes, I am aware of the law. Article 33, right? But I'm really not officially employed by United Press. I'm not on their payroll. It's just an informal verbal arrangement. The bureau chief is an old friend of mine, and I'm just going to be helping him out. He's short-handed right now, with a man on vacation, and I'm just sort of doing him a favor. If I happen to write a story he can use he'll pay me out of petty cash. I'm not interested in working full time, and I certainly am not interested in breaking the law. I'm really here on vacation, to relax and enjoy your beautiful country, explore the history and the mountains and the beaches." Careful, Harry thought, slow down. Don't lay it on too thick.

"I'm really not interested in the technical aspects of your arrangement with United Press. That's not my concern. I'll leave that up to the people at Gobernación, and frankly, I think they have more important things to worry about right now, more serious affairs of state.

"But I am interested in the death of a certain man. I am, after all, a detective in the homicide bureau. I'm talking about a sudden death, a shooting. I would like you to tell me what you know about that event. I believe you know what I'm talking about?"

Here it comes. I wish he would open a window and let in a little fresh air. "How can I help you?"

"I believe you were at the Bar Restaurante 33 on Avenida Juárez last Thursday. Is that not correct?"

"Yes, I was there. I had supper there."

"You had supper with a young lady, correct?"

"Yes."

"A man was killed there Thursday evening. I believe you're aware of that?"

This guy's clever, Harry realized. He's working me. He's trying to trip me. Keep it simple. "Sure, I'm aware of that. It's been in all the newspapers."

"Yes, but I believe you know more than the newspapers have reported. The manager, Fernandez, said you went back to the men's room and nearly tripped over the body—Sergeant, turn right at Calle Victoria."

Suddenly the cigar smoke is not so bad, Harry realized. Gonzalez has cleared the air for me. He's going to turn right. He's not taking me to jail, he's taking me for a ride around the same loop Corbett did. I'll give him a little information, but not too much. I'm sure as hell not going to tell him that I know who did it. And I guess he's not interested in the dead cowboy on the elevator.

"Yes, after dinner I went back there. I had to take a leak. I nearly tripped because I was trying to be careful where I walked. I didn't want to step on anything or upset the crime scene."

"That was very thoughtful of you. And tell me, what did you observe?"

"Well, I saw the body, of course. As you say, I nearly tripped over it. I saw he had been shot in the chest. Or stabbed. I couldn't be certain which. I saw blood on him and blood on the floor."

"Anything else?"

"Well, nothing that occurs to me now. I was trying to be careful where I stepped, but I did notice that some of the blood on the floor had been smeared, like someone already had stepped in it."

"Yes, the victim, for certain, and perhaps the killer. Anything else?"

"Well, I did notice a splatter of blood on the wall, on the bullfight poster. I guess that means he had been shot?"

"Yes. Blood and a bullet in the bullfight poster. We were able to determine from the trajectory that the killer was shorter than the victim."

"Or perhaps the killer fired from a crouching position? Or from the hip? Or maybe the killer was down on the floor?"

Gonzalez laughed. "Yes, yes, of course. Those are all good possibilities. You should be a detective, Harry. May I call you Harry?"

"Please do." What took him so long, Harry wondered? They always call you by your first name. It's a way of intimidating you. Like when I got that speeding ticket on the turnpike.

"Did you know the man, Harry?"

Careful with this one. Did I know him, as in did I know his full name, address and date of birth? Were we formally introduced? "No, I didn't know him. Have you been able to identify him?"

"Yes, as a matter of fact, we have. The killer tried to make it look like a robbery, hoping we would not be able to identify the victim. The killer did a thorough job, and left us very little to work with, but because of diligent detective work, we've been able to identify the victim as a Russian citizen named Sergey Ivanovich Vasiliev. Like you, he was in Mexico illegally."

"You mean he was a Russian wetback?"

Gonzalez laughed. "Yes, I guess you could say that."

"What was he doing here?"

"Well, I'm certain he wasn't here to spread good will. We've been able to establish that he was a member of the MGB, the Russian Ministry for State Security. His suit coat helped us identify him. We were able to trace the coat to a tailor shop in Madrid where he bought clothing on several occasions when he lived in Spain."

"How were you able to trace the label?"

"We traced it through good old-fashioned police work," Gonzalez replied, a touch of pride registering in his voice. "I told one of my men to check several tailor shops right here in Mexico City and inquire if they recognized the name on the label. Two of the local tailors never had heard the name, but two of the others were able to identify it immediately as a well-known Madrid haberdasher.

"From there we learned one of the names he used, and with that name we were able to trace him to Mexico and confirm the final identification through our Russian contacts here in Mexico City."

"How did he end up here in Mexico?"

"He fought for the Loyalists in the Spanish Civil War and remained in Spain for a few months following the War. He came to Mexico thirteen years ago and burrowed into the daily life here. He had been living here, masquerading as a private citizen, ever since."

Harry tried not to smile when he heard that. "What was he doing here? I mean, what was his job as a private citizen?"

"We're not certain of everything he was doing, but we know he worked for a time in a bakery in Coyoacán and also as a clerk in a men's clothing store here in Mexico City. Using one of his cover names, he also worked in a travel agency. Apparently he lived well, better than a simple clerk should be able to afford. He had a new car and an apartment on Insurgentes, not far from the Plaza México. We know he visited several other cities on various occasions, notably Acapulco, Tampico, Veracruz, Guadalajara, Monterrey and Manzanillo. He seemed to be particularly interested in visiting industrial centers and seaports, but he also liked to visit Taxco and Cuernavaca. He also made at least two trips back to Europe."

"You kept pretty good tabs on him."

"Yes, he's been a person of great interest to our government."

"Was he a spy?"

"Well, I guess you could call him a spy. The definition of 'spy' is nebulous, just like so much of the work they do. But a more direct answer to your question is yes, he was a spy."

"You say you recovered a bullet from the bullfight poster, and also another bullet?"

"The bullfight bullet passed through his body," Gonzalez said, "and the other bullet was still in his body. At first, our forensic experts had difficulty identifying the origin of the bullets, but they now have determined Vasiliev was killed by two 7.62 millimeter bullets fired from a Tokarev TT-33 pistol."

"That sounds like it might be a Russian gun."

"Yes. It's a pistol favored by many of the MGB agents. Isn't it ironic, Harry? Isn't it ironic that what we have here is a case of one Russian spy killing another Russian spy?"

Yes, Harry thought, it certainly is ironic. This guy was killed by another Russian spy—did Rosa tell me the whole story?

"You could identify the gun from the bullets?"

"Many guns fire a seven-sixty-two, but the Tokarev TT-33 bullets are distinctive. Our forensic technicians tell me the size of the bullet is unusual.

"I don't mind if the Russian Communists, or the Russian spies, eliminate each other," Gonzalez continued. "They've been doing it for years. In one celebrated case back in 1940 a Stalinist agent came to Mexico and killed Leon Trotsky with an ice ax in Trotsky's house in Coyoacán. Trotsky was living here in exile. I was just a rookie in the detective bureau then, and I was assigned to that case. Imagine, the assassin split Trotsky's head open with an ice ax. That was a very bloody case."

"I can imagine. Did the blood in the Restaurante 33 help you identify the Russian?"

"Not really. We had no prior knowledge of Vasiliev's blood type, but our pathologists determined his blood was type 3-B, and the blood splattered on the floor and the wall also was type 3-B. There was no other blood in the room."

"Did he have a gun?"

"Oh, I'm sure he carried a gun in his line of work, but as I said, there was no gun on his person. The killer removed everything."

"So the killer was very thorough."

"Very thorough," Gonzalez emphasized. "We don't know the name of the killer yet, but we know that this was the work of a highly-trained professional, someone who knew just what to do, when to do it, and how to do it. The killer removed things from the victim's pockets, trying to make it look like a robbery, trying to throw us off the track, but we were not fooled by this clever diversion. Yes, this was an execution by a highly-trained assassin."

Harry smiled when he heard this, and he wondered about Rosa, and he thought about what Corbett said earlier about people hiding in plain sight. She's a very talented girl, in a lot of ways, and she sure knows a lot about flowers, but a highly-trained professional assassin? Could be, but that's one skill she sure as hell wouldn't have learned in music school.

"I suppose Fernandez would just as soon have the Russians do their killing someplace other than the men's room in his restaurant."

"I'm sure he would. Sometimes they do it on the street or in the back alleys, sometimes out in the country. Sometimes it's in the back seat of a car, or maybe they do it right in the victim's home, as they did with Trotsky. They kill with guns or with knives, they strangle with garrotes or bare hands. They use poison. They use any means at their disposal, and whatever they use, or wherever they do it, they are very proficient. They never miss.

"The Vasiliev assassination last Thursday was a particularly audacious crime because it involved gunfire in a very public place, during the supper hour in a crowded restaurant."

"Yes, I'd say that was a very bold crime. One of the earlier newspaper stories said you thought there might have been a third person back there?"

Gonzalez smiled. "Ah, yes, the theory of The Third Man. A possibility in the beginning, but we ruled that out when we were unable to verify any indication of a third person.

"Then, when we traced the suit coat and the bullets, and identified the weapon, we ultimately came to the conclusion that it was a dispute between two MGB agents. Over what, we can only surmise. Perhaps a disagreement over tactics, or even politics. They don't always agree on everything. Or maybe it was a dispute over a woman." Gonzalez snickered, and blew a cloud of smoke. "Often there is a woman in a case like this."

"Yeah, how do they say it in French, *cherchez la femme?*"

"Yes, 'look for the woman.' We did that at first, but the clues brought us back to the unknown Russian agent. And there is another possibility. Perhaps Vasiliev fell out of favor with Semyon Denisovich Ignatiev, their leader back in Moscow, and Denisovich ordered another agent to eliminate him."

"That's one sure way to give a person the pink slip."

"The pink slip?"

"Yes, where I come from, when you give someone the pink slip you're giving him the boot, kicking him out the door, telling him that his services are no longer required and his employment has been terminated. It's a gentler way of firing someone without using a gun."

Gonzalez grinned. "Of course, kicking him out the door. The pink slip. Very well put, Harry. You Americans have a way with words.

"But now it's time for me to move on. We of the Federal District police have done our work, and now I'm turning my file over to the PGR, the Federal prosecutor, and to the DFSN, the Federal Directorate of National Security—that's the new government branch that deals directly with espionage. They're the ones who verified his identity. I'll let them pursue it further.

"Yes, it's time for me to move on. I have other cases to investigate, like the murder tonight right here in the Hotel Del Prado. Another messy case."

Harry's back stiffened, and the pain in his side surged when the sergeant made the turn onto Humboldt. Gonzalez doesn't want me for that Bar 33 thing after all, Harry realized. Gonzalez is looking at me for the body in the elevator. How the hell did he know?

CHAPTER 66

"You say there was a murder tonight, right here in the Del Prado? I heard a commotion in the lobby a little while ago, but the waiter said someone had a heart attack. What happened?"

Gonzalez blew a cloud of smoke. "It was more than just a heart attack. A man was killed in one of the elevators. Somebody chopped him on the side of the neck. The blow ruptured his carotid artery. He bled to death, died on the spot, on the floor of the elevator. That's why I'm still here now, so late in the evening."

"You're kidding. On an elevator? Right here in the Del Prado?"

"On a service elevator, away from the crowds. Apparently it was just the two of them on the elevator, the victim and his killer."

"When did this happen?"

"Earlier this evening. My sergeant and I had been here looking for you. We left for supper, but before we had a chance to eat we received the call about the corpse on the elevator."

"You were in the hotel looking for me?"

"Yes, we've been looking for you since Friday, not to arrest you, just to talk to you about the Bar Restaurante 33 incident, to ask you a few questions."

"Who was the man who was killed here tonight?"

"He was someone who was well known to us. He was a street hustler, a pistolero who did odd jobs for people. You might say he was a contract killer. Originally he worked on a ranch in Jalisco. He also worked as a roustabout in the oil fields, and he was a labor organizer.

No family, as far as we can tell, probably not many friends. He won't be missed."

"You say he was a pistolero?"

"Yes. He usually carried a gun, and we believe he was responsible for three or four deaths here in the Capital, hired to do the killing. We've picked him up several times on suspicion, but we never have been able to pin anything on him. He never was carrying a gun when we picked him up, so we were not able to register his gun or check for ballistics in any of those cases. We never knew what kind of gun he owned."

Gonzalez tapped his cigar ashes into the ash tray. "I'm happy to have him out of the way now. The killer, whoever he was, did us a favor. We won't have to worry about this guy any more. I'm always happy when someone takes a low-life such as this man off the street. It makes my job so much easier. The city will be a much safer, more peaceful place without him around. And I'm always happy to close a messy case like this, and stamp it *Caso Cerrado*—Case Closed. I won't have to deal with it anymore."

"You say he had no family or friends who would miss him, but he must have had a patron who hired him to do those killings."

"That's true, his patron will have to find another hired gun now to do his dirty work."

"And you say he usually carried a gun, but not tonight?"

"Correct. All we found tonight was the knife next to his body on the floor in the elevator. Imagine that, a pistolero without a pistol. I guess he was smart enough to realize that gunfire would attract attention in the Del Prado. His killer also was smart enough to avoid gunfire."

"But the dead man had a knife?"

"Yes, his initials were carved on the handle. Blood on the tip of his knife indicated he wounded his killer in a futile fight for his life."

The semi-darkness and the cloud of cigar smoke masked a sly grin on Harry's face. "Do you think the killer might have taken his gun?"

"Perhaps. That's a distinct possibility."

"Who could have done it?"

"We know it wasn't a robbery. His wallet and his keys and a substantial roll of cash were still in his pockets. We believe it was a disagreement with one of his criminal cohorts."

Harry smiled to himself when he thought about that "substantial roll of cash." *The guy's pay for killing me? I wonder how much I was worth.*

"You mean he was killed by another pistolero? What were they doing in the Del Prado?"

"Well, they certainly weren't socializing with the international crowd, that's for sure. Not the way he was dressed. He would have stood out in his cowboy clothes. They no doubt were targeting a wealthy visitor, probably a foreigner. The hotel is full of wealthy people tonight, important people from all over the world."

"Then they were in the right place at the right time."

"Yes. Like the saying goes, if you want to catch fish, you go to the river or the ocean."

"What was the dead man's name?"

"His name was Jaime Calderón."

"Could the killer have been a hotel guest, rather than another pistolero?"

"Perhaps, but I doubt it. Not where the murder took place, in that service elevator. Of course, we have no idea where they got on the elevator, at the bottom or the top or anywhere in between. His body was discovered when the elevator doors opened down in the garage."

"But his companion didn't use a gun? Or a knife?"

"No, he just beat him to death, apparently with one or two well-placed and well-delivered blows. The killer must have been a powerful man to do such lethal damage in the confined space of an elevator cabin. It's unfortunate that it happened in such a fine hotel as the Del Prado."

"Yes, it certainly is."

Most unfortunate that it happened with me as the target, Harry thought. *Next time it could be anywhere—in the hotel or out on the street. Or in the men's room in a restaurant. Or the back of a taxi. Or out in the country.*

CHAPTER 67

"Thank you, Harry, for your cooperation in this matter," Gonzalez said. "You've been most helpful."

"How have I helped?"

"Oh, you've been very helpful, in an indirect fashion. From the beginning I suspected that you and your lady friend were involved in the killing at the Bar Restaurante 33. I wanted to bring you in and lock you up and question you. I was looking for you right from the start, and that kept us on our toes.

"Then I learned you were trying to solve the case yourself. I learned that you came back to the restaurant the next day, questioning the bartender and the manager, much like a police investigator. And you identified yourself to the manager without hesitation. I talked with those people. I talked with your bureau chief at UP. I talked with your friend Duarte. I talked with staff people at the Comé and here at the Del Prado. All of this convinced me you were not the one.

"All along, of course, we also had been looking in other directions. We had been pursuing certain clues, such as the distinctive bullets and the label in the suit coat, and we were successful in identifying the weapon and the victim."

"Sounds to me you've got the case pretty much wrapped up."

"Yes, we've closed the book on this one. Like I said, I'm always happy to close a case and move on to other things."

Harry decided it was worth a try. You never know until you ask the question. "Then it's probably time to let people know about your diligence and success in solving the mystery of the man at the Bar Restaurante 33. Why don't I write a story about it, let the public know?"

Gonzalez laughed as he relit his cigar. "Cheap cigar won't stay lit. That's exactly what I had in mind. You might have wondered why I'm giving you so much information. Your story would have widespread international interest. It would demonstrate that the Kremlin's presence in Mexico is shaky at best, with dissension in the ranks, and it also would demonstrate that the police in Mexico City are capable of solving even the most complicated cases. You can say that the police were diligent in tracking down the most obscure clues. And you can add a unique personal angle, of course, by revealing that you were there when the crime occurred."

Harry coughed on a cloud of cigar smoke. "You would expect me to say I was there when it happened?"

"Of course. You know more about it than any other reporter. You were the only reporter on the scene. You saw the body, you can describe the scene. Yes, I think you should write it. The Bar Restaurante 33 story is your story."

"Okay, I'll write it, but I might have to leave out the personal angle. I can't write a story tonight that says I was right there at the murder scene last Thursday night and saw the body on the floor. That would look kind of funny, me sitting on the story that long. Any good reporter would've pounced on it right away."

"You know, I wondered about that, Harry. That's when I first suspected you, or your girlfriend, or both of you. Why didn't you break the story right away?"

"How could I? I just got in town. I hadn't even been over to the UP office. How was I going to do a story? Who was I going to file it with?"

"Yes, I see what you mean. You didn't have a job yet. Well, I crossed you off my list as a suspect when I determined the facts of the case."

Gonzalez took a long draw on his cigar and blew another cloud of smoke. "You can say you held off because the police asked you to, and that'll be the truth, because I don't want you to write anything until the PGR tells me I can release it. We solved the murder part of the case, but they still want to know more about Vasiliev's activities here in

Mexico. It's in their hands, and they're working on it right now. They'll notify me when it's okay to release the information. I would appreciate it—in fact I insist—that you hold your story until I tell you. I'll call you when they tell me it's okay to release it."

"And you just wrapped up the case tonight, so it's still a fresh story."

"Yes, it's still fresh—very fresh. We just got the final confirmation on Vasiliev's identity this evening. Other reporters, like your friend Duarte, have been following the case, but you're the first to ask me about it since we closed it." Gonzalez grinned. "Of course, you didn't ask me until after I told you most of the details, but that's a minor technicality."

"I could file a story right now and slug it *Hold for Release*. My lead would say 'police tonight solved the mystery' or something like that."

"No, wait till I tell you."

"I could phone it in right now, and tell them not to move it on the wire until I give the go-ahead."

"No, Harry, wait until I give you the go-ahead. Personally, I'd like you to do the story right now, and get it out to the public, but it's not my call. I'll call you tomorrow."

"Tomorrow? It's already tomorrow. It's Tuesday morning now. It's past midnight."

"So it is, so it is. Time gets away when you're busy on a tough case. I'll give you the go-ahead just as soon as I get the word from the Federal officials."

"Okay, and when I file the story I'll use all the information you gave me just now, including Vasiliev's name and all his background, right? And how you and the detective bureau were able to solve the case? The gun and the label in the coat and all those clues, right?"

"Of course, by all means. I leave it up to you how you handle your presence at the scene of the crime."

"I'll stay out of the story. I don't want to tell the whole world I was there when it happened."

"Quite a few people already know. Fernandez, for one, and the other people who saw you at the Bar Restaurante 33. And I believe you told Duarte and Prescott, correct? And, of course, your dinner companion certainly knows you were there."

"Yeah, you're right, but I don't want the Russians to know. I don't want them coming after me. I don't want them to think I saw something they didn't want me to see."

"Like who the killer was? But you can't identify the killer by name."

"But they don't know that. I won't even put my byline on the story. I can describe the scene, but I'll quote you for the description—the bullet in the bullfight poster, for example, or those tall Aztec screens, and the body stretched out on the floor, and all that stuff."

"That would be fine."

"And I won't file anything until you tell me. Trust me."

"Oh, I know I can trust you Harry. We understand each other. You're here in our country as a tourist on a tourist card, and I wouldn't want you to do anything that would jeopardize your tourist status, would I? I'm sure you don't want Gobernación to apply Article 33. After all, you haven't had an opportunity to see Acapulco, have you?"

"That's right. I want to spend some time on the beach."

"Of course Duarte and the other reporters will call me as soon as they see your story. They can do the follow-up coverage."

"Standard procedure," Harry said. "Duarte and I joked that we might have to solve the case ourselves, just like the writer in the movie, *The Third Man*."

"Ah, *The Third Man*, an excellent movie. Orson Welles. You can tell Duarte you ran into me here at the Del Prado in the middle of the night and that you asked me about the case. He'll call us, of course—Sergeant, pull up to the curb just beyond the entrance."

"But what about Calderón, the dead cowboy?" He's not a federal case, is he?"

"No, just a local matter. Right now, the management people here at the Del Prado want to say it's just a rumor, nothing but a rumor. They want to say somebody had a heart attack. The management wants to insist that nothing sinister happened here tonight."

"But it's too late for that," Harry said. "People are talking about it. A waiter told me about it. That Englishman in front of the hotel just now, he was talking about it. The story is out. The hotel might insist, but the word already is out."

"Yes, you're right about that. The hotel says it's nothing but a rumor with no confirmation, but that's the way it is with a good story, isn't it? You can't keep a good story down. The hotel people can't expect to keep it quiet for long. In the morning, when reporters ask us about the dead man in the Del Prado, we'll have to respond. You're the first reporter to inquire, Harry, so you might as well write the story, while it's still fresh."

"Okay, let me ask you a few more questions right now."

"Go right ahead, but what more can I tell you? You've been asking me questions, you've been interviewing me right here in my car. You know just about all there is to know. I've told you the cowboy's name, where he came from. I've told you his background. I've told you where and how he was killed. I've told you our determination on who the killer was, although we don't know his name. I've told you everything I know about him."

"You said Calderón worked in the oil fields, and he was a union organizer. You mean he was an organizer specifically for oil workers union?"

"Enforcer might be a better word."

"Do you think this might have been a union job? Do you think he might have had some connection with those fires at Pemex installations the past few weeks?"

"Perhaps. We've considered that possibility. Knowing what we know about his background, anything is possible."

"Didn't the Communists have a role in organizing the oil workers' union, back in the early days?"

"You're suggesting he was a Communist?"

"Was he?"

"Yes, he was a Communist, an active member, but his chief occupation was petty crime, with a special aptitude for contract killing."

"Who did he kill, and who hired him?"

"We never had anything on him that would stick. No hard evidence, just suppositions. The problem was we never could tie him to a weapon. Two of his supposed victims were in the oil business. There definitely could be a petroleum connection.

"This is your story now, Harry. Ask a few questions around the hotel, and see what more you can learn. As far as I'm concerned, the case of Calderón the cowboy is closed. We've completed our investigation, and closed the file. I'm sure I'll have another homicide to dig into when I get to my office in the morning. And I'll call you and give you the go-ahead on the Bar 33 story as soon as I get the word from the federal authorities."

The sergeant opened the rear door, and Harry stepped out into the fresh night air. "By the way," Gonzalez said as he handed Harry his business card, "when you write your stories about these killings—both of them—be sure you get the spelling and the title right."

CHAPTER 68

Harry drew a deep draft of fresh night air. He worked his way into the hotel and through the lobby, his eyes constantly sweeping the faces in the crowd. He made quick stops along the way to chat briefly with several hotel guests. He also talked to the doorman, the cigarette girl (another pack of Camels), a waiter, and a clerk at the reception desk.

The hotel employees all had heard about the incident. The waiter said it was a terrible thing. Roberto, the doorman, said he didn't understand how the cowboy could have slipped past him, said he must have come in through the garage or through Sanborn's. The desk clerk said the man on the stretcher might have been over-served in the bar. One Englishman said he'd heard that someone fell and injured his back; another heard it was a heart attack. A man and his wife from Guadalajara said nothing as terrible as this ever had happened before at their favorite hotel.

No one was able to provide any solid information, which was all right—Harry didn't expect any, he had all the information he needed for a good story. But they all found out that the guy from United Press was nosing around, asking a lot of questions.

Harry asked a bellhop to show him where the crime took place, "in the interest of diligent journalism." The police had cordoned off the area around the elevator down on the garage level. While the bellhop was chatting with a hotel security officer, Harry was able to stick his head through the open door of the elevator and look around.

The dimly-lit cabin had not been cleaned. A large concentration of dried blood, plus a couple of scraps of paper that might have fallen out of Calderón's pockets, remained on the floor. Harry assumed the police must have looked at those papers and found nothing of interest. They removed the body, but they were not in a rush to remove anything else. It was only logical to assume that, in their hurry, they might have overlooked a crumpled photograph or two on the floor of the cabin.

Back in his room, Harry dropped into the chair by the window, called the UP office and introduced himself to the overnight man.

"Oh, yeah, you're the new guy. You called earlier with a couple of stories from Veracruz. Good stories. You got something else on the fire?"

"No, this one is a bit different."

Harry dictated a story about the bloody murder in the luxurious Hotel Del Prado. Many of the details in his story were quotes from Detective Captain Victor Gonzalez Moreno (be sure to get that name right), including the identity of the dead man, Jaime Calderón, who was well-known to the police as a pistolero and a suspected contract killer.

Harry quoted Gonzalez on the determination that the victim was killed in a fight with another street thug. He quoted Gonzalez on the theory that the two of them were in the Del Prado to rob one or two of the financial gurus in town for this week's monetary conference. For a touch of levity, Harry dropped in the detective's remark that the two thugs were in the Del Prado to "augment their own monetary funds."

Harry felt a twinge in his side when he included the detective's speculation that the killer must have been wounded in the fight, as indicated by the blood on the tip of the dead man's knife. And he smiled when he quoted the detective's observation that the "killer must have been a powerful man to do such lethal damage in the confined space of an elevator car."

For color, Harry gave the rewrite man a couple of paragraphs describing the gala setting for the murder: the international crowd, the music, the banners, the flags draped over the balcony railings, the formal attire of many of the guests, the festive air. And he gave him a few tidbits from "guests and employees" who "wished to remain anonymous." Most of the anonymous comments were drawn from his own personal recollections of the incident.

For drama, Harry included a quote from an attractive young woman who wondered how such a terrible thing could happen "right here in this hotel, while my friend and I were sitting here in this lounge—perhaps the poor man was having a cocktail or a sandwich right there at that next table."

And for added drama, Harry ended with the detective's statement that "he's always happy to put the *Caso Cerrado* stamp on a messy case like this."

"Great story," the UP man said when Harry finished. "Anybody else have this yet?"

"Not yet. I just happened to bump into Detective Gonzalez here in the hotel as he was wrapping up the investigation, and he gave me the details. I think we ought to move it right away, before someone else gets hold of it. Can we make the morning papers?"

"It's almost one o'clock now, but we'll make it all right. I'll have to put your byline on it. You were on the scene, you were part of the story, right there in the middle of all the action."

Harry's side hurt when he laughed. "Hey, I don't make the news, I just write about it."

CHAPTER 69

The taxi passed an all-night taco stand, and the smell of cooking food drifted into the back seat. Damn it, Harry thought, I never did get that chicken sandwich. Maybe I can get something to eat in this Indianilla place.

"Where is this Indianilla place?" Harry asked. "And what is it, some kind of all-night restaurant?"

"It's not far, Señor, just a few blocks. It's open all night and all day, but it's not a restaurant. Indianilla is where the streetcars and trolley-buses come home to rest at the end of a busy day, worn out from criss-crossing the city all day. In the old days, trams and streetcars were built right there at Indianilla. Now the barns are used for repair and maintenance. But I'll bet you're going to Indianilla to visit the *Abuelitas*."

"Who are the Abuelitas?"

"Ah, yes, the Little Grandmas, the little old ladies in the courtyard outside the repair barns. They're out there every night, serving thick hot chocolate for the maintenance workers in the car barns and for the streetcar motormen and conductors when they pull in at the end of their runs, but they also serve it for the drunks who come here after a night of carousing."

Harry knew he wasn't a streetcar conductor, so he figured he must fit into that last category. He hadn't exactly been carousing, but he decided a cup of hot chocolate would taste damned good anyway.

"This place is a real find in the middle of the night," Harry said as he settled in at a little table in a quiet corner of the courtyard. "It's like an oasis in the middle of the desert."

"Yes, there's a lot of activity here, but it's also quiet and secluded. And there's a lot of history. Unfortunately we tend to take these rumbling old streetcars for granted. We see them everywhere, every day, and we curse them when they clang their bells and chase us off their tracks, but we forget that so many people rely on these monsters to get around. Not everyone can afford to drive a car. I thought this would be a good place for us to meet rather than a hotel lobby or a bar or a restaurant. No one will bother us here. Did you read the material?"

"Sure did, as soon as it was delivered. I brought it with me."

"What did you think of it?"

"Looks like a routine biography, the kind that's released to the press when someone is hired or gets a promotion or makes a speech or wins an award—or dies. Or maybe when he gets arrested, or something like that."

"That's what it is, all right, but it's not routine. A couple of significant details are missing, facts that I thought you should know. First, take a look at those paragraphs outlining his education."

Harry reached into his coat pocket and pulled out the sheets of paper. He scanned down the second page. "Says he studied engineering at the National Autonomous University here in Mexico City, then he received a masters degree from the University of Texas in Austin. Also did graduate work at the Polytechnic Institute in Mexico City. Quite an impressive background."

"Yes, it's very impressive, but take a closer look. Take a look at the dates."

"Says he got his degree from the National University in 1933, and his masters from Texas a year later, in the spring of 1934. Then he got his graduate degree from the Politécnico in 1937. That's three years later."

"That's right. Three years later. Now, skip down here, and look at this sentence."

"Says he joined the Compañía Mexicana del Petróleo El Águila in 1935."

"That's right, but there's a significant omission. What's missing is the date he joined the company. I happen to know he joined El Águila the sixteenth of December in 1935."

Harry took a sip of his hot chocolate. "You're kidding. That's eighteen months after his master's degree in Texas. He took a long vacation? A year and a half?"

"He was in Moscow all that time," Isabel said, "but it was no vacation. He spent eighteen months over there, studying geology and hydraulic engineering at a technical institute."

"This doesn't say anything about Moscow. He wants to keep his Russian education in the background, but a lot of people go to foreign countries to continue their studies. That's not unusual. After all, he also studied in Texas."

"No, it isn't unusual, and back in the Thirties it was okay to study in Russia. Diego Rivera went to school there, too, but everyone knows he's a Red. He certainly doesn't hide it. He flaunts his Communism and his atheism."

"Yeah, like the mural he did for the Del Prado, the one that said 'God does not exist.'"

"Correct. But right now, during all the confusion and the conflict of the Cold War, it's not such a good idea for an executive at a company like Pemex to be a Communist."

"So you think this guy is a Communist?"

"Yes, he is. He never talks about politics, at least I've never heard him say anything. Of course, I'm not that close to him at work. Now look at this paragraph down here."

Harry read the final paragraph, then read it again. "Says he's married and the father of three children—two sons and a daughter. He's a family man. That's always a nice touch. There's a problem with that?"

"No, not at all. There's no problem with him being a family man. As you say, it's a nice touch. The public can identify with a good, loving family man, the doting father of three beautiful children. But this biography is for the press and for public consumption, so naturally, there's no mention of his *casa chica* in Morelia."

"His little house? He has a vacation home?"

"Not exactly. It's not a vacation home. Velasco has another family in Morelia, a mistress and two small children. The casa chica is a macho thing, not uncommon with wealthy Mexican men. It's a way of proving their machismo, their manliness. Velasco's casa chica is supposed to be a secret, of course, and it certainly is not something he wants to be made public.

"No," Isabel continued, "I never would expect his casa chica to be mentioned in a press release, but I wanted you to see this second omission, Harry. I think it's important, I think it's something you should know."

"How do you happen to know about it?"

"Oh, we secretaries have a way of knowing these things. Secretaries always know what's going on."

"Secretaries would make excellent spies. Maybe you should apply to the government for a job."

Isabel laughed, her first departure from her solemn demeanor since she arrived at Indianilla, and she took a slow sip of her hot chocolate. "Well, maybe I am a spy, but if I really am a spy, I wouldn't be able to tell you, would I?"

"No, I guess not. You'd have to keep it a deep, dark secret."

"Yes, a deep, dark secret. Oh, I have thought about it from time to time. I suppose it might be an exciting job, and maybe I could do double duty, and keep my present job with Pemex. And maybe I would be doing something useful for my country."

"Well, you're already doing a little bit of that kind of work now." Harry said. "For all I know, your name is not Isabel, and you *are* a spy, and your job at Pemex is just a cover."

"No, I'm just a concerned citizen, Harry, and I'm concerned about something that I see as a potential problem, and I thought you should know because you're in a better position than I am to tell the story, if it should become necessary. I know a lot of newspapermen—you know, the people who call our office, and the ones who come to our press conferences, but I think you're the one I want to confide in. You're new here, and you don't have any preconceptions, like all those people on Bucareli."

"But you hardly know me."

"I'm a quick judge of character, and I could tell on the telephone that I like your character."

Harry felt the need to press on. "So Velasco is well-paid at Pemex? Does he make enough to support two families?"

"I'm sure it's a struggle. He has a good salary, but I'm sure he wants more, or needs more. As the children grow, the financial pressure builds. Right now, he has a big expense facing him in a few weeks, a birthday party for his daughter."

"Yeah, he mentioned it the other night, but Aguilar has the same thing coming up."

"That's right, but Aguilar has only one house and one family to worry about. Can I get you another cup of hot chocolate?"

"Sure, thanks. Those little grandmas make a good brew."

"Yes, it's like a witch's brew."

Harry laughed, and he recalled what he thought after their first telephone conversation. She's anything but a witch, and she sure as hell is not ugly. "So you think he's feeling the financial pinch?"

"His mistress in Morelia works, of course. She works in a small dress shop. I suppose that helps, but I'm certain he's under tremendous financial pressure."

"Does his wife know about this double life?"

"I'm not sure. I've met her on a few occasions, and she's a decent woman, a good mother and a good Catholic who would never consider divorce. As long as he takes care of her and her children and her home, she won't cause him any trouble."

"But how does he juggle two houses and two families? He must wear roller skates."

"His job requires him to travel to Pemex facilities in various parts of the country, just like his trip to Veracruz yesterday, so that gives him a good excuse to be away from home. He hops back and forth to Morelia, either by car or by air. He has his own airplane."

"I know. I saw his plane in Veracruz. My pilot pointed it out. But why are you telling me all this, Isabel?"

"I thought you should know about it. I love my job, Harry, I love my country, and I don't like what I see happening. It's been bothering me for quite a while, but I didn't know what to do about it. I didn't know until yesterday, that is. When I learned how bad the fire was in Veracruz, and the deaths of those men, I decided I had to do something."

CHAPTER 70

Isabel smiled as she stirred the thick chocolate. "I couldn't really talk to anyone else. I can't tell my boss, I have no real evidence. I can't tell the police, but when we talked on the phone yesterday you sounded like a decent person, and I decided then and there that I liked you. You're a man of action, and I like a man of action, a man who knows what to do and when to do it.

"And when I read the stories you wrote, I could tell you're also an honorable man, a man of principle. I believe you were genuinely disturbed by what you saw and what you learned in Veracruz. I could tell, from what you wrote and the way you wrote it, that you have compassion, you have a conscience and a good heart."

If Isabel had looked carefully in the subdued light of the courtyard lamps, she might have seen that Harry was blushing.

"I know you'll be writing more stories," she said, "and I thought you should know the truth about Velasco."

"I appreciate your concern, Isabel, but I need to know more about what's going on, and I'd like to know how Velasco is involved. Are you convinced he's a Communist?"

"He spent eighteen months in Russia. I believe his education went beyond just science and engineering, I believe his studies might have included indoctrination by the Communist Party, and perhaps even training by the secret police. He came back here during those turbulent years leading up to the petroleum expropriation, during the Cárdenas years, when the Communist Party was building strength here."

Harry took a slow drink of chocolate, studying Isabel's face as she talked. Yup, she definitely is not an ugly old witch. Anything but. She's the kind of girl I expected to meet in Mexico: a native-born, dark-eyed, dark-haired Latin doll. So different in appearance from Rosa, the Russian-born, blue-eyed blonde. Both are beautiful, each in her way, and they share a passionate patriotic love of Mexico.

"But who do you think could actually be setting the fires, setting off the explosions?" Harry asked. "Velasco wouldn't be doing it himself."

"Well, it has to be someone who knows what he's doing, someone who has worked in the oil fields."

Harry reached in his pocket and pulled out the picture of the man on the marble slab. "You mean someone like this guy?"

Isabel made a quick sign of the cross—the Roman way, Harry noticed. "My God, he looks … *he looks like he's dead.*"

"He is dead. He was the third victim in Veracruz. Do you recognize him?"

"I can't be sure, it's difficult to tell from the picture, in this soft light, but he does look familiar. Velasco would know someone like this, someone who could do whatever needs to be done."

"And you think Velasco needs more money to maintain his double life. But if he needs money, if he's short on money now, where did he get the money to pay this guy?"

"That's a good question. It's obvious he's not doing this by himself. Someone else would have to supply the money."

"The Communist Party people?"

"Of course, they have plenty of money."

"But how would setting the fires help Velasco?"

"He would like to be the hero, you know, and make a big show out of solving the mystery. He would like to take credit for putting an end to the fires, and have a press conference, and put out a press release and let the public know what a wonderful thing he has done in saving Pemex by stopping the fires, and Pemex would reward him with a bonus and a promotion. I think he even sees himself replacing Señor Bermudez as the head of Pemex."

"A power grab."

"Yes. He was hanging around the public relations department this afternoon, asking questions about how press releases are written. I had a glimpse of something he wrote himself, the rough draft of a press release."

"Tell me, Isabel, this idea has been gnawing at you?"

"Yes. I thought his casa chica was just a peccadillo that was none of my business. I thought I should just let it be, that I shouldn't try to force my moral values on someone else. But the fires during the past few weeks set me thinking, and the Veracruz fire ignited my anger. I made up my mind, Harry. I realized Velasco is an evil man—and I don't mean just because he has a casa chica and a mistress. I decided he's a real danger, a threat to the integrity of Pemex and the stability of Mexico."

"I'd say you're right about that."

"Yes, and I'm telling you now because I can't talk to Señor Aguilar about it. He would say the casa chica is none of my business, and he's right, of course. He would think I was being paranoid about Velasco's connection with the fires. I have no proof, and I can't very well go to the police or the PGR with only a suspicion."

Harry spooned the last bit of chocolate from the bottom of his cup. "How can I thank you for this, Isabel?"

"Don't worry about that, Harry. I'm just glad to be able to help."

"Well, under the circumstances, I think we should forget about the driving lessons for a while, but I'll give you a call at your office first thing in the morning."

Isabel looked at her watch and laughed. "In the morning?"

"Yeah, I guess it is morning now. I mean later in the morning. Are you going to be all right getting home now, at this hour?"

"Oh, don't worry about me, Harry. I'd like to give you a ride back to your hotel, but I don't think it would be a good idea. I think it would be better if you took a taxi. And my trusty little green car will get me home without any trouble."

CHAPTER 71

Harry picked up Detective Gonzalez' message at the reception desk and read it as he walked toward the elevators. In his room, he sat in his favorite chair by the window, lit a cigarette, and read the message again. Okay, he murmured, Gonzalez says he wants to get the word out to the public, and he wants me to write the story.

With a few hastily scribbled notes in front of him, Harry called the UP office. "Got another one for you."

"Another dead body at the Del Prado?"

"It's a dead body, all right, but not at the Del Prado. This one was in a restaurant. It happened last Thursday, but the police just wrapped it up tonight, barely an hour ago, so it's still a fresh story. They just gave me the go-ahead to file it, and right now we're the only ones who have it."

"Great. Another exclusive. I'm ready when you are."

Harry began to dictate. The lead to his story said the Federal District police, through meticulous detective work, have cracked the mystery of the brutal killing that occurred last Thursday evening in the back hallway of the Bar Restaurante 33. The police, working with the Federal Directorate of National Security, were able to identify the victim as Sergey Ivanovich Vasiliev, an agent of the Russian secret police, the MGB, who had been living and working underground in Mexico for many years.

Harry quoted Detective Capt. Victor Gonzalez Moreno on the painstaking work of the detective bureau in tracing the label in the victim's coat pocket to a tailor in Madrid, where Vasiliev had been stationed before coming to Mexico.

Through skillful forensic work, Harry said, the police were able to identify the Russian Tokarev TT-33 pistol and the distinctive bullets used in the crime, leading to the determination that the killer also was a Russian agent, not yet identified.

Harry smiled when he added the detective captain's observation that "it's ironic that what we have here is an intramural crime, with one Russian spy killing another Russian spy."

Harry paused. "Give me a minute," he said, "there's one detail I want to get straightened out in my head."

That bit about one Russian agent killing another, Harry wondered, was that conjecture, or did Gonzalez base his comment on solid information? Did he have someone specific in mind? Did Rosa tell me the whole truth, and nothing but the truth?

Harry continued with a paragraph that said "this reporter" happened to be having dinner in the Restaurante 33 the night of the killing. He made no mention of his dinner companion, implying he was alone.

He described the gruesome scene from his own recollection—the blood splatters on the floor and the wall, the bullet buried in the sand of the Manolete bullfight poster, the body with the blood-soaked shirt stretched out in the open doorway to the men's room. He mentioned the tall screens depicting the Aztecs' bloody human sacrifice, an oblique suggestion that there might be some sort of connection.

He included a line confessing that he nearly tripped over the body—quite by accident, of course. He explained he was trying to step carefully, to avoid contaminating the crime scene. This last bit, he thought, would add a bit of drama.

Harry wound up with a sentence explaining that the police had told him to withhold the story until now "in the interests of national security."

"That should do it," Harry said, "but I think we should emphasize why we're four days late with the story. Move that last sentence up higher, and put it right after the lead. Get it in the second paragraph."

"Good idea," the night man said. "You're in the story, so I'll have to put your byline on this one, too. Geez, you're right in the middle of the action again, just like with that Calderón piece."

"And like I told you before, I wasn't in the middle of the action, I just happened to stumble on it. How are we on timing?"

"It'll be close, but I think we can still make the morning editions. The Calderón story was no problem. Say, are you going to have another story for us later today?"

"No, I'm not anticipating anything, but who knows? I might stumble on another one. Anyway, I'm going to be playing golf this afternoon."

The night man laughed. "Well, maybe you'll stumble on a body out there in the middle of a sand trap. If you do, be sure to use the rake."

The long day finally caught up with Harry. Exhausted, he leaned back in his favorite lounge chair, kicked off his shoes, and put his feet on the ottoman. His feet ached, his stomach gurgled, the wound in his side burned. His eyelids flickered as he struggled to keep them open, his head bobbed as he fought to stay awake. His mind wandered.

This has been one hell of a day, Harry reflected. A few ups and a few downs … Arnie says it's all down hill … hot chocolate was good … Isabel's worried … so is Rosa … great time with Rosita … gotta see her tonight … couple of good stories from Gonzalez … good Veracruz stories too … cowboy gave me a scare … gotta keep my eyes open … Commies hiding in plain sight … crazy talk at flower shop … lots of booze … flowers for the people … what the hell's that all about? … food's gone … party's over … Pedro clears the table … clears the table … clears the table …

"*That's it!*" Harry cried out. Wide awake now, he jumped up from his chair, looked at his watch, and grinned.

CHAPTER 72

The back room at the Florería Roma smelled like a cheap cantina, with the stench of stale cigar and cigarette smoke, rotting cheese, day-old chorizo, pungent cilantro, spilled liquor, and half a dozen sweating human bodies. In one corner of the room a rotary fan was running full-speed. The alley door was ajar and the window was open wide, with a healthy breeze ruffling the curtain. But none of this free-flowing air seemed to help.

And right now, nobody cared. Miguel was asleep on the day bed, an empty Cardenal Mendoza bottle beside him, his faux foot resting comfortably on a pillow, his strident snoring competing with the rattling of the rotary fan.

Waiting for the telephone to ring, and fueled by an evening of abundant brandy, Miguel had stayed the night at the Florería Roma.

Pedro pushed through the back door, and cursed when he saw the body asleep on the day bed. "Miguel. You still here? Wake up, damn it! Get up! It's late! What're you doing here now?"

Miguel sat up with a start. The empty brandy bottle rolled to the floor. "Wh-what …? Oh… is that you, Pedro? What happened? What time is it?"

"What happened? Whadda ya mean, 'what happened?' You passed out, pendejo, that's what happened. You had too God-damned much to drink."

"No, I didn't pass out," Miguel muttered, forcing himself to swing his legs over the side of the bed. "I just stretched out here to rest my eyes while I waited for Orozco to call."

"And did he call?"

"No, not yet. He should be calling any minute now. What time is it?"

"It's time for you to get your ass off that sofa and get moving. Call Orozco right now. Or go find him—find out what happened to Sergio. We have to know."

Pedro tossed Miguel's bedside bottle into a trash can. "Come on, get up. Get moving. María Elena will be here. She's late, but she doesn't need to see what a pig pen this place is, and she doesn't need to know how bad it smells in here. The shop should be open now, and customers will be coming."

Miguel made his way to the sink and stuck his head under the faucet. He let the tepid water run over his head, soaking his scalp and his neck and his face.

"Why is that window open," Pedro asked.

"The window? Oh yeah, I guess I opened the window to let in some fresh air. I must have left it open when I fell asleep. The smoke was so thick in here I couldn't see from one side of the room to the other."

"You didn't have any trouble seeing where the brandy was stored. Now call Orozco."

"I'll call him as soon as I clear my head of that damned brandy. I need a couple aspirins. Just give me a minute or two."

"You need more than a couple of aspirins. You need black coffee, and lots of it. You were attacking the brandy last night like it was your last bit of life blood. Come on, get your ass in gear. We've got things to do today. And why was the back door open?"

The telephone rang, and Pedro grabbed the receiver on the first ring. "It's for you," he said, holding his hand over the mouthpiece. "It's your friend Orozco. I could hardly hear him, he whispers so softly."

Miguel grinned as he took the phone. "He loves to play the role of a spy or a private investigator. He loves sneaking around in the shadows."

The grin disappeared as Miguel listened. "You're absolutely certain? That's all you know? No details? Okay, call me as soon as you have more information."

Miguel dropped into one of the chairs by the table, his face the color of the pewter coffee carafe Pedro held in his hand. "Orozco says Sergio was shot. He says he was killed Thursday night in the back room of a restaurant on Avenida Juárez. That's all he knows. He said he'll call later if he learns more."

"Son of a bitch. Sergio was shot. That doesn't tell us much, but at least we know he didn't die of natural causes."

"It's the same thing, Pedro. Being shot is a natural cause of death in his line of work. But the big question is, who shot him?"

"Wait a minute! Thursday night? A restaurant? On Juárez? Maybe it was the Restaurante 33. My God, Rosa was at the Restaurante 33. She had dinner there with Harry Banister. She came in here to the shop after dinner.

"María Elena and I were working here in the workroom," Pedro continued, "getting the baskets and urns ready for the press conference. But Rosa didn't say anything about Sergio being at the restaurant, and she didn't say anything about anyone getting shot."

Miguel pounded his fist on the table. "Of course she didn't. It must have been the Restaurante 33, and it must have been Banister! He shot Sergio. I never did trust that gringo."

"Why would Banister want to kill Sergio? Banister just arrived in Mexico Thursday night. He didn't even know him."

"Banister claimed to be a reporter. He said he came to Mexico looking for work, but perhaps he's something more than just a reporter. Perhaps he actually did know Sergio, or at least he knew who he was."

"Yes, that's possible," Pedro said, "and if he knew who Sergio was, I'm sure he knew more than that. But what if it wasn't Banister? Who else could have killed him?"

"That's a good question. It could have been a DFSN agent. The Mexicans might have blown Sergio's cover."

"Or it could have been a Russian agent. He was not a likeable man, and I'm sure he had enemies inside the MGB."

Miguel snickered. "Or maybe it was an angry husband, or even a woman."

"It could have been most anybody," Pedro said. "We just don't know, and it's no good speculating. The police will have to figure it out.

"Meanwhile, let's get this placed cleaned up before María Elena gets here. Banister said he'd be back today to talk about what he can do for us, but we'll have to keep a close eye on him from now on. If he's the one who killed Sergio, he's a real danger to us."

Miguel laughed. "He's not a danger to us. You won't have to worry about him any longer. I've already taken care of that, just like you asked me to."

"What do you mean, just like I asked you to?"

"When you gave me his picture Friday night, after you came back from the Brazilian embassy. I arranged for my friend Jaime to follow him. I gave him the picture. Banister won't be giving us any trouble."

"What're you saying? You already set it up?"

"Of course. I told you all along I didn't trust that gringo. He was dangerous. When he left here last night, I knew he had to go. He heard too much while he was here, too much information. But don't worry, Jaime's been following him for the last couple of days. He knows where Banister's been, and he knows what he's been doing, and by now he's taken care of everything. Jaime's a good man."

"For Christ's sake, Banister was with us at dinner Saturday night, and he was in Veracruz all day yesterday. Did your friend follow him to Veracruz?"

"I don't know, but I called Jaime after you left yesterday, and I told him to go ahead and finish the job. Jaime knows his business and he'll take care of Banister, if he hasn't already. That gringo is a dead gringo now."

Pedro's face turned red with rage. "You fool! You shouldn't have done that. You were too quick. You should've waited. I had a plan for him."

Miguel laughed. "A plan? What plan? You don't mean writing some kind of God-damned press release for your phony trade association?

What good would that do? What could he say in a press release that we can't say ourselves?"

"But he's a writer, he has a way with words."

"So he's a writer. What makes him a writer? Because he has a typewriter? Big deal. Anybody can be a writer. Give me a typewriter and I'll show you who's a writer. Anyway, we don't need him. We don't know who he really was. He was dangerous, he was a threat, and I've taken steps to eliminate the threat."

"Damn it, Miguel, I wish you hadn't done that. I brought up the trade association at dinner for his sake. That was just a ruse to keep him on the string. My plan for him went beyond writing a press release. He wants to see the country, I was planning to use him as a courier, and take Rosita off that assignment. She's done enough. She needs a rest."

Pedro's voice dropped to a whisper. "Poor little Rosita. She really had an eye for him."

"Poor little Rosita? She'll be better off. Think about it, Pedro. All Banister wanted to do was get in her pants."

"But she's just a child, an innocent child."

"*Mierda*. She's not so innocent anymore, Pedro. She's a big girl now. She knows what's going on in the outside world. She knows what her father was doing in Spain. She knows what's going on around here. She may not know all the details, but she knows what we're doing, and you're the one who introduced her to this new world."

"What do you mean? All I did was give her a job selling flowers after her mother died."

"Yeah, you gave her a job selling flowers, but you also persuaded her to do a few other things for you. Running errands. Taking trips. All the way up to the border. Down to the coast. Delivering packages. Doing all your dirty work. You pulled her into our circle."

Pedro sat down at the table. His face went blank, and his head dropped. "Yes, you're right about that. I've asked her to do more than a child should have to do. But those were simple tasks, putting her in no real danger."

"She's in real danger now, Pedro, we're all in danger until we finish this thing. We have to look at all the possibilities. Remember what you said earlier, the advice Colonel Gutierrez gave us when we were fighting the Fascists in Spain. We have to keep our eyes open for enemies all around us."

Miguel paused, and he laughed a quiet laugh. "It just occurred to me. Sergio was a threat to her. Maybe she shot him."

"That's ridiculous," Pedro said. "Why would Rosa want to shoot him?"

"Why not? Did she know who he really was? Did she know he was a Russian agent? Did she know what he wanted to do?"

"I don't think she ever knew his true identity, but she did know he wanted to take her to Moscow. She knew he had arranged a scholarship for her to study music at the conservatory in Moscow."

"Pedro, you sentimental old fool. He never told you? There was no scholarship. That was just a ruse to get her to go with him. Sergio wanted to screw her, and then blackmail her, and press her into service with the MGB, and bring her back here to Mexico as a deep cover agent under his control. You never figured that out?"

Pedro slumped in his chair. His scissors, gripped tightly in his fist, pointed to the ceiling. "No, I knew nothing of Sergio's plan. If I had known, I would have killed him myself."

"Of course he never told you. He didn't trust you. He thought 'good old Tío Pedro' was too close to her, too protective, too sentimental. You believed his story about a music scholarship because you thought it would be a great opportunity for her, yet you must have known she didn't want to go to Moscow, even to study music."

"Yes, I knew she didn't want to go. But Rosa? A killer? My little Rosa Blanca? No way. I watched her blossom from just a little child, and grow into a beautiful young woman. There's no way she could be a killer."

"What does it matter? She's a survivor, Pedro. You and I were not killers when we joined the struggle in Spain, but we learned what we had to do to survive. Her father was not a killer when he came to Spain, and he learned what he had to do."

"But unfortunately he didn't survive."

"Right now it doesn't matter who shot Sergio. The important thing now is that we have to be careful. Like the colonel said, we have to keep our eyes open, constantly on the alert, watching for enemies that might be coming at us from any direction."

"The colonel gave us excellent advice," Pedro said quietly, and he smiled as he recalled Rosa's rumpled appearance, and the pair of sagging roses on her lapel, when she came to the Florería the night of Sergio's death. "Yes, Rosa truly is a survivor."

CHAPTER 73

Pedro jumped up from the table. "Okay, Miguel, let's get moving. We've got things to do today. You get on out of here—go home and get some aspirin. Take a shower and get yourself cleaned up. I'll try to straighten up the place before María Elena gets here."

"I'm already here." María Elena announced as she came in through the alley door. She put her purse on a chair, laid a couple of newspapers on the round table, and set a paper bag next to the newspapers. "Here, help yourselves. I brought you a half-dozen fresh *buñuelos*."

"Thank you, María Elena. That's very thoughtful," Pedro said. "A doughnut would taste good right now."

Miguel was on his way to the door. "Thanks, I'll pass on the pastry."

María Elena stepped in front of him. "Hold on. You might want to stay long enough to enjoy one doughnut."

"No, I have to run. I have things to do."

She shoved the copy of *Novedades* into Miguel's hands. "Well, you might want to see what's happening out there in the civilized world. I've marked a couple of stories I think you should read."

Miguel took the newspaper and sat on the edge of the day bed. He kept his thoughts to himself as he read the story about the dead man in the Bar Restaurante 33. Good riddance with that sleazy Russian scumbag out of the way. I never did like him. Banister wrote the story, so he was at the restaurant, just like we figured, but he didn't kill Sergio. Banister might have seen who the killer was, but it doesn't matter now because Banister's a dead man, too. Jaime got him last night, or he'll get him today."

Miguel started to get up from the day bed, but he sat down again when he spotted the story about the dead man at the Del Prado. "Son of a bitch," he muttered, but once again he kept his thoughts silent as he read the story. Somebody killed Jaime last night. Banister wrote this story, too. That means Banister's still alive. Maybe Banister killed Jaime. But who else might have done it?

"Sure you won't have one little buñuelo, Miguel?"

"No, I have to go," he said, tossing the paper on the table. "There's something I have to take care of. Right away." He slammed the alley door on his way out.

María Elena wiped the table top with a semblance of a clean napkin and sat down. She removed a cigarette from a polished silver case, placed it in the end of an elongated cigarette holder, and lit the tip. She leaned back in her chair, blew a perfect smoke ring into the air, and then dramatically stabbed the center of the circle of smoke with her cigarette.

"My God, it looks like you *cabrones* had a wild orgy in here last night—and it smells like it, too. Booze, garbage, and smoke. Worse yet, cigar smoke. Only thing missing, I suppose, were the women. Or did you have the whores in here with you, too? That old day bed looks like it really had a work-out. How many whores did you have here, Pedro? One? Two? Four? And I see lots of empty bottles. I hope you didn't run out of brandy, Pedro. I know how you like your brandy."

Pedro was stunned. What kind of language is this? It's not like her. How does she get off talking like that? Has she forgotten where she is, and who's in charge here?

In an attempt to downplay María Elena's outburst, and to change the subject, Pedro asked a simple question: "What's in the newspapers this morning?"

María Elena slid the copy of *Novedades* across the table to Pedro. "Here, read this story."

Pedro's face went blank when he read how the police had solved the perplexing case of the assassination last week in the Restaurante 33.

He was surprised when he saw Banister's byline, and he was shocked when he saw the identity of the victim. He was relieved when he read the detective's remark about "one Russian spy killing another Russian spy." Somebody got the slimy son of a bitch, one of his own kind, and Rosa's in the clear. Thank God it wasn't La Rosa Blanca. I've been worried about her ever since that night.

Another story on the same page raised a couple of puzzling questions: Miguel's friend is dead, and Harry wrote the story, which means Harry is still alive. The story says the police believe one of Calderón's "criminal cohorts" killed him, but what if Harry actually was the one who did it? And if so, who the hell is this Banister guy?

"My God," Pedro said, tossing the paper aside. "Sergio's dead. The police say he was shot by a Russian agent. Last Thursday. How could this be? He was supposed to be here last night."

"That's right, Sergey is dead. Poor fellow, it looks like he missed a good party last night. He's been out of circulation for a week, but now that his death has been confirmed, I've been put in charge."

Pedro had considered María Elena to be a well-meaning, hardworking clerk in his flower shop during the past few months—not too attractive, not too bright, sometimes good-natured, sometimes gruff. He always figured she was someone who didn't know a whole lot about flowers, someone who followed directions cheerfully. But who does she think she is? What the hell is she talking about now?

To cover his confusion, Pedro laughed. "What are you talking about? What do you mean you're in charge? This is *my* store, and I'm in charge here."

"I'm not talking about the store, Pedro. You can have this insignificant little flower shop and these putrid flowers. My God, sometimes I wish I could toss these stinking flowers in the trash can. You can have all this, if it keeps you busy, if it makes you happy. I'm talking about the Party's operation here in Mexico."

María Elena stood up and sauntered over to the sink, waving her cigarette holder in the air as she strolled around the room, piercing the occasional smoke ring to emphasize her words. "Now that Comrade Major Sergey Ivanovich Vasiliev is dead, I've been named to replace him. I'll be giving the orders from now on, coordinating with our top man at the embassy here in Mexico City. I'll be the direct link to Moscow for this project. You were expecting Sergey to bring you the latest word from Moscow last night. Unfortunately, he didn't make it to your meeting. From now on, you'll get your orders directly from me."

"Who the hell are you, anyway?"

"I am Captain Yelena Mariya Petrova of the Ministry for State Security. I was placed in your flower shop by the MGB."

"What do you mean, you were placed here? I hired you myself."

"Technically, that may be true, but I was sent to you for the interview. It was all arranged."

"But how could they arrange something like that?"

"We have our ways."

"You mean you were planted here to spy on me?"

"Let's just say that Moscow thought your flower shop would be a good place for me to be working, not specifically to spy on you, but as a cover while I perform my regular duties. A small, insignificant little business that no one would suspect. Your shop was selected because of your Party affiliation."

Pedro was on his feet, his heart racing, blood rushing to his face. "You're a God-damned Russian spy, and you've been here in my flower shop, spying on me, while I've been doing a faithful job for the Party."

Yelena spat as she continued her restless circuit of the room. "You've been rubbing elbows all these years with the debilitated Communist Party of Mexico. A scattering of dilettantes and dreamers, who lack the dedicated conviction of the international party. Yes, you've been faithful, like a little puppy trailing after his master, hoping for a table scrap, sniffing at Sergey's heels for your orders and your orts.

Pedro was simmering. "I didn't take orders from Sergio. I get my assignments directly from my control here in Mexico City. He's the one who tells me what has to be done, and when, and where. He tells me who I should contact to complete the task, and he provides the money. From there, I take care of the rest of it. I make my own decisions."

Yelena poked another smoke ring with the tip of her cigarette. "You've been nothing more than a minor messenger boy, delivering payments to the operatives who were selected to light the fires and set the explosions. You've been nothing more than a conduit, delivering funds and directives from the man who runs the technical aspects of the local operation, the man who recruits the arsonists and picks the date and the time and the location for each strike."

Pedro cursed as he tossed an empty bottle into the trash can. "As a matter of fact," he said, "Sergio didn't give me orders. I got my orders from a better source. Sergio had other problems."

"Perhaps that was part of his problem. He was distracted, busy with other things. All the wrong things. He had become too accustomed to the decadent lifestyle here in Mexico. He was letting important details slide. He liked to live the resort life, he and his horses and his whores. We cannot permit that kind of behavior. Sergey wasted too much time. He was not paying attention to details. He was not in control of the situation."

"I can't believe it. You've been such a good worker here in the flower shop."

She laughed. "I did what I had to do, for the good or the Party and Mother Russia. You've been telling me what to do here in the Florería Roma. Now the situation is reversed. From now on I'll be telling you what to do."

Pedro took a platter from the round table and set it in the sink. "I didn't take orders from Sergio, and I won't be taking orders from you. This is my shop, and as long as you're here you'll continue to take orders from me. My assignment is an important job. My control tells me what needs to be done, and I take care of it. Without me, the fires would never happen."

"Without you, someone else would be doing it, and what you've been doing—those fires and explosions—are nothing more than mere distractions."

"These fires are more than just 'mere distractions.' They're an important part of the plan, and yes, the fires are the harbingers of things to come, and the ultimate plan goes well beyond these early fires. I don't believe you have any idea of what the final plan is all about. I believe you're just bluffing in an effort to make your job sound more important than it really is."

Yelena laughed a low, guttural laugh, and stabbed another smoke ring as she continued her circular route. "You say that as if you, yourself, are a part of the master plan. All you know is dribs and drabs. All you have to do is perform your job for the local party, see to it that the payments are delivered to the right person, and after that it's out of your hands. The Party could get along without you.

"As a matter of fact, you haven't even been doing your job. You've had the impertinence to ask poor little Rosa to do the hard part for you, asking her to make those pay-off trips to Nuevo Laredo and Veracruz and those other places, putting her in danger while you sit here in the safety of the Florería, plucking petals from daisies and humming old zarzuela tunes. My god, your constant humming nearly drives me crazy."

"I asked her to help because I couldn't take the time. I couldn't afford to be away from my cover here in this shop. This flower shop is important. The flower shop is a center of activity, where my comrades can convene in confidence. I asked her to help because I believed she would be honored. I believed she would want to participate, just like her father did in Spain. I fought alongside her father in the great struggle in Spain, and incidentally, I took a bullet for the cause."

"But that was years ago, old fool. Since then, Rosa has been corrupted by her mother and her religion, and by the bourgeois life style here in Mexico, just like Sergey was. She never has been a true believer in our glorious cause. She's a nice enough girl, but she's just a naïve child. She's a romantic dreamer, she and her damned flowers and her mariachi music, and incidentally, her infatuation with that American reporter is a dangerous thing. Banister has been poking his nose in all the wrong places, snooping around where he shouldn't be. He's become a liability, and because of her infatuation with him she also has become a liability, and we have no patience for such people."

Yelena continued her nervous pacing. "And you were never part of the real international struggle. You were fighting for the Republicans in Spain, not for Mother Russia, and come to think of it, you didn't fight for Mother Russia in the Great Patriotic War either, as I did."

"We were fighting for a just cause in Spain. We were fighting to defend the elected government of the Spanish people. We were fighting Franco and the fascists, and Miguel and I, in particular, were fighting for the preservation and the autonomy of our beloved Basque homeland."

"You failed us in Spain, you and the International Brigade, those starry-eyed adventurers who came from America and the other capitalist countries to help you. The Irish and the Polish. The Mexicans and the Swedes and the Czechs and all the rest. The bullet you took in your arm didn't help us in the grand struggle, Pedro."

"And bullets are everywhere in this world. Sergey Ivanovich took a bullet last week—in fact, he took two bullets, and perhaps it's a good thing. It's good that he's been eliminated. He was a liability. He had become a danger. Whoever killed him did the Ministry a great favor."

"Did you a favor? What do you mean, did you a favor? Wasn't he a valued comrade?"

"He was a malingerer, a hindrance. He was an impediment. He was not performing. He had strayed from the true path. His death was a good thing. He had to go."

"But who would have killed him? According to Harry Banister's story in the newspaper this morning, the police say he was killed by a Russian agent, one of your own."

"Our investigators have been looking into it, believe me. There are many possibilities."

Pedro dropped an empty bottle into the trash can. "But who would benefit by his death? Who would want him out of the way?"

"It could be anyone who is a traitor to the cause, a trouble-maker, perhaps a double agent. Simply put, an enemy of the Soviet. A capitalist pig, perhaps an American or an English assassin, or perhaps a Dutch agent, or an agent of the CIA. Yes, of course, the CIA. The Americans have agents operating under cover here in Mexico right now, as we speak."

Yelena laughed, that same abrasive, guttural laugh. "I suspect your friend Banister might even be a CIA agent, operating right under your nose, romancing poor Rosa. Don't worry, Pedro, the MGB will find the killer, and take the proper steps. And the MGB will take whatever steps necessary to deal with inquisitive threats such as Banister."

"I'll tell you who could benefit from Sergio's death," Pedro said. "It could be a captain in the MGB who would like to be promoted to the rank of major. It could be someone who would like to take over the job of a superior officer. Someone who is ambitious, conniving, and devious. Someone who has put personal cravings and desires ahead of the Party's goals."

Pedro set an open brandy bottle on the ledge in the front of the armoire. "Yes, I'll tell you who could profit from Sergio's death. It's someone who's tired of working in an insignificant little flower shop, selling pretty petunias and stuffing baby's breath into a putrid pot. Someone who no longer wants to grovel and smile at the rich ladies from the fancy houses in the Lomas and say 'Good morning, ma'am. Is there anything I can do for you, ma'am? How can I be of service to you, ma'am?'"

Yelena stopped her frenetic pacing. She took a long draw on her cigarette and blew an incipient smoke ring. The breeze from the rotary fan next to the day bed immediately dispersed the smoke, sending it in all directions, destroying any chance for her smoke ring to take shape.

A startling thought struck Yelena as the smoke drifted away: Pedro is right. I could be their prime suspect. Everything Pedro says is correct. I complained to Moscow that Sergey was no longer reliable. I complained about his drinking and his whoring. Semyon Denisovich is aware I'm hungry for a promotion, and hungry for Sergey's job. Semyon knows I'm restless, snipping dead dahlias here in this fucking flower shop. And Semyon also knows I have a Tokarev TT-33.

"The MGB should not have to look too far," Pedro continued. "Whoever killed Sergio made a serious mistake, and no doubt will make another mistake. I'm sure the MGB investigators are very thorough, and they'll find their man—or woman, as the case may be."

Yelena's face turned red, her eyes glistened. "What are you saying, Pedro? Are you suggesting that *I* could have killed him? That's absurd. Last Thursday night I was here with you, remember?"

"You were? That's strange, María Elena—or whatever your name is—I don't remember, I don't recall you being here."

Yelena moved across the room and picked up her purse, pushing the window shut as she passed by. "Of course I was here. I was here all evening in the workroom, helping you prepare pots and urns for that Pemex press conference."

"No, María Elena, you were not here. I did all that work myself. I had to prepare all those baskets and urns and bouquets by myself. I had to tie those ribbons and trim those stems and water those flowers because there was no one here to help me."

Pedro opened the armoire door and pulled out a pistol. He turned to face Yelena, but he was too slow. She already had a gun in her hand, and she fired one shot. Pedro instinctively squeezed the trigger of his gun as he crumpled to the floor in front of the armoire, blood oozing from a hole in his upper chest. The open brandy bottle crashed to the floor next to him, breaking, and spraying his face with Cardenal Mendoza. He smiled a faint smile as he licked the brandy from his lips. A farewell kiss, he thought, from high on the cold mountain of my ama lur, my beloved homeland.

Yelena spat. "Die, old fool. Die here, in your stinking flower pot. You have plenty of flowers to make a proper blanket to cover your casket." She slammed the door on her way out.

CHAPTER 74

The sudden sound of the telephone disturbed Harry's restless sleep. Still in a fog, he let the ringing continue for a moment or two while he tried to clear his head and clear his throat. Then, to stop the annoying noise, he answered the phone.

"Hello, Harry. This is Gilberto Gomez in Veracruz. I hope it's not too early, but I thought you might be interested in what the harbor looks like this morning."

"I'm glad you called," Harry said, suppressing a yawn. He grabbed a pencil and a piece of hotel stationery, and shifted into his interrogation mode.

"Okay, so tell me, what's going on?"

"How many?"

"Where?"

"Who do you think they are?"

"You're kidding. How big?"

"So what do you make of it?"

"I agree with you, although it does sound like a wild idea. Many thanks, and please call me if you get more information. I'll be in and out, but I've got your number."

Harry hung up, and he sat for a moment on the edge of the bed, digesting what he had just heard. Not good, he decided. Have to keep in touch with Gomez. Right now, a shower, a *cold* shower, would be a good idea, and some clean clothes, and a little breakfast. I haven't had a decent meal since those chicken burritos yesterday at the Pozo

Hondo, and there's a lingering question about the decency of those damned things.

Before he could do anything, the telephone rang again.

"Mario?"

"Yeah, it's me."

"What's going on in Veracruz? All calm?"

"Things aren't back to normal yet. It'll be a week or so before the refinery is back in full operation. The damage was more extensive than we realized yesterday, more than just a lot of smoke and fire and excitement. Today we're trying to get the last of the debris cleaned up, and now the action has shifted out of town—there was a fire last night in Acapulco. Incidentally, your favorite restaurant, the Cantina Pozo Hondo, is open for business as usual, and I just had breakfast there."

"Still smells bad?"

"Always has and always will. But there's one bit of information I thought you should know. I showed the dead man's picture to the fellow I had breakfast with, and he recognized him immediately. He remembered seeing him working at the refinery in Salamanca a year or so ago. He was a drunk, and he couldn't do his job, so they fired him. The medical examiner at the clinic here said he was drunk Sunday night, and he didn't do a very good job of blowing up the refinery."

"But he did manage to kill himself, though."

"Yeah, and a couple of other men, too."

"Did your friend remember his name?"

"His name was Paco Cabrera, but everyone called him *Paco Poco Peso*."

"Paco Poco Peso?"

Mario laughed. "Well, it was either that or Poco Peso Paco. They say Paco would do just about anything for a handful of pesos."

"That job Sunday night should've been worth a hell of a lot more than just a few pesos. Any idea who paid him?"

"No, but Paco was just a roustabout, so it must've been someone with the technical expertise to know how to do it."

"Like someone who works for Pemex?"

"Probably, either now or in the past. Someone who knows his way around. Someone who could have told Cabrera what to do, and how to do it, and even when to do it, but apparently Paco just plain screwed up."

"And you saw Paco last Saturday at the cantina, right? You said he was having lunch with a girl who was trying to hide under a black wig."

"That's right, she must have been the one who brought him his instructions and his money, but nobody knows who she was."

"So now you have to connect Paco to the girl and connect them both to the guy who supplied the money and the instructions?"

"Well, either we will or the police will, when they learn Paco's name—or you will, Harry. It would make a hell of a story if you could make the connection yourself."

"Yeah, you're right. I'll see what I can do. You say the police don't know Paco's identity yet?"

"No, I just found out myself."

"Okay, sit on it for now. The police don't have to know just yet. Don't tell them. Don't tell anybody. I have an idea. I might be able to make the connection. Thanks for this update, Mario, and I'll get back to you."

Mario answered one question for me, Harry thought. Now I know the name of the guy who caused the damage in Veracruz. I know who brought him the money, and I know she got it from Pedro, but I don't know how Pedro fits in. Who was his source? A lot of questions still floating around out there, and the answers most likely are just like those Russian agents: they're hiding in plain sight. I guess I'll have to look in plain sight if I want to find the answers.

But the first order of business, Harry decided, is breakfast—a good breakfast. "Huevos rancheros, hot coffee and cold orange juice," he told the room service operator, "and send up a copy of *Novedades* with the food."

Harry took a shower, got dressed, and pulled his collection of photographs from the dresser drawer. He smiled when he saw the picture of Paco Cabrera. He looks peaceful, Harry thought, stretched out on his marble slab. Paco Poco Peso ... anything for a handful of pesos. But here's a new question to wrestle with: Paco Cabrera is dead, so who did the job last night in Acapulco?

The ringing of the telephone interrupted Harry's meditation.

"I'm in the cantina, having a cup of coffee," Alberto said. "Can you make it over here?"

"I don't know, I had a long night, and I'm slow getting started today."

"I guess you did have a long night, and a busy night. We carried four of your stories this morning. I tried to call Gonzalez just now, but he's not in. He's probably out running around on another homicide already. You really got to him last night. How did you manage that?"

"Just lucky, I guess. You could say I was in the right place at the right time, but I didn't get to Gonzalez, he got to me."

"You mean he finally found you?"

"Yeah. He was here at the hotel investigating the elevator killing, and he gave me the details on that one and also the details on the killing last week in the Bar Restaurante 33."

"What did you have to do, buy him dinner? Buy him a drink? Slip him a fifty?"

"No, nothing like that. He saw me, and he said he wanted to ask me a few questions. At first, I was afraid he was going to run me in, but he said he wanted to close the book on both those cases, and he wanted me to write the stories to get them out to the public as quickly as possible, before the inevitable rumors could do too much damage."

"Well, your stories sure caused a hell of a lot of damage for me. My editor doesn't like it when we get beat, especially by a wire service. And you and I were going to solve the one at the Bar 33 together, as a team, remember?"

"Yeah, but I couldn't turn him down, and I couldn't say, 'wait just a minute, Captain, while I call Alberto and get him out of bed.'"

"No, you're right, but now I need to get a couple of good follow-up pieces. I left a message for Gonzalez to stop in here for a cup of coffee. Why don't you join us?"

"I just called room service and ordered breakfast. Say, I've got a quick question for you, Alberto. What does *hamacas* mean to you? Does the word have a special meaning? Some kind of a code or a hidden meaning?"

"Not that I know of. A hammock is just a comfortable place to relax in the shade of the palm trees, winging gently in the breeze. It's a place to take a nap, to fall asleep. If you're very careful, you can even make out in a hammock. A hammock is a tropical thing, thanks to the Indians of the Caribbean. Why?"

"I heard someone mention hammocks yesterday. I couldn't hear everything he said, he was climbing into a car, but I did hear him tell his driver he wanted to go to the hammocks."

"Ah, *The* hammocks. That's different. There's a hotel in Acapulco called Las Hamacas. It's out on the afternoon beach, away from the crowds, away from downtown, and it's where President Alemán and a lot of the government people like to stay when they go down there."

"Acapulco! That's it!"

"What's this, another hot tip? Follow your nose? Follow the smoke? And who's going to Las Hamacas?"

"A guy I met at the Brazilian embassy. An army officer. I never did catch his last name, but he looked like he might be somebody important. Anyway, that fire in Acapulco last night gives me an excuse to get down there and check things out, and while I'm there I can hit the beach and maybe do some fishing."

"Wait a minute. You can't go running off to Acapulco. You're supposed to be playing golf today, remember? Two o'clock at Churubusco, and you'd better be there."

"Golf can wait. Right now, I don't have time for golf."

"What do you mean, you don't have time? I thought you came to Mexico to play golf."

"You're right, I did, but I do have other interests, you know, and sometimes they get in the way of each other. I smell a story, and like I said, this gives me an excuse to get down to Acapulco. Churubusco and Golf will have to wait."

"But we're both dead with the pro at Churubusco if you don't show up, and I'm dead with our ad salesman."

"Better to be figuratively dead at a golf club than literally dead in an alley—or an elevator."

CHAPTER 75

The shop was closed when Rosa arrived. The shutters were down and the *Cerrado* sign still hung on the front door. Someone should be here by now, she thought. Pedro should be here, or María Elena. And what about Miguel? I'm late, the morning is half-gone, but the shop should be open by now. What's wrong?

Rosa used her key to enter, and the sweet scent of flowers immediately raised her spirits. Things can't be all that bad, she decided, as long as flowers such as these continue to blossom and thrive. She moved slowly through the shop to the workroom, instinctively snipping a fading bloom with her fingernails as she passed a dahlia basket. Everything looks good, ready for us to open for business. But where are the others?

Rosa opened the first of the two doors leading to Pedro's meeting room. She hesitated when she opened the second door. The odors of last night's party were a shocking departure from the familiar floral aromas in the front of the shop. The floating fragrance of flowers that followed her fought to overpower the smell and the smoke in the meeting room.

Tentatively, she called out. "Pedro? Miguel?"

No answer.

"Is there anyone here?"

Still no answer.

Slowly, she moved into the cluttered room, her hand shielding her nose and her mouth. Then, from across the room, somewhere near the antique armoire, she heard a muffled moan.

"Rosita?"

Pedro was spread out on the floor in front of the armoire, his face drawn and pallid, his shirt soaked in blood.

"Rosita, is that you? Come, over here …"

Rosa hurried over and knelt by his side. *"Pedro! What happened?"*

"Rosita. Take my hand … I've been shot."

"What are you saying? Who shot you?"

"María Elena."

"María Elena? Why? When? Why would she do such a thing?" Rosa folded her rebozo to form a pillow and gently slipped it under Pedro's head.

"I don't know. Rosita, let me tell you something … María Elena is impostor. María Elena is dangerous."

"What do you mean?"

Pedro struggled to speak as pain contorted his face. "Stay away from María Elena. You're not really involved now … just a few little packages … don't get involved with the Russians … don't let them trap you …"

Rosa wiped Pedro's brow with the loose end of her rebozo.

"Are you saying María Elena is Russian?"

"Yes. Stay away from her, Rosita. Stay away from Communists. I was part of their schemes. I was trapped, I was duped. I'm sorry I used you, Rosita. You are not part of their evil schemes."

"Don't try to talk now, Pedro. I'll call a doctor."

"No … it's too late for doctor … doctor can't help now. Call Harry … find Harry … he'll know what to do … Harry knows detective. Rosita, water the flowers. Take care of the flowers, and they will bloom."

"Where's Miguel? Did he see what happened?"

"Miguel knows nothing. He was here all night, slept here, but he left when she came. No one here, just María Elena and me. Be careful, Rosita."

"Let me get a doctor. I'm going to call the police."

"Too late for doctor ... won't do any good. Listen. Call Harry's detective. Tell him. He'll know what to do."

Pedro coughed, fighting for air. "Rosita ... talk to Morales ... call him. He has papers. He'll tell you. Stay away from Russians, Rosita. Don't let them trap you."

"I'll be careful, Pedro. Who is Morales? Tell me what?"

Pedro reached out and took Rosa's hand. "Look in armoire ... Find number in my desk. Call Morales. He has papers ... Be good to the flowers, Rosita, and the flowers will be good to you ..."

Pedro coughed, blood seeping from the corner of his mouth. "Call Harry ... talk to Harry's friend."

"Who is Harry's friend?"

"Gonzalez. Talk to Detective Gonzalez."

Pedro coughed again. "And talk to Morales. He has papers. Be good to the flowers and they'll be good to you. Feed the flowers, Rosita, and flowers will bloom. Time and flowers wait for no man."

Pedro uttered a quiet cough. His fingers went limp and Rosa's hand slipped away. His eyes closed and his breathing stopped.

"Pedro! Tío Pedro!" Rosa made the sign of the cross, leaned forward, and gently kissed Pedro's forehead.

CHAPTER 76

Alberto's right, Harry thought, I can't go running off to Acapulco. Not yet, anyway. Not until I talk to a few people, ask a few questions, and get a few answers. Right now, it's time to work the telephone.

Harry opened the crumpled piece of yellow paper he had picked from Jaime Calderón's pocket—the cowboy's portable telephone directory. He scratched out one of the numbers, remembering how Calderón's wife-or-whatever cursed when she answered the phone last night. Well, she won't have to worry anymore about her man Jaime coming home late.

Harry dialed the second number on the list, the one that didn't answer last night. After ten or twelve rings he hung up and put a question mark next to the number on the yellow sheet. Might have to try that one later, he thought.

Next, Harry tried the third phone number, the one he was dialing last night when the bellhop knocked on the door. A woman answered, and Harry's immediate reaction was to hang up, but he held on while she repeated the greeting. He wanted to be sure he heard the name right. He swallowed hard and proceeded with the logical question,

"Is he there please?"

"I'm sorry, he's not in. Who's calling?"

"This is Harry Banister."

"I'm sorry, he's out of town."

"Is there somewhere I can reach him?"

"No, he cannot be reached. Can I help you?"

"He'll be in later?"

"I don't believe so."

"When will he be back?"

"I don't know. He'll be gone all day."

"Thanks. I'll try again later."

"Would you like to leave a message?"

"No, there's no message."

"I'll tell him you called."

Harry cursed as he hung up. Another answer drops into place, he thought, but a new question pops up.

Next, Harry unfolded a soiled paper napkin and dialed the number he had jotted just a few hours ago.

"Good morning, is Isabel there?"

"She's not here just now. Can I help you? Would you like to speak to Señor Aguilar?"

"Well, I really wanted to speak with Isabel. She'll be in later?"

"I don't know. Is there a message?"

"That's all right, there's no message. I'll try again a little later."

"Is this Mr. Banister?"

"Yes, it is. I take it Isabel mentioned my name?"

"Yes, she and I are close friends, and I'm covering her telephone for her this morning. I guessed that it might be you, judging by your accent. She talked about you several times yesterday. She said she was going to teach you how to drive our glorietas, and she said she was going to meet you for a cocktail after work. She sounded very excited."

"Well, we never did get around to doing the traffic circles, and we never did have a cocktail but yes, we did talk. She told me she's concerned about the fires at Pemex facilities around the country, and she said she's particularly concerned about potential problems with one of the Pemex executives."

"Yes, I know what you're talking about, and I know who you're talking about. Like I said, she and I are good friends, and right now I'm worried about her. She should be here, or I should have heard from her. I tried to phone her but I haven't been able to get an answer."

"You don't have any idea why she's late? Maybe she's not feeling well."

"No, she would have phoned by now. Señor Aguilar is concerned, too. We're very busy this morning, preparing a statement on last night's Acapulco fire. And I understand our mutual friend also wants to make a statement, and he wants us to put out a press release for him."

"A press release? What does he have to say that's so important?"

"I'm not sure of the details, but Isabel saw a rough draft. She told me he wants to name the man who's been setting the fires and the explosions. He wants to expose the man and then take credit for solving the mystery. He wants to be a big hero."

"Is the press release ready to go?"

"Oh, no, not yet. He wrote the draft, but it would have to be edited, maybe even rewritten, and put into proper Spanish, and approved by Aguilar and the other top executives. And he hasn't put the man's name in yet. He wants to do that at the last minute."

"Tell me, what is your name?

"My name is Juana."

"Juana, do you think you can delay this press release? Hide it in drawer? Re-check his spelling, re-check the grammar. Don't let it get out till you hear from me. Better yet, lose it in a waste basket or kill the damn thing altogether."

"No problem. I'll think of something. I don't think he's here right now anyway."

"Good. I'll call again later this morning. And I'd like to catch up with Isabel."

"Call this same number. If she's here, she'll answer. If she's not here yet, I'll answer."

"Okay, Juana, and please call me at the Del Prado as soon as you hear from her. If I'm not in my room, leave a message for me. If I'm gone, I'll call and tell you where I can be reached."

The answers have been hiding right in front of me, Harry thought, but where the hell is Isabel? She said she picked Indianilla last night because it would be secluded, better than a hotel lobby or a bar. But how safe was it?

Harry finished his eggs and got dressed. He picked up the two photos he had taken from the cowboy: the Polaroid picture of himself and the glossy portrait of a man named Ivan Booth. That's not a bad picture of me, he thought. Looks like it's a copy of a copy. Whoever made the first copy did a sloppy job masking out all those flowers in the background. It's easy to figure out where the picture was taken, but who took it? And more important, who made the copy? How did it wind up in Jaime Calderón's hands? And how many more copies are still floating around out there?

Harry flipped the two pictures face-down and studied the handwriting on the back. The names on these pictures were put there to help Calderón identify his targets, and the name on the back of my picture sure as hell worked. The cowboy recognized me when he saw me last night.

But what's the connection between Booth and me? Who is he? Why are we both on the cowboy's hit list? The writing on the back of Booth's picture says he's a Negro, but his picture shows he's a white man. And what's the significance of the number thirty-nine on the back?

Here's the scary part: Calderón is dead, but his patron is going to hire someone else to finish the job. Or he's going to try to do it himself. There's still a ton of questions out there, and I'd better come up with the right answers pretty quick.

CHAPTER 77

"I'm calling from a window phone, Vladimir. I don't have much time, so I can't say very much. There's been a change in my plans."

"I guess so, Lena. I saw Banister's stories in the morning papers. Now we know what happened to Sergey Ivanovich, and I know why he didn't show up for the meeting last night. But who killed him? The police say it was the MGB."

"The police could be wrong, Vlad. They don't have all the facts."

"But they have the bullets. They can figure it out from—"

"They might have the bullets, but they don't have the gun. They can't be sure. Listen to me, Vlad. That's not important right now. What's important now is that we proceed. What's important is that we don't fail. We must move forward."

"Everything is on schedule for me, Lena. I just have to make one minor adjustment."

"Good. And what's important right now is what's going on over at the Florería Roma. Somebody killed Pedro. Somebody shot him."

"When? Who shot him?"

"I don't know. Last night. This morning. I'm not sure."

"He was alive when I left the shop last night. He and Miguel were still there. Do you think Miguel might have done it?"

"It's possible. Or perhaps someone broke in during the night and shot him. A burglar. And yes, Miguel might have done it. I also think it might have been that American reporter, Banister."

"Of course, the nose of a tiger. You said he could be dangerous. He was at the meeting. He dropped in unannounced, hoping to see Rosa. Pedro let the meeting get out of hand, with too many people doing too much talking, too many wild statements, and I think Banister heard more than he should have."

"I think I'll go to the shop now, Vlad. I still have to maintain my cover there. I don't have much time. I'll know more after I get there."

"Who will run the flower shop now that Pedro is dead?"

"I don't know. Perhaps I will. Perhaps I can take it over in the interest of the Party. It makes an excellent cover, a base of operations for my work. I think I'll take over. Yes, that's it, I'm taking over the Florería Roma and I will run it myself."

"You don't know much about flowers, do you?"

"I know enough. Miguel can help me, and Rosa can help. Or Pepe, the porter. Yes, the porter. He knows what to do. They'll need to keep their jobs."

"Is the shop open now?"

"I don't think so. I haven't talked to anyone over there. Rosa might be there."

"Are the police there?"

"I don't know. I don't believe so. Nobody's called the police yet. Incidentally, I'm taking over for Sergey Ivanovich. Yes, I'm in charge now. Moscow will approve. Yes, Moscow will promote me. Everything will proceed on schedule. The fires might be over, but everything else will proceed—Vlad, I have to get off the phone now. I must hurry. Someone just walked up behind me. I don't have much time. Someone wants to use this phone. I don't have much time."

Yelena hung up. She ignored the coin dish next to the telephone and stepped out into the street to hail a taxi.

Vladimir thought about it. He wondered why Miguel would have shot Pedro. Miguel had been hitting the brandy pretty heavy all evening, but he and Pedro were close friends, from the old days in Spain. Miguel looked up to Pedro as his jefe, his leader. No, I don't think Miguel would have done it.

And I don't believe Banister would have done it. The American had nothing to gain from Pedro's death. Yelena says she's on her way to the flower shop now, and she tells me she hasn't talked to anyone at the shop, and she says no one has called the police. How does she know that? How does she know Pedro is dead? How does she know he was shot? How could she know so much while she knows so little?

And Vladimir wondered how much Pedro really knew. Yelena said yesterday that Pedro knows only about his own assignment, and that he might have known only "dribs and drabs" about the other project. Maybe I should go to the shop myself and see what's going on there. The police will take care of Pedro's murder, and Banister can write about it for his wire service. Yelena will bask for a while in the glory of her elevated stature in the Ministry. By tomorrow, all of this will be old news, and the fires will be old news, their ashes drifting in the breeze. And who knows, perhaps Yelena will be old news. By tomorrow afternoon, the world will be focused on the latest news.

CHAPTER 78

Harry picked up the copy of *Novedades* that came on the breakfast cart and took a quick look at the sports section. He smiled when he saw that the Yankees took a game from the Red Sox. Almost over but the shouting, he thought.

Then he turned to the main news section for the important stuff. A page one story on the fire in Acapulco, this one at a tank farm on the edge of town. Heavy damage, but no one injured. Police say it looks like it was accidental. The police must have missed something when they looked it over, Harry thought. But who set this one, with Poco Peso Paco Cabrera stretched out on a marble slab in Veracruz?

The two homicide stories, late as they were, also made it to page one. The two feature stories from Veracruz ran on the jump page, next to the bottom half of the Acapulco fire story. Harry chuckled when he read the headline on one of his stories: *Saboteurs: Red agents or Red Planet aliens?* That story might raise a few chuckles, and also a few questions.

Novedades gave prominent play to the meetings of the International Monetary Fund and the World Bank opening tomorrow at the Palacio de Bellas Artes and continuing into next week, right here at the Del Prado. Harry realized this was going to be a big story when he saw the list of fifty-some nations participating and a summary of some of the topics on the agenda: rapid world population growth … persistent inflation … development of transportation and electric power …

balance of payments disequilibrium … food production … exchange rate stability. Water and oil also expected to come up in the discussions.

This is pretty heavy stuff, Harry thought, and it looks like it's going to be boring to boot. Balance of payments disequilibrium? What the hell is that all about? This kind of financial mumbo-jumbo would put me to sleep in a hell of a hurry. I hope Prescott doesn't ask me to cover any of this, but it should make a great story for the business sections of newspapers here in Mexico and in the States and also in all those other countries.

Novedades also ran a full page of photos and thumb-nail biographies of some of the important financial gurus from around the world who will be taking part in the conferences. Mexican president Miguel Alemán, who will make the opening address tomorrow, rated the biggest photo on the page. He's a financial guru in his own right, and *Novedades*, is a big supporter of Alemán. Why not, Harry thought, since he owns a piece of the paper.

The men on this picture-page have a ton of financial power, Harry decided. Men like Horacio Lafer, Minister of Finance for Brazil and chairman of the board of governors of the World Bank. He'll be serving as chairman of the meetings. And this American, Eugene Robert Black, the former president of Chase National Bank. Now he's president of the World Bank. That's real power. And this one …

Holy Christ!

Harry dropped the paper. This is more than just a routine business story, he realized. This is front page stuff.

"Damn it," Harry muttered when the telephone rang. "No more calls."

But he couldn't resist. He picked up the phone.

"Harry, I'm at the flower shop."

"Good morning, Rosita. How are—"

"Harry, something's happened. Pedro is dead. He's been shot."

"*What? Pedro shot?* What happened? Who shot him?"

"I came in just now and I found him lying on the floor, dying. He said María Elena shot him. He was still alive when I got here, but he was struggling to breathe."

"María Elena? Why?"

"I don't know. He was failing fast, Harry. He died barely a minute or two after I got here. He'd lost a lot of blood. I asked him when she shot him, and he said he didn't know, but he said it seemed like it was hours ago. The poor man, he was just lying there on the floor. He couldn't move, he could hardly speak, and he barely could breathe. He said he was just lying there waiting for someone to come."

"But why did she shoot him?"

"He didn't say, but he said María Elena is an impostor. He said she's Russian, and I should avoid her. He said she's dangerous."

"I guess so. Anyone with a gun is dangerous." Jesus, Harry thought—another Russian, hiding in plain sight. "Anybody else around? Anybody else know he's dead?"

"No one else was here when it happened, just the two of them."

"How long have you been there?"

"Just a few minutes. I called you right away."

"Okay, that means no one else knows yet."

"Harry, I'm frightened. I need you. What if she comes back now? Can you come over?"

"I'll be there as quick as I can, Rosita. What does the place look like?"

"It looks like there was a wild party here last night, and it smells like it, too."

"I know, I was there, and it was breaking up when I left. Any signs of what happened this morning?"

"Just Pedro's body, lying on the floor. There's a broken bottle on the floor next to him. I think maybe he was trying to clean up the room when she shot him. And there are copies of today's *Excelsior* and *Novedades* on the table. She always brings the papers when she comes to work in the morning."

"That's good. That'll show that she's been there. Is the shop open or closed now? I mean, are the shutters on the front windows still down?"

"Yes, the shutters are down and the *Cerrado* sign is still on the door."

"Okay, that's good. Let's keep it that way. Where's Miguel?"

"I don't know. He should be here soon. Pedro said he was here when María Elena arrived this morning, but he left right away. The shop should be open for business, but we can't open now. We can't open today with Pedro dead. Shouldn't I call the police?"

"Yes, but wait a few minutes."

"I have a better idea, Harry. Why don't I come to your hotel room now?"

"That's a great idea, but not right now. Later. Is there anything else I should know?"

"Yes. He said you know a detective named Gonzalez."

"I'll call Gonzalez when I get there."

"Oh, there's one other thing. He told me I should talk to someone named Morales. He said I could find his number in his desk. I don't know the man."

"Okay, you can call him later. Now sit tight, and don't touch anything. I'm on my way. Wait five or six minutes and then call the police. Make it eight minutes."

Harry gathered his collection of photographs, business cards, scraps of note paper and napkins with scribbled names and numbers and stuffed them in his pockets. He threw a few things into his duffle bag, pulled the rest of his cash out of the golf ball pocket, left the room, and made his way down to the garage. Eight minutes later he pulled up to the curb and parked, half a block down from the Florería Roma.

CHAPTER 79

The police hadn't arrived yet, but Harry could hear their sirens approaching. He went around to the back of the shop and entered through the alley door.

Rosa rushed over and pulled Harry close, her arms tight around his neck. "Oh, Harry, I'm so glad you're here. Poor Pedro. He tried to hold on, but he couldn't, he'd lost so much blood."

Harry gave her a quiet kiss, and kissed a tear on her cheek. "You've had quite an ordeal, Rosita. It's no fun watching a man die."

"He was a good man, Harry. He just got mixed up with the wrong people. He was a Communist, yes, but that was not a political commitment for him. He joined the party in Mexico because he thought it was the thing to do, sort of a social club. He just followed along with the crowd. He wasn't really a violent revolutionary. He didn't want those fires to kill anyone, or hurt anyone. That wasn't supposed to happen."

"I know, Rosita. I understand. A lot of good-intentioned people get trapped in the Communist party's intrigues, like houseflies in a spider web."

"He just wanted what was best for people, and he thought what he was doing somehow would help. He loved his flowers, and he just wanted people to enjoy his flowers."

"I know, Rosita. That's the way I had him figured—listen, the police are here. They're rattling the front door."

Detective Capt. Victor Gonzalez and his sergeant opened the rear door of the flower shop and walked right in. Behind them came two uniformed patrolmen. Twenty paces behind came two ambulance technicians carrying a stretcher and a kit with a red cross stenciled on the side. "Someone called to report a shooting," Gonzalez said. "Who placed the call?"

"I called," Rosa volunteered quietly.

"Good morning Victor," Harry said, stepping forward to shake hands.

"Ah, Harry, good morning. Fancy meeting you here." Gonzalez already was moving over to Pedro's body, making a quick visual assessment of the room as he walked. "I heard on the police radio band that there had been a killing at the Florería Roma, so I decided to come over here and look into it myself. Shot once in the chest, I see. Who is this man?"

"He's the owner of the flower shop," Harry volunteered. "His name is Pedro Yzaguirre."

"And how do you happen to be here now, Harry? You seem to turn up conveniently, whenever there is a dead man."

"Rosa called me right after Pedro died. She was afraid, she didn't know what to do. She was afraid the killer might come back. I told her she should call the police and I hurried over."

Gonzalez turned to Rosa, and when he saw her blond hair and blue eyes, he decided she must be the good-looking güera who had dinner with Banister at the Bar Restaurante 33. "And what can you tell me about this?"

Rosa gave him the bare facts. "I arrived for work this morning, and Pedro was lying there in front of the armoire, barely breathing, failing fast. He'd been shot. He told me María Elena shot him, and then he died."

"And who is María Elena?"

"She works here, part time."

"And where is she now?"

"I don't know. Pedro was alone when I arrived. She was gone."

"Naturally. Where do you think she would be now?"

"I don't know. I have no idea. At home, maybe. Hiding somewhere."

"And when did this take place?"

"This morning, just a little while ago," Rosa said, pointing to the round table. "She brought those newspapers. She always brings the morning papers with her when she comes in."

Harry watched as the sergeant and the ambulance crew performed a cursory examination of Pedro's body. They checked his pulse to confirm that he really was dead. They looked for an exit wound and, finding none, decided the fatal bullet was still in the body. They lifted his body onto the stretcher, leaving a white rebozo, a broken brandy bottle, a pistol, and a splotch of blood on the floor where Pedro had been lying. Some of the blood still was fresh, some was dry, and some was fortified with brandy.

The ambulance crew wasted no time. They lifted the stretcher and took it out the back door. Pedro was gone from his beloved flower shop.

"Aha," Gonzalez said, "the removal of the decedent's body reveals several clues. And whose rebozo is that?"

"It's mine," Rosa said. "I tried to make him comfortable in his final moments."

"That was very thoughtful of you. And helpful to me in my investigation of this case."

"How does her rebozo help your case?" Harry asked.

Gonzalez turned to face Rosa. "When I arrived, I was confronted with the possibility that you actually might have been the killer, young lady, blaming the crime on someone else. It's not unusual for a killer to call the police immediately after the murder and report the crime. They mistakenly believe they can divert suspicion in this manner. Your embroidered initial 'R' on his temporary pillow, however, dispels any such thought. If you had shot him, you would not have been concerned about the comfort of his head.

"Now, then, what can you tell me about the gun?"

"That must be Pedro's gun," Harry said.

The Sergeant was holding the gun, sniffing the muzzle. "It's been fired recently, Captain. One round is missing. It looks like a Gabilondo Llama. A Spanish gun."

"Yes, Pedro was Spanish," Rosa said. "He came to Mexico after the Spanish Civil War."

"The irony of it," Gonzalez remarked. "He fought in the Spanish war, and lived to tell of it, but ultimately he died fighting for his life right here in his flower shop. He was able to fire one shot, but her bullet was the deadly one. Sergeant, see if you can locate the bullet from his gun. It must be somewhere on the other side of the room. Obviously they were having a serious disagreement."

"Obviously," Harry agreed.

"I thought she was a good employee here at the shop," Rosa said, "but apparently something went wrong."

"Yes, apparently," Gonzalez said, "and it looks like there has been some kind of a party here. What can you tell me about that? Could this crime have anything to do with the party?"

"No, that was last evening," Rosa said, "but it wasn't really a party. From time to time, Pedro would invite some of his friends in for a few drinks and a snack. All men. They would talk about politics and sports and things like that. Men talk. María Elena would not have been included in that."

"No, of course not. Perhaps Pedro and María Elena argued about who was going to clean up the mess from the party."

"We have a porter who will do that," Rosa said.

"That's good. I always like to have the crime scene cleaned up after a murder, after we've completed our work. Sergeant, what have you learned?"

"We can't find any trace of the bullet from the Spanish gun."

"Perhaps the porter will come across it when he cleans the room. If you men have finished your work here, you can move on. We have a full schedule this morning. Just a few more questions and the sergeant and I will be leaving, too."

Harry moved to the round table and pulled out a couple of chairs. "Victor, before you leave, I have something I'd like to show you. You too, Rosita."

Gonzalez spoke first. "Harry, you were able to get both your stories into print this morning, and you summed up the information very well. You even had a few things in your Calderón story that I didn't know myself. That was good reporting, almost as if you had been there yourself."

Harry forced himself not to smile. "Yes, after you left the Del Prado, I wandered around the lobby and I talked to a few people, some guests and some employees. Interesting what you can pick up with a few pertinent questions. I even went down to the garage to check out the elevator, the scene of the crime."

"What? You went down to look in the elevator cabin? Wasn't it cordoned off?"

"Yes, but I thought I should take a look at it."

Rosa interrupted. "Pardon me, but I haven't had a chance to see the morning papers yet. What did I miss?"

Harry handed Rosa the main news section from *Novedades*. "Take a quick look at these two stories. These are the homicide cases Captain Gonzalez is referring to, Rosita. He solved them both, the Bar Restaurante 33 case from last Thursday and the body in the elevator. Brilliant detective work. He and I bumped into each other late last night in the Del Prado, and I phoned both stories over to the UP office. Victor, is there anything new on either of those cases?"

"No, nothing new. We still have to finish the paperwork. Always there is paperwork, but as far as I'm concerned those cases are closed, and getting the stories into the newspapers so fast certainly helped put the lid on them. Thanks again for your cooperation, Harry. Like I said, we solve one crime and move on to another. Already this morning, we have four new cases. But what is it you want to show me?"

"Victor, you told me you're always happy to close a case, and stamp it *Caso Cerrado*. You said you're always glad you won't have to deal with a murder case after it's been solved."

"Absolutely. I'm always happy to close any case. Reopening a homicide case can present new problems that could be just as thorny, or even worse, than the first time around."

"Like the case of Jaime Calderón, for example?"

"Absolutely. Like I said, that case is closed. I don't like to waste time going over a case that's already been solved. Anyway, I know there's going to be another one to worry about. As a matter of fact, one of our new cases this morning is the kind of murder I never like to see."

"You mean there are some you actually like to see?"

"I didn't mean that the way it sounded. They're all bad, but in the homicides you wrote about, the victims were unsavory, undesirable characters. Evil men. One of them was an enemy of our country, the other was a thug, a hired killer. The world will be a better place now, without either of those two men. They won't be missed."

Gonzalez lowered his voice and continued. "But frequently the victim is an innocent person who did not deserve to die. That's the kind of case I never like to see, like the young woman whose body we found this morning. She had been shot twice in the head, execution style. She was sitting behind the steering wheel of her little green car."

Harry felt a sudden stab of pain in his side, and his spine stiffened. His throat clogged and his eyes blurred. He swallowed hard, and he cleared his throat, and he managed to utter a quiet question. "A little green car?"

"Yes, an English car, a Morris Minor."

"Where was that?"

"She was parked on a street in the Colonia de los Doctores, not far from the Indianilla car barns."

"How long had she been dead?"

"The medical examiner said she had been dead for six or seven hours, which put the time of death between one-thirty and two-thirty in the morning."

Pieces falling into place, Harry thought, and questions being answered, right before my eyes. Poor Isabel. She knew what she was doing. She was trying to help her country, trying to do her job. A sweet girl, really. She did her espionage work well. She had the facts, she wanted to help. She saw something that was not right, and she had the guts to do something about it. And she wanted me to help her. Well, the best thing I can do to help her now is take care of that son of a bitch Velasco, one way or another.

"Poor girl," Rosa said. "What a terrible way to die. Do you know who she was?"

"I'll have to talk to the officers working the case," Gonzalez said. "We do know, from a parking tag on her car, that she worked for Pemex."

"Pemex has been in the news a lot lately," Harry said, "and most of it is bad news. Those fires around the country are bad enough—there was another one last night in Acapulco. Three people were killed the other night in the Veracruz fire. And now this."

Harry paused to clear his throat again and catch his breath. "But this one is different. It sounds like this was a personal killing, a hateful killing, although you have to wonder if it might have some connection with the fires. So this is a murder you'll definitely want to solve."

"Absolutely. We want to find María Elena, of course, the woman who shot Pedro. That's a top priority, but this poor girl also is at the top of our list. I said we had four new homicides this morning, five with Pedro. The others were people who were killed in bar brawls. Those cases are easy to take care of. These two cases, Pedro and the young girl from Pemex, are the ones we don't like to see."

"Then I suppose preventing a murder can be just as important as solving a murder."

"Absolutely. Prevention is always a good idea, but what are you getting at, Harry? You said you have something to show me. Do you know something I should know?"

CHAPTER 80

Harry handed a photograph to Gonzalez. "Victor, I ran across this picture last night. I believe this man's life is in danger, and I believe you can do something to prevent his murder."

Gonzalez looked at the photo, flipped it over, and read the writing on the back:

Ivan Booth – Negro – 39 –

"When I first saw the name scrawled on the back," Harry continued, "I thought it was 'Ivan Booth,' but when I saw this same picture in *Novedades* this morning, with his name in the cutline under the picture, I realized I had made a mistake. I had misread the name. Either that or someone made a mistake writing the name. The man's name is not Ivan Booth. His name is Ivar Rooth."

"Ivar Rooth," Gonzalez repeated. "Yes, I can see how you could misread the name, the way it's written here, but who is Ivar Rooth?"

"He's the managing director of the IMF, the International Monetary Fund."

"He's a very important man, indeed," Gonzalez said, "with a very important job. But are you certain who he is? The information on the back of the picture is contradictory. The man in the picture is not a Negro, he's white."

"You're right, he is white, he's Caucasian," Harry said. "As a matter of fact, he's Swedish. Here, let me show you what I mean. Take a look at this picture-page in *Novedades*. These men are all here in Mexico

City for the annual meetings of the governors of the IMF and the World Bank. Here's Ivar Rooth's photo right here, the same picture you have in your hand. Same face, same man."

Harry was excited. Pieces were falling into place. "That word 'Negro' on the back of the photo does not refer to Rooth's race or his skin color. In fact, it has nothing to do with Rooth. That word, in English, means black, and in this case it's Black with a capital 'B.'"

Harry pointed to another picture on the page. "It refers to this man, Eugene Robert Black, the president of the World Bank."

"What you're saying is this photograph actually has two names written on the back."

"Exactly," Harry said. "Two names. One of the names just happens to be translated to Spanish. You told me Calderón was a pistolero, a paid assassin. I believe this picture was his ticket for a double-header, Rooth and Black."

"Calderón? What's does Calderón have to do with it? Where did you get this photo?"

"I found it on the elevator."

"The elevator? That elevator was cordoned off. My men are very thorough. How could they miss something like this lying on the floor of the elevator cabin?"

"Maybe it was the poor lighting."

"Are you telling me Calderón had this picture?"

"I can't think of any other way the picture could have turned up on the elevator, can you?"

Gonzalez frowned. He sat motionless, his eyes shifting between Harry's face and the picture. After a moment, he spoke. "Banister, you son of a bitch. I think maybe you're right. I think this picture was Calderón's ticket for a double-header, as you so graphically put it. Only one face, but two names. Two targets. Two kills. But what's the significance of this number thirty-nine on the back of the picture? I don't believe it's his age."

"Permit me," Rosa said. She took a ballpoint pen from her purse and drew a vertical line between the two digits. "You're right, Captain, it's not his age. That doesn't mean thirty-nine. That's a date, *3/9*, the third day of the ninth month. You Americans, Harry, would read that as March the ninth, but we Mexicans read it as the third of September."

"Good girl, Rosita," Harry said. "With the stroke of a pen you've given us the date for the double kill. This picture told Calderón not only who to kill but when to do it. Tomorrow is September the third, or, as you put it, the third of September, and tomorrow is the opening ceremony at the Palace of Fine Arts."

"Calderón is dead," Gonzalez said. "He's not going to kill anybody. But somebody else is going to try it. We already have planned for heavy security at the Palacio de Bellas Artes, both local and federal police. It's a big event, and President Alemán is going to be there. We can crank up the security a few notches, put more men on it. But who hired Calderón, who gave him this picture, this assignment?"

"I think I can help you on that one, Victor." Harry pulled out the crumpled piece of yellow paper. "I found this on the elevator, and I tried calling these telephone numbers—"

"Hold on there a minute, Banister. You found that on the elevator? Are you telling me my men missed that too?"

"Must have been the poor lighting. So I tried calling the numbers this morning. Two of them where no help, but the third number turned out to be the office of an engineer at Pemex named Humberto Velasco. His secretary told me he's out of town."

Gonzalez nodded, and stared at Harry. "Of course, the poor lighting. I'll have to admit, Harry, when I looked at the crime scene last night, I had difficulty focusing on some of the details. I'll have to tell the management people at the Del Prado to do something about fixing that poor lighting. It's hard on the eyes.

"But let me get this straight. You're telling me Calderón had Velasco's telephone number, so you think Velasco hired Calderón to kill these two foreign bankers?"

"That's right," Harry said, "and maybe a few other people as well. And I believe Velasco might be the man behind the fires. Get Velasco, and the fires will stop."

"Humberto Velasco is one of our customers," Rosa said. "In fact, we have a job scheduled for the Velasco family for the end of September. A quinceañero for their daughter."

Harry pulled another sheet of paper from his pocket and handed it to Gonzalez. "Victor, here is a list of names of some of the people mixed up with Velasco in this scheme. Names and dates, and a few notations. I believe their plan, in a word, is to create a wave of terrorism and death with a series of devastating Pemex fires, while Velasco grabs control of Pemex, along with a Communist takeover of the government here in Mexico and a Communist incursion into the United States, triggered by a pair of high-level assassinations and a concurrent explosion to disrupt the opening of the World Bank and IMF conferences at the Palacio de Bellas Artes, causing chaos and panic in the financial markets of the Western world."

Harry paused. "I guess that's more than one word, isn't it?"

Gonzalez looked at the sheet of paper and shook his head. "Don't tell me you found this on the floor of the elevator too."

"No, that's my handwriting you're looking at. You might say this was a joint project with Pedro. He put the list together, and I copied it on that piece of Del Prado stationery, just the way he wrote it."

"I recognize one name at the top of the list. Sergey Vasiliev. We don't have to worry about him anymore. And Paco Cabrera. He's dead, too. Velasco, or course, is on the list, and you say we still have to worry about him. Who are the others?"

"Some of those men were at Pedro's meeting last night. Miguel, of course, and José García, Jorge Bustamante, and General Suárez. Obviously, Sergey Vasiliev didn't make it to the meeting, but I believe he was the group's leader, their connection to Moscow. The other names I don't recognize."

"So Pedro kept a detailed journal of his activities," Gonzalez said. "Names, places and dates."

"That's right," Harry said. "He was very meticulous. He had the dates for all the fires, even for the fire last night in Acapulco."

"What are these notations next to some of the names? You put 'PBA' next to José García, for instance, and '$$$' next to both Bustamente and Velasco."

"I copied them just the way Pedro wrote them," Harry said. "I don't know about the PBA, but the peso sign, or dollar sign, means money. Velasco supplied the money to Cabrera, along with the instructions on where to strike the match."

"The 'PBA' could mean the Palacio de Bellas Artes," Rosa volunteered. "Maybe that means José García is supposed to be on hand tomorrow for the opening of the economic conference. And Jorge Bustamente is a professor of economics, so maybe he's supposed to be there, too."

"But we don't know what their assignments are," Harry said. "Maybe one, or both, of them have been picked to hit these two targets, now that Calderón is out of the way. This could be during the opening session, or even before it begins."

"But who picked them? I mean, who is in charge?" Gonzalez asked. "Sergey Vasiliev is dead. Who's giving the orders now? Velasco? Suárez? Bustamente?"

"Or someone who's not even on Pedro's list," Rosa suggested. "Someone we don't know about."

"Okay, let's concentrate on the ones we know," Gonzalez said. "I'll pass this information along to the Federales, and they can pick up García and Bustamente today, before they have a chance to do anything. And maybe we should bring in the CIA to help us, since one of the assassination targets is an American citizen."

"The CIA?" Harry asked.

"Sure. I'll let you handle that, Harry, since you've already been in contact with them."

Harry tried to hide his surprise, but he couldn't conceal the hint of a grin. "Me? How did you know that?"

"They're not the only ones capable of collecting information. We know Corbett has been trying to recruit you. Has he had any success?"

"Not yet, but after everything I've seen in the past twenty-four hours, you never know what might happen."

Gonzalez nodded, and smiled. "Now then, what's the General's role in all of this? How does he fit in?"

"Well, it must be something military," Harry said. "Maybe he's planning a march on the National Palace. Maybe he's planning to launch a revolution."

Gonzalez laughed. "Sounds far-fetched, but this whole damned thing sounds far-fetched. Those fires must have had some purpose, and what better purpose than to create terror and prepare the nation for something wild?"

"Pedro kept a detailed journal," Rosa said. "This must have been bothering him, weighing heavily on his conscience."

"I believe he went along with this gang just to see where they were going," Harry said. "I believe he was going to blow the whistle on them, but María Elena killed him before he had a chance to do anything."

"What do we know about this María Elena?" Gonzalez asked. "What's her background? Her name's not on his list."

"She's Russian," Rosa answered. "Beyond that, we don't know much. She only worked in the shop for a short time. She didn't know much about flowers. She spoke excellent Spanish, and I thought she was Mexican. She had me fooled."

Harry looked over at Rosa and smiled. "Imagine that, a Russian girl living here as a Mexican. She had us all fooled."

"We may never know her motive," Gonzalez said. "Meanwhile, my sergeant and I will move on now to our next case."

CHAPTER 81

Professor Jorge Bustamente closed his office door and picked up the telephone receiver.

"Vladimir, did you see the newspapers this morning?" José asked. "Did you know Calderón was killed last night?"

"Yes," the Professor replied. "I read the story."

"And Sergey Ivanovich has been dead for nearly a week."

"Yes, I saw both those stories," the Professor said, "But Calderón! That idiot! What was he doing in the Del Prado, two days before his assignment? He could have blown his chance for a clean hit tomorrow. Someone in the hotel could have recognized him."

"He was there on another assignment, Vlad. He was there to kill Banister, but obviously he failed. Velasco wanted to get rid of Banister. He said Banister caught up with him in Veracruz, and all but accused him of setting the fire himself."

Vladimir laughed. "Banister was right on target. I don't know if he realized how close he was. But he's dangerous. He knows too much. He heard too much last night at the flower shop. There was too much idle talk before Pedro was able to cut it off."

"Velasco is nervous, and rightly so, and he probably thinks getting rid of Banister would settle his nerves. And Jaime knew he could find Banister in the hotel."

"But he messed up. Banister is still alive, and Calderón is dead."

"Maybe Calderón was there to set up his moves for tomorrow's job, to familiarize himself with the layout of the hotel."

"Bullshit. He's been in the Del Prado before, he knows the layout."

"Maybe he was there to pick up extra cash from one of those visiting bankers."

"Hah, that foreign cash would not have done him any good."

"You're right about that, Vladimir. Which of the sleazy cantinas he hung out in would accept French francs or British pounds for a bottle of Dos Equis beer?"

"But more to the point, what value will that money have in France or England when our plan is put into play? The Western nations will cry for our help when their currency crashes and becomes worthless. The collapse of the IMF and the World Bank will destroy the Western world's dependence on the dollar and the pound sterling. There will be a rush of nations pushing each other out the exit doors, resigning from those tools of capitalism."

"Right. Poland already started the exodus by withdrawing—"

"Bah! They never should have joined in the first place," Vladimir said. "That was in 1945, when the Great Patriotic War was just over, before Moscow was able to solidify the Eastern bloc. Czechoslovakia also joined back then. But Poland soon realized that the IMF and the Bank are nothing but a grotesque Western plot, controlled by the old wealthy banking families of Europe and the United States."

"Like the Rothschilds?"

"Possibly. I have not been able to verify their involvement in this capitalistic combine, but it certainly would not surprise me. Mainly, it's a display of Anglo-American power. The Poles soon realized that the Bank, in particular, is top-heavy with Americans and is operated almost exclusively by English-speaking executives and staff. If you don't speak English, you're not part of the club. The Poles felt the whole structure was designed to bring Poland and other Eastern bloc countries in line, under the iron heel of the United States."

"But the German Federation and Japan, and even Jordan, joined barely a month ago, and Burma earlier this year," José said. "Could that be a sign of growing strength for the Bank and the IMF?"

"They're too late. The whole thing will be falling apart, like a house of cards, when our plan kicks into high gear tomorrow. There'll be a frantic run on the World Bank as frightened member nations rush to withdraw their deposits."

"What about tomorrow's targets, Vlad?"

"Just a slight change of plans. With Calderón gone, I'll have to handle it myself."

"You?"

"Yes, unless Velasco can come up with another shooter within the next few hours."

"But it's his job to take care of the killing."

"Yes and no. He hired one man, but that man is dead. Velasco's main interest is Pemex. Actually, Velasco's main concern is Velasco. His interests are right here in Mexico, his concern is mainly to provide for himself. He's greedy. He wants Pemex for himself. My concerns, and yours, are much broader. Our goals are international in scope. We can't wait for Velasco to provide us with another hired gun. Besides, I have the equipment, I have the experience, I have the eye, and I have the will."

"I've never pictured you as an assassin, Vladimir. I've always pictured you as the quiet, studious, professorial type, lecturing your students or burying your nose in a book in the library."

"Ah, you know what they say about a book and its cover. It's the pages on the inside of the book that matter. I'm more than just an academic. My studies of economics have enlightened me to the severity of the problems in the world today, and have led me to the knowledge and the decision that revolution is the only solution.

"Because of my position as a professor of economics, I have an observer's pass for the conference, and this will give me entrée tomorrow at the Del Prado. I'll be able to move around the hotel unimpeded. One of my students is a porter at the hotel. I'll take care of those men in the morning, in their rooms at the hotel. The bodies won't be discovered until later."

"In their rooms?"

"Yes. Meanwhile, all of the other conference participants will be in their seats in the Palace of Fine Arts, waiting for the arrival of those two men, and someone will have to announce that there will be a slight delay in the opening."

"Excellent," José said, "so my explosion will take place when the hall is full of capitalists."

"Precisely, and what is your plan, José? They'll have a ring of security around the Palacio de Bellas Artes so tight that a mosquito won't be able to get inside without an official name badge."

"Fortunately, I have that proper name badge, and I'll have no difficulty moving around inside the Palacio at will, early tomorrow morning, and planting the explosives. And believe me, it'll be a work of art. People in Cuernavaca will be able to hear it, and I'll be able to hear it with them, because by then I'll be in Cuernavaca, enjoying a scotch at a table in the square."

"Excellent, the Professor said. "All of this will serve notice that there are deep cracks in the seemingly impenetrable curtain of dollars and pounds that separates the capitalist countries of the West from the glorious future of Communism. The Party will prevail."

"A brilliant plan, Vladimir. Brilliant."

CHAPTER 82

"I'm coming with you, Harry."

"I think you should stay here, Rosita. This is something I have to do by myself. I don't know how long this will take. You take care of the shop, there's plenty for you to do right here."

"No, the shop will remain closed today, out of respect for Pedro. The shop will be all right. Besides, I don't want to stay here right now—I'm afraid María Elena will come back."

"Okay, but we'll have to move fast. The day's nearly half over now. I don't know what's going to happen and I don't know when we'll be back."

"I'm not going to worry about that, Harry, as long as I'm with you."

"What about the flowers?"

"The flowers will be all right. I just want to get away from the shop for a little while. I've got everything ready here. Pepe cleaned the meeting room and got rid of the trash. I checked all the stock on the selling floor and in the workroom, and I watered everything. I hung a wreath on the front door with a card that says 'we are closed today in memory of our beloved owner, Don Pedro Yzaguirre Mendoza, may he rest in peace.' The shop will be fine."

"Okay, that's good," Harry said. "What about Miguel?"

"He'll see the wreath. I left a note for him. I told him what happened. I tried to call him but I couldn't reach him. I'll talk to him later. He and Pepe can handle anything that might come up. I made a couple of calls to cancel today's appointments. Everything will be fine."

"Okay, you've been busy. While you were doing all that I made a few telephone calls from the other room—"

"Naturally."

"And I'll fill you in on the details as we move along. Let's go."

"I met a fellow in the bar the other night," Harry explained as he drove off. "He said it's good publicity to have his cars out on the streets and the roadways where people can see them. Sort of like a rolling billboard, advertising on wheels. He offered me the opportunity, and I took him up on it. So where do I turn?"

"Head south on Insurgentes. We'll pass the bull ring and the new University City, and down the road a bit we'll pick up Highway 95. We'll stay on Highway 95 all the way."

"How long will it take us?"

Rosa laughed. "Harry, the way you drive, it won't take long at all. They're building a new superhighway, but it won't be ready for a while. President Alemán is scheduled to cut the ribbon and dedicate it in November, but even that first section will only go as far as Cuernavaca."

"He's a real politician, ending his term with flair. He'll be memorialized on plaques all over the country. Say, we'll have to stop somewhere along the way and get some coffee. I didn't get much sleep last night."

"I wondered about that. You were up late with Detective Gonzalez, and up late filing those stories. What did you learn on the phone before we left?"

"I talked to Gonzalez. He already had turned over a copy of the list to the Federal people, and he said they're making good progress. He said they recognized many of the names immediately, and they're working fast to identify the others."

"That list! Harry, I'm confused. There were people we both knew on that list, like Professor Bustamante and Gen. Suárez, and also José García. And, of course, Paco Cabrera. Pedro was dealing directly with Cabrera, and so was I, but I didn't realize until today what Cabrera was doing."

"But Calderón's name wasn't there," Harry said. "That means Pedro didn't know him, so he didn't know that Velasco was paying

Calderón to be a killer. The thing I'm not clear on is how Calderón got my picture. I know the original Polaroid snapshot was taken the morning I came to the flower shop, and someone made a copy, or maybe two copies."

"It was Pedro's Polaroid camera, so he might have taken the picture," Rosa said, "but Miguel was in the shop that day, and so was María Elena. Any of them could have taken the picture."

"And any of them could have made a copy," Harry said. "But I think it was María Elena who made a copy, and passed it on to Velasco."

"And then Velasco gave it to Calderón."

"Or maybe Miguel passed it on, although I'll have to admit, Rosita, I did suspect it might have been you."

"Really?"

Harry smiled. "Just for a little while."

"Harry, you told Gonzalez that you and Pedro worked together to write the list. What was that all about? You said it was a joint project. When did you meet with him?"

"I didn't. I didn't really say we worked together to write it. I said it was Pedro's list. I saw it, and I copied it."

"But when did he show it to you?"

"He didn't, and I didn't really tell Gonzalez he did, but I wanted Gonzalez to think he did. I wanted him to believe that Pedro was planning to expose those bastards. I wanted Gonzalez to think that Pedro was not really a part of the conspiracy, that he was not a dangerous revolutionary, that he was a true patriot."

Rosa leaned over and kissed Harry's cheek. "That was sweet of you, Harry."

"And who knows, maybe he really was a loyal patriot. He sure didn't agree with everything they were discussing at the meeting last night. It sounded like he was just going along with the crowd."

"So when did you see the list?"

"This morning. Just a few hours ago. The list and the dates were all in Pedro's pocket notebook. I saw the notebook on the table during the meeting last night, and I noticed how carefully he guarded it. A couple of times, when José or the Professor was ranting, he wrote something in it and slipped it into his shirt pocket. Then I noticed him put it into a drawer when he was declaring an end to the meeting. I was curious, so I went back to the shop later—actually, it was early this morning, about two-thirty."

"Oh, Harry, you're kidding. At two-thirty in the morning? You broke into the flower shop like a common burglar? How did you get in?"

"Well, I didn't know if I would be able to get in. I gambled. And I didn't really break in. I went around to the back, and the window was open. One lamp was on. I looked in, and Miguel was asleep on the day bed. I climbed in the window and took the notebook out of the desk drawer."

"And Miguel didn't hear you?"

Harry laughed. "Are you kidding? He was out cold. He was snoring so loud, and that rotary fan was making so much noise, I could have knocked over the armoire and a chair and a tray of glasses, and he wouldn't have heard it. I was gone in less than two minutes. I went back to my room and copied the names and dates and all the other pertinent information. Then I fell asleep, and I slept for a few hours till the damned telephone woke me."

"How were you planning to put the notebook back?"

"I hadn't really thought about that. I guess I won't have to worry about it now."

"Did Gonzalez have any other news when you talked to him?"

"Yeah, he said the feds have a tail on Jorge Bustamente and José Garcia, but they're not ready to pick them up yet. They want to verify their identities first. And they want to identify more suspects, and see who else they can connect to this group, and sweep them all in at the same time, later today."

"They can't wait too long," Rosa said. "Remember that number on the back of the photo."

"That's right. Tomorrow's the day for the double-header, but they'd like to close things up tonight, to take the pressure off tomorrow's big event at the Palace of Fine Arts."

"How about Velasco? And General Popinjay?"

"He said they haven't been able to locate them, but they're working on it. That's why we're on the road now, Rosa. I believe they're both in Acapulco."

"I was going to ask why we're going to Acapulco today, with so much going on in Mexico City, but I thought you would tell me when the time was right."

"Well, there's a lot going on all over Mexico, not just in the Capital. When I arrived at the flower shop last night—the first time, that is—I overheard Suárez tell his driver he wanted to go to Las Hamacas. I since learned that Las Hamacas is the name of a hotel in Acapulco where a lot of the government people like to stay. So I figure the General must be there. Then, before we left, I called Arnie at the airport."

"He's the pilot who flew you to Veracruz?"

"Right. He said he wouldn't be able to help me today because he had to do some routine maintenance work on his plane, but he told me Velasco flew down to Acapulco yesterday."

"But you saw Velasco in Veracruz."

"That's true, and right after I saw him he came back to Mexico City, and then he flew to Acapulco. Not once, but twice."

"Twice? Why twice?"

"He lost Cabrera in Veracruz, and he didn't have anyone to do the job in Acapulco, so I think he had to go to Acapulco to do it himself. I asked Arnie what time he flew, and he said he didn't know, but he would try to find out. He said there are no secrets among the charter pilots. Everybody knows where everybody else is flying."

"But maybe he came back home today," Rosa said. "Maybe he's back in Mexico City."

"No, I think he's in Acapulco. Arnie said Velasco's plane was not in its usual tie-down spot this morning at the airport in Mexico City."

"So what happens when we get there? Neither one of us has a change of clothes."

"I have a few things in my duffle bag. When I left the hotel this morning I didn't know what was going to happen or what I was going to do or how long I might be gone. You can pick up a few things in the shops when we get there."

"And what do we do when we see either of those men?"
"I don't know. We'll figure it out as we go along."
"So you don't know how long we'll be in Acapulco?"
"Not really. We'll just see what happens."

CHAPTER 83

Rosa opened her eyes when Harry pulled into a gas station in Chilpancingo. "How long have I been sleeping?" she asked.

"Probably not long enough, but every little bit helps. While they're filling the tank we can get out and stretch our legs and use the restrooms, and maybe get a snack. And as long as we're here, I think I'll make a couple of phone calls."

"Naturally."

"What would you do without a telephone?" Rosa asked when they were back on the road again.

"I don't know. I think I have a congenital affliction," Harry laughed. "Some people are born blond, some are born smart, and some are born good-looking, but I was born with a telephone stuck in my ear, and I've never been able to get rid of it. Doctors tell me they can't do anything about it, surgery won't help, it's inoperable. But it sure comes in handy when I need to get some answers. I call it a 'tool of the trade.'"

"What did you learn just now?"

"I called the Del Prado and picked up a few messages. One was from Arnie. He called just thirty minutes after we left the flower shop. His message said our mutual friend made his first flight to Acapulco at six o'clock last night. He landed back in Mexico City around thirty minutes past midnight, refueled, and flew out again about three o'clock in the morning."

"But why did he come back to Mexico City? And why did he rush back to Acapulco?"

"The explosion and fire in Acapulco were not a problem," Harry said. "The story in the paper this morning said the explosion was just before ten o'clock, so he had plenty of time to fly down there, set it up, make the turn-around, and fly back to Mexico City. He didn't have any problems in Acapulco. I think his big problem was in Mexico City."

"That's a lot of flying in the middle of the night. His problem in Mexico City must have been very important."

Harry was silent. He was thinking, his eyes dead ahead. Yes, Velasco's problem must have been God-damned important. Something that couldn't wait. Something he had to handle himself. The *bomberos* in Acapulco would put out the blaze at the tank farm, but the problem in Mexico City required his personal attention.

"Are you awake, Harry? Don't fall asleep at the wheel. If you're too tired, pull over and I can take over the driving."

"Sorry about that. I'm all right, I'm wide awake. I've just been thinking. So much going on, and I'm trying to sort it all out. I was thinking about Velasco's second trip. Why did he fly back to Mexico City in the middle of the night? What was so damned important to him?"

"He had business to take care of?"

"Yeah. Personal business. His Pemex life and his personal life are tangled up together. Rosita, I think Velasco killed the girl in the car. The girl in the little green car."

"Velasco? Why do you think that?"

"I met her yesterday. She worked in the public relations department at Pemex. Her name was Isabel. She was wise to him. She knew he was a Communist. She knew he was the man behind the fires—"

"The man who was supplying the money to Pedro! The money I gave to Cabrera. My God."

"Yes. She knew he planned the fires, and set them up, and paid for them, and now that Cabrera is dead he wants to take credit for stopping them and be the big hero. Isabel saw the rough copy of the press release he had written announcing his grandiose achievement. He wants to kick Bermúdez out and take control of Pemex."

"Velasco, a hero? That monster! He's anything but a hero. Velasco's a villain. He's a killer. He's the one responsible for those three deaths in Veracruz. And now you say he killed the girl in the little green car. And he wants to take credit for stopping the fires? What a terrible man. Will the press release go out?"

"No, I talked to someone over there at Pemex this morning, and it's been killed. Stuffed in the trash. But I think he knew Isabel had seen the rough draft, and he was afraid she would screw things up for him."

"Now she's dead, but he's not going to be the hero."

"Right. we won't be down here very long, Rosa. We'll just take care of business and then get back up to Mexico City as quick as we can."

"What is our business in Acapulco?"

"I don't know yet. I want to talk to Velasco, and I want to talk to the General, and see what kind of story I can write. Maybe it won't amount to anything. Anyway, this is a nice way to get away from Mexico City for a little while."

Harry wanted to steer the conversation away from Velasco and murder. "By the way, Rosita, did you ever figure out who this Morales fellow is? The man Pedro told you to call?"

"Oh, yes, I was going to tell you later, Harry. I found his telephone number in the desk, just like Pedro said, and I called him while I was waiting for you this morning. Licenciado Morales is my mother's attorney, and he's been processing her will. He has papers for me to sign in a day or two. He said there are no complications, and since I'm her only heir, everything will pass to me."

"After his cut, I'm sure."

"Oh, he told me one other thing, Harry, and this was really a shock. He told me my mother owned the Florería Roma. Pedro had been leasing it from her all this time. Can you believe it? Pedro was so proud of the flower shop. He always referred to it as *his* flower shop, and he took care of it as if it really was his. All his friends, and all our customers, thought it was Pedro's flower shop."

"That's great, Rosita, I'm happy for you. You deserve it."

"He said my mother bought the shop years ago as an investment, and she leased it to Pedro when he came to Mexico to help him get established. She knew that Pedro had worked for a florist in Bilbao before the War in Spain, so she knew he had some experience in the business."

"And you never knew anything about the lease?"

"No, I never knew. She never said anything, and he never said anything. I think they kept it quiet so he could run the shop the way he wanted. Everyone thought he was the owner. He did such beautiful floral arrangements, Harry. He was a true artist. I'm going to miss him. He was a puzzle at times, and he could be demanding. Somehow he got mixed up in those terrible fires, and mixed up with those terrible people, but in his heart he was a good man."

Harry glanced over to his right, and he could see moisture in Rosa's eyes. There was a bond, he realized, between Rosa and her Tío Pedro. "Yes, he was a good man, Rosita."

"She let him run the shop, although I can recall some arguments they had from time to time about the business. How to do this and how to do that. Little things, not so much about flowers but about the shop, the business. Nothing serious, just little differences of opinion. I thought she was just meddling, but now I know why."

"I wonder if she really knew what was going on in the back room of her flower shop," Harry said. "Did she ever know what kind of mischief Pedro and his Commie friends were brewing in the back room? All of those clandestine meetings, people sneaking in and out through the alley door, Pedro's double doors to muffle the conversation? All their wild conspiracies?"

"Harry, she hated the Communists. I'm sure she never would have approved, but she might have suspected. She didn't like any of those people who came to the back room, at least the ones she knew about. I know she didn't like the Professor, and I know she didn't like Sergio. She knew he was trying to take me to Moscow, and she fought with him about that. They used to argue in Russian, hoping I wouldn't understand what they were saying."

"And Velasco? How about him?"

Rosa was silent for a moment, and then she spoke. "She thought he was the worst of the lot. She didn't think the flower shop should even do business with him."

"Maybe you could change the name of the flower shop, give it a fresh start. Maybe you could call it La Rosa Blanca?"

"My father's nickname for me? I'd have to think about that. Harry, you said there were several messages for you when you called. What were the others?"

"Oh, yeah. One was Corbett, the guy at the CIA. He's been trying to get me to work for them."

"Are going to do that?"

"I don't know, maybe. I suppose I could help them, and I guess I could use the extra money. I'll call him later. The other call was from Gonzalez. I called his office, and they transferred me to his mobile phone. He told me they found the missing bullet from Pedro's pistol."

"You mean they went back to the flower shop and searched again?"

"No, Gonzalez said they found it in the middle of Chapultepec Avenue, in the body of a woman who collapsed out in the middle of the street. Witnesses said she was staggering, and she was trying to wave one hand, trying to stop a taxi cab."

Rosa made a quick sign of the cross. "My God! María Elena?"

"Yes." Harry smiled, and shook his head. "Isn't it ironic, that Pedro's final act on earth was to take the wraps off a Russian spy who was working right there under his nose in your flower shop? The police had searched the back room looking for Pedro's stray bullet, but it wasn't a stray bullet at all. It found its mark, right on target. It just took a little longer to do its job."

Rosa closed her eyes, and looked down at her folded hands. After a moment she spoke softly. "I asked Pedro why she shot him, and he said he didn't know. But now we have to wonder, did she intend to kill him, or was it the other way around? Did he want to kill her? I wouldn't blame him if he did."

"Gonzalez said she was the aggressor. The angle of entry in Pedro's chest indicates they both were standing when she fired, and the entry wound on her body proves he was on his way down when he fired. There was no doubt about it, she fired first.

"Gonzalez also said she had two sets of identity papers, her fake Mexican papers and her MGB card. She was a captain in the MGB. And he said she had a pistol in her purse, a Tokarev TT-33, with one bullet missing."

Rosa perked up. "There she was, a Russian agent, hiding right in front of us."

Harry drove by the Acapulco airport as he approached the town. A typical tropical afternoon shower was falling on the field. He spotted Velasco's Piper Tri-Pacer parked on the tarmac next to the terminal. Busy little plane, he thought. Its wings must be tired.

"Velasco's in town, but we don't know where he is, so let's go to Las Hamacas and see what develops. I'll see if I can get us a room."

"Do you think we'll have to stay overnight?"

"I don't know. We'll see what happens. As long as we're here, we might as well see the town, maybe hit the beach."

CHAPTER 84

"Here, take this room key," Harry said. "You do what you need to do. Relax, make yourself comfortable. Do a little shopping if you need anything. I just want to look around the lobby and see what's going on."

Harry made a beeline for the bar, sat on a stool with a full view of the room, and ordered a Carta Blanca. No one was sitting on the veranda during this late-afternoon shower, but the covered area was bustling with a dozen or so army officers and fifteen or so civilians. Most of the army people were in uniform, a few were in casual slacks, and several were in sandals, bathing trunks, and tee shirts or sports shirts.

Harry hardly had a chance to taste his beer when a man in a bathing suit got up from a table and headed for the door to the lobby. At least Harry assumed he was wearing a bathing suit. An extra-long, loose-fitting guayabera hung down almost to the man's knees, effectively covering the presumed bathing trunks and anything else he might want to conceal.

"Good afternoon, General Suárez!" Harry said as he slid off his stool and stepped in front of the man, thrusting his right hand toward his chest. "How are you? Nice to see you again. Remember me? I'm Harry Banister. We met at the Brazilian embassy last week. Say, that certainly was a nice reception, wasn't it? Delicious *camarão tempura*. Those Brazilians certainly do know how to entertain."

The General's face showed a sudden look of surprise and apprehension. What the hell is this all about, he wondered. Is this guy armed? What's he going to do, and what's my best defensive move? Do I stand my ground, do I retreat, or do I attack?

The General chose to stand his ground. He automatically extended his right hand and shook Harry's hand. Second nature. It's what an officer and a gentleman does in a social situation.

"The flowers looked so nice at the Brazilian party, didn't they?" Harry continued. "Our friend Pedro Yzaguirre did the flowers. Say, this certainly is a beautiful hotel, isn't it? So tropical, out here on the afternoon beach, away from the Caleta crowd. Will you join me in a beer? A cocktail perhaps?"

The General was confused, but he was impressed. This guy really comes on strong. Pushy, but I like that, I respect him for that. He's tough. He's aggressive. He would be a good officer. I could use more men like him. "Yes, I remember you. Banister. You're the American newspaper reporter. What brings you to Acapulco, Banister?"

Harry had a reasonably firm grip on the General's elbow—not too firm, just enough to guide him to a table. "Why don't we have a seat here? These tropical showers are like clockwork. Every afternoon. You can set your watch by them."

"Bring me another tequila, double," the General said to the waiter. "That's right, Banister, the afternoon showers are very punctual this time of year."

"Are you going for a swim, my General? It's a great way to get your exercise."

"Yes, I am planning to go for a swim when the rain lets up, although I don't mind swimming in the rain. You're going to get wet anyway, so a little rain won't hurt. I try to swim every day, wherever I am."

Harry laughed. "That's so true about the rain. A little bit of rain won't hurt you when you're in the ocean. You're already wet anyway, but so many people abandon the ocean and head for cover when the rain starts. Say, I stopped by the Florería Roma yesterday afternoon, and Pedro said—"

"You were at the flower shop?"

"Yes. Pedro said you had just left. I'm sorry I missed you. We had a spirited discussion after you left. Sergey Ivanovich never did show up, but otherwise things are right on schedule. José García and Professor Bustamente were really wound up about their assignments. They're ready to do their thing. Jorge seems to have a firm grasp on the economic plan." Drop a few names, Harry thought. That always helps. "How about you, my General? Everything on schedule with you?"

The General frowned. What were they talking about at the flower shop, he wondered, and how much does this guy know? He calls Sergey by his Russian name? "Yes, I read about Sergey. Too bad. But what were you doing at the flower shop?"

"Pedro invited me. He said he wants me to be a regular part of your group. He wants me to write a pamphlet or a press release, or keep a journal of the group's activities, and maybe do some driving. Yes, he thought I could be a courier, and deliver packages to Humberto's new man in the field. Humberto lost a good man in Veracruz, you know. I hope that doesn't mean the end of the fires. The fires certainly are important. They're doing a great job, getting attention and agitating the public."

Gen. Suárez was squirming in his chair. What's this all about, he wondered. Why wasn't I informed? Who the hell is this Banister fellow? How much does he know? He's strong. I like that. He's forceful. We need more men like that. I could use him. "Humberto's man was a drunk. He messed up his assignment in Veracruz. There's no room for drunks in this operation."

"You're absolutely right about that, my General. I agree with you whole-heartedly."

"And Humberto is a fool, relying on a drunk like that." The General leaned forward and laughed. "He's a fool in a lot of other ways, too."

"But Humberto took care of everything quite well last night here in Acapulco, didn't he? I mean, the fire was a success? Plenty of damage."

"God damn it, no! Things did not go well last night. Velasco is an ass! That was a debacle. Entirely too much damage. The idea is to create some excitement and big headlines in the newspaper, frighten the people, not to destroy the whole God-damned tank farm."

"Yeah, I guess the damage was pretty severe," Harry said.

The General was getting warmed up. "And then Velasco disappeared. Where the hell did he go? That was stupid. He was the ranking Pemex official on hand. He should have been here. He should've been available to talk to the local authorities. I don't know where he disappeared to."

Harry saw an opportunity. "I think he flew back to Mexico City."

"What? In the middle of the night?"

"I think there was something he wanted to take care of in Mexico City. Some sort of personal business."

"What the hell are you talking about? Why would he go back to Mexico City in the middle of the night? He was back here again this morning. I saw him at breakfast."

"Something about a press release he wants to put out, something about a statement he wants to make about the fires."

"What's he doing making a statement to the press? That's not his job. What does he have to say to the press? Pemex has people for that."

"Well, as I understand it, he wants to put out a press release that says he's been doing some investigating and he's discovered who's been setting the fires—"

The General was simmering. He rapped his empty tequila glass on the table in anger. "What the hell does he mean by that? He knows damn well who's been setting the fires. He hired the guy!"

Harry nonchalantly signaled the waiter, and motioned to the General's empty glass. "Well, I hope this will not mean the end of the fires, with Velasco's point man dead. We need those fires. Will Humberto have to do it all himself, like he did last night?"

"No, this is not the end of the fires, and Velasco's press release is premature. From now on the fires will be handled differently, and from now on Velasco won't be involved at all. I have a skilled munitions expert who can expedite the next one, and I will supervise everything personally. I'll have to replace Velasco, one way or another. He's an idiot, anyway."

Harry's mind was racing. This could turn out well, with these two guys working against each other. I may not have to do anything, just let nature take its course.

"I know Pedro's been getting his instructions from Velasco, and doing what he's told to do," the General continued. "Pedro is a good man. He's a florist, and a fine one at that, but he's not a military man, and he's not trained as an undercover agent."

The waiter brought another double tequila, and the General quaffed it in one gulp. Harry took a sip of his beer.

"From now on Pedro will be getting his orders directly from me," the General said. "From now on the fires must be carefully controlled. Velasco's fires were not well planned, they were not strategically selective. The fire in Veracruz was a fiasco. There was a danger it could have damaged the port facilities, and we're going to need that port and those docks for the next phase of the operation."

The General was fuming, and his voice was rising. "We must not burn the hand that feeds us, Banister. Pemex is vital to our success. We're going to need Pemex fuel for everything that's coming up. Yes, I'm on schedule, and these men here in the bar are my loyal officers, ready to do my bidding."

"They look like a fine group of officers."

"But there are too many civilians in here right now, Banister. Let's take a walk, where we can talk freely. What I have to say is not for the ears of those civilians. You never can tell who might be sitting among them. As a matter of fact, what I'm going to tell you is known by only a handful of my junior officers."

"The rain should be letting up, let's take a walk down by the beach."

Harry glanced over his shoulder and spotted Rosa and Velasco as they sauntered across the lobby. What the hell is she doing, he wondered.

Rosa looked across the lobby and saw Harry and his new friend as they made their way toward the front door of the hotel. Where's he going with General Popinjay, she wondered.

Harry and his new friend crossed the road and stepped onto the beach. The rain, however, had not stopped, and lightning over the water indicated a storm was moving in. A rumble of thunder in the distance indicated the storm was still a few miles away. Harry silently counted the seconds between a flash of lightning and the subsequent clap of thunder—one Mississippi, two Mississippi, three Mississippi, four Mississippi, five Mississippi, six ….

The sand was soaked, and the footing was treacherous. The two men moved gingerly toward a row of large canopies and took shelter under one of the vacant canopies, where they were dry and reasonably comfortable in a pair of folding hammock-like sling chairs. A few brave souls walked the beach, and a few more huddled under nearby canopies.

"Getting back to the business at hand," the General continued, "there will be two or three more fires, and I'm picking the time and the place. Frankly, Velasco screwed up. His man in Veracruz was a drunken buffoon, and Velasco himself is no genius, but we have to move on to the next phase."

"The fires are doing a good job stirring up the public, creating unrest," Harry said, "but I believe we need more."

"I think you're right, Banister. And it will be necessary for me to take control of Pemex, for the good of the nation, for the good of Pemex, for the good of the people. The oil belongs to the people, not to the bureaucrats at Pemex. And it sure as hell won't belong to Velasco."

"Absolutely."

"Yes, it will be necessary for me to take over Pemex, and there will be a brief interruption of production and deliveries. For a brief time, people will not have gasoline for their cars. The wealthy will not be able to buy fuel for their limousines or their yachts or their airplanes. Deliveries of vital goods will be curtailed. Food, medicine, clothing, liquor, beer—all the necessities of daily life and all the luxuries the wealthy crave. Buses and taxi cabs will not be able to operate. Private companies will have no fuel for their trucks."

"But people will be unhappy," Harry said.

"Yes, there will a great public uproar, but it's all for the good of the nation."

"Of course, for the good of the nation," Harry agreed.

"The seaports will be closed, the airlines will not fly. I'll control the military, and I'll decide who will have fuel. I'll control the railroads because I'll control their fuel, and I'll use the railroads for vital troop deployments. And, believe me, Banister, there will be strategic troop movements."

"It's a bold plan you have, my General, and I'm confident you can do it."

"Yes, it is a bold plan, indeed. I can't do it alone, but I'll have help. That's why it's essential that we maintain control of the seaports."

"Seaports like Veracruz?"

The General hesitated. "Yes, ports like Veracruz. And Acapulco, Tuxpan, Mazatlán, Tampico, Manzanillo ..." He hesitated again, and then he continued slowly. "I'll be receiving a surge of valuable support through these vital port facilities. Personnel and armaments."

Holy Christ, Harry realized, this guy wants to take over the whole God-damned country, not just Pemex. Unidentified ships, flying unknown flags, waiting to dock in Veracruz, just like I saw yesterday, just like Gilberto Gomez described on the phone this morning. Ships with troops, ships waiting for a signal from General Suárez.

Harry continued his quiet count. One Mississippi, two Mississippi, three Mississippi, four Mississippi, five ... "And how does Velasco fit into this?"

"He knows all this, of course. He's been part of the master plan. But his main interest is his personal goal of controlling Pemex. His personal greed. My interests are much broader. Yes, I want to control Pemex, as well I should, but I see important opportunities here in Mexico and beyond, and my opportunities are supported by the Kremlin and the international Party."

"But Velasco stands in your way."

"Nothing stands in my way. I'm ready to move forward. Nothing will stand in my way, Banister. Nothing. No one—not Velasco, not the Mexican armed forces, not the DFSN—no one will stand in my way! Not even you, Banister!"

"Me?"

"Yes, you. I know why you're pumping me for information, for details. I know what you're doing, I know who you are and who you're working for!"

The storm was moving in. One Mississippi, two Mississippi, three ...

CHAPTER 85

Talk fast, Rosa told herself. Catch Velasco by surprise, and keep him off guard.

"Señor Velasco, what a surprise. I didn't expect to see you here today. Is Señora Velasco with you? I've been meaning to call her. I have some new ideas for your daughter's quinceañero. I'd like to show her the drawings."

Velasco was surprised. And confused. Something's wrong, he thought. Pedro didn't send her down here. Cabrera got everything he needed for the Acapulco job when she gave him the Veracruz package. What the hell is she doing here? "Rosa! What are you doing in Acapulco? Did Pedro send you here?"

"Oh, no, Pedro didn't send me. Why would he send me? In fact, he didn't even know I'd be coming today. But I am glad I bumped into you. Is Señora Velasco with you?"

"No, the Señora is not with me." What the hell is this girl doing here, he wondered. Pedro said she never knew what was going on, never knew what was in those packages she delivered. He told me she thought it was all about flowers. She never knew she was part of the fire operation. What's she doing here?

Rosa smiled. "Oh, so you're alone. Well, maybe I could have a few minutes of your time, and I can sketch a few—"

"How did you get here?" he interrupted. "Who did you come with? Are you alone?"

He's nervous, Rosa thought. That's good. But he's surprised to see me. That's good, too. "Well, I am alone right now. I came down with a friend, but he's not around now. I don't know where he is. Maybe he went to the beach. Or perhaps he's in the bar. I'm alone right now. So what brings you to Acapulco, Señor Velasco?"

"There was a fire last night at the Pemex tank farm out on the edge of town. I came down to see what the damage was like."

"Another fire? Oh, my goodness. You certainly have had bad luck lately."

"Yes, we have, and that was a very destructive fire last night. It did a lot of damage."

"Such a pity. Isn't there anything you can do to stop these horrible fires? They've been happening all over the country, and I read in the paper that three people were killed in one of them. Veracruz, wasn't it? That was so horrible. Oh, it would be so wonderful if you could find a way to stop them."

"Yes, they have been terrible, and very costly for Pemex and the Mexican people. But as a matter of fact, I have put a stop to them. I've been investigating, checking all the clues myself, and I've solved the mystery. I've discovered who's been responsible for the fires. It was a difficult task, but as a matter of fact, I'm going to release a statement that identifies the person responsible for the fires. Yes, when I get back up to Mexico City tomorrow, I will have a press conference and explain to the press and to Mexico and the world how I was able to accomplish this, how I was able to save Pemex."

"Oh, that's wonderful, you're going to release a statement?"

"Well, Pemex has to put out the press release, but the statement will come from me. In the statement, I'm naming the criminal who has been traveling all around the country setting the explosions and starting the fires."

"Oh, that's wonderful, Señor Velasco—"

"Call me Berto. We don't have to be so formal, Rosa. After all, we're friends, and you've been working for me. I know you work for Pedro, but he works for me. Yes, the nation and the President will be grateful, and Pemex will breathe better with this problem off its back."

Rosa caught her breath to keep from saying the wrong thing. There are so many other names I could call him besides Berto, she thought. "Of course, Berto. Pemex should give you a medal. Better yet, they should give you a promotion."

"Yes, the story will be in all the papers tomorrow." A sudden thought struck Velasco. She's alone, so why not give it a try? She looks like she'd be a good lay. A young, fresh, sexy body, nice firm tits, ready for the taking. And she's alone. What have I got to lose?

"Rosa, I have to meet the local Pemex manager later this evening, but right now I have a couple of hours of free time. Maybe you could show me those sketches?"

"Oh, I'd love to show you a few of my new ideas. I didn't bring my sketchpad with me—heavens, you'd think I could carry it in my purse, this purse is so big. My sketchpad is at home. I planned on showing the sketches to Señora Velasco later this week, but—"

"She's not with me. I'm alone."

"Well, I could do some rough sketches for you right now. I'll have to see if I can get some paper in the gift shop."

"Paper? How big? I have plenty of paper in my room. That's no problem. I can get plenty of paper for you."

"My, it's so noisy here in the lobby. So many people. There must be something going on in the hotel. So many army uniforms."

"Yes, the lobby is crowded. Maybe we could get a table in the bar, and I could buy you a drink."

"The bar? Oh heavens, no, the light is not very good in the bar, and there are so many people in there. And the tables are not very large, and it would be difficult for me to do my sketching on such small tables. Anyway, that's where my friend is, if he's not across the street at the beach."

"Why don't we go to my room?" Velasco said. "I'm sure I have plenty of blank paper in my room, and the light would be much better there. And I could call room service and have them send us a cocktail."

Rosa clenched her teeth, and tightly clutched her purse. "Yes, let's go to your room."

CHAPTER 86

"Victor, what are you doing here in Acapulco?"

"I might ask you the same question," Detective Gonzalez said. "What are you doing here?"

Harry's mind raced to think of a clever answer, but he couldn't come up with one. Better give him a simple response, he decided. "Rosa and I drove down here to get away from the flower shop. She wanted to get out of there. She needed a change of scenery after everything that happened earlier today."

"Well, I came down here to see a dead body. A man was shot this evening, here in the hotel. I received a call from the Acapulco police asking for my help. My sergeant and I flew down right away, and when we arrived, they told us they had discovered a second body."

"Two bodies? Can't the local police handle it?"

Gonzalez moved toward a corner of the lobby. "Let's sit over here so I can use this ash tray. Ordinarily, yes, the local police could handle it, but this is not exactly a local matter. Both of the dead men were on that list you gave me."

"You're kidding. Pedro's list? Which ones."

"Humberto Velasco and General Suárez. Velasco was killed in his room here in the hotel, and Suárez was killed on the beach."

"You're kidding. Both of them dead."

"Yes. The list keeps getting shorter. Velasco was supposed to meet the local Pemex manager for dinner, but he didn't show up. The hotel security officer went to check his room and they found him sprawled on the floor. He'd been shot twice, once in the stomach and once in the chest. There aren't many clues, except for the bullets. Do you have any ideas?"

"Me? No, I wouldn't have the foggiest. What do you know about the bullets?"

Gonzalez laughed as he relit his cigar. "I believe the bullets that killed Velasco came from one of those damned Russian Tokarevs. Those pistols keep popping up everywhere."

Harry laughed. "Well, I'm sure it wasn't María Elena's gun."

"No, that's for certain. There was another gun on the floor near his body. We believe it was his gun. We're checking for fingerprints to be certain."

"Had the gun been fired?"

"Yes. Three times. We found one bullet in a pillow on the bed. The other two bullets had been fired earlier, and were not part of this scene. The two Russian bullets that killed Velasco and also the bullet we found in the pillow are downtown now at the Acapulco police headquarters."

"I think the gun you found on the floor is the gun Velasco used to kill the girl in the little green car."

Gonzalez rolled his cigar between his thumb and his index finger. "You think Velasco killed her?"

"Yes. I think you'll be able to confirm that when you get back to Mexico City and make the forensic comparison. She knew he was a Communist, she knew he was responsible for the fires. She knew about his plans to have a press conference and be the big hero, and his plans to take over Pemex. She knew a lot more. I think Velasco found out she was going to expose him."

"But he's been here, in Acapulco."

"Not all the time. Check his plane. I think you'll find he's been doing a lot of flying, yesterday and today."

Harry wanted to move on, and steer the conversation away from the Velasco killing. "Now, you say the General's body was found on the beach?"

"Yes, his body was discovered by a tourist who went down for a swim after the storm. He saw someone slouched in a sling chair under one of those big canopies. He figured the man was sleeping. As he approached, he realized there was something wrong, the way the man was doubled over, sideways in the chair, so he ran back to the hotel and told the desk clerk."

"You're kidding. Wow. Just like in the movies."

"Yes, it does sound rather melodramatic. Suárez had been shot once. We believe it's possible that he, like Velasco, was killed by a Russian gun, but of course we'll work with the Acapulco people to verify this, and we'll confirm it when we get back to Mexico City. As a matter of fact, we'll be leaving in just a few minutes, as soon as our plane is fueled and ready."

Gonzalez laughed as he clipped the end of a fresh cigar. "It's like I told you, Harry. It's another case of Russian agents killing each other. Soon there won't be any left, which is all right with us."

"Russian agents? Do you think the general was a Russian agent?"

"Most likely he was a renegade Mexican who sold out to the Russians. There's no way a Russian could have been an officer in the Mexican army. He was on your list, Pedro's list. The federal people will have to sort out the details."

"I think he actually was a Russian, Victor."

Gonzalez shook his head. "A Russian who was a Mexican army officer? A general, at that? I find it hard to believe, Harry. A clerk in a flower shop I can understand, but a general in the army? That would be quite a trick."

"Not at all, if he was born in Mexico or his parents brought him here at an early age. He was in his mid-thirties, I believe. Thirty-five years ago would have been right about the time of the Russian Revolution. If he was born here or born in Russia, either place, but then raised here and educated here, with that fake Suárez de la Garza identity, he could have pulled it off."

"That's an interesting observation, and we should be able to check it out with no trouble."

"Did he have a gun?" Harry asked.

Gonzalez blew a cloud of smoke as he laughed. "Harry, do you believe in signs, portents?"

"I believe in stop signs when I'm driving in the city."

"The General's right arm was hanging down over the side of the chair, limp, with his index finger pointing straight down, pointing at a gun that was partly buried in the sand. It was almost as if he wanted to be sure we found it. The gun had been fired once."

Gonzalez paused and slowly blew a cloud of smoke. "Of course there was no way to know where the bullet went."

Harry smiled. "Might have gone right into the ground, or off into the heavens. But tell me, Victor, what about the other names on the list? Any progress with them?"

"Yes, the Federales picked up Professor Bustamente—Vladimir something-or-other, I've got his full name in my notebook. He was a Russian, a card-carrying Communist. They picked him up at his home a few hours ago. They found several hand guns and also a high-powered sniper rifle with a telescopic sight. They found a scholarly treatise on the World Bank and the IMF, with a list of names of executives and area managers, member nations, information on deposits, and so on.

"They also found a list of telephone numbers, some of them the same numbers that were on Pedro's list, and also a couple of phone numbers in Moscow. And they found three pictures he had clipped from the newspaper, pictures of Black, Rooth and Lafer, the man from Brazil."

"The professor was a good student," Rosa said, "and he certainly had done his homework."

"Yes, and like a good professor, he lectured the arresting officers on the evils of capitalism and the perils of the Western monetary system."

"These guys never give up," Harry said.

"And neither do we. The Federal police found José García just a few hours ago, standing on the steps of the Palacio de Bellas Artes. He talked tough when they confronted him, and he told them all about his plans for blowing up the Palacio tomorrow. And then he blew himself up, and part of the steps along with him."

"A big hole?"

"Just a small hole. A small man and a small hole. They'll have it fixed in no time."

"Was he a Russian, too?"

"Yes. He'd been living in Mexico for nearly twenty years. A lot of Communists came into the country during the Cárdenas administration."

"How about Miguel?" Rosa asked. "Did he come back to the flower shop?"

"No, he never did. The DFSN agents went to his apartment, and his landlady said he moved out in a hurry. She said he had to take care of a sick relative somewhere in South America."

"Miguel doesn't have any relatives," Rosa said. "He's always moaning about being a lost sparrow. Pedro was like family to him, and with Pedro dead, I guess he felt more lost than ever. He was never really happy here in Mexico."

"What was Miguel's role in this?" Gonzalez asked.

"Whatever Pedro asked him to do, although I'm not sure he really understood everything that was going on."

"Tell me, Harry, how did you happen to be here in Acapulco tonight when these things happened? You always seem to show up when there's a dead body or two lying around. How do you always manage that?"

"Oh, you know what they say about reporters. I guess I just have a nose for news. If there's a good story, I can sniff it out."

"You came to Mexico for a vacation, but it seems like you're working all the time. I suppose you'll want to file a story on these killings?"

"Don't you think I should?"

Gonzalez shrugged his shoulders. "I don't see why not. Talk to the local authorities, ask a few questions, but I think you already know most of the answers."

"Can I quote you? On the theory of Russian agents killing each other, for instance?"

Gonzalez laughed. "Of course. You can fill in the details."

"Yeah, you're right, I am supposed to be on vacation. From now on I just want to lie on the beach and catch some sun and play a few rounds of golf. Maybe I'll go out on one of those charter fishing boats in the morning and do a little deep sea fishing."

"Good idea, but look out for the sharks." Gonzalez relit his cigar and grinned. "By the way, Harry, you might want to stop downtown at the *Cruz Roja* clinic and get your arm taken care of properly. You wouldn't want to get an infection. And when you get back up to Mexico City, you might want to get that hole in your sleeve patched. Maybe you can take it to the tailor on Bucareli—you know, the one who's fixing the hole in your other sport coat."

Back in the room, Harry took three more aspirins. He sprinkled the last of his sulfa powder on the wound in his arm and covered it with a couple of fresh Band-Aids. Looks kind of sloppy, he thought, but it'll do the job for now.

Harry popped the cap on his last bottle of Carta Blanca and called the UP office in Mexico City. "I have a story for you," he said to the overnight man. "Put an 'Acapulco' dateline on it."

"You're down there now? Are you on vacation, or did you stumble on another body?"

"A little of each. I might go fishing tomorrow, and it's two bodies, not one."

Harry gave the UP man the story about the two dead Communists. He quoted Gonzalez on the determination that the victims were killed by fellow Russian agents, and that one of the dead men, a Mexican national, had killed the girl in the little green car. He fleshed out his story with comments on the tank farm fire, the thunder storm, and the army officers convened in the Hotel Las Hamacas. He included the Gonzalez statement that "those Russian guns keep popping up everywhere."

When Harry finished dictating, the overnight man said, "Boy, you're right in the middle of the action again. Seems like you're always part of the news as it happens."

"No, it's like I told you before, I don't make the news, I just write about it."

CHAPTER 87

"I feel better now," Rosa said. "I'm glad it's over. What a horrible experience. I don't think I could go through that again."

"I know, Rosita. Like I told you the other night, killing is not very pleasant, but sometimes it has to happen. We respond to a critical situation, and we do what we have to do."

"I made a mistake, Harry. I mentioned your name. I'm sorry, it just slipped out. I said I came by car, and I said you drove, and Velasco went wild. He was afraid you would come after him. He mumbled something about Isabel, and he said he killed her, and he said he was going to have to kill you, too, because you know too much."

Rosa paused, closed her eyes for a brief moment, and continued. "And then he pulled a gun out of his brief case. He was waving it around in the air and ranting like a lunatic. 'This is the gun I used to kill that bitch,' he laughed. I mean, he really laughed, Harry, as if it was some kind of a joke. And then he yelled, 'this is the gun I'm going to use to kill Banister, and this is the gun I'm going to use to kill you,' and then he fired at me. I couldn't wait for him to take another shot, Harry. I couldn't take any chances, so I shot him. That man was crazy."

"So you used your mother's gun again?"

"You know I did, Harry. It was the only gun I had. I was terrified, and after he fired that shot over my shoulder, I knew I had to shoot right away, before he could shoot again."

"Good thinking, Rosita."

"But I will have to get a new purse. Those holes are so obvious."

"I'll buy you a new purse, and you're right, he was crazy."

"Yes, he was living a double life. He was a Pemex executive and also a Communist agent."

"A *triple* life is more like it," Harry said. "He had a casa chica with a second family in Morelia—a mistress and two small children. Maybe if I talk to Aguilar about it, Pemex can find a way to help that poor woman. She was a victim, too."

Rosa leaned over and kissed Harry on the cheek. "That would be nice, Harry, very thoughtful of you. That man was truly evil."

"All those people who came to the back of the flower shop were evil—and dangerous. Their plans were insane. I know Sergio was their leader, their nominal leader, but it seems like they had no real leader. It seems like they were all working against each other. Even with help from Moscow, they never could have pulled it off."

"But the threat was real, and the fires were real," Rosa said. "Those men were killers, and there was always the possibility that one of their plans somehow might have succeeded. Which gun did you use?"

"I used Sergio's gun, the one he dropped when you shot him last week. I must confess, Rosa, I lifted the gun from your purse while you were asleep in the car on the way down here."

"I know. I noticed the gun was missing, and I knew you must have taken it. But why didn't you use your gun?"

"My gun?"

Rosa smiled. "Yes, your gun, or should I say Calderón's gun? When I read your story in this morning's paper, I thought that must have been you fighting with Calderón on the elevator. And you told me you were attacked by a mugger?"

"Well, he was sort of a mugger, depending on your definition of 'mugger.' I figured it would be better—more consistent, let's say—if I used a Russian gun. I figured it would be easier for the police to wrap up the case. Of course, I didn't know I was going to use it, and I didn't know you were going to shoot Velasco."

"But weren't there other people on the beach?"

"Yes, there were people sitting under a few of the other canopies, and there were people walking on the beach. The storm was still a few miles away."

"Weren't you afraid?"

"You bet I was, Rosa. I was afraid he would find out I was just stringing him along, and obviously he did. I was afraid he would shoot me, if he could get at his gun. I didn't know if Sergio's gun would work. I was afraid one of the General's subordinates would come down to the beach and interfere. I was afraid the storm would mess things up. I didn't know what the hell was going to happen."

"So what did happen?"

"Suárez realized he had told me too much. I think it was something I said about the ships in Veracruz. He was sitting on my left, and his guayabera was wet from the rain and it was clinging to his legs. We were both slouched down in those damned sling chairs, and he went for his gun, but he had trouble getting it out of the holster. He had to try to sit upright and turn sideways in his chair in order to get the gun and shoot with his right hand. He couldn't get a good shot, just enough to nick me in the arm. My gun—Sergio's gun—was in my coat pocket, and I was able to get it out in a hurry."

"But weren't you afraid of the noise?"

"Nobody could hear the shots, the thunder was so loud, and I timed my shot to coincide with a clap of thunder on the Mississippi River."

Rosa sat up straight. "What on earth do you mean by that? The Mississippi River?"

Harry smiled, and pulled her close. "It was dark on the beach. I'll explain it to you when we're alone in the dark." He reached over and turned off the lamp.

Rosa lifted her head and kissed him again. "I don't want this to end, Harry, but all good things must come to an end, it seems. I should get back to Mexico City. I should open the flower shop and see to the flowers, and I should meet with attorney Morales and sign those papers."

"Good things never really end, Rosita. Sometimes they get interrupted or delayed, put on the back burner for a while, but the good things in life always seem to return. And you're right, we both have a few things to do. I'll have to return the car, and I have to tie up a few loose ends."

"And what are you going to do then, *mi amor*? Do you think you'll want to help me at the flower shop?"

"No, the flower shop is your baby, Rosita. I don't do flowers, but you'll do just fine. You have a passion for flowers, and you'll do a great job. You'll make the Florería Roma flourish, and it'll be the best damned flower shop in all of Mexico.

"But me? I came to Mexico for a vacation. I wanted to see the sights, I wanted to play golf and lie on the beach and soak up the sun. Well, I never did play golf. I did get to the beach, but there was no sunlight, just flashes of lightning, and it wasn't as much fun as I thought it might be."

Harry kissed her again, and squeezed her shoulder. "But the best part of coming to Mexico, *mi vida*, was meeting you."

"But we never did go to Xochimilco, Harry. And you never saw the Pyramids."

"I know, Rosita, but Xochimilco will always be there, and so will the Pyramids. And so, thank God, will the Palace of Fine Arts."

"So what will you do?"

"I don't know. Sidney said there's something brewing down in Guatemala. Something about a plan to distribute land to the peasants. Something to do with bananas. Maybe there's a good story there. Maybe I'll go down there and check it out."

"Guatemala's not too far away," Rosa said, a wistful tone in her voice.

"No, not too far at all. No place is very far nowadays, with the speed of those modern jet planes."

Harry perked up, and laughed. "And hey, remember the night you taught me how to do the mambo?"

She smiled, but in the soft glow of the candle Harry could see tears in her eyes.

"Yes," she said quietly, "the mambo. You learned to do the mambo."

"Well, maybe I'll go down to the land of the tango, and learn how to dance the tango."